Archie Blue Sky

by

Diarmid MacArthur

TO MARK

VERY BEST WISHES

This is a work of fiction. Names and characters are the product of the author's imagination and any resemblance to actual persons, living or dead, is entirely coincidental.

ISBN: 978-0-244-32801-6

PublishNation
www.publishnation.co.uk

for my girls,
Joanie, Kirsty and Lindsay.

The heavy oak door slammed behind him and he stepped out in to the soft, relentless West of Scotland rain, the kind that appeared merely as an extension of the heavy grey sky above and seemed to seep into your very soul. Without either hat or jacket, he was soon soaked and the rain streamed down his face, mixing with his own tears. He could not have explained whether these were tears of anger, sorrow or frustration and he turned his face skyward as if in a vain attempt to wash them away. But after a few seconds, he lowered his head once again and headed towards the sleek black car that awaited him, on this occasion bringing him not the slightest morsel of pleasure or joy as he entered and closed the door with the characteristic, solid Germanic "thunk." He sat for a few seconds and tried to control his emotions but there was nothing he seemed able to do to prevent the red mist descending. The temper that he had spent most of his adult life kept well under control was now consuming him, burning like a fire in his chest. He gritted his teeth as he switched on the engine and gunned the car out of the drive, scattering gravel across the well-manicured lawn. As he sped along the quiet street, the fire gradually turned to a coldness as the chaos of his thoughts focussed on one single goal – revenge.

PART 1
PLANET LOH
THE PAST

Chapter 1

Samian sighed and sat upright, easing the muscles in his back. He was weary and, quite frankly, he was relieved that this would be his final project. He was already well past his allotted timespan of ninety cycles and, in addition to becoming more aware of the aches and pains that invariably accompanied an extension such as his, he was getting increasingly lonely as more and more of his friends and associates embarked upon their one-way journey to what was euphemistically referred to as "The Terminus", the large and deceptively innocuous-looking building just outside the city in which, after ninety cycles of productive and worthwhile existence, life ceased, or was "terminated". This feeling of solitariness had been exacerbated by the loss of Benna, his life partner of more than sixty cycles who, sadly, had succumbed to a rare and incurable virus some cycles previously and he still really missed her badly, both emotionally and physically; she had been an affectionate and loyal companion and had produced a daughter and two sons, of whom he was extremely proud. However, they were, of course, unable to offer the level of companionship that he had grown used to over the years and, had he had the choice, he would willingly have gone at ninety. Recently, too, his younger son and his daughter had gone "off-planet" and only his eldest remained, this circumstance serving only to increase his loneliness. His situation was unusual; as chief weapons technologist (and, according to some, the most innovative and talented ever) for the ruling Atra faction, he had been granted extra time to complete his current project, although "granted" was not necessarily how he saw it. If the Atra said you stayed on, you stayed on - no question of that!

Samian 1 Klassarius, to give him his full title, had entered the weapons technology unit, located in the city of Sal in the 19th Division, in his 24th cycle, having graduated from Jesencta College in advanced weaponry and technological sciences. He came from a long line of weapons designers, stretching back as far as anyone could remember. Maybe it was a genetic inheritance, maybe just the fact that his family, especially the boys, grew up handling weapons, tinkering with them, improving them and understanding them. Maybe (as some suggested) it was just that the Klassarius clan possessed a sadistic streak that thrived on inflicting pain and suffering on others. But Samian definitely had an edge over his siblings and his contemporaries. As a younger man, he had come up with some amazing innovations, one of which, the PTT (or perceived threat transmitter) was legendary and had been instrumental in the rise and consolidation of the power of the Atra. His species being moderately telepathic, Samian was able to develop a system that rapidly scanned the mind of its victim, determining the primary cause of fear within this individual, assimilating that information then re-transmitting it to the victim, sending him into a blind panic, believing his worst fears were about to be realised - it might be drowning, falling, even being attacked by insects. The telepathic powers his race possessed were relatively limited and this weapon harnessed and amplified these to devastating effect. It had taken him, along with his hand picked team of specialists, almost six cycles to create the weapon in its final form, having tested the various prototypes along the way on a variety of prisoners, some political, some prisoners of war, some just good, old fashioned criminals, of which there were many on the planet Loh. Some had survived, although not necessarily in the same frame of mind as they began the test. Others didn`t, being, quite literally, frightened to death. Some committed suicide, unable to live with the continuous feeling of impending doom that the early forms of the weapon instilled. But finally Samian achieved success, with a usable, small handgun sized version of the PTT that could be adjusted at the turn of a dial to either scare someone off or to terrorise them to the extent that their brain shut down and they died of heart failure. This latter scenario was eminently suitable for the Atra as it allowed them to carry out assassinations with impunity - it was very convenient (and co-incidental, though no-one dare mention the fact) that so many of their enemies just happened to die of a sudden and unexpected heart-attack! And, of course, the Atra managed to turn this to their advantage, citing "genetic inferiority" as the reason for these deaths. As a result of this invention, Samian rose quickly through the ranks both socially and in the weapons development unit, finally attaining the elevated position of Chief Technologist at the tender age of thirty nine cycles. His father, Samian 2 Klassarius, had not attained this position until fifty one cycles and his grandfather, Samian 3, until fifty four, so Samian 1 was well pleased with his progress.

Ultimately, however, the PTT was a niche weapon as, in battle, soldiers still preferred a more traditional approach that left towns and cities in ruins and the corpses of their enemies strewn over the barren battlefields. The PTT remained as a specialist weapon, used mostly by the Civil Guard in local disputes for the immobilisation and apprehension of thugs and minor criminals but occasionally it was deployed if someone needed to be "disposed of" without fuss and bother. And, of course, where something of this nature exists, there will be those who develop the antidote, in this case a small headband-style electronic shield that initially prevented the incoming transmission from reaching the wearer`s brain but, eventually, was developed to "feedback" the transmission to the perpetrator, causing reverse exposure to the weapon. Such a device didn`t come cheap and the average criminal couldn`t generally afford it, (although the more organised managed to steal a fair quantity) so initially it was used by those in higher places who felt that they may be political targets. However, eventually nearly everyone who considered themselves at risk of assassination from the PTT collaborated and developed a tiny neural implant that rendered them totally immune from its effect, thereby relegating it firmly to the armouries of the local Civil Guard offices.

Samian had continued to invent and develop a variety of other, more sophisticated weapons and had hoped that, when he reached eighty cycles, he could retire and spend his last ten in relative peace and tranquillity, in the company of his beloved Benna, travelling the safer areas of the planet and possibly even making an excursion or two to some further flung areas of near-space. But it was not to be. Benna had died when she and Samian were only seventy-nine (most couples chose partners of the same age to ensure that they attended the Terminus simultaneously) and then, when he reached eighty, the Atra President, Mossala 4 Fensh, expressed a wish that Samian stay on past his retiral date as he, personally, "needed his help". Samian was under no illusions as to what this meant. For some time there had been a growing movement of resistance to the Atra`s rule, which was, in effect, a fiercely defended dictatorship. Recently, there had been rumours that these so called "resistance fighters" had access to sophisticated weaponry and the Atra were looking to ensure that they were adequately defended. Who best to turn to than one of the greatest weapons designers of the last hundred cycles? So Samian really had little choice. No retiral, no partner, the only "benefit" he had been offered by the President was the possibility of an extension, which he now found himself in, with few friends and little spare time. (And, of course, the un-mentioned alternative – forced labour in some vile penitentiary, where refusal to comply would be rewarded by a series of extremely unpleasant punishments.)

There was little else in his life now to interest him, other than his eldest son, who was starting to show considerable promise as a weapons technician. Samian was more than happy to pass on as much of his skill as he could to the boy, as, after all, his extensive knowledge and experience would all die with him- little of what he had developed was recorded due to his ability to memorise plans and details photographically. Nowadays he often didn`t go back to his apartment at all, preferring to sleep in his private living space in the high-security weapons unit on the 20th level of the military research facility. In fact, he almost thought of it as home now and there were too many reminders of happier times in his luxurious living space anyway, just serving to make him melancholy. And these were slightly troubling times, with rumblings of dissent amongst the non-Atra populace. No, nowadays he was safer and happier here, working amongst the familiar tools of his trade, commanding the minuscule micro-drones - he almost thought of them as his family - and instructing his son in the finer arts of weapons manufacture. And he truly believed it was an art, despite the end result, the death and carnage that his inventions inevitably wreaked. His weapons were beautiful and sophisticated, especially this latest one. He looked down at his work, the culmination of his long and distinguished career. It was indeed, truly beautiful, he thought. A dull, pewter-like sphere with polished highlights, about forty centimetres in diameter, fashioned from Cealon alloy, a mixture of precious and extremely rare metals found on a planet at the edge of far-space. Its surface was elaborately engraved (much of it by hand) with patterns, creatures and ancient writing. These engravings served to conceal the many hidden orifices that would open on the command of its user and also contained a cryptic code decipherable only to a very select few. On the top of the sphere, where Samian was carrying out the final tasks in its completion, was a space about 6 centimetres square and on his workbench lay the covering panel with twenty eight countersunk holes around the periphery, eight along each edge. The panel was exactly curved to match the rest of the sphere so that, when in place, it would form a totally smooth casing, broken only by the screw holes. The corresponding threaded holes in the sphere itself, that would hold the lid in place, were a random, but precise, mixture of left and right-hand threads. The very existence of such outdated and basic technology in Samian`s workplace was an anachronism but it had become his trademark. No matter how advanced the weapon, somewhere upon it there would be a little piece of ancient technology such as this. He liked to think of it as testament to all those who had gone before, designing the basic weapons of history with their limited technology. The handle grips of the PTT, for example, were similarly held in place by little gold-coloured screws and those that had been fashioned for senior officers even had carved, hardwood handles, similar to the ancient pistols their forebears had used. To create a weapon as advanced as that which he had nearly completed, then to attach the final access panel using screws and a screwdriver, appealed to Samian`s quirky nature. The fact that the screws had to be undone in a particular order to avoid a contained but lethal gaseous emission also appealed to him - after all, you couldn`t simply let anyone take your life`s work apart and have a look at the innards! It would, of course, have been much simpler to use tiny drones to micro-weld the metal then use nano-burrs to make the join entirely invisible, but Samian loved the idea of an access panel, enticing the unwary into what lay inside then zapping them with a burst of Radic gas that would leave them in convulsions for the few moments before death if they got the sequence wrong. Perhaps, he thought wryly, his family did, after all, have a predilection for violence and suffering!

He picked up a device that resembled a hypodermic syringe, although the main part contained a wealth of micro circuitry visible through the clear casing. The thin needle-like portion was, in fact, a transmitter that sent instructions to the massive army of micro-drones that had carried out the internal work on the sphere. Of course, all the actions they undertook had been carefully planned, co-ordinated and programmed by Samian - they were merely acting on his command, constructing the weapon from inside, dancing to his music! And now it was nearly done. He wondered if, when it was finally finished, he might have a small excursion to the Division of his birth, perhaps in the company of his eldest son Lumian. Having reached the suffix "1" the family first name changed and started again at nine - this was the way of things. Lumian 9 Klassarius. Had a ring to it! He and Benna had thought long and hard about the name and finally settled on Lumian, her distinguished grandfather`s name. He had been a great warrior in his day and they both felt it would be an honour for their first-born to bear the legendary name of Commander Lumian 9 Prussin. Young Lumian already had a son, Lumian 8 and he, too, would carry this great name, as would his male descendants until they, too, finally reached "1". Samian wondered if, by then, any of his descendants would remember him and decide to name their first born son "Samian 9". Probably not, he reflected.

His son, Lumian 9, was already showing signs of becoming a great weapons master. Perhaps he didn`t share Samian`s flair for the extraordinary, perhaps he didn`t have the eye for the fine detail, but he was a hard worker and had come up with a few interesting and usable ideas. Samian, however, was less sure of his son`s political leanings. It didn`t do to cross the Atra and, whilst Lumian didn`t openly say anything against them or their ideals, there were times when he seemed less than happy to be in their employ. The Atra, of course, liked to pretend that the society they presided over was free and open to democratic opposition and that they could, theoretically, be voted out if the population so desired. But everyone knew that this was a load of bullshit - anyone opposing them seemed to come to a sticky end somehow, usually suffering a sudden and fatal heart attack (great thing, the PTT...). Samian didn`t delve too deeply into the politics and the morals of the system - after all, a weapons master cannot afford to have too many of the latter - but Lumian did sometimes question the freedom of their society and Samian worried that, one day, he might open his mouth in front of the wrong person and find himself carted off unceremoniously to a few cycles in a labour camp somewhere in far-space, possibly mining the very metals for the Cealon alloy that he had used for the sphere - wouldn`t that be an ironic circumstance for Samian to take with him to the Terminus!

Samian pressed a small sensor on the side of the instrument that sent a message to the last battalion of micro-drones who had been sealing the final chamber and devouring the minute pieces of construction debris. Even with the powerful electronic loupe in front of his eyes, he could only just make them out, scurrying on his command into their tiny receptacles where they would remain, de-activated, until called on once more for duty, an altogether unlikely scenario. Anyway, that would be beyond Samian`s responsibility - once he handed the weapon over to the Atra military commander, that was it. Finished. Maybe just time for his quick sentimental trip then off to the Terminus. All operating instructions would be passed over, along with full schematics of the mechanism- presumably as this was his last assignment, they wanted some form of written instruction as he would no longer be there to advise them! The select few in the Military who would have access to the weapon would ensure they were fully conversant with these instructions, then they would guard the weapon carefully until its deployment. There was just one small thing. When compiling the technical specifications he had, somehow, omitted the part about the screws, their sequence and the Radic gas. Damn!

With the micro-drones finally at rest Samian lifted the small cover panel and placed it over the open space. Although extremely light, it fell in to place with a most satisfying "click" and fitted like a glove. Beautiful! He could not help but feel a sense of pride in his work and he took great pleasure in the feel of the metal, cool and satin smooth, the engravings barely discernible to the touch. Perfect! He briefly wondered how many convicts had died to ensure that he had sufficient metal to construct this precious orb in front of him. Still, it was their own fault for committing crime, or for getting caught. Either way, he didn`t really care. The tiny silver screws sat in a small segmented metal case, precisely labelled and aligned as they would go in to the panel. Each had a simple circular arrow next to it to show the direction of tightening and a number to show the sequence in which they should be placed. When the final screw was inserted and tightened, using a micro torque driver (a highly prized and collectable antique) to ensure exact insertion and tension, the weapon would then be effectively booby-trapped for anyone trying to open it. This applied to multiple attempts. The Radic gas generator would repeatedly emit its deadly vapour through four slots, almost invisible amongst the engravings, that would flip open for less than a second, for up to two hundred discharges, after which there was a mechanism that would automatically lock all the screws, totally preventing the panel from being removed. Cealon was a notoriously hard metal, almost impossible to penetrate. Any attempt at forced entry would result in a self destruct mechanism being activated that would completely fry the innards as well as anyone unfortunate enough to be within about ten metres of the explosion. Samian was nothing if not protective of his work!

The old designer lifted the micro torque driver and paused. This, then, would be his final act, his greatest work. It would all end with a screw and a screwdriver - basic tools and yet the ultimate symbol of everything he had achieved, how his forebears had created their empire, their travelling craft, their basic yet deadly weapons, their reactors. It would also be the end of life as he knew it on his world, the planet they knew as Loh. But that was not his concern. He had been given a remit and he had fulfilled it. Magnificently! He placed the driver in the first compartment (marked with the ancient Loheni symbol for “1”) and pressed one of the buttons on the side of the tool. Immediately the screw jumped to the end of the driver and self-aligned its three crossed slots to fit the blade. He lifted it and placed it in the corresponding hole. Although he knew the sequence off by heart, he still double-checked the container to ensure he turned the screw in the correct direction. He pressed the relevant operating button on the side of the driver then moved his thumb to the button at the end of the handle. The screw torque had already been preset and, with a very soft whirring sound, the driver proceeded to propel the screw into the sphere until it reached exactly the correct tension, after which it switched off. Samian still took pleasure in watching the tiny threaded object disappear into its hole - there was an almost sexual quality about it, a perfect coupling, a full insertion. Just like he and Benna, especially in their younger days. Couldn`t leave each other alone! To his absolute amazement, a tear dripped from his eyelid and landed on the side of the sphere, running down the curve without leaving a trace. `Come on now, you old fool` he murmered out loud, `this, of all times, is not one for sentiment.`

One by one he lifted each screw and meticulously placed them in the correct hole, tightening each in the correct direction with the torque driver. Once in place, the screws were so smooth and fitted so perfectly that they could hardly be seen, just as the join in the casing was barely visible. He came to the last screw, the keystone of the self protection mechanism- once it was in place the whole system would be activated. He placed it in the hole but paused just before he pressed the button. Had he heard a sound? Despite an aural bypass and implant a few cycles ago, Samian`s hearing wasn`t what it had been. The transmitter, which would only have been designed to take him to ninety cycles, probably needed replaced but there had seemed little point - hardly anyone conversed with him these days anyway. It was long after the department had closed and the security in Samian`s inner sanctum was extremely tight - only a privileged few were authorised to be there at any time, far less at this time of night. But there it was again, like a whisper, the faintest of footsteps. He turned, his hand still paused on the driver. A familiar figure stood at the doorway, facing him.

`Hello father.`

`Lumian! What are you doing here? Strictly speaking you are well off limits at this time of day. You know your authorisation only covers standard working hours. How did you manage to get past security?`

`I am well beyond letting any of that bother me now.` Lumian said. `As for security, let us just say they were otherwise engaged!`

His expression, his father thought, could best be described as grim. He felt a slight frisson of panic run down his spine. What had his son got himself involved in?

`What do you mean, Lumian? Tell me.`

`There is not really time just now, father and, anyway, you will find out soon enough. We have come for the sphere.`

`We!` exclaimed Samian. `To whom are you referring? And what do you mean "you have come for the sphere". Do not be absurd.`

Another sound at the door and two more figures entered Samian`s workshop. Like Lumian, they wore the grey jumpsuits and matching self gravitating boots of far-space operatives. However, their outfits lacked the usual insignia of regular flying crew. Instead, round the upper part of their right arms, they each wore a simple dark green armband, adorned with a silver badge bearing two black letters, EC. Samian shuddered involuntarily – he knew exactly what these letters stood for and what they represented. If caught wearing the badge Lumian would have effectively signed his own death warrant. He recognised one of the men as Lumian`s old friend Camali, but the other, older man (a bit of a ruffian, by the looks of it) was a stranger. Samian didn`t like the look of him at all.

`You cannot come in here` Samian shouted. `This is a private space. You will find yourself in great trouble if you do not leave immediately! Get out! Get out, now before I summon Security! And Lumian, for the love of all that is sacred to you, take off that armband before someone sees you!`

Lumian simply shook his head and raised his right hand and, for the first time, Samian realised he was holding something. *Surely not!* Yes, it was a PTT pistol. This was getting ridiculous. Samian smiled wearily at his son.

`Lumian, I hardly think that is going to work!`

`No?` replied Lumian. `Oh yes, father, I know all about the neural implant you had a good many cycles ago. The one that neutralises the effect of the weapon. And I also happen to know that it was you that invented it in the first place, then quietly sold the technology to the opposition. For a great deal of money, too, or so I am led to believe.`

`Oh, come on now, do not play the naïve, innocent child with me! I do not remember hearing you complain about the rewards, Lumian. All the holidays, the education, the lifestyle. We lived a life of great privilege and luxury. Did you honestly think all of that came from my position as chief weapons designer? Although my position commanded an excellent salary, you know that nearly everyone does a bit of work on the side from time to time. Like it or not, that is the way in our society so there is no point in climbing on to the moral high ground now. It is a bit late, do you not think?`

Lumian snorted in disgust. `And there was I thinking that, perhaps, somewhere deep in your soul, you had a moral conscience, that maybe you had allowed the opposition to have the technology to prevent further assassinations and to allow just a little bit of genuine democracy creep into our lives. Turns out that, after all, you are just a mercenary bastard. But I guess I already knew that`

`Aah, if only life were that simple, Lumian` Samian sighed and shook his head. `Now, come on, stop all this foolish nonsense. I will allow you and your friends to walk out of here and we will say nothing further about it. Put away that weapon before someone gets hurt. Do you even know how to use one in anger, Lumian?` His hand was still holding the driver, thumb hovering over the button, but he didn`t want to waste the moment, didn`t want to miss the final turn of the screw, the tiniest of clicks (which he probably wouldn`t hear anyway) confirming the activation of the self defence mechanism.

Lumian gave his father a look of disgust. `Well, there is one way to find out. And you are also forgetting something, father. I am the next generation of designer, I am your son, after all. And, guess what, I have made a few modifications of my own. I guess you could call it a "bit of work on the side."`

`Lumian, we have not got time for this` hissed Camali. `We need to get out of here. Now.`

Samian suddenly started to feel vaguely uneasy. Beads of sweat appeared on his brow. He couldn`t quite place the source of his fear, it was more a feeling of dread. His free hand started to shake. *Surely it is not the PTT?* Lumian smiled ruefully.

`As you see, it has been adjusted to over-ride your wonderful neural implant. Also, it no longer needs to feed on your specific personal fear. It just induces a general feeling of dread. I will turn it up and demonstrate. Or you can just let us take the sphere. What is it to be?`

Samian now started to feel an overwhelming sense of panic. He looked at his son with an expression somewhere between terror and pleading, yet somewhere in the back of his mind was a strange sense of pride at the boy`s achievement. Lumian had bviously turned up the transmitter on the weapon, demonstrating once again its amazing, debilitating power. He started to feel unfocussed, disorientated. He fought the urge to scream. But he was a strong, stubborn man and there was steel enough in his character to command his thumb to press the button on the driver and start the descent of the final screw.

`Lumian, quickly. He is closing the panel.`

Lumian used his thumb to notch up the setting on the PTT to maximum, causing Samian to let out a scream and collapse on the ground. Camali and the other man rushed over to the sphere. The screws looked as if they were all securely in place. Or was one a fraction higher than the rest? They couldn`t tell.

`Shit!` exclaimed Camali `I do not know if it is fully in place or not`

`We will find out soon enough` Lumian said softly. He was kneeling over his father now, not knowing if he was alive or dead and not really wanting to find out. He made to feel for a pulse, then retracted his hand as he thought better of it. `I did not want it to end this way, father. I am so sorry.`

He stood up as the other two carefully lifted the sphere and placed it into the specially designed cradle that they would use to carry it. Fortunately, it was very light - yet another of Samian`s trademarks. When they had secured it safely inside its container (custom built by Lumian in anticipation of this very moment) they placed both in a scruffy looking holdall, originally an expensive luxury item of luggage but now looking well worn, far travelled and fairly inconspicuous. They were going to need all the camouflage they could muster, after all. Once it was all securely stowed, they lifted the holdall and its contents by the two side handles and made for the door. Lumian lagged behind, almost reluctant to leave. He had the feeling he had missed something and, also, this would probably be the last time he set eyes upon his father, either alive or dead.

`Come on, Lumian, we need to get out. The guards will be changing shift soon. Hurry!`

Suddenly he realised what it was he had forgotten - the case that contained the sequence for the screws. He ran to the table and lifted it, then bent down to retrieve the driver that was still clutched in the old weapons master`s hand. He shoved them in the large pocket on his right thigh and as he stood and made for the door he turned one last time to looked at the stricken, shrunken figure of his father, lying slumped on the floor. Although he had many faults he had been a great man and, deep down, Lumian was proud of him, despite his dubious morality and the responsibility he carried for countless deaths. He only wished his father had felt the same about him. As he turned to follow his accomplices, he whispered

`Goodbye father.` Then, almost as an afterthought he added `I love you` before rushing from the room, making sure the door was closed and locked behind him.

Samian`s eyes briefly flickered open

`I love you too, Lumian`

But it was more a thought than a spoken phrase. And, anyway, Lumian was gone.

Chapter 2

The city of Sal was a sprawling community of about four million souls, of whom Lumian was one. The centre was, for a relatively modern city, unusually attractive, with gardens, watercourses and spectacular high rise buildings housing shopping malls, offices and luxury apartments. As cities went it was also particularly safe, in a large part due to the fact that it was home to the military command of the Atra faction. The outer city limits consisted mostly of barracks, armouries and both civilian and military spacecraft ports for internal, near-space and far-space flights; as with most travel centres, the space ports, especially those serving far-space, had heavy security to prevent any forbidden movement. However, due to the central location of the military command centre and its associated offices, the city itself boasted a higher proportion of Civil Guards than most other major settlements - as the saying goes, the Atra liked to keep their friends close and their enemies closer! And, recently, the ranks of the perceived "enemies" had been swelling, as the populace finally became disillusioned with the ruling faction`s dictatorial and, more often than not, brutal methods of government. This undercurrent of resistance, of course, had been going on for a very long time and minor uprisings were not uncommon on Loh. The last, just twelve cycles ago, had been relatively small and quickly quashed but, for the last ten cycles or thereabouts, a much more organised, motivated and numerous opposition had been forming. Historically, and like those in many other worlds and societies, the ranks of these smaller uprisings had traditionally consisted mostly of academics and students who, in reality, stood little chance against the highly organised, well informed and well equipped Atra internal security forces. But this new opposition was different. People from every walk of life, including political and military, had finally had enough of the dictatorship and numerous, clandestine and highly illegal meetings were taking place to discuss how best to attempt a coup. However, no matter how the subject was broached, no matter how the idea was packaged, it really all came down to one issue - Tribalism.

Lost in the mists of time (although, with a bit of delving and palm-greasing, the information was available in the restricted section of the national historical archive, if anyone was really interested in finding out) the planet Loh had been inhabited by numerous different tribes and, as would be expected, they fought. Repeatedly. On occasions, they nearly wiped each other out until, finally, one tribe managed to gain superiority in most areas of the planet - the few areas that remained outside their rule were barely worth their attention, being either barren or frozen, although some hardy souls resided there, eking out some form of life in the harsh conditions. This tribe was the Atra, physiologically and psychologically stronger han the others and naturally the superior race. For millennia they dominated, sometimes by force but managing in the most part to co-exist with the remaining tribes reasonably peacefully, on occasion seeing off unwelcome attention from hostile off-planet species. Although the other tribes may have resented this domination, nonetheless the Atra offered them a level of protection that they, themselves, could not provide. But, like many tribal systems, they liked to keep their blood lines pure and, as is often the way, after a time (and a good bit of in-breeding) some of their less pleasant genetic traits started to come to the fore. Their desire for dominance and their blood-lust were the two most obvious and, eventually, Loh`s populace plunged into repeated conflicts as the other tribes attempted, unsuccessfully, to overthrow the Atra. The principal opposing tribes were the Erti and the Cathalla but, despite strong alliances, they just did not have the might or the resources to overcome the power of the Atra.

Here, the history of Loh becomes increasingly tragic, with atrocities such as attempted genocide, horrific bombing campaigns, chemical warfare, all in an attempt by the Atra to finally eradicate their enemies. But, even with their superior strength, they failed, mainly due to the cunning and resourcefulness of the other tribes and, eventually, an uneasy peace developed, albeit in the form of a dictatorship under the Atra "faction" (as they were known by this time, the term "tribe" being deemed archaic). The status quo had thus remained until the appearance of the current resistance movement, which had adopted the name EC, being the initials of the original opposition tribes. And they were, for the first time in centuries, a real threat to this status quo. The times were, indeed, changing.

As is often the case in such circumstances, practically anyone in a position of senior authority was a member of the Atra faction, carrying the same genetic codes that created their inherent strengths. Similarly, the opposition factions each had their own unique genetic codes and, with routine regular genetic sampling, the national security database (accessible, of course, only by the Atra) could easily identify who belonged to whom. Thus, anyone applying for a position of even minor authority in the governing structure but who did not "belong" to the Atra was unlikely to get very far. Nowadays, everyone carried a minute genetic code and personal identity implant under the skin on the back of their left hand (inserted shortly after birth and, being carefully engineered to attach to the bone, unable to be removed without considerable damage) which allowed instant identification to be carried out by means of a simple scanning device linked directly to the database. As well as their other traits, the Atra were thorough!

A stranger walking through the central gardens of Sal, browsing the shops full of exotic produce and artefacts or dining and drinking in one of the many excellent restaurants would think it a most sophisticated and wonderful city. The different factions were visually indistinguishable, other than a slight difference in height and build, the Atra being marginally taller and broader than the others. But the more astute residents could feel something, a slight undercurrent of discontent, and the Civil Guard were on the alert. It was rumoured that the Atra were working on some highly secret deterrent but, of course, such rumours frequently abounded about what events were forthcoming on both sides of the political fence. But there was something...and Lumian knew exactly what that something was;

Revolution!

After all, it was he who had started it, all those cycles ago! Well, not exactly on his own but it was his own small, secretive resistance cell who had initially been responsible for this ever increasing movement. It is said that "knowledge is power" and Lumian had knowledge, gleaned first-hand from watching his father at work. Initially Samian had remained tight-lipped as to the ultimate purpose of his weapon but as Lumian began to suspect that what his father was constructing was the "secret deterrent" referred to, he made sure that his interest and admiration grew. He finally managed to piece together enough information to realise that the sphere was somehow designed to commit total genocide, applicable to all non-Atra genetic groups. When he had shared this information with his cell, they had immediately decided to share it with the other cells and within days it was common knowledge amongst the resisting factions. They knew they had to act. Quickly. If they didn`t the outcome was certain. - all inhabitants other than Atra would cease to exist.

It hadn`t been easy, of course, and there had been enormous risk involved. Lumian was an excellent weapons technician in his own right but he had swallowed his pride and, abandoning his own current projects, had shadowed his father carefully on the pretext of wishing to learn "the true way". Although Samian traditionally worked in great secrecy, entrusting only small portions of his work to others, after a while his ego could not resist showing off to his eldest son, who appeared to hang on his every word. Slowly but surely Lumian built up a picture of what his father was constructing. The near-photographic memory he had inherited from Samian was a huge asset, of course, and he would go home at night to his luxury 60th floor apartment and carefully note down everything he had seen that day. The picture eventually built up and, although the mechanism devised by Samian was incredibly complex, the method of use was very simple. A sample of the genetic code of a given group was placed in the sphere where it would be analysed in minute detail. This information would be used to produce a wave of highly specific radiation that would be emitted as an unseen and unfelt pulse, causing a change in the genetic code of the target group. The nature of this change could be pre-determined but, ultimately, the plan was to ensure it would be fatal to that specific group. They may develop various forms of terminal cancer, they may have sudden heart seizures, almost any fatal disease or condition could be programmed. But it would be unstoppable - once the pulse was transmitted, anyone with that specific genetic code was doomed. There was a range outside which it would not work but this was large, somewhere in the region of a two hundred kilometre diameter. All the Atra had to do, however, was move the weapon about to the necessary plotted locations and, within a few years, all opposition would be destroyed and they would be left as the sole inhabitants.

Despite all the attention he had paid to his father`s labours and despite his detailed, memorised plans, Lumian was still not entirely sure exactly how it worked but, one thing was certain. If his father had built it, it would, most definitely, do exactly what he intended it to, making it one of the deadliest and most horrifying weapons ever imagined. And now, here he was, walking casually through the centre of Sal, on a dry, warm evening, heading for far-space departure port 5, carrying this grim weapon in a slightly tatty holdall.

He was absolutely terrified!

Chapter 3

The adrenalin-fuelled rush of excitement that had provided Lumian with the necessary courage when he and his two accomplices had stolen the sphere had long since worn off and he was not only nervous but also extremely upset at the outcome, not knowing if his father was alive or dead. The thought that Samian would soon have been taking his final journey to the terminus anyway was of little comfort to Lumian and, although he had followed his conscience, doing what he believed was morally correct, nonetheless he was riddled with guilt. Perhaps he was as not as strong of character as he had imagined, but there was no going back now. He glanced nervously over one shoulder then the other, to ensure that his friend, Camali, and the other man were still shadowing him. The older man was a highly experienced combat pilot, now flying far-space craft through the trans-space conduit system. His name was Gara 4 Theasak and Lumian was aware that he had been a highly decorated and high ranking member of the military. However, like many others, he was among those who felt the Atra had pushed their dominance to the limits and he was now rebelling. They were lucky to have him on their side - if anyone could get them, along with the device that was banging against his right knee, off the planet then it would be Gara. But they still had a long way to go and getting the device out of the military research facility was only the first challenge.

They were approaching the transit station where they would catch a shuttle to the space-port; Lumian could see the long, floodlit building with the high level anti-grav tracks leading out of either side. He was just passing the Haff fountain, a massive replica of their planet, supported on three large crystal columns, that was alternately washed with red and blue liquids, signifying the change from bloodshed to the dubious and dictatorial peace of the Atra, the blue liquid representing the faction colour, supreme against all others. It was particularly beautiful at night and as Kii, their sun, had long since set, the liquids were now glowing in the subtle lighting that was transmitted up through the crystal columns. Its significance, however, only served to remind Lumian of the purpose of his mission. He walked past the training academy for the military then the massive, dark faced tower of the military headquarters itself, an imposing building fronted with wide steps leading to a series of carved columns depicting the military history and numerous victories of the Atra. It was guarded by four ceremonial guards in their dark blue uniforms, with scarlet piping, who carried carried the Juftai, the ceremonial sticks that their ancestors would have used to duel with one another, but Lumian knew that other, more lethal weapons were undoubtedly concealed elsewhere on their persons - as always in his world, nothing was ever what it seemed. As he passed the steps he tried not to stare up at them, attempting to look like any casual passer-by, but he was sure they were looking at him, at the holdall he carried. Was he becoming paranoid? But then he was past them and they continued to pace back and forth, gazing straight ahead into the night. He approached the long, gradual slope up to the station, upon which were a few travellers, some returning home from work, others off on expeditions or journeys, none of which would be as significant as his. There were also a number of Civil Guards patrolling the area but, nowadays, this was routine for the centre of the city and he tried to disregard them. He climbed up the wide steps and entered the main hall. A quick glance re-assured him that his companions were still there.

Their mission had been meticulously planned over the last three cycles, down to the smallest details such as individual staff rotas at key locations, shuttle times, access routes, security codes, everything that could act as a barrier to their free passage off the planet with their deadly cargo. They had sympathetic "sleepers" in many areas of security and they hoped to gain a clear passage through the various security levels that would ultimately allow them unhindered access to the far-space port. Their safety also depended, of course, on the theft not being discovered and, whilst Samian had mostly worked alone and had few visitors, there was always the possibility that one of his small, but trusted, group of staff might try and contact him, in which case the alarm would be raised and a full scale man-hunt would ensue. This was a scenario that he managed, so far, to shut out of his thoughts but, as he stood in the transit hall, Lumian glanced nervously about, looking furtively at the few late-evening travellers. Who were friends, who were enemies? Nowadays, there was no reliable way of knowing what any one of the population felt, where their loyalties lay.

Fortunately he didn`t have long to wait, as the shuttle service, even at this hour, was frequent. The sleek, silver vehicle glided silently into its bay and, once the doors opened, he climbed aboard, sitting next to a window. He was aware of the other two boarding through different doors but they sat in separate areas simply as a matter of protocol and avoided any recognition of, or eye contact with, one another. The shuttle pulled out of the station and glided softly and silently along on its anti-grav track, speeding them to the first of the security gates that would allow them access to the main space-port complex. The shuttle stopped and the doors flicked open. An armed security operative, carrying a small scanner, stepped into the shuttle and those on board lifted their left hand for him to check the implant that each inhabitant carried inserted under the skin on the back. Lumian hoped that the central database for these scanners would have been suitably modified to allow them access - unless you had a specific journey booked, whether local or space, you would be unable to get past this first stage. The operative didn`t even look at Lumian, just quickly scanned his hand and passed on to the next passenger. Lumian breathed an internal sigh of relief. One other hurdle down. A good few more to go.

The shuttle moved on to the main security concourse, a high and brightly lit space with an enormous glass roof, where the next, and possibly most hazardous, obstacle lay. He would have to check the holdall containing the sphere through one of the main security scanners that lay between the concourse and the ports themselves. A great deal of time, effort and money had gone into creating a complex, virtual sub-net within the holdall. When passing through the scanner this would project an image showing that the contents were merely a couple of changes of clothes along with some shoes and a few personal belongings, just enough for a short holiday off-planet. The recognition computer would, hopefully, pass the holdall as "clear" and he would simply collect it at the other side. The weight of the virtual contents matched exactly that of the sphere (at least, according to Lumian`s calculations) so that no discrepancy should be apparent. Despite the many trials that they had carried out, however, they were never able to include anything exactly resembling the unique construct of the sphere and the worry was that one of Samian`s obtuse inclusions may generate a background image that would show behind the virtual sub-net image. Alas, there was only one way to find out. He had been specifically instructed to look for scanner 19 as this would be overseen by another sympathiser on this particular day, at this particular time. The hope was that, if anything untoward did show, a manual search would probably be instigated and the security guard would turn a blind eye. However, there was no guarantee that, if the sphere was detected, it wouldn`t trigger a "concealed weapons" alert, at which point their plans would terminate and he would find himself on trial for treason. Not a re-assuring thought.

There appeared to be some sort of minor delay, as a result of which there was a short queue at scanner 19 – a fellow traveller was already having a manual search carried out. As he joined the few people in front of him, he hoped that their mission hadn`t been discovered. Also, he was feeling somewhat conspicuous as a number of the other scanners appeared to have no one at them at all. This was the kind of action that might attract undesired attention. Fortunately, he moved on quickly and, within minutes, was placing the tatty old holdall on the scanner tray. The scanner blade lifted and did a top sweep, rotated through ninety degrees and did a second top sweep. It then did the same at all four sides, at which point it started to emit a rapid, high pitched bleeping sound. Lumian resisted the temptation to run and did his best to appear surprised and entirely innocent – no easy task, as the sweat was pouring off him and his hands were visibly shaking. The "friendly" security officer should, hopefully, be able to get him past this point.

An attractive young woman in the smart Transit Security uniform of crisp pale-blue shirt with blue epaulettes and tightly fitting dark blue trousers crossed over to Lumian`s scanner. This wasn`t the operative he had expected - it should have been an older man. That was it, game over. He stood where he was, acutely aware of the physical manifestations of his fear. His two companions, carrying no baggage, were already through the scanners and were standing separately from each other. They appeared to be ignoring him but he knew they would be as anxious as he was. The young female security operative approached him and smiled. Inexplicably, Lumian noticed that she smelled nice. She reached over to the holdall, lifting one of the handles and Lumian was very aware of her blouse stretching across her curvaceous body. Then he noticed that under the handle was a small metal ball, attached by a short wire to the loop that secured the handle to the body of the holdall. Despite their extensive and careful preparations, all the calculations and the science, none of them had noticed it. How costly would a tiny oversight such as this prove to be, he wondered.

`It looks like you have got an old travel security tag there, sir` she said.

She pulled a small device from one of the pockets of her immaculate uniform shirt and passed it over the ball. With a tiny click it released the wire and she lifted it off.

`It should have been removed following your previous trip. I am very sorry for the inconvenience. The scanner will activate again and I am sure it will be fine this time. Have a good journey.`

As she turned, Lumian managed to blurt out a quick "thanks" as the machine started its second scan. He watched the guard walk away, conscious of her shapely legs and pert behind under her tight blue uniform trousers. Was all this excitement increasing his sexual appetite, he wondered? But it was with an overwhelming sense of relief that he watched the scanner repeat its cycle, at the end of which no alarm sounded. A small mechanical arm reached out from the base of the scanner unit, attached to which was a similar silver ball to the one that had just been removed. Using its sensors the device located the handle loop and quickly attached the ball with the same short wire. A voice then said "Clear to proceed", Lumian walked through the personal body scanner, which showed up nothing, lifted the holdall and approached his associates. His heart was pounding and he was soaked with sweat, but he had made it through the most difficult part. To be honest, he was astonished, and extremely relieved, that nothing more serious had occurred!

The three finally acknowledged each other`s presence, feeling that it was now safe to travel as a team. They set off on the short walk that would take them to the internal shuttle station for the space ports and, as they passed the Security station the attractive security operative caught his eye and smiled at him. His heart fluttered again but he simply smiled back and moved on. This was certainly not the time or place... This time they had to wait a bit longer until a shuttle eventually arrived and when the doors had flipped open they entered and sat together. Lumian had the holdall in his lap and the three said nothing to each other; each was lost in his own thoughts about recent events and possible future scenarios as the shuttle glided silently towards the base station for far-space port 5. It wasn`t long before it stopped and the three stood up and exited.

They were now entering Gara`s domain and he moved confidently in the familiar surroundings. He led them swiftly to the check-in area for Port 5, the access gate reserved exclusively for privately owned far-space charter craft and again staffed, hopefully, by operatives sympathetic to the resistance cause. There were further checks and document inspections to undergo but Gara had assured them that, having cleared the main security area, these were mere formalities and they would have no problems whatsoever in boarding his far-space craft. As far as anyone was concerned, they were two holidaymakers seeking a bit of far-flung excitement - some of the more distant planets offered services and substances that were strictly illegal on Loh! Again, their hand implants were scanned and, in what seemed like no time at all, they passed through this final checkpoint, walked along a short corridor, through another sliding door and, at last, they exited the building. It appeared that fortune, along with what seemed like most of the security staff, was on their side. Lumian reflected that the revolution was apparently spreading even wider that he and his immediate associates had hoped.

The night was clear and it was still warm from the departed sun`s heat. It was good to breathe the fresh air again after the claustrophobic atmosphere of the terminal building and Lumian looked up to the night sky where he could see the stars twinkling despite the glow of the light pollution from Sal`s urban sprawl. Far up in the sky he could just make out the inner perimeter shield buoys flashing blue and white, marking the limit of planetary manoeuvring speed. After that, barely discernible, were the rows of green and red lights disappearing into the stratosphere, marking the near-space and far-space routes, the latter heading directly towards the distant, invisible and mysterious (to Lumian, anyway) trans-space conduit. The port was still quite busy, as it handled inter-space freight as well as passengers and the freighters tended to use night time slots to avoid the heavy charges imposed during peak passenger hours. The freight terminus was a good bit away but he could hear the rumble of their powerful thrusters as they moved themselves in and out of the many cargo bays. In the opposite direction lay the military facility but he avoided looking in that direction as if doing so might give be tempting fate. He knew, however, that the fastest and deadliest craft were stationed there - he himself had designed the latest weapons systems for the new Hosil class fast-response fighter, after all! From a storage bay under the canopy they took a small anti gravity hoverer onto which they climbed, then Gara pointed it towards a large, sleek looking craft parked some distance out on the private berthing pads. As they sped across the flat expanse and approached Gara`s craft, Lumian could see its name "INTARIA" emblazoned on its side, along with its registration "1171 LOH GARA 4 7" proclaiming its home planet and its ownership. Gara put the hoverer down and, once they had alighted, pressed the return button that sent it speeding back to the space-port. *No going back now.* Gara placed his hand on the recognition panel, the door of the craft gently lowered to form a short ramp and the three climbed up into the ship.

The Intaria was a Wik class 7 far-space fast cruiser, designed for the stresses of trans-space conduit travel. It had been extensively upgraded and was extremely luxurious, as befitted a craft that usually transported wealthy citizens for off-planet rest and recreation. It contained a sumptuous lounge, into which they stepped, which was lit with a dull green glow. As soon as they entered, it seemed to beckon Lumian to sit and relax - probably some tele-subliminal de-stress program had activated on entry, he supposed. "Come" it seemed to whisper "Relax. Sit, we will take care of you, unwind you." But he knew he had to stay alert so, with considerable difficulty, he ignored the call of the comfortable looking couches. As they passed into the forward crew space, the feeling of disappointment that the lounge transmitted was almost overwhelming, as if he had disappointed it and hurt its feelings. Gara noticed his expression.

`Sorry Lumian, the program activates automatically. Hang on` he leaned forward and touched a small pad. Lumian immediately felt the beckoning cease. `Is that better now?`

`Much better, thanks, Gara. It has been a very long day. Oh, how I could just have sat and fallen asleep.`

`Time for that later, my friend. First, we need to get this abomination safely stowed, then we have to get to the conduit portal before the loss is discovered.`

At one side of the crew space a short flight of stairs descended to the lower service area, down which the three of them climbed and walked back along the lower section, arriving at a pressure sealed door. `Cargo bay` Gara stated. Again he placed his hand on the security panel, they heard the door unlock then it slid open. They entered the bay which had a catwalk around the walls and two large, securely closed doors in the centre of the floor. Above them, two dull silver cylinders that resembled missiles sat in their launch cradles.

`I take it that these are not still armed?` exclaimed Lumian, recognising them as the old and obsolete type 15 electron-pulse torpedoes.

`Of course not` laughed Gara. `These have been converted to what we call "drop drones". It allows us to drop..em..things on to planets without having to enter their controlled zones or make a landing.`

`What things` asked Lumian, absently.

`Oh, just things` said Gara with a mischievous grin. `Probably best you do not know.`

He went to a panel at the side of the bay and placed his hand on it. The cradle holding the nearest drone hummed gently as it moved its payload across to where they stood then stopped. Gara placed his hand on a slightly depressed area on the surface of the drone and a small panel slid back to reveal a keypad, into which he entered a sequence of numbers. The top of the casing split into two parts and folded open, revealing a hollow chamber with what resembled a small convex turntable, identical in size to Samian`s sphere, projecting up from the lower surface. Meanwhile, Lumian and Camali were unpacking said sphere from the holdall and the protective harness that had screened it. Lumian held it at arms length and looked at it, wondering again whether his father was dead or alive. This was his final legacy and they were about to dispose of it as best they could. Once they had put sufficient distance between them and Loh, they would attempt to open and dismantle it - quite possibly losing their lives in the process.

Lumian took the sphere to the drone and placed it carefully on the podium. Gara touched the panel again and a number of projections appeared from the lining of the drone, moving inwards until they all touched the sphere.

`There, that should hold it.` Gara said. `It is fully gravity buffered so it should be safe there, no matter what.`

He carried out another few tasks in the innards of the drone then he straightened up and touched the panel again - the casing closed with a hiss and a faint click. Then he pressed another sequence of numbers and the cover of the small panel slid shut. Gara stood back, surveying the drone, and said

`Right, that is it safe and secure. For the time being, anyway...`

They left the bay and climbed back to the main deck, passing through a door into the control area of the vessel. Gara pointed to two of the four seats that faced ahead towards the wide slit of the forward viewing panel, which continued round to the sides of the craft, ending just behind their seats. It was already activated and Lumian could see the spread of the space-port ahead of them, with the lights of a few craft coming and going against the night sky.

`As you may know, it is not a window as such.` Gara explained. `It is a screen that transmits the forward view in real time. Much safer, especially once we are in the conduit.`

Gara placed his hand on the panel that was glowing white on control console. A soft, sexy (Lumian thought) female voice said

`Welcome back, Gara 4 Theasak. Glad to have you on board. Can you please ask your guests to confirm their identity?`

`Place your left hand on the panel please.` Gara said to Lumian. He did as he was told. A small bar flipped up from beside the panel and passed quickly over the back of his hand.

`Welcome aboard, Lumian 9 Klassarius. You honour us with your presence, being such a distinguished guest. I hope you have a pleasant journey and enjoy your destination.`

Lumian removed his hand and, although he expected the craft to recognise his identity, he was slightly unnerved that it also recognised his position. He looked at Gara with some concern.

`Will this not transmit our identities to the authorities?` he asked, a note of alarm in his voice.

Gara smiled. `Perceptive, my friend, but that is all taken care of. No-one knows you are here except the four of us.`

`Four?`

`Yes` smiled Gara. `The fourth being the Ship, of course! Now you, please.` he said to Camali.

Camali placed his hand on the panel and the procedure was repeated.

`Welcome aboard, Camali 8 Calfarr. I hope you enjoy your break from the Justice Assembly and enjoy your journey with us.` The voice seemed, somehow, less friendly.

Camali was what was known as a "facilitator" with the Justice Assembly, ensuring that trials of those accused of political crimes against the faction went according to plan and that the accused was found guilty - yet another of the Atra`s methods of ensuring the repression of their opponents. In recent times his position had been the subject of an investigation as he had appeared too lenient, resulting in the occasional release of political prisoners. This was not to his superiors` liking and he reckoned it was time for him to go.

Gara placed his hand back on the pad. The computer spoke again.

`Gara, please state your destination.`

`Trans-space conduit 7 VFF 65.`

`Do you wish to initiate full automatic control at this time?`

`Yes please.`

`Do you wish to initiate full or partial telepathic override at this time?`

`Full please.` he said, picking up what looked like a fine metal headband and placing it over his grizzly, grey hair.

`Telepathic control activated, operational on request. This will override automatic control. Do you wish to initiate manual override at this time?`

`Yes please.` A panel slid open on the console and a short handle slid out. Gara placed his right hand on it. A second panel opened and an identical handle slid out. He placed his left hand on this.

`Manual override confirmed, control paddles activated, operational on request. This will override automatic control. Please manually test paddles.`

Gara moved the so called "paddles" and Lumian could see that they moved in every direction and could also rotate.

`Paddles fully functional.` said the voice. `Do you wish to activate launch sequence at this time?`

`Yes please.`

`Activated.`

They could hear the faint hum of the propulsion and navigation systems as they started to come on line. Lumian was aware of what felt like a shudder of anticipation run through the vessel and he somehow imagined that the Intaria was maybe excited! However, he couldn`t quite decide if he was excited or simply plain terrified...

`Gara, you will now be contained.`

Gara sat back in his seat as a series of very thin, padded but highly flexible strips formed a cage round his body and legs and self-adjusted to ensure that he was immobile in his seat. His arms were still free and he could use telepathic control to move the seat as required.

`Containment implemented. Lumian, you will now be contained.`

Lumian sat back and felt the same process being applied to him. Strangely, it didn`t feel nearly as bad as it looked. But, as the cage tightened around his legs, he could feel something pressing into his thigh. `Shit!` he thought, remembering the torque driver and the little box he had lifted containing the sequence for the screws that would allow access to the sphere. He should have placed it in the drop drone with the weapon. Too late now, it would just have to stay there in the meantime.

`Containment implemented. Camali, you will now be contained.`

Camali was similarly held in place. Lumian wondered what thoughts were going through his friend`s mind.

`Containment implemented. Gara, do you wish to proceed with your flight?`

`Yes please.`

`In which mode?`

`Full automatic. Check for available take-off portals and proceed. Once free of the atmosphere, proceed to designated conduit entry portal then pause for further instruction.`

`Proceeding as requested. Artificial gravity activated. Gravitational acceleration buffer activated. Proceeding at standard manoeuvring speed to take-off portal seven eight.`

The craft lifted off the ground and skimmed noiselessly across the surface of the space port. Lumian didn`t like to disturb the pilot (nor did he wish to appear ignorant) but, as everything appeared to be functioning automatically, he risked a question

`Gara, what exactly is a take-off portal? I have heard the term but I suppose it has never been relevant for me to find out what it meant.`

`Ah, my friend, I forgot that you would have probably made any flights using the traditional method. As you know, escape from the planet`s atmosphere uses a large amount of power. The take-off portals emit energy pulses that form something resembling a tunnel in which the craft flies, using minimal power, until it has reached open space. In my business` he paused and smiled wryly `well, my former business, at any rate, time is money and my clients usually want to get to their destination as quickly as possible. It is an expensive option but, fortunately, one I can afford. Now, here we are. Ready?`

With barely a shudder the craft raised its nose skyward and moved effortlessly towards the belt of lights floating in space that Lumian had gazed at earlier. He looked out the side of the screen at the tilted view of his planet. The lights of Sal stretched into the distance, flashing and glowing, people going about their business, be it good or bad. He wondered if he would ever return. The scene diminished rapidly as they approached the final security barrier, after which they were free to go wherever they chose. Surely it couldn`t be this easy, Lumian thought to himself. Then a harsher male voice spoke, making him jump and sending a rush of adrenalin through his system. Was this it...?

`Craft Intaria. Registration One one seven one. Loh Gara. Four seven. Please confirm immediate destination.`

`Trans-space conduit seven V F F sixty five`

`Please confirm passengers.`

`Seli six Ofti and Mag two Pilis` He turned to his companions, grinned and winked. There seemed no end to this man`s ingenuity and skills!

There was a pause, broken only by background sound from the control orbiter. They held their collective breaths. Surely nothing could go wrong now.

`Intaria, you are now clear of take-off portal containment and free to proceed to the entry portal for conduit V F F sixty five. There are no craft waiting at the portal. You may proceed at will. Safe journey.`

`Thank you.` said Gara and they breathed a collective sigh of relief.

`Passing inner-space barrier.` said the sexy voice, as Lumian was now thinking of it. Definitely a heightened sexual awareness, he reflected. The craft swung slightly to face the two lines of flashing red beacons that disappeared into what looked like infinity.

`Clear of inner-space barrier. Initiating acceleration level six towards conduit. In three, two, one...`

Lumian felt his chest tighten before the gravity buffer kicked in and negated the acceleration effect. The craft was now propelling itself at a high speed to the conduit. Suddenly a red light flashed above the front window screen. The harsh male voice spoke again.

`Attention all craft in vicinity. This is a class one security alert. All craft must report back to their relevant docking area with immediate effect. Repeat, all craft must return to docking area with immediate effect. Please be aware that military craft have been deployed.`

The red light continued to flash. The sexy voice said

`Security alert noted. Returning craft to docking station.`

`Implement manual override. Immediate effect.` Gara shouted.

`That will be in contravention of protocol. Confirm security alert noted.`

`Confirmed. Security alert noted. Manual override. NOW.`

`Gara, I must warn you that you will be in contravention of a direct security order. Military craft have been deployed. You will be at risk.` the voice sounded concerned.

`Noted. Risk accepted. Now, let us get out of here.`

Gara played the paddles with the consummate ease of the experienced pilot that he undoubtedly was. Lumian could feel another pressure wave on his chest as the craft accelerated to maximum speed. The beacons now appeared as a single red line on either side of the craft.

`Need to move it, now.` Gara said quietly. `These guys do not hang about at manoeuvring speed. They will be off the mark and on our tail.`

`Can we outrun them?` Camali asked, concern in his voice.

`Never tried it with a Hosil before!` smiled Gara. The man seemed totally unflappable. `Certainly this would beat the military craft that I used to fly but the new Hosils... mmm, not too sure. Still, we have got a bit of a start and I have a few tricks up my sleeve. Bet none of them have done a full speed dive into the conduit.`

`What do you mean?` asked Lumian, feeling a bit alarmed. He had never travelled in the conduit but he knew it was a risky business and the sound of diving "full-speed" into it did not appeal to him at all.

`Well, normally when you reach the portal you stop, orientate yourself then fly in at a very shallow angle. Safest way. But we will not be stopping tonight. Straight in, full speed. Should be exciting.`

This was probably the most Lumian had heard Gara talk and the man was obviously in his element here, no wonder he was such a venerated fighter pilot. However, Lumian didn`t find the prospect at all exciting and, by the expression on his face, neither did Camali. He had never fully understood the complexities of the trans-space conduit but now most certainly wasn`t the time to ask.

They heard a faint "blip" sound and, in response to an unspoken telepathic command by Gara, four fine metal strips slid up from the console and a three dimensional display of their current location appeared between them. The Intaria showed in the shape of a craft at the centre of the display and they could clearly see the forms of three smaller craft, in a "v" formation, behind them.

`This is the latest thing in proximity sensors` commented Gara. `Cost a fortune, I can tell you, but I think it will prove to have been worth it.`

A flat screen then rose up from the console, this time showing the position of the conduit. Invisible to the naked eye, the radiation showed as what looked like a white spiral against the dark of the screen. Below the image the distance counted down, along with the estimated time to reach it. The view suddenly changed to show a map of their proximity to the conduit. Alongside the other sensor, it seemed that the gap between them and the conduit was closing slower than the gap between them and the pursuit craft. Another small panel appeared out of the console, again in response to an unspoken command by Gara. He moved his left hand and pressed several small buttons.

`Good old fashioned stuff that they will not be expecting!` he said in a remarkably cheerful voice.

The main screen suddenly shifted to a rear view and they could see the distant lights of the three Hosil craft that were pursuing them. Suddenly they heard a commanding voice say

`Vessel Intaria. This is Commander Setris, Airspace Security. Halt immediately. I repeat, halt immediately or we will open fire. I will not issue further warning. I repeat, halt im...` The transmission stopped as suddenly as it had begun. At the same time, a multitude of flashes appeared on the display screen.

`That will slow them a bit` chuckled Gara. `Good old fashioned electrostatic grenades. Take their automatic systems down for just long enough to get us to the portal. So much for latest technology, they forget the old stuff, think no-one uses it anymore. Hah! They underestimate old-timers like me!`

Sure enough, the gap between them and their pursuers started to widen. The conduit looked a lot closer. Sexy voice spoke

`Approaching portal. Suggest slowing craft to align portal entry.`

`Not today, Baby!` Gara shouted.

`Danger! Approach angle too steep. Abort! Abort!` An audible warning started to chirp loudly, almost drowning out the noise the craft was making as it started to vibrate. Lumian was grasping the arms of the chair and he could feel his teeth chattering together – he didn`t know if it was the movement of the Intaria or just good old-fashioned fear! Gara ignored the urging of the sexy voice. `Hang on, guys, it will get a bit rough now.`

Understatement...!

Chapter 4

Despite the artificial gravity, the gravitational buffers and the seat restraints, Lumian felt as though his body was being torn apart. The craft was resilient but he could hear some alarming creakings and groanings as it ploughed straight into the trans-space conduit at full throttle. Gara was fighting with the two control sticks, obviously preferring to control the vessel manually - possibly the fully automatic system could not cope with this course of action anyway. He continued to grip the handles of his seat and turned his head slightly to see Camali looking equally terrified. Gara seemed to be too pre-occupied to show emotion and he was staring intently ahead, with occasional glances at the various small monitor screens that now projected from the console. The main screen showed what looked like reddish-white sparks that seemed to pass extremely rapidly - gone were the red guidance lights and the comforting twinkle of distant stars. Gara suddenly pulled the two sticks hard back and the craft seemed to stand on its tail. No sooner had this happened than he pushed the right hand one forward, making the craft spin alarmingly. Lumian threw up all over the floor.

`Do not worry` shouted Gara above the almost overwhelming noise the craft was making `quite common to feel a bit sick with this manoeuvre. Nearly in, then it will become a bit calmer.`

A bit sick! He thought he was going to die. The alarm continued to sound and the computer`s voice spoke with a sudden urgency – somehow it didn`t sound sexy anymore!

`Structural integrity weakening to forty five over a hundred. Vessel requires to be stabilised soon or it will destruct.`

`Noted!` shouted Gara. A final twist of the control sticks and, suddenly, all the noise and random movement stopped and they appeared to be almost still, floating in a grey mist. Gara released the paddles, sat back in his seat and let his breath out, as if he had been holding it throughout the entire manoeuvre.

`We are in! Return to full automatic control. Advise when approaching any known sector portals.`

`Full automatic control restored.` responded the voice, with what sounded like a sigh of relief.

Lumian and Camali sighed as well. Gara said

`Release all safety constraints.`

The securing straps on the seats retracted and all three were free once again. They stretched their aching limbs, which had been tensed up throughout the alarming flight. Gara looked at Lumian and smiled.

`Rough trip, eh? I take it this is your first time in the conduit?As you can see, it is not for the faint hearted. You did well to remain conscious, my friends. Many passengers would have passed out long ago!`

Lumian and Camali simply nodded. Neither had the energy or the inclination to make conversation. Gara continued.

`Yes, it can be a bit bumpy at the best of times. Today was a bit of an emergency, though, as there was not really much choice with those fighters on our tail. Anyway, I doubt if they will attempt to follow us - well, not that way, anyway. Not got the stomach for it, these young pilots. Our good fortune!`

Camali spoke, his voice hoarse. Lumian suspected he may have been screaming at one stage.

`So, Gara, what exactly is this conduit? It seems that we are hardly moving now, if at all. How exactly does it transport us?`

Gara chuckled. `Ah, if only you knew...we are travelling at a speed far greater than you have ever travelled before, multiple factors of the speed of light, believe it or not, although our ship is doing little other than keeping us stable and on course. The conduit is situated within the material that forms about eighty hundredths of our universe, unseen but most definitely there. It spreads across the entire universe in an invisible network and, with the correct knowledge and a good vessel it can take you almost anywhere you want to go. But only if you know how to use it correctly. One small mistake and, well, your atoms will simply be absorbed into the energy of the conduit. You will be gone...forever!`

`Obviously you do know how to use it` commented Lumian `and only too well, my friend. I must compliment you on your flying. Most impressive, most impressive indeed!`

Gara smiled and inclined his head.

`Thank you, Lumian, it is nice to be appreciated. Now, I think it best if you two go back and clean yourself up, you are in a bit of a mess! Back through the lounge, left hand side. Should be fresh towels.`

`What about the...` asked Lumian, looking at the vile puddle on the floor.

`Do not concern yourself, it will self-clean. Every eventuality is catered for here! Off you go.`

The two friends stood up, carefully avoiding the mess on the floor which was already being removed by a couple of cleaning drones, exited the bridge and walked slowly back through the lounge area. Although it still looked comfortable and relaxing, the programme that Lumian had found almost irresistible upon entering the vessel had been de-activated and they passed through without any effects, reaching the after quarters of the ship. Lumian would have liked nothing better than to flop down in one of the large, soft couches and have a sleep but he needed to clean up and he knew that there was still much to be done before their mission was over.

The two friends easily located the facilities and the door to the toilet area slid open upon their touch, opening on to a large, softly lit room. The walls were covered in what Lumian recognised as a bio-sterile polymer that would require minimal cleaning and, to his surprise, a pile of luxurious, soft, fluffy white towels were neatly folded on one of the surfaces, just next to two large white wash-basins. The entire unit appeared to be crafted from a marble polymer that sparkled in the diffused light – another expensive item, he reckoned and he wondered just exactly who Gara`s passengers normally were. He presumed that the surfaces had their own anti-gravity system as he would have expected the towels to be scattered over the floor. He ran the cool, crystal clear water into one of the basins and splashed his face, noticing that there was a subtle scent, like mountain herbs and forest foliage. This obviously wasn`t ordinary water! He felt the reviving effects immediately, then dried himself off on one of the towels before starting on his soiled flying suit. Fortunately, the material was water repellent and self-cleaning (to an extent, although it would have struggled with the large green stain down the front) and, after a few moments, he considered his image in the large mirror behind the basins and deemed it acceptable - for duty, at any rate! He briefly considered that the stains made him look almost battle worn and he smiled wryly! He turned to his friend who had completed his own ablutions.

`That was the worst journey of my life, my friend.` `Mine too. But Gara...well, I do not think any one else could have piloted the craft the way he did today. Amazing.` Camali replied, drying his hands. He turned to face Lumian.

`Tell me, other than sick, how are you? It has been a very difficult time for you, Lumian. I never had the chance to say how sorry I am about your father.`

He reached out and grasped Lumian`s arm in a gesture of friendship.

`Thank you, Camali. Yes, it was a terrible situation, made even worse by not actually knowing if he survived. I thought he mumbled something as I left but I was in such a hurry...` his voice trailed off and he gazed down at the floor. Camali squeezed his arm harder

`Well, the hardest part is over now and hopefully we are safe. Obviously the theft of the weapon has been discovered and I wonder if, perhaps, this will have provided the catalyst for the long awaited revolution. Now that the threat of annihilation has been removed. I believe it is our time at last, Lumian, time to overthrow the corruption that we have lived with for far too long. But I fear it will be a long and difficult struggle and your father will be the first of many casualties on both sides.`

`Indeed` replied Lumian sadly`and I hope that, once we have safely disposed of the abomination stored below we can return and join in the fight. Somehow, though, I feel there may be more to come before then. It has all seemed just a bit too easy so far, despite our preparations. I am certainly glad that Gara is on our side.`

He managed a wry smile but, before Camali could respond, a further alarm sounded and they heard the pilot`s voice. It had a sense of urgency.

`Back to the control room, my friends. We have got company, I am afraid.`

Lumian and Camali rushed back to the control room and, safely back and fully secured in their seats, they watched in growing horror as the image of a single Hosil fighter gained on them. Gara explained again that, although they didn`t seem to be moving, they were, in fact, caught in the central channel of the conduit, the field of which was moving extremely fast. However, the ship behind them was using its own propulsion system to gain on them. This was a very dangerous move, he said, but they were obviously prepared to risk it in an attempt to get closer.

`They do not dare to use weapons in the conduit. That would be suicidal. But they know we must make an exit at some stage and they will attempt to follow us out. Then we will be at great risk.`

`Is there nothing we can do?` Lumian asked, panic sounding in his voice.

`Oh yes, of course there is. As I said before, these young guys fly by the book. Never seen real active service, you see, just floating about bothering the locals! Not me, though. I did not get where I am flying by the book. Just wait and see!"

His two companions didn`t like the sound of this but they had no choice but to trust him. *I think he is slightly mad*, thought Lumian.

Suddenly, a crackling voice came over the intercom.

`Vessel Intaria, as you will be aware, we are in pursuit and we have a superior craft to yours. It is pointless to try and escape.`

`We will see about that` mumbled Gara.

The voice crackled again.

`As always, Gara Theasak, you always assume you are better than the rest. It would seem that age has not dulled your ego.`

Gara`s head snapped up from the console and his eyes widened in astonishment. He opened his mouth as if to speak but the crackling voice continued

`Yes, I can almost see the look on your face. You thought I had vanished long ago. And yet, here I am, in pursuit. Gaining, in fact. And you think I will be afraid to fire my weapons, am I correct? Hah!`

There was a sudden flash from outside the Intaria and the vessel lurched violently to the left.

`Shit` Gara shouted, as he attempted to stabilise his ship. `What is that madman doing? They must have some extremely advanced weaponry to risk firing in the conduit!`

He shot Lumian a look – given the pilot`s comment about the weapons, he knew exactly what Gara was thinking. Lumian ignored the look, though, now was certainly not the time for a discussion on the finer points of the Hosil fighter`s armaments! Instead he asked

`The pilot seems to know you. Who is he?`

Gara glanced at him again, a grim expression on his craggy face.

`A ghost` he muttered. Then in a clearer voice `Joch six Jocha. A former commander of mine. Presumed killed on an early mission in the conduit. But, apparently, the information was inaccurate.`

`Is he good?` asked Camali

Gara paused before replying. `Mmm. Taught me everything I know. Which means he probably knows exactly what I am going to do next.`

`And what exactly is that?` asked Lumian. His panic was increasing by the minute.

Suddenly the ship`s sexy voice announced.

`Exit portal 7 approaching. Do you wish to exit at this portal?

`Yes please` replied Gara.

`Initiating portal deceleration sequence.`

`Over-ride!`

`Gara, that is dangerous, The ship is already weakened and is presently re-generating. Deceleration sequence recommended.`

`Noted. Implement full manual over-ride`

There was a definite pause as if the vessel was considering Gara`s request. Then the sexy voice responded

`Implemented, Good luck, Gara,` the ship responded wearily.

`Thank you.`

He grasped the paddles once again as he regained manual control of the craft. Lumian closed his eyes and gripped the arms of the seat tightly, hoping to keep control of his stomach, although there was little left in it!

`Where will this portal take us?` Camali managed to ask between clenched teeth.

`I do not have any idea` replied Gara `and I am sorry, but this is going to get bumpy again. Probably worse than the first time. Hang on!`

`Final portal exit approach. It is now or never, Gara. Please be careful.` The ship`s voice was even less sexy this time – in fact, it sounded decidedly strained.

Gara pulled the paddles back towards him and, at the same time, pulled them up from the console. The others were immediately thrown forward despite the gravity buffer. They also felt that they were being pulled down into their seats as the ship rose up very quickly. The misty grey of the conduit appeared to be speeding away from them and, in it, they noticed the vague shape of another craft flash past underneath them. As it did so, Gara twisted the paddles and shoved them forward. Immediately they plunged from grey mist into a darker, red mist that appeared somehow more dense.

`This is the peripheral sector, where the energy field slows down. Normally we move through this slowly to decelerate.` shouted Gara over the noise. `No time today, I am afraid.`

The ship was being tossed around like a cork in a storm. Lumian opened his eyes to see what looked like swirls of pink and red ribbons on the screen ahead of him, apparently moving in entirely random directions, and he suspected that the vessel was completely out of control.

`If you feel like saying a prayer to whatever you may believe in, then now would be the time.`

Lumian found this advice neither encouraging nor re-assuring! He glanced at his friend but Camali`s eyes were tight shut. Lumian decided that this seemed like the best idea and closed his own once again, then opened them as he realised that, actually, he would rather see where his demise lay. Gara managed to regain some small amount of control over the Intaria. The ship`s voice was almost inaudible over the noise when it announced

`Structural integrity down to thirty seven over a hundred. Critical level. Abort! Abort!`

`Not just yet!` Gara shouted, twisting the paddles one more time.

And they were out.

Silence! Floating in the darkness of space. Stars twinkling re-assuringly. The conduit invisible behind them, as if it didn`t exist.

`There. I think that will be the last we see of them` laughed Gara, the relief on his face clear to see. `They have missed the portal and cannot follow us now without coming out at the next one then re-entering and making their way back to this one. For all that he thinks he knows me, Jocha never saw that one coming. We will be well away by then, even if they are faster. Take them ages to find us, if ever!`

`So what just happened back there?` asked Camali as his breathing returned to something like normal.

`Well` said Gara. It is complicated, but as I said, the conduit is really part of the dark, invisible matter that makes up a lot of space. There are different layers, different energy fields, if you like and, with care, you can slide in and out of them and travel vast distances very rapidly. But, as you can see, it can be hazardous! Fortunately, due to the nature of my, em, businesses, I have had the Intaria strengthened considerably to allow it withstand sudden exits, like the one we just performed. I am not completely familiar with the Hosil craft, but I do not think it is strong enough to carry out the same manoeuvre. We normally pull out very slowly. Today, however, we could not hang about so I plunged the ship in at a much steeper angle. The secret is knowing what you can get away with without totally destroying the ship. I suspect we were quite close today. But not close enough and here we are!`

`So you do not think the Hosil fighter could follow us out?` asked Lumian.

`Ah well? Who knows! An old pilot`s trick, one that I suspected these boys might never have seen, but then again, Joch...Anyway, you let them gain on you then, right at the last minute, put the ship into full reverse thrust, pull it up as fast as you can and hope for the best. Then full thrust to get out, no slowing down if you want to make it out through the portal. That is why I asked you to pray! They shot right past underneath us, as you may have noticed, and, by the time they realised what had happened they had missed the portal altogether. Puts a bit of a strain on the old girl, though` he reached forward and patted the console in front of them, smiling as he did so.
`So where exactly are we?` asked Lumian.

`Not sure, but we will find out in due course. First, how is my girl doing?`

The sexy voice sounded exhausted. `Not well, Gara. Some serious hull damage which is re-generating, power charge badly depleted. But she will survive. As always, it would seem.`

Was that sarcasm? thought Lumian

They sat for a short while, resting and regenerating themselves while the vessel attended to its own, apparently extensive, damage. At length Gara said

`I am going to get something to drink. You guys thirsty or hungry?`

`Something to drink would be great, Gara. Thanks. And well done back there. You are an amazing pilot. Really!` said Lumian.

`Just a drink for me too,` said Camali `not much appetite. And I agree totally with Lumian. What a job! No one else could possibly have done what you did today.`

`Ah, it was nothing. All in a day`s work` laughed Gara, obviously delighted at the praise. He exited back to the lounge and the two friends were alone again. They sat in a stunned silence for a short while before Camali spoke.

`Well, that is the hardest part over, I think. I hope! Once the ship has recovered a bit I would imagine we will be moving somewhere safer, then we can have a better look at your father`s...device. Are you going to attempt to destroy the bomb, Lumian?`

`I am not sure but think so. And, alas, that may yet prove to be the hardest part, my friend, despite my knowledge and my preparation for this very moment. Fortunately I remembered to lift the box containing the sequence of the screws.` he chuckled, patting the pocket on his thigh. `I cannot believe that my father still used such archaic technology. It was always his trade mark, though. What a man!`

They sat in silence again, remembering the old weapons master. Lumian was gazing at the screen ahead of him, when he noticed a small flashing light appear in the small three- dimensional display. Just as he was about to draw it to his friend`s attention, the Intaria`s voice spoke.

`Incoming vessel approaching. Hostile craft. Hosil fighter.`

Gara was back in a flash and in his seat.

`Harnesses on!` he shouted. Suddenly they were all locked back in their seats, A vague crackle became audible, difficult to make out at first. Then

`You see, Gara, you think you are so smart. Always so confident in your own abilities. Not so smart now, though. Now, stop your craft, before it stops itself, and prepare to be boarded. You are defeated. By the master!`

`Shit!` Gara shouted and thumped the console in front of him. `Manual control. Weapons online`

`Insufficient power for weapons.`

`None?`

`No, I am sorry, Gara. Power was badly depleted by the voyage and has also been deployed for repairs. Hull is intact but still weakened. Weapons systems are inoperative.`

`What about manual weapons?`

A pause. `Manual weapons?`

`Yes. Missile gun at lower rear`

`So that is what that odd piece of junk is!` There was another pause `Apparently functional. But it requires manual operation.`

`Okay. Lumian, I am really sorry but, after all, you are the weapons expert! You need to get down below, past the bay where the drop-drones are located and along to the rear of the craft then into the small compartment marked "Do Not Enter". In it is a seat and a manual plasma missile gun. You will need full space equipment as the gun portal will be open to space and de-pressurised. There is a suit behind you. I take it you have been in full space gear before?`

Lumian nodded. He had worn a full suit many times before on weapons tests and, although he wasn`t greatly fond of open space, he could tolerate it and was familiar enough with the operation.

`Camali, help him. Open harnesses two and three.`

Their harnesses unfastened and the two stood up. Beside the door a panel slid aside to reveal six lightweight full space suits. Between them they quickly managed to get Lumian fully suited up and when they had finished he checked all life support functions - they were fully operative. Gara spoke in his headset

`Right, down you go. Once you are in I will talk you through the operations of the gun. Quickly. Camali, back in your seat. I suspect this will get messy before too long.`

The intercom crackled again.

`You can play all the silly games you like. We are a superior vessel with advanced weaponry, as you have seen in the conduit. Your vessel does not even have the power for your weapons system. Oh, my apologies, Commander, of course, you are a civilian craft, you do not have weapons, do you? Now, stand down or we will open fire. Do not think for a minute that I will hesitate. You are a traitor, Gara. You should be ashamed...`

`Switch off intercom!` Gara shouted. Joch`s monologue terminated abruptly.

Camali had returned to his seat and was immediately strapped in as Lumian descended the stairs and made his way back along the lower deck of the craft. The entrance to the drop bay slid open and he walked round the catwalk to the back corner where the door that Gara had mentioned stood, clearly marked "Do Not Enter".

`Gara, I am at the door.`

`Good.` the door slid open to reveal a tiny cabin with a chair similar to those in the main control area. However, in front of this was a large, forbidding looking weapon, the likes of which Lumian had only seen in reference books. Still, it looked pretty deadly, if a bit antiquated. He climbed up into the seat.

`Right, I am seated.`

The obligatory harnesses closed round him and the door behind him slid shut. It was dark and he felt a bit claustrophobic so he switched on his visor lights which shone eerily on the large weapon. Then the wall in front of him slid silently open and he was staring out into space, with nothing between him and the airless void. *Shit!* He turned the light back off.

`Listen carefully` said Gara, his voice re-assuring in Lumian`s ear. `On the right is a lever. Pull it down to activate the gun.`

Lumian located it and pulled it down. Arrays of lights appeared and he felt it vibrate slightly as the various systems came on-line.

`Now, in the centre is a handle with a red button on the end. Do not touch it yet, but have you located it?`

`Yes`

`Good. Now, hold the handle. The button is the firing mechanism and is activated by your thumb. DO NOT press it until you are ready to fire. Am I clear? We do not want to give ourselves away just yet.`

`Yes, you are clear.`

`On the left is a handle with a green activation button for the sight. It will self-locate on your helmet visor. Press the button now.`

Lumian did so and the sight mounting moved towards him and touched his visor, moulding to the shape and forming a seal.

`Now, with your left hand, hold the aiming handle. You can rotate it to zoom the sight in on your target, which should show on the sight screen as a small red dot. Do you see it?`

`Yes, I see it` Lumian twisted the handle to zoom in and gasped audibly as the image of the Hosil fighter appeared, immediately much larger in his field of vision.

`The rangefinder shows below the image. If it is red, it is out of range. If it is blue, it is within range. Do not fire until it is in range, it will just waste ammunition and alert them to the weaponry. Which, I may add, we are not really meant to possess!`

Once again, the symbolic red and blue

`I am ready. What now?"

`First, we are going to try and get away, although that is somewhat unlikely, given our depleted energy reserves. However, despite Joch`s bravado, I suspect their craft will have suffered as well. If we can get near enough to a planet where we can land, then we might have a chance. If all else fails, we jettison the drop drone, hope they do not see it, and lead them as far away as we can. But a bit of old fashioned missile fire will be the last thing they expect. I am counting on you, Lumian.`

That didn`t make Lumian feel any better.

Gara pushed the ship forward as best he could given the depleted power sources. The image of the fighter continued to grow larger.

`But how did they get here?` asked Camali. `I thought they overshot the portal.`

`Different craft.` replied Gara. `The one immediately behind us must have had a shadow. A shadow that Joch was piloting, the sneaky dog.`

`A shadow?`

`There would have been a second craft flying behind the first, very close and flying in perfect tandem, mimicking every move so that it would show as a single craft on our scanners. It requires great skill which, unfortunately, Joch possesses. It was a bit of insurance against the manoeuvre we carried out. After all, by that time he knew it was me, knew what I might attempt - you see, it is a kind of trade mark of mine. When we pulled up and the leading craft overshot, the second craft slowed up and exited the portal behind us, using the same manoeuvre. Smarter than I took them for and perhaps he is right about me. Too arrogant, that was always my trouble. Still, we can always hope for a bit more luck now, it has been on our side so far. Lumian, they should be coming into range very soon.`

Sexy voice. `Power now down to thirty parts over a hundred. Maximum speed no longer possible.`

`Ah, shit! Sooner than I had hoped,` exclaimed Gara. `Right,

Lumian, over to you. They should be in range.`

Lumian placed his thumb on the button, moved the gun to bring the Hosil into the central part of the sight and noted that the rangefinder had turned blue. He pressed the button. A stream of yellow plasma missile fire streaked from the barrel of the missile gun and, almost immediately, he saw what looked like sparks fly from the left wing of the fighter. Its nose suddenly pointed up as it pulled away from its pursuit, briefly revealing its lower surface. Lumian fired again, scoring another hit on its underside. Although he wasn`t sure it had much effect, he shouted out loud.

`Well done, Lumian!` yelled Gara. `It will not have done much damage but it will slow them down a bit and will have given them a shock. This vessel is not supposed to be armed with such weapons, after all! Keep watching, give them

another dose when they get back on our tail. I think there is a planet nearby that might do the trick. I am changing course now.`

Lumian felt a slight movement and saw the orientation of the stars change. The Hosil fighter had climbed out of sight until he could no longer see it. He kept scanning the sky, moving the beautifully balanced missile gun with minimal movements of his left hand. It really was a work of art. He moved his head back and, when the visor retracted he looked under the machine and saw a small plate with printing on it. He switched his visor light on and peered at it, just making out the tiny print that said

Plasma Missile Launcher.
Maximum delivery 50 rounds CCC
Designed by Samian 3 Klassarius.
Weapons Master.

His great grandfather.

He sat upright in astonishment, staring out into open space.

`Lumain! Hosil coming in, right hand side. Are you on it?`

`Yes!` He quickly pressed the button that brought the sight back on to his visor and rotated the zoom handle. *Oh shit.*

He fired another burst at the fighter and saw it take evasive action, easily dodging the yellow stream. He heard Gara speak again.

`Hold fire, Lumian, they are wise to us now. Do not waste any more until they get a bit closer.`

Suddenly Lumian saw the Hosil appear immediately behind them and open fire. He knew, of course, exactly what its weapons were capable of and braced himself. But, at the very last second their own ship suddenly dropped alarmingly and there was no impact. *Shit, Gara`s good!* Then he became aware that the vessel`s nose had dropped and it was plummeting downwards. His orientation of space changed and he saw the Hosil streak past above the rear of their vessel as Gara shouted

`I am going to eject the drone. When they come around again, give them a few bursts to keep them occupied. Wait for my command.`

A few seconds more of steep descent and the ship levelled off. Lumian was aware of a slight vibration as the drop bay doors opened, then he saw a small, silver object appear briefly behind them before powering off towards the planet below, which was still out of his line of vision.

`Right, here they come!` shouted Gara, suddenly pulling the ship`s nose back up. `I am heading for that moon, might get a bit of cover. Lumian, do me a favour and knock that son of a bitch out of the sky for me!`

Suddenly, and before Lumian could reply, he felt the craft lurch violently to one side and, as it did so, he saw the Hosil appear back in his sight for an instant before pulling below them. He tried to fire but it was too fast and he felt another impact on the Intaria, which, judging by its movements, now appeared to be out of control.

`Gara, are you there?`

Nothing.

`Gara!` he shouted.

Another impact and he knew that they had been hit again, although he had no idea how badly damaged they were. He knew his failure to communicate with Gara didn`t bode well, though, but he tried once more.

`Gara! Camali! Can you hear me?`

There was a faint crackle, then he heard the pilot`s voice.

`I am here, Lumian, but we are not in good shape. We are going down. Do what you can. I am sorry .`

The ship started to descend with a slow spiral motion and Lumian now knew for certain that it was no longer under Gara`s control. He couldn`t see the fighter and presumed it was just waiting for them to hit the moon that Gara had mentioned. Still, he kept his eyes on the sight, just in case. The ship twisted and, suddenly, the Hosil was right in the middle and very close. He pressed the trigger but, once again, it evaded his fire, pulling up sharply and out of his line of vision. As it did so, the Intaria gave another violent twist and Lumian found himself facing straight towards the fighter`s propulsion exhaust - he pulled the trigger and held it there, watching the plasma stream disappear inside the glowing violet cylinder until, suddenly, the whole rear of the Hosil fighter exploded, parts flying in all directions. Despite his predicament he yelled out loud

`For you, Gara!`

The shout, however, quickly died on his lips as part of the Hosil`s stabiliser assembly spun towards the Intaria and sliced the rear portion, including half the missile bay, away from the remainder of the ship.

As Lumian plummeted towards the small moon, still encased in his prison of the weapons compartment, he saw the remains of the stricken fighter hit the surface and explode in an enormous fireball that illuminated the barren surface. As the orange-tinted ground came up to meet him he briefly had time to wonder about Gara and Camali. *Probably dead, but at least the sphere is safely out of reach. For now. Ah well, it is all over...*

`Yes!`

She hadn`t imagined it – there was definitely something transmitting a signal. Weak and intermittent, nonetheless there was a small light flashing on the display with a series of characters below it. She scanned them quickly and allowed herself a slight, enigmatic smile. Was this fate, or just luck? Almost imperceptibly she shook her head. She believed in neither, having taught herself just to accept whatever happened without question. But it was curious that the signal happened to be emanating from a planet not too far away and had, apparently, just started. Well, at least further investigation would relieve the monotony, the boredom and the...no, she wouldn`t dwell on that at present.

She set a course for the source of the signal, the planet just visible as a tiny blue sphere in the centre of the virtual display projected in front of her. It appeared to be a part of a small solar system and, as her craft altered its direction, she felt an unfamiliar surge of excitement rise in her stomach and her smile widened...very slightly!

PART 2
PLANET EARTH
THE PRESENT

Chapter 5

It was always the smell that reached him first. As Detective Inspector Archie Blue, Paisley Division of Scotland`s Police Force, ascended the dirty, graffiti-scrawled stairwell of the tenement in the town`s Seedhill road, he could detect the characteristic rancid smell that was all too familiar to those of his particular speciality. A mixture of dirt, urine, unwashed bodies, alcohol, stale tobacco smoke and dope, on this occasion very slightly tainted with a fainter, yet more sinister, smell. That was why he was here, of course. An elderly neighbour, some poor old pensioner forced by circumstance to eke out her last few years, or perhaps months, surrounded by drug addicts and alcoholics, afraid to leave her house and venture through the filthy close to the outside world. She had heard some sort of disturbance the previous evening, not an uncommon occurrence in itself, but when she had decided to brave the stairs and head out for some shopping that morning, she had noticed the door of the flat opposite hers was open. She had barely seen the occupants since their arrival several months previously, she had told the uniforms, but their door was always firmly closed, she assured them. Sure enough, the officers had entered the flat, found two bodies in suspicious circumstances and Archie had been informed.

He arrived at the open door and nodded to the young uniformed officer who was standing guard. Before he stepped inside, he took the usual precaution of pulling covers over his shoes and donning a pair of disposable gloves – wouldn`t do to contaminate the crime scene, there were too many sharp defence lawyers all too ready to find the most minor technicalities that could free their wealthy (and usually guilty) clients - Archie had seen it happen too often to take any chances and the last thing he wanted was to fall foul of the Procurator Fiscal`s office by ruining a conviction! He crossed the threshold and walked down the short hallway, only vaguely aware of his shoe covers sticking to the filth of the carpet as he did so. The door to the living room was open and two white-suited scene-of-crime officers were busy, one with a Nikon digital camera and the other with the usual bag of tricks looking for any vestige of relevant evidence. The other figure present was his good friend, pathologist Sam Clayton, who was standing in front of an old dining room chair and bending over the body sitting in it. The doctor, a tall, ruddy-faced man with what could only be described as a truly magnificent moustache, turned and beamed as Archie entered. He more resembled a farmer inspecting a newborn calf than an on-duty pathologist inspecting a corpse.

`Ah, Archie, my boy, and how are you on this fine Monday morning?`

Before Archie could answer, the Doctor moved to one side, revealing in full the subject of his scrutiny. Archie looked at the body then back at the pathologist.

`Yes, another one, I`m afraid.`

Tied to the chair, hands lashed behind its back, was the body of a man of indeterminate age. He was stripped to the waist and there were unpleasant and fresh-looking bloody wounds on his torso. However, the most striking feature was the fact that, stuffed up his nostrils, were two fingers, forming a crude inverted “V-sign”. Archie knew before he even approached the body that these would turn out to be the victim`s pinkies, sheared off with bolt-cutters and stuffed, bloody end first, up the nostrils immediately prior to strangulation. As he approached, he could see the now-expected nylon clothes line round the victim`s neck, undoubtedly the method of his murder. He knelt down and gazed at the slightly bloated face, then turned to the pathologist.

`Usual cause of death then, Sam?`

`Yes, Archie. Death by strangulation, probably late last night. A wee bit of torture first, then the ceremonial removal and placement of the digits, followed by strangulation. Just the right amount, though.

Alas, death wouldn`t have been too sudden.`

Archie looked again at the face.

`I know this guy. I think, anyway.`

He turned as footsteps announced another presence in the room.

`Mornin` Boss. Christ! No` another one!`

`Morning Cam. `Fraid so, usual modus. Have a look. I think we know him. Well, knew him, anyroads.`

Detective Sergeant Cameron Wilkie, Cam to all (except his long-suffering wife, Tracey, who glared at anyone who dared to call him anything other than "Cameron"), knelt down beside his superior and gazed at the face.

`No` a pretty sight. But, yeah, I would pit money on it bein` Gaz Cochrane.`

`Yep, what I thought too.`

He stood up and approached one of the SOCOs who, having finished his photography, was searching the detritus in the flat.

`Anything?`

`No` much, Sir. Looks like this guy was almost off the radar.` he shouted to his colleague who was now through in the bedroom. `Anything in there, Stu?`

The other SOCO came through holding some papers and handed them to Archie.

`Stuffed in the drawer of a wrecked chest of drawers. You`re right with your identity, Sir.`

Some social security papers revealed that the occupant was, indeed, Gary Montague Cochrane, aged 42, unmarried with no dependants.

`Montague?` exclaimed Cam. `Fuck sake! Bit grand for a wee bugger like him, is it no?`

`Aye, you just never know. I`ll leave you to it, Sam. Let`s have a look at the other one then.`

They crossed to the room where the second SOCO had been working and surveyed the scene. If Gary Montague Cochrane`s corpse had been gruesome, the second was entirely tragic. On the floor in the corner of the filthy bedroom, and in the absence of any structural bed frame, was a mattress covered by a pile of grubby sheets and blankets. Huddled in this, naked and filthy, was the figure of a girl. It could have been a child, or teenager, but as they approached they could see from her face that she was older, perhaps mid-twenties. She was emaciated and skeletal and Archie shuddered involuntarily as he recalled pictures of the victims of the Holocaust rescued from Auschwitz. Not for the first time he silently asked himself how this could happen in a seemingly civilised society. Her left arm was crooked with the deadly syringe still dangling from the vein. Either a dirty fix or just one hit too many. Archie gazed at the face, gaunt and white, with the start of smoker`s wrinkles around the mouth. And yet, even in death, even in these vile surroundings, there was a faint transparent beauty and serenity about her, as if she wasn`t really human at all but almost elf-like. And, as with Cochrane, Archie felt there was something vaguely familiar about her. He gazed down at her, hoping she was at peace.

`Recognize her, Boss?` asked Cam, noting Archie`s vaguely puzzled look..

`Nope, don`t think so, Cam. Its just something...no, can`t place it. Maybe she`s been lifted for soliciting. You?`

Cam leaned over and scrutinised the pathetic heap of skin and bones with a grimace. He shook his head.

`Naw, reckon she`s jist another poor wee junkie.` He turned to the SOCO`s who were standing behind them. `Anythin` on this one, guys?`

`Nothing Sir. Just a few clothes and a scruffy bag. Nothing to identify her at all, just some fags, change, keys to the flat. Not even a mobile. Again, its like she doesn`t exist.`

`Not far wrong there. Can`t really call this an existence.` mumbled Archie. `Cover her up, guys, give the poor lassie a wee bit of dignity. She was someone`s wee girl once, don`t forget that. Keep looking, there`s usually something, somewhere.`

He turned back to his DS

`Right Cam, I`ll head back to the office, you go and have a wee word with the old biddy next door. Doubt if she`ll have much to tell us, sounds like the poor old soul was petrified out of her wits. Still, you never know, we need all the help we can get.` He turned to the Pathologist as he left.

`Sam, will you let me know if anything turns up at the post-mortem?`

`I certainly will, my boy, I certainly will. Although I doubt if there will be any great surprises but I`ll keep you posted. On a lighter note, we must get together for a wee dram tasting soon. I`ve got a lovely 18 year old Glendronach that I know you`re just going to adore. And, of course, you are most welcome too, Cameron.`

`Aye, thanks, Doc, I`ll see.` Cam looked away as the Doctor winked and Archie stifled a grin. He was irrepressible, was Sam Clayton. Camp as a row of tents, a truly brilliant pathologist and one of the kindest and funniest men Archie had ever met. The two were close, if slightly unlikely, friends. However, his relationship with the Detective Sergeant was strained, to say the least, and the good doctor knew exactly which of Cam`s buttons to press. As they left the flat, having removed their protective clothing, Cam turned to Archie

`Honestly, boss, I do not know how you have anythin` tae do wi` him ootside work. The guy`s...well, he`s...`

`He`s a true gem and a good friend, Cam, you should give him the benefit of the doubt. And he`s got one of the best malt cellars I`ve ever seen. Listen, maybe you should come along next time. I think he really likes you!`

`Aye, that`ll be fuckin` right!` Then, as he saw Archie`s face break into a grin, he took a pace back and aimed a kick at his boss`s backside with his size 11s!

***

Archie was sitting at his desk, glowering at the pile of paperwork he was leafing through, when Cam returned. He looked up

`Any joy?`

`No` wi` Mrs Macleod, Boss. Christ, it`s criminal! Her wee flat`s like a palace, spotless, beautiful furniture, plants, just lovely. But she`s stuck in the middle o` aw these scumballs living in Social Security rentals, hasn`ae a hope of selling up and there`s nowhere else for her tae go. No family, nothin`. And its no` just the junkies and jakeys. She says she`s sure there`s something going on with kids up the back o` the close. She`s seen a few dodgy characters taking a kid up, then a few minutes later a car appears an` another one disappears up the close after them. Ten minutes, the whole caravan`s aff again before there`s time for us to arrive. Makes you sick. But she`s got nothin` more tae tell us. Never spoke to the neighbours, sometimes bumped into the girl but she never said a word. Mrs Macleod wondered if she was foreign. Christ, I feel that sorry for her.`

Not for the first time Archie realised that, under the tough, gruff exterior, Cam was capable of great compassion and sympathy for the victims of the crimes they were obliged to investigate. He would never have dared to tell Cam this though!

`I know what you mean, Cam. But, unfortunately, she`s the least of our worries. This is the fifth one of these killings in the last two months. I was just checking the files. Sixth of July, John Connelly. Twenty fifth, John Brogan. Fourth of August, Steven Allan. Twenty ninth, Zak Christie. And now Gaz Cochrane.`

`Aye. All small time dealers, all Dillon`s boys.`

Dillon`s boys!

Until a few years ago, Callum Dillon had been "the Man", one of the West of Scotland`s most notorious criminals dealing in drugs, prostitution and anything that was stolen, all fronted by a taxi firm, a scrapyard and a chain of coin-op tanning salons. All text book stuff. His only redeeming feature was he refused to have any involvement with child prostitution or exploitation, coming down hard on anyone who crossed that line. Dillon was seemingly untouchable until one day he just simply wasn`t there any longer. Gone. Vanished. Just like that. His custom built, luxurious house in Bridge of Weir lay empty until it was finally re-possessed by the bank, his Range Rover sat un-moving until it was dealt with in a similar fashion. His partner, Sandie McGrath was questioned repeatedly until her innocence could no longer be disputed, after which she quietly slipped off the scene, with little or no funds of her own (well, none that the Police could trace) to show for her ten years with "the Man".

And then came Blok.

Six foot six, about twenty stone, cropped black hair, he arrived from some vague and undefined Eastern European country and conveniently stepped into the vacuum left by Dillon. Some said his nickname derived from his origins (Eastern Bloc, easily mis-spelled by those he associated with). Others claimed it came from his lack of emotion, resembling a block of stone (equally easily mis-spelled!) But Blok he was to all, except when called in for fruitless questioning, when his full name of Gregor Czarneki was recorded on the police files.

Looking back, it now seemed too much of a co-incidence that he had conveniently arrived just as Dillon disappeared. But, with no body, no evidence and, most certainly, no witnesses, there was nothing the Police could do, except watch and wait. Unfortunately, as well as being big and brutal, Blok was also cunning and had managed to remain one step ahead of them and free to go about strengthening his criminal empire. That was when the killings had started, all of the victims being Dillon`s men, although Blok had recruited a good few of those higher up the food chain – local knowledge always came in handy, after all! Up until now, the victims had all been the small time dealers and distributors who had thought that, perhaps, they could make it on their own. The method was always the same. Tied in a chair with cheap clothes line, available in any pound shop, the victim was brutally interrogated, slashed with some sort of surrated-edged blade, then his pinkies were severed and stuck up his nose in the characteristic "V" fashion before he was strangled slowly by another piece of clothes line. It was brutal and sent two very clear messages. The first to any other minor criminals who thought about furthering their careers – don`t mess with Blok! The second, to the police – up yours, you can`t catch me! As Archie thought about it he clenched his fist in anger, but he knew that wasn`t the way, anger just clouded his vision. They had to watch and wait until, sooner or later, he would put a foot wrong and they would have him. Hopefully sooner, he thought. He might even get deported back to wherever he came from, save Scotland the bother of accommodating him for twenty five years. Anyway, a man like Blok would thrive in jail, his size and brooding presence would quickly establish him as the top dog, even in the likes of Barlinnie or Peterhead.

But it was proving to be a long wait.

`Oh, jist one other thing` said Cam, digging something out of his trouser pocket. `Nearly forgot! We found this. Stuffed doon the back o` the mattress.` He placed a cheap, pay-as-you-go mobile with a cracked screen on the desk. `Unfortunately, its oot o` charge.`

`Good stuff, Cam, at least its something. See if you can get someone to charge it up and have a look at any useful numbers, track them down if you can. With a bit of luck we can find someone who can identify her. Gonna be a tough call, though.`

`Ok boss, no problem. Coffee?`

`Aye, cheers, Cam. Get us a biscuit. Chocolate. Need something to sweeten the day!`

Chapter 6

It was lunchtime. Not being a huge fan of the canteen and preferring to eat in his office, Archie had just swallowed the last mouthful of Marks and Spencer`s finest BLT sandwich and was washing it down with Barr`s finest Irn-Bru (sugar free, of course) when Cam pushed open the door and came into the office, looking very pleased with himself. The Tunnock`s tea cake could wait! The DS sat down across the desk from him and Archie looked at him questioningly. Cam grinned.

`Result. We got the phone fired up an` there`s a list o` numbers, one o` which is "Mum". We traced the number an` its registered tae this name and address. Upmarket area, it would appear.` He passed a piece of paper over to Archie, who deciphered the DS`s scrawl to read

Mrs Karen Whiteford
Highfield House
Duchal Road
Kilmacolm.

His heart plummeted to his boots. Cam stared at him.

`You ok, Boss? Look like you`ve seen a ghost. Dae you know her?`

Archie paused before replying. He put the paper on the desk , sighed heavily then looked up at Cam.

`Do me a big favour, Cam?`

`Aye sure, Boss. Whit is it?`

`Can you make the call please, mate. I can`t talk to this woman over the phone. I`ll explain in the car.`

Cam looked quizzically at Archie but didn`t comment. If the big man needed a favour...

`Aye Boss, nae problem. D`you want to head over straight away?`

`Yeah, I`ll see you downstairs in five minutes, unless there`s no-one home. Let me know.`

Cam left to make what was always the worst call in the life of a cop and Archie sat at his desk, head in his hands. After a few minutes, he shook himself, stood up and grabbed his jacket then headed down to the car park. As he crossed to where his car was parked, he experienced the vague (and slightly guilty) thrill that his black Porsche Panamera always instilled.

***

Fifteen minutes later they were heading to the expensive Renfrewshire suburb of Kilmacolm, reputedly home to the highest proportion of millionaires in Scotland (including a few in whom Archie and Cam had more than a passing interest). Cam broke the unusual silence – the two were close friends and conversation was never usually an issue.

`So Boss, I get the feeling there`s a wee story here. You want tae tell me before we get there so`s I don`t look like a prize twat?`

Archie paused for a minute, then spoke in a flat tone.

`Karen Whiteford, or Karen McMillan, as I knew her. Way back. We had a slow dance at a school disco in second year then went steady until we finished sixth year. We were inseparable and everyone thought we would get married.`

`So whit happened?`

`Life, Cam, that`s what. I went to Glasgow Uni to study English and Politics. She went to St Andrews to study medicine.`

Cam considered this. He had joined the Force straight from school and was a bit suspicious of higher education.

`But it`s no` that far, surely? If it wis somethin` special.`

`Well, I thought it was. Then suddenly, she met this guy who had been a couple of years ahead of us at school. Gordon Whiteford. He was in third year medicine by this time, top of his class, a real high flier. Went on to become a leading Paediatrician, he`s had papers published, the full works. He was there, I wasn`t and he became flavour of the month, year, whatever. Next thing, they were engaged and that was that. We lost touch completely. Until now, that is. Didn`t even know they stayed here, last I heard they were down south somewhere. I didn`t even know they had any family until now.`

`Fuck sake!` exclaimed Cam, shaking his head. `No wonder it wis a shock when you found oot who the mother wis! Listen, Boss, d`you want me tae handle it? We can go back, I`ll pick up a WPC, do the usual routine.`

Archie shook his head.

`No, Cam, thanks anyway. I owe her this much. We meant a lot to each other a long time ago so this is the least I can do. Her husband`s a decent guy too, very highly respected. I kinda knew him, we played rugby in the school team. It`ll be a tough one, though.`

He lapsed into another silence as he concentrated on his driving and Cam refrained from any further interruptions until they were cruising slowly along Duchal Road. It was wide and lined with trees, behind which the large Victorian sandstone villas nestled in their immaculate grounds. By this time the rain had come on heavily, making it harder to find their destination. He gazed at the expensive properties on either side of him.

`Must be doin` awright tae live here, though. I reckon these are well over a million apiece, easy. There it`s there, Boss. Highfield House.`

A semi-circular driveway cut through a row of copper beech trees, identified by the sign carved into the stone gate-posts.

Archie slowed down and turned into the first of the two entrances and the sparkling granite gravel crunched under the wide tyres. He pulled up behind a silver Mercedes coupe with a personal plate, KW 1. He had noticed a dark blue Bentley parked at the side of the beautiful blonde sandstone building with a similar number, GW 1. The cost of the two plates alone would just about have bought his own, somewhat indulgent, Porsche Panamera. The two policemen got out of the car and climbed the few steps to the heavy oak door. Archie looked at Cam and took a deep breath.

`Here goes.`

He pressed the bell and they heard a distant, sonorous chime from somewhere deep within the palatial house. The door opened and they were met by a tall, lean man with dark hair, greying at the temples. He was dressed in that casual, elegant way that oozed class and money. A pair of expensive rimless spectacles sat on his clean-shaven face, which, at this moment, looked drawn and haggard. But he managed a slight smile as he extended his hand.

`Archie. It`s been a long time.` His handshake was firm and oddly re-assuring. A good bedside manner, Archie supposed.

`It has, Gordon. I`m so sorry that it had to be in these circumstances.`

Gordon Whiteford briefly lowered his eyes.

`Yes, well, you`d better come in.` He stood aside.

`This is Detective Sergeant Wilkie.`

Cam extended his hand, but only nodded and didn`t say anything as the Dr Whiteford shook it.

`Well, this is, of course, a terrible shock but, alas, not entirely unexpected, as you can probably imagine. We tried everything but, in the end, poor Lucinda just seemed hell-bent on a course of self destruction.`

Archie winced inwardly at the mention of the name. Lucinda had been his mother`s name and she and Karen had been very close. His mother was heartbroken when the relationship ended and he couldn`t help but wonder if there was any significance in this choice for her daughter. Of course, maybe she just liked the name; he certainly wasn`t going to ask. Gordon Whiteford took their rain-soaked jackets and briefly disappeared into what appeared to be a cloakroom – there was no sign of any other outerwear cluttering the walls. He came back out and attempted a smile, although Archie thought it looked more like a grimace of pain.

`Right, come this way, please.` he said, leading them through the large, tastefully decorated hallway. Archie was vaguely aware of a chandelier above his head and, as he looked, he could see Cam glancing about him, obviously well impressed by the surroundings which included several original and expensive looking paintings, all with their own individual picture-lights. Gordon led them along a short corridor, leading to a glass door that opened out on to a huge conservatory, running the whole width of the rear of the house. It looked on to what Archie quickly estimated to be about half an acre of perfectly manicured lawns, gravel pathways, lush shrubberies and an enormous pond with a central fountain. But it wasn`t the conservatory or the garden that held his attention. Perched on the edge of a beige leather settee was an attractive, natural ash-blonde woman with large, tear-filled hazel eyes set in a perfect oval face. She stood up and uttered a single word, `Archie,` before bursting into a fit of sobbing and, to his astonishment, falling into his arms. He didn`t know where to look. Gordon Whiteford turned to Cam.

`Can I make you a tea or a coffee, Sergeant? I think we`ll leave these two to catch up a bit.` He exited the conservatory, leaving Cam with little choice but to follow.

A door led off the corridor that they had come along and Cam followed Gordon Whiteford through it into the kitchen. It was enormous. Cam reckoned it was about the size of the whole ground floor of the house he shared with his wife and his infant daughter. It had a large, central breakfast bar, a table with six chairs and most of the walls were lined with solid-wood units, under which were pristine white tiles. More expensive-looking prints were hung tastefully on the remaining, untiled walls, along with a huge pin-board plastered with family photographs and memorabilia, a very human touch in the quasi-clinical environment. The overall effect was dazzling though, even on this dull day.

`What can I get you, Sergeant?`

`Coffee please, Sir, if it`s no trouble. Milk and two, thanks.`

`Funny, isn`t it. In times of emotional stress, collapse even, we cherish the comforting solidity of a hot drink. I remember when my own mother died, I went in to the hospital room where her body lay and my father was sitting beside her, drinking a cup of tea. Quite bizarre, really.`

Cam noticed that he was getting no ordinary coffee. One of the modern, Barista-style machines was hissing and spluttering and he could smell the delicious, sharp tang of real espresso as it filtered down into the white china cup. Gordon crossed to an enormous American-style fridge and, opening it, asked

`Milk or Cream?`

`Oh, a wee splash of cream would be lovely, thanks very much.`

`White or brown sugar?`

This was getting very slightly ridiculous, but Cam was very aware that, in times of extreme emotional stress, people often responded with an over-compensation of normality. Who was he to question it?

`White will be just fine, thanks.`

Gordon spooned two measures in the cup from an elegant silver sugar bowl and passed it to Cam.

`Can I get you a biscuit, a scone, perhaps?`

`No, thank you, I`ve no` long had my lunch. Coffee is just fine. It smells absolutely delicious.`

`Yes, these machines are wonderful. Can`t beat a really good coffee, one of life`s little pleasures. So, how did it happen? Did she suffer much?`

More like it.

`No sir, I don`t honestly think she did. You know she was found with a syringe in her arm?` Gordon shook his head

`No, I wasn`t aware of that. Heroin, I take it?`

`Well, we`re still carryin` out an analysis of the contents but I suspect it will prove to be heroin and either contaminated or else extremely pure. It looks like she became unconscious very quickly, probably didn`t feel a thing in the end.` What else could he say? He certainly wasn`t going to go into detail about the filthy, squalid flat where the girl had been found.

`Well, I suppose that`s something. We tried everything, you know. It all started at Art School, she got in with the wrong crowd. At first it was just the occasional joint, then she moved on to cocaine. I guess she just had one of those addictive personalities. Latterly she was injecting heroin. Tried to hide it, of course, but we`re both doctors, the signs were all there. We had her in re-hab last year and thought she had finally cleaned herself up, but then she moved in with some vile man almost twice her age and...well, here we are, I suppose. I have to confess that this hasn`t come as a great surprise, you know. I suspected it was only a matter of time...` he looked away. Cam made no reply.

`I haven`t told our son yet. I suppose that`s the next step.`

`You`ve got a son?` Cam asked. At least that was something.

`Yes, Ewan, he`s studying medicine at Glasgow. Following in the family footsteps, I suppose you`d say. He stays in a flat in the West End. I`ll go up and see him this evening - he`ll be devastated...`

The doctor broke off suddenly and glanced towards Cam.

`Are you married, Sergeant? Do you have any family?`

`Yes, sir, I do. I`ve a wee girl called Abigail, eighteen months old.` He suppressed a smile or the offering of any further details. He felt it wasn`t appropriate.

Gordon Whiteford suddenly turned to face him, grabbed his arms and gazed straight into his eyes with a look of such intensity that it almost set Cam back on his heels.

`Watch over her, Sergeant. Always. Look out for her, find out where she`s been, who she`s been with. If she comes in late, find out why. And never let a day pass without telling her you love her. Will you do that!`

Cam managed to stammer `Aye, of course` when they heard a door open and heavy footsteps in the hall. Gordon let go of the Sergeant`s arms and they looked expectantly at the kitchen door. But the footsteps passed and, suddenly, they heard the loud slam of the front door. They briefly looked at each other in surprise then headed out into the hall, where they could hear Mrs Whiteford sobbing quietly in the conservatory. But they turned in the direction of the front door and Gordon Whiteford opened it just in time to hear the engine of the Detective Inspector`s car scream and witness its departure as the wheels fought for purchase on the gravel of the driveway, scattering chips in all directions until, suddenly, it lurched forward and disappeared out of the exit and down the tree-lined street, narrowly missing a parked delivery van as it briefly slithered on the water-slicked tarmacadam. They stared in astonishment, then Cam turned to Gordon, spread his hands in disbelief and said, quietly

`Well, that`s a first!`

Chapter 7

Cam was feeling decidedly uncomfortable and trying his best not to keep looking at his watch. There had been no response to his calls to his superior officer`s mobile and he reckoned Archie had been gone about fifteen minutes, although it seemed like an eternity as he sat in the luxurious surroundings of the Whiteford`s conservatory, attempting to make some kind of small talk. He had finished his second coffee and was vaguely needing the toilet when the doorbell rang - he suppressed a `Thank Christ`, instead standing up hopefully. Gordon led the way to the front door after Cam had said an embarrassed goodbye to Karen Whiteford but, when he opened it, there was no-one there. However, they could both see the shape of the Porsche through the trees, parked at the side of the street. Cam turned to Gordon and said

`I`m really sorry, Dr Whiteford. I`m sure there`s an explanation. I`ll go and have a word wi` DI Blue. Give me a minute.`

`No, Sergeant. There`s no need, I fully understand the situation, no explanation is needed and I think it best if you just leave it at that.`

Cam hesitated but decided to say nothing. The doctor brought the jackets out and handed them to Cam, who put his own on. He frowned questioningly and was about to change his mind but before he could speak the Doctor continued.

`Go and speak to your friend, for I am fairly sure that he is, indeed, your friend. He will explain everything to you. At least, I hope he will.`

He extended his hand and Cam shook it.

`Well, okay Sir, if you say so. I really am so sorry for your loss. We will, of course, keep you informed.`

`Informed? Oh yes, the PM, etcetera. Will it be Sam Clayton who carries it out?`

`Yes Sir, it will. Do you know him?`

`Yes, indeed I do. An excellent man. He`ll probably do me the courtesy of contacting me personally. Anyway, Sergeant Wilkie, I appreciate your time. I know you understand what a shock this is to us, but your own task is not an easy or a pleasant one and you have been most sympathetic. Please tell Archie not to worry. And remember what I said about your daughter. What was her name again?`

`Abigail, Sir. And I will. Thanks again.`

By the time he was down the steps the heavy door had closed behind him. Despite jogging down to the waiting car, the rain was streaming off his jacket by the time he reached it and slipped in to the passenger seat. Archie was gripping the wheel, staring straight ahead; he neither spoke nor acknowledged Cam`s presence. The sergeant was furious.

`So, Boss. D`you mind explaining just whit the fuck happened back there? Mind whit I said about me no` looking a total twat? Well, guess what? I did! What`s this all aboot, eh?`

Archie made neither move nor reply.

`Hey, did you hear me? Archie, for fuck sake, are you ok?`

Still no reply. Cam considered the situation briefly, then said

`Okay! Fine! The silent treatment. Listen, I hav`nae a clue whit`s goin` on, but you`re in one hell of a state. You want me to drive?`

Without a word, Archie got out and walked round the rear of the vehicle. Cam did likewise but, to avoid passing he walked around the front – he was seriously pissed off at his Boss. He got in to the driver`s seat and, once they were both secured, he set off, a bit more sedately this time. He knew Archie well enough to know when to keep silent and this was one of those times, but he was angry at the way he had been treated and he wanted some kind of an explanation. However, they arrived back at Police HQ without a word being spoken and, as it was still pouring, Cam pulled into a space as close to the entrance as he could get before killing the engine. He sat for a few minutes, then turned to Archie.

`Ok Boss, whit now?`

Archie finally responded.

`You go on in, Cam, I just need a bit of time.`

`Aye, okay, fair enough.`

Cam got out and ran the thirty yards or so to the entrance. But by the time he got there, the Porsche had fired up again and was speeding off towards the exit. Cam gazed in astonishment for the second time that day,

`Fuck me!` he exclaimed, shaking his head as he turned and entered the building.

***

Archie leaned forward on the leather settee and gazed, unseeing, at the view before him. One of the reasons that he had bought the old, converted farm cottage, high above the sleepy little Renfrewshire village of Lochwinnoch, was for this very view. The large, bi-fold doors faced almost due south, down across the fields and trees to Castle Semple Loch and the rising terrain beyond. It was dark now and the lights of the houses and the various farms and properties dotted about the countryside twinkled comfortingly in the clear night air. But tonight there was no comfort for Archie Blue, other than that contained in the three-quarters empty bottle of Glenfiddich that sat on the table in front of him. With an unsteady hand, he splashed another inch of the golden liquid into the crystal tumbler sitting on the table and swallowed about half of it before sitting back on to the cushions, gazing unseeingly out into the darkness. His reverie was interrupted by a banging on the door, which he ignored. The banging was repeated, more forcefully this time.

`Fuck off!` he muttered.

More banging, and a shout.

`Open the fuckin` door, Archie. It`s bloody freezing out here. And wet. I`ve been soaked enough for one day. C`mon! Let me in!`

It was Cam. Archie stood up unsteadily and turned to go to the front door but he caught his foot on the leg of the couch and came crashing down, catching his head on the edge of the large dresser that sat against the side wall. He moaned and was vaguely aware of blood trickling down his face.

`Archie, for fuck sake, what`s going on. Mate, are you okay? Open the door, for Christ`s sake.`

Archie managed to get up, stumble his way along the hall and unlock the door before collapsing in a heap on the hall floor. Cam managed to squeeze past him and get behind him, lifting him up beneath his armpits.

`Come on, mate, let`s get you back through an` intae a seat. Christ, it`s been a while since I`ve seen you this bad.`

Cam managed to get Archie back on the sofa, where he lay down groaning and clutching his head. Cam turned on a side light and Archie winced at the brightness.

`Dearie dearie me, you`re a right mess, Boss. Listen, you stay put, I`ll get a towel, clean you up then organise some strong coffee for us both.`

Cam knew his way around the house well enough and soon had Archie sitting up, holding a towel and a bag of ice over what was turning into a large, purple swelling. He went back to the kitchen and returned a few minutes later with two large, steaming mugs of coffee and a packet of chocolate digestive biscuits.

`Right, son. Get some of that down you. I reckon we need tae soak up some o` that fine malt whisky that you`ve obviously been sampling.`

Archie managed to eat about four biscuits and swallow two gulps of coffee before he threw up.

After Cam had cleaned Archie, the couch, the floor and made some fresh coffee, the Detective Inspector was looking very slightly healthier, although he sat with his head cradled in his hands, moaning softly.

`I`m so, so sorry Cam. That was above and beyond. I really appreciate it.`

`Och, no problem. Anyway, its no` the first time!`

Archie actually managed a slight grin.

`Aye, I suppose its not. Thanks anyway, I owe you one.`

`Naw, Boss. What you owe me is an explanation.`

There was a pause.

`You`re right, that`s exactly what I owe you.`

`I`m listening...`

Archie sat up and swallowed a slug of coffee. He gazed at the floor.

`She was mine.`

`Who was? What do you mean?`

`The girl. Lucinda. She was mine.`

Cam paused as it sank in.

`Naw! The lassie in the flat. No way! How could she be yours? You said you hadn`ae seen Karen Whiteford, or whatever she was, since school. That makes it somewhere aboot thirty odd years ago.

That lassie was in her twenties. Anyway the Doctor said she was his daughter.`

Aye, well, turns out she wasn`t.`

Cam said nothing. He just stared at Archie in disbelief.

`So, we went to Uni, different towns, just kinda drifted apart. I heard Karen had hooked up with Gordon Whiteford and, yeah, I was a bit hurt but it was as much my fault as hers. Too busy to keep in touch. And there were girls up in Glasgow, you know...`

Cam knew!

`So, I got over it, it wasn`t a big deal in the end. Then, in fourth year, a crowd of us went through to St Andrews for a golf weekend.`

`But you don`t play golf, Boss.`

`Aye, well, it was just an excuse for a piss-up really. Sounded like a good idea but I think the most we managed was a game of putting at the Old Course putting green. Then, on the Saturday night, guess who I met in a pub. None other than Karen McMillan, as she still was, although she was engaged by this time. Well, we were all pretty well gone and, next thing I know its Sunday morning and I wake up in her bed. Both naked. Don`t even remember anything about it. To be honest, I don`t know if she did either.`

`But that`s nothing tae go by, Archie. She was engaged - surely she wis sleeping with Gordon?`

`Well, there`s the thing. Turns out his family were Brethren and he had a very moral upbringing. Didn`t believe in sex before marriage, apparently, wanted to wait until they`d tied the knot and it seems that Karen was happy enough to go along with it. Come to think of it, that was probably why the two of us ended up...well...you know. Poor girl must`ve been desperate. And drunk. Anyway, two months later, she did the test and I`m the only guy in the frame.`

`But he must have known.`

`Oh aye, of course he knew. Karen told him the whole, sorry story. But he said he still loved her, it had just been a moment of weakness and he would happily take the child as his own. All about "turning the other cheek", that kind of stuff, you know? Anyway, they moved the wedding forward so she wouldn`t be, well, "showing" I think they put it. No wonder I didn`t get an invite, mind you.`

`So you`re certain.`

`Yup. So`s she. Absolutely no doubt. I was the only guy she`d slept with. Poor wee Lucinda was hers and mine. My own kid.`

And the flood gates broke.

***

It was well after midnight before Cam managed to get Archie calmed down and into his bed. He waited until he heard his friend start to snore before heading back downstairs and clearing up the remaining mess. The room was stinking of vomit and whisky and he left a small side window on the catch in the hope that it might be a bit fresher in the morning. He made to pour the remnants of the Glenfiddich down the sink then thought better of it – Archie would probably need it before too long. As he went out into the hall, on an impulse he opened the drawer in the little cabinet behind the door and smiled grimly as he reached in and took out a spare set of door-keys...just in case. He switched off the lights then left as quietly as he could before starting the drive back to his home in Paisley. He had never in all his life felt so glad to be returning to his wife and his daughter but his heart was breaking for the big man, his friend, Boss and now a bereaved father. Cam shouted

`Fuckin` bastards. You fuckin` bastards` and thumped the steering wheel in fury.

Chapter 8

He must have left the light on in his bedroom; the brightness was searing his eyes, even behind his closed eyelids, dragging him back to consciousness from a very dark place. He half opened one eye and realised that the light was, in fact, coming from the window. He half opened his other eye, triggering a wave of nausea before realising that his body felt as if it had been hit by a truck. His head was pounding and, initially, he struggled to recall what had happened. He sat up but felt so dizzy that he collapsed back on the bed, reaching his hand up to locate the source of the headache. He winced as he felt the tender lump on his forehead then, suddenly, the memories flooded back and he closed his eyes and groaned. He lay for a few minutes, then sat up again, more slowly this time, got out of bed and shuffled carefully to his en-suite where he risked a look in the mirror to see if he looked as bad as he felt. He did! He splashed some cold water on his unshaven face and returned to the bedroom where, sitting back on the edge of the bed, he suddenly noticed the time - 11.45a.m.

`Shit!`

He stood up too quickly and his legs nearly buckled under him, causing him to fall back heavily on the bed. A vague memory managed to infiltrate his brain of Cam saying something about not going in to work. The phrase "no` way you`ll be fit for anything tomorrow." seemed to come to mind and the way Archie was feeling, Cam was correct. He lay back down, closed his eyes and, almost instantly, fell asleep.

When he woke for the second time his clock showed 3.14p.m. and, when he sat up, he definitely felt a bit more human, although he still had a thumping headache. He made it to the shower without collapsing and, half an hour later, he was sitting at his kitchen table with a steaming mug of sweet tea, a couple of painkillers and two slices of toast. Although he was hungry, his throat was still raw with the combination of whisky and vomiting. Also, his stomach was decidedly tender and he didn`t want to push his luck too far. But any discomfort paled into insignificance compared to the hurt he was feeling at yesterday`s discovery and, once again, he felt the swell of uncontrollable rage surge up inside him.

Archie had always had a temper. At school, there had been the occasional incident where someone had pushed him just that little bit too far, causing him to lash out and, whilst many would argue that he was just showing normal male teenage aggressive tendencies, the problem was more that, once he had started, he didn`t know when to stop. However, his apparent, if occasional, lack of self-control became more of a problem when a fellow pupil was hospitalised as a result of Archie`s frenzy and his parents had struggled to convince the head teacher not only that Archie deserved to remain at the mildly-prestigious Paisley Grammar School, but also that the police should not be involved as it would seriously damage Archie`s future prospects. The school reluctantly agreed, although more to save their own reputation than that of their pupil. A prolonged and stern talking-to from his father followed, in which Archie was left in no doubt that, should he wish to get anywhere in his life, he would need to learn to control his temper. Throughout University and in his subsequent years of police service he had managed, despite frequent provocation, to repress what his father had called the "red mist" , but this particular set of circumstances was pushing him beyond all reasonable limits. He gazed at the mug of tea and tried to focus his thoughts. Raw anger was no good; after all, although he knew who was ultimately responsible for his newly-discovered daughter`s death, he could hardly just walk round to Blok`s house, (always assuming he had given the police his correct address) knock on his door and smash his face, much as he would have liked to do just that. No, this called for a far more measured approach, with good hard evidence, a solid case for the Procurator Fiscal and a long conviction. He reached for a notepad and pen and started jotting down his thoughts and trying to craft a plan of some sort. At least it kept his mind off his grief; and his headache!

Like many people suffering from the feelings of desolation caused by bereavement, Archie lost all track of time and, to his surprise, it was 7.15p.m. when Cam called him on his mobile.

`Hey Boss!` the DS said in a slightly sombre tone. `How`re you doin`? Feelin` a bit better, I hope?`

`Yeah, slightly, Cam. Still got a hell of a bruise on my head though. Listen, mate, I really appreciate all you did last night, it couldn`t have been very pleasant for you.`

`Aw, no problem, Boss. You`d have done the same for me. I hope!`

`Aye, of course I would! Listen, Cam. Could you just keep the...well...situation to yourself in the meantime. Don`t really want word getting out, you know what it`s like in the office.`

`No worries, Boss. No` a word, I`ll leave any of that to you.`

`Also, I`m going to take the rest of the week off. I just need time to get my head sorted, know what I mean.`

There was a pause before Cam replied.

`Aye, sure thing. Listen, Boss, you`re not planning on anything daft, are you?`

`Like what?`

`Well, like you were pretty upset last night, rantin` aboot revenge and retribution. No` words you usually hear a responsible Detective Inspector throwin` aboot. I just...well, I wouldn`ae want you to be thinking o`...em...taking the law into your own hands, if you get ma meanin`.`

`Aye, fair comment, Cam, point taken. No, that was just the whisky talking - don`t worry, I`m under control, I just don`t want to come in and have to pretend that life`s normal at the moment. It`s not.`

`No, I reckon it isn`ae an` I`m truly sorry, Boss. Okay, no problem, I`ll let the powers that be know you won`t be in `til next week. I`ll try an`come up with somethin` believable! Reckon you`re owed, anyway, as far as I recall you`ve no` had a day off sick in your career. And when wis the last time you took a holiday?`

`True. I was supposed to be heading down to the Lake District the weekend after next, catch some fresh air and do a bit of hill climbing. Don`t know now, though, I`ll wait and see.`

`Naw, Boss, you should definitely go! It`ll do you the world o` good, up some God-forsaken mountain in the wind and pissin` rain, cold, hungry an` knackered, with only some scabby sheep for company. Cannae beat it!

Archie actually managed a chuckle at his friend`s remarks (although the resulting pain in his head made him wince) before they said their goodbyes and he suddenly realised he was ravenous.

***

And so the next few days slipped by, with the hours and days seeming to blend into a single, bleak entity as Archie struggled to come to terms with two simple facts; he had discovered that he was a father and his daughter was a recently deceased drug addict. He could think of little else and, in fact, he tried to think of little else for, if he kept these two painful thoughts to the fore, he could repress his burning desire for revenge. Well, almost...

Cam phoned a couple of times to check he was okay – he told his friend he was fine but it was a lie - he was far from okay. He struggled to put his feelings into words; he was hurt, both at his loss and at the fact that Karen hadn`t told him he had a daughter. Maybe he could have done something to help - then again, maybe not! He was also trying to control the fury that he felt rising inside him when he thought of those responsible for Lucinda`s death. Another whisky always helped, though...

It was just an idea at first. Due probably to a combination of shock and of the drastic change to his normal routine, he was struggling to sleep and, on Wednesday night, he decided to drive into Paisley, assuring himself that it was just a bit of reconnaissance. He circled about the town centre and some of the seedier areas, looking for any recognisable vehicles or faces but the town was bleak and deserted and, after a couple of fruitless hours, he gave up and drove home. The next night he repeated the exercise but, again, to no avail. It was almost as if the criminal fraternity knew of his intent and were all staying indoors and he decided he would have to widen the search. It never even crossed his mind that his black Porsche Panamera, his one big indulgence in life, was a pretty conspicuous vehicle and any self respecting criminal would soon make themselves scarce upon its approach.

***

High up on the Gleniffer Braes, the range of steep, rolling hills behind Paisley and its environs, lies the so-called "car park in the sky", accessed from the steep (and aptly named) Sergeantlaw Road.

Offering spectacular views across the extensive flood-plain all the way up to Glasgow in the east and over to Ben Lomond and the distant Highland mountains in the north, the car park was a daytime favourite with dog-walkers, kite-flyers and those just wanting to get some brisk, fresh air and a great view, particularly of what appeared to be toy aeroplanes taking off from Glasgow Airport. At night, however, it became more of a trysting-place for the young, "hot-car" set, avoided by the more respectable citizens. Then, once their time had passed, it was reputed to be an occasional, secluded meeting place for the exchange of illicit substances and sometimes worse, although it was a long time since any arrests had been made here – any vehicles on the road below were visible in plenty of time to allow a hasty escape.

Having grown up in Paisley, Archie was entirely familiar with the area and was only too aware that an approach from down below would be easily noticed. Instead, he drove along the narrow back roads, over the hill from the small Ayrshire village of Gateside, parking in the roadway to an abandoned farm about half a mile across the braes from the park, then made his way on foot over the rough moorland to arrive at the raised ground behind the car park itself. He was dressed for the occasion, in a warm, black waterproof jacket, black "Crag Hoppers" trousers and dark climbing boots, with a black woollen hat pulled low over his short, sandy-fair hair. He had left it a bit later, being a Friday night, as he knew that the park would be filled with twenty-something guys with cropped hair and tattoos, showing off their souped-up Subarus, Astras and Corsas to each other and their respective skin-tight denim-clad ladies. By 2.00a.m. they had all departed and the car park was deserted. He lingered for another half hour and, chilled to the bone, he was about to leave when he heard a car slowing down to enter from the road. It looked like a dark-coloured Audi or BMW and his pulse quickened. It drove to the end of the park and Archie waited to see if any other vehicles approached. After another fifteen minutes, during which there were no further entrants to the park, he crept along to where the solitary car had stopped and listened. He could hear noises, certainly, but they were most definitely not related to any kind of drug exchange and the steamed-up windows confirmed that this was simply a couple after nothing more than a bit of illicit physical pleasure. He hung around until 3.30 then called it a day and made his way back to his car, sitting with the heater on for ten minutes in an attempt to thaw his frozen hands.

The exercise was repeated on Saturday night, with very similar results. This time, however, four cars made the later arrival and he witnessed what he realised was a spot of "dogging", with several participants and several observers. This was certainly the place to see the sleazier side of life and Archie crouched in the damp grass feeling disgusted and thoroughly miserable. He lingered until the last car had gone and had just turned to begin his weary trudge back over the moorland when he heard the growl of a large vehicle making its way up the hill from Paisley. He stopped and crouched back down, pulling his hat even lower, just in time to avoid the sweep of headlights as a black Range Rover entered the deserted car park. It headed to the far end and, at first, he presumed it to be another set of late-night rompers, although the dark-tinted windows prevented him from seeing any of the occupants. As he surreptitiously made his way towards it, he heard a second vehicle approach and watched as a white Porsche Cayenne glided along and parked beside the Range Rover, both switching their lights and engines off. The doors opened and there was a short, inaudible conversation, but he could definitely see a package of some description being passed between two of the occupants, who stood between the vehicles – in the darkness, and to his annoyance, he was unable to identify either of them. Following this brief exchange, the drivers returned to their respective vehicles and, as they approached the exit, Archie crept closer to the park to try and catch the registration numbers. The Range Rover passed first but it was travelling fast and still had its lights switched off, making it impossible for him to see the plate. The Porsche followed at a similar pace but, just as it passed him, it stopped suddenly. Archie crouched lower in the grass, afraid that he`d been spotted, but the driver just crossed to the grass, pulled down the zip of his jeans and proceeded to relieve himself, just a few yards from where Archie knelt. He held his breath and stared at the man. Stocky build, cropped black hair, narrow-set eyes, he was definitely familiar. Then it came to him. Kevin King, former lieutenant of Calum Dillon and strongly suspected of having had a hand in his disappearance, presumably on the instructions of his new boss, Blok. This was a result indeed, especially as he had a valuable package of some sort in his car. There was nothing Archie could do as this was an entirely unofficial stake-out, but he would phone Cam as soon as King had left, give him a tip off. The man finished his business, zipped up his jeans and turned back to his car when there was a loud "ping" from Archie`s phone as he received an e-mail – he was sure he had switched it off but apparently not. He swore under his breath as King turned sharply back and stared into the darkness. He reached in behind his jacket and spoke in a gravelly voice

`Some cunt there, eh? Come on oot, ya fucker, have a wee word with yer uncle Kevin.` He pulled out a short knife, held it in front of him and moved slowly forward. Archie remained crouched, figuring the element of surprise might help him. King was almost upon him when Archie jumped up and punched as hard as he could, sending the other man flying down on to the grass. He was back up in an instant though, blood pouring from ruptured lips but still clasping the knife. He dived forward and lunged with the blade, Archie just managing to avoid being stabbed in the stomach.

`So its a fight yer after, eh? Come on then, matey. Who the fuck are you, anyway? Spying on yer poor auld uncle Kevin, were ye? Whit are ye, a cop? I fuckin` hate cops, me!`

King circled and Archie stepped back to avoid another strike, but his opponent sensed this and charged straight at him, grabbing him round the waist and trying to stab him in the back. Archie deployed an old trick. He dropped like a stone out of the other man`s grasp to a kneeling position then punched upwards, between King`s legs, with all the strength he could muster. King howled with pain and doubled over, dropping the knife as he fell to the ground clutching his crushed testicles. That should have been the end.

But the red mist had descended.

Archie didn`t know how long it had gone on for, but when he came to his senses, King was curled in a foetal position and totally inert, his face a mask of blood and virtually unrecognisable. Archie stood back and gazed down in horror. He realised that the pent up rage, frustration and grief that he had held in for the last five days had been taken out on the body in front of him and he didn`t know whether King was alive or dead, although the latter seemed a distinct possibility.

Right, Archie, don`t panic...

He looked quickly about – nothing, no-one in sight. King`s Porsche was still sitting with the driver`s door open, the motor running. He quickly ran to it and, pulling a tissue from his pocket, turned off the engine and the lights, then carefully closed the door with his elbow. He went back over to King – the man still wasn`t moving and Archie reached down to check for a pulse then thought better of it. He stood up, took a last look at the inert figure then turned and ran across the moor back to his car, starting it up and gunning it off along the rough track and on to the main road. Once home, he poured himself a huge tumbler of "own-brand" whisky (the Glenfiddich was long-finished) and swallowed it in one gulp. Then he sat down on his couch, head in hands, and moaned softly to himself. If the week had started horrifically, it had just got worse. Much worse.

***

Sunday passed in a vague blur, with Archie`s emotions swinging wildly between panic, fear, guilt and desolation. Despite the lateness of his return, he hadn`t slept at all well, with images of the inert King and of his own, dead daughter floating in and out of his mind. He dozed fitfully during the day, expecting at any moment the arrival of some of his colleagues to arrest him for criminal assault at least, murder at the worst. But the day passed uneventfully, with no visitors and no phone calls and, by eleven o`clock that evening he decided he should try and get himself back into a routine and face work in the morning, no matter what consequences the day may bring. He downed a nightcap, a hefty glass of a newly opened bottle of Bowmore, reflecting briefly on how, over the past week, his drinking habits had changed from social to necessary. He would have to be careful – he had seen too many cops acquire a dependency on alcohol to allow them to function and he had enough problems at present without becoming an alcoholic. He headed up to bed and managed some semblance of a night`s sleep before his alarm roused him at 7.00a.m. Monday morning, the start of a new week.

The first coffee of the working day sat in front of him when Cam knocked and entered his office, a slight grin on his face. There wasn`t much that could keep his DS down for any length of time.

`Hey Boss, nice to have you back. How`re you doin`?`

`Aye, not too bad, Cam, getting there.` There was no way he was going to say anything about the events of the previous Saturday, even to Cam, There were limits to a friendship.

`Good stuff, good stuff.` Cam sat on the chair opposite Archie. The DI spoke.

`So, anything new in my absence?`

`A couple of things, nothing major, but all part of the picture.` He slapped a folder down on the desk and, suddenly, it was business as usual – well, for the time being.

***

As the week progressed, the sick feeling in Archie`s stomach started to recede and he realised that the key to his survival, in any shape or form, was to keep himself busy. He still started every time the phone rang or when someone knocked on his door but he was starting to think that, just maybe, Kevin King had somehow survived the vicious assault and managed to get himself back in his car and away from the scene. Otherwise, surely he would have heard about it – the body of a local gangster turning up in a car park would have landed on his desk immediately. No, perhaps it wasn`t as bad as he had thought – after all, he had been tired, it had been dark, King had deserved it...he was surprised at just how easy it was to find excuses for what he had done and ignore the fact that he was a Detective Inspector who had carried out a serious assault on what would be viewed as an innocent member of the public, albeit one with a stash of illegal substances in his car, wielding a knife and trying to stab him. Mitigating circumstances, perhaps, but still not enough to justify the brutality of the assault. As to the other matter...well, the best description he could have given was numb. He was dreading any further contact with the Whitefords, although he knew he would need to speak to them at some point to update them on their enquiries, despite the fact that there was precious little to tell.

On Tuesday they had carried out a raid on a disused factory near Linwood, where a local couple, walking their dogs late the previous evening, had seen a van unloading what they thought looked like “suspicious”packages. It turned out to be outdated chicken carcasses, a matter they quickly turned over to Environmental Services. On Wednesday, Cam tried to round up some of their usual informants but to no avail. No-one wanted to be seen within half a mile of the police, far less speaking to them. They were getting nowhere and there was a general sense of deep frustration in the air.

Archie had taken his first sip of coffee on Thursday morning when he was summoned to the Superintendent`s office. His stomach lurched – was this finally it? He downed the rest of the coffee, burning his mouth in the process.

A few minutes later he was staring blankly at the nameplate - “Superintendent Alexander Hamilton”- as he knocked, before the customary “Come!” summoned him. He opened the door and his boss looked up and smiled, somewhat grimly, Archie imagined.

`Ah, Archie. Have a seat.`

Archie sat down across from the Super. The room was sparse, with a few official photos and the usual collection of files. Not much personality, all very ordered and tidy, much like its occupant. Hamilton (the Hamster, to his detractors) was a tall, elegant and somewhat vain man; no matter where he was, media conference or crime scene, if he thought he was going to be on public display his well-pressed suit, immaculate white shirt and carefully chosen tie would look as if they were just out of the cleaners. Today, however, he was in the more mundane black polo shirt that had taken over from the traditional uniform. He signed a letter, placed his pen down and turned his grey eyes to Archie.

`So, Archie, How are you? I believe that you`ve had a bereavement of some sort?

Archie felt the hostility rise inside him. You either suffered a bereavement or you didn`t – there wasn`t “some sort”. He tried to conceal his feelings.

`Yes Sir, the daughter of a friend, I`m afraid.`

`I`m sorry to hear that. Anyway, on to business. Where are we at with these murders?`

`Well, I`m afraid we`re not making much headway, Sir. Of course, we know who`s behind them but there`s nothing we can tie down, no-one is talking. This new guy, Blok, they call him, well, he`s really sent out a very strong message. Keep quiet, toe the line or be killed.`

Hamilton sighed. `Ah yes, Blok.`

He sat back in his chair as if choosing his words carefully.

`Archie, as you probably know, I`m due to retire in the not-too-distant future. I`m getting pressure from Lydia, my wife, wants to do a bit of travelling – we`ve got a daughter in New Zealand, a couple of grandkids we`ve hardly seen. I`d intended to stay on for a bit longer but, well, you know how it is...?`

Archie didn`t, but he just nodded – Hamilton didn`t like to be interrupted.

`Anyway, I would really like to get this sorry mess tidied up before I leave rather than pass it on to my successor.`

He stopped and Archie got the feeling he was struggling with what to say next. Hamilton rubbed his hands over his face, sighed again then leaned forward on the desk and looked straight at him.

`I`ll be quite honest with you, Archie, I`ve had enough. This isn`t the force I joined, not the job I signed up for.`

He sat back again.

`I was just like all the other new recruits. Full of it, out to get the bad guys. Oh yes, I`d be the one to make a difference! But it`s all a pile of shite, Archie, really. All red tape, political correctness, criminals getting off on technicalities, organised crime on the up. What difference have we made, tell me? Tell me it`s not all a complete waste of time.`

Archie was stunned – this display of candour was certainly not what he had expected.

`Of course it`s not, Sir - we are making a difference! Bear in mind that these murders are all small time villains – much and all as it`s wrong, at least they`re not poor, innocent folk. We`ve pretty much shaken off the tag of the murder capital of Scotland.`

Hamilton shook his head

`I really wonder, though. And all this "Scotland`s Police" nonsense – just a massive cost-cutting exercise. And our new Chief Constable? Bit of an odd bugger, that one, if you ask me. No-one seems to know much about him.`

Archie was starting to feel slightly uneasy – what was he expected to say? Hamilton continued.

`Anyway, Archie, I`d really consider it a personal favour if you could clear this matter up before I retire - it would be really nice to leave on a high. Probably be a good chance of promotion to Chief Inspector too, I`d think. I`d put in a word, of course...Anyway, don`t let me keep you.`

The formal tone returned for his dismissal and Archie stood up and left, still totally taken aback at Hamilton`s words and thoroughly relieved that the "other" matter hadn`t been on the agenda! He went back to his office via the coffee machine and sat down to ponder their next move. The pressure was really on now! He decided not to tell Cam about the conversation – perhaps another time.

By the time he got home that night he realised that his life had resumed a pattern of sorts and, following a plate of macaroni and cheese and a couple of hours in front of the television he managed a reasonable night`s sleep without recourse to alcohol.

Chapter 9

Big Dunk hated Friday 13th. Not that he was superstitious - no, it was just that things often seemed to go tits up on Friday 13th. Even before he opened the curtains of the Neilston Road flat he shared with his partner, Anna, he knew it was raining. Between the "clank-clank" of the cars and buses passing over the loose drain cover outside the entrance to the tenement block, he could hear the swoosh as the vehicles drove through the puddles and over the wet tarmac. Pulling the curtains open and peering out confirmed this. It was pissing down, that good, old fashioned, West of Scotland rain that you knew was on for the day. Two minutes outside and you were soaking. Bad start!Things got worse when he discovered that Anna had used all the butter and the only remaining block was lurking in the freezer. His attempt at de-frosting it resulted in a dish full of yellow liquid that he ended up pouring onto his toast. Dunk wasn`t good with kitchens!

His breakfast finished, he dumped his dishes in the sink, lifted his flask, grabbed his lunch box from the fridge, (two rolls and cheese, a Mars bar and a packet of salt `n`vinegar crisps) pulled on his most waterproof jacket and headed downstairs. His ageing Vauxhall Astra was parked just around the corner but, as he suspected, he was soaked by the time he got to it and, as soon as he sat down and shut the door the windows started to steam up. He breathed a sigh of relief as the engine burst into life and he turned the fan up full. Even so, it was a couple of minutes before he could safely drive and he just knew he was going to be late.

He encountered the usual snarl up at St. James interchange and, as he approached the Red Smiddy roundabout he started to get the feeling that something wasn`t quite right - the car wasn`t responding as he felt it should and was pulling slightly to the left. Reluctantly, he stopped, put on the hazards and got out, receiving a long blast on the horn from the BMW driver behind him. Dunk gave him the obligatory finger then headed round to the kerb.

`Aw fuck!`

The tyre was about two thirds down. No way it would get him to the site, he was going to have to change it. In the rain, on a busy road. He kicked it to see if that helped – it didn`t! As he opened the boot he hoped the spare was up to it.

Big Dunk hated Friday 13th.

He arrived at the building site in Erskine, where he was employed as a JCB operator, forty minutes late, filthy and soaked to the skin. Andy, his boss, had his Mr Angry face on.

`What the fuck time do you call this, eh, Dunk?`

`Sorry boss. Got a puncture just at the Red Smiddy. What can I say?` He spread his hands and shrugged.

`Aye, well, just so long as you make it up and don`t bugger off early like you usually do on a Friday, eh! We`ve got a schedule to keep to.`

`Aye, no worries, boss.`

Andy was okay, really, one of the boys at heart, just under pressure from his own boss, a man Dunk hated. He usually came out with him and the rest of the lads for a few pints on a Friday, supported the right football team too and Dunk didn`t really want to let him down. He`d planned to go for a few pints today after work before meeting Anna for a curry and the pictures but an extra half hour wouldn`t do any harm. Hey, she`d used all the butter, after all! He left the office, made a quick visit to the somewhat unpleasant-smelling toilet facilities then, after pulling on a pair of waterproof over-trousers, he grabbed the yellow high-vis jacket hanging up in the staff room. The one with "Big Dunk" emblazoned on the back in indelible marker.

The rain was still teeming down as Dunk walked round to the compound where his JCB was parked. The puddles were starting to join together and he reckoned there would be some serious flooding before the day was out. He climbed up into the cab, made himself comfy then started the big diesel tractor up, let it warm up for a few minutes then shoved it into gear and trundled round towards the area where he was clearing scrub land and topsoil and digging out foundation trenches.

HomeFree were a relatively new outfit, resurrected Phoenix-like from some of the casualties of the most recent recession. They had bought one of the few remaining undeveloped pockets of land at the eastern end of the town of Erskine which, in the last decade, had pretty much become a dormitory town for its larger neighbours,

Paisley and Glasgow. The development of Erskine had started in the eighties just east of Rashielee Light, an old marker buoy on the south edge of the river and, once this latest batch of houses was complete, it would stretch almost to the Black Cart river and Renfrew. Big Dunk couldn`t really get his head round how companies could fold then re-appear leaving a trail of debt behind them. Didn`t seem right. Still, he had a job again after a few years on benefits, he had a cracking wee girlfriend and an okay flat in Paisley. Even had a week in Majorca booked for later in the year - aye, things were starting to go a bit better at last.

As he approached the main development area, the usual, vague feeling of unease crept over him. The origins of this feeling lay many years ago when Dunk had been doing a bit of drainage work on a farm near Inchinnan. The farmer had a nice looking wee daughter called Susan and, after a couple of weeks, he had plucked up the courage to risk her father`s wrath and ask her out. They`d gone steady for about eighteen months and he got to know the family reasonable well. Her Mum was a right character. Loads of great stories, a foul mouth (and temper too, as Dunk discovered when they crept in after a party at 2.00a.m. on a Sunday morning) but a brilliant sense of humour. When they had started developing the land at the end of Erskine, down next to the Clyde, she had said

`No fuckin` way I`d buy a hoose down there. Not for a pension!` she had stated in her usual colourful way.

The World War Two German bombing raids on Clydebank, on the north side of the River Clyde, on the 13th and 14th March, 1941, are notorious. The numerous docks, shipyards and factories in the area (including the legendary "Singer" works) were always going to be a major target but, unfortunately, centres of industry such as Clydebank were also centres of high density housing, in this case tenement flats. When the bombers came on those two fateful nights, the attack was relentless and ruthless and the civilian casualties were terrible, with over five hundred dead and over six hundred seriously injured. Only seven houses were left completely undamaged, leaving nearly thirty five thousand people homeless. The River Clyde is narrow at this point and a large number of the German bombs fell on the south shores where the land was low-lying and soft, frequently plugging themselves in the mud and not exploding. The army moved these further down the river to a point near where the Erskine Bridge now stands, defusing them and removing them from the site. But the farmer`s wife had been born and raised in the area and was convinced that they hadn`t got them all.

`Aye, its only a matter of time before some poor bugger digs one up in their gairden or, worse, someone`s hoose goes up wi` a huge bang. Naw, you`ll no` catch me livin` doon there!`

Eventually Dunk and Susan had drifted apart and he hadn`t given her mother`s expletive-peppered observations any further thought until, many years later, he got the job with HomeFree, when her words came back to haunt him. The first day he went out on the job, faced with undisturbed grassland and scrub and with Clydebank visible just across the river, he was literally shaking as he scooped out the fresh soil, waiting for the explosion that he had convinced himself would come. But he had now been here two months and nothing had happened. As usual, he tried to put the thought out of his mind and set off to clear some more ground and maybe get a trench or two started, although at this rate they would resemble miniature canals!

It was nearly lunch time and the cheese rolls and crisps were calling to Big Dunk - his stomach was rumbling. He`d give it another fifteen, make up a bit of the lost time and keep Andy happy. He pulled the handle and lifted the jib of the big digger, moved it forward to the next section, lowered it and started to drag the bucket back. It snagged on something. By now they were into a roughly wooded area, although the trees were relatively small, mostly willow and birch. As well as numerous rocks, some enormous, the ground was a tangle of roots. He lifted the bucket and tried again but it wouldn`t shift whatever it had snagged on. One more go.

`Aye, that`s it, move, ya fucker!`

Whatever it was shifted about a couple of feet then stopped dead, lifting the back end of the JCB off the ground and tipping Dunk over the controls.

`Holy shit` he shouted, easing the arm back up so that the tractor levelled itself, then killing the engine.

He opened the door and climbed down into the dark, clinging mud, so deep it was almost running over the top of his Dickie workboots. He waded and squelched his way round to the front of the tractor and looked at where the bucket had stuck. It had wedged behind a long, cylindrical object that the heavy rain was starting to wash clean. It was a dull silver colour, smooth, with what looked like a couple of fins attached to it at the end sticking out of the quagmire.

`Ohhhh shit! Shit! Shit!` Big Dunk screamed, turning and stumbling back through the mud in the direction of the site offices.

Chapter 10

As Archie drove to work on Friday morning (through the seemingly inevitable pouring rain) he supposed he should get the dreaded task over with and call round or phone the Whitefords that day. There was no point in putting it off any longer and he knew that, at the very least, he owed them the courtesy of an update on the investigation into their daughter`s – his daughter`s -death. He vaguely glanced at the car stereo, unusually silent as Archie was a great lover of classic 70`s rock music and would normally have had his music blaring as he sang along. This week, though, he hadn`t felt in the mood and had switched the system off. He suddenly noticed the date in the corner of the screen - it was Friday 13th. Archie wasn`t in the least bit superstitious but, given recent events, he did wonder what the day might have in store for him. After all, he certainly hadn`t seen the Superintendent`s comments the previous day coming! He arrived at Paisley Police headquarters in Mill Street, found a space and jogged up the steps into the familiar, institutional atmosphere.

It was past lunchtime but, his appetite having deserted him, he was still sitting at his desk with the third (and now cold) coffee of the day in front of him, staring despondently out of the window at the grey Paisley rooftops, slick with the heavy rain that continued to fall. They had really made very little progress during the week and he was now fairly certain that he knew the reason why. Anyone with any knowledge or information that may be of use to the police was petrified of the fearsome Blok and the recent spate of murders had sent a message loud and clear to anyone who dared to oppose him or cause him any trouble. The usual informants were running scared, Blok`s gang representing a far greater menace than Scotland`s finest, whose worst threat was a couple of years in a warm and reasonably comfortable cell with three meals a day and access to the latest Playstation! Their enquiries were going to become increasingly difficult and the thought depressed him, especially now that his involvement was personal as well as professional. He briefly wondered if he should request that he be taken off the case but discarded the thought immediately. Revenge would be his at any price.

His mood was not helped by the co-incident organisation of a "boy-band"concert at Hampden Park (he hadn`t even heard of them) an international athletics event at Glasgow`s prestigious venue, The SSE Hydro, and a high profile SNP conference at the adjacent Scottish Exhibition and Conference Centre. Did these organisations never liaise with each other? A whole squad of Paisley cops were up in Glasgow re-inforcing the numbers and, if anything went seriously wrong on home territory, then there was going to be a big problem. His department was already a bit short staffed due to an amount of "re-deployment" following the amalgamation of all Scotland`s various Constabularies several years ago and some of his officers were having to cover regular policing duties rather than carry out the investigation work that they should be doing. The ring of the phone on his desk roused him from his gloomy reverie and he was somewhat relieved to notice that it hadn`t made him jump. He picked up the receiver.

`DI Blue.`

`Hello Sir, Control room here. Sorry to bother you but we`ve just had an odd call.`

`Odd how?` asked Archie, trying to keep the annoyance out of his voice. Detective Inspectors shouldn`t be bothered by "odd"calls!

`Well, Sir` the female civilian employee continued `It`s from the site manager at HomeFree Building in Erskine. He says he thinks one of his JCB drivers has dug up a World War Two bomb.`

Archie actually held the receiver away from him and looked at it in astonishment. He lifted it back to his ear

`Are you having a laugh?`

`No Sir, honestly, it`s just come in. I can`t locate the uniform Inspector, I think he`s at a meeting in Glasgow with Superintendent Hamilton, you seem to be the only senior officer available so I thought I`d better let you know. The man was quite agitated.`

Archie sighed and shook his head. This was a piece of nonsense, but he supposed it wasn`t really the girl`s fault.

`Okay, thanks, leave it with me. Can you get someone to bring up the details of the site, names, phone numbers, etcetera?`

`Certainly sir, I`ll organise it right away.`

`Oh, and I suppose you`d better find out how we get in touch with the Army. If it really is a bomb, we`re going to need them.`

Archie hung up the phone and stared back out of the window, shaking his head. It wasn`t often he was at a loss but an unexploded WW2 bomb...Christ, this was just what he needed!

Within five minutes, a uniformed WPC had delivered a sheet with the names of the building company, the site manager, phone number and postcode for HomeFree. There was also a scribbled note saying "A Major Donaldson from the Royal Regiment of Scotland will be calling you back within five minutes." Already Archie was on Google, looking for information on the area and the possibility of unexploded bombs but nothing was coming up. He had phoned his Detective Sergeant, who had reacted in a similar fashion when Archie had given him the information.

`You`re kidding me on, Boss. A bomb! Hey, I suppose it makes a change frae trying to get sense oot o` a feart junkie though!`

Archie winced at Cam`s choice of words but he couldn`t blame the man. After all, the tragedy was exclusively his. He suddenly remembered the Whitefords and felt an enormous pang of guilt. Of course, it wasn`t exclusively his, not by any stretch of the imagination. He managed to push the thoughts out of his mind as Cam continued

`I`ll be right along, but how come we get landed wi` this shite?`

`Couldn`t locate any senior uniformed officers apparently, Cam. Probably all up in Glasgow, sookin` in with the politicians and looking for an MBE! Bet a lot of them are sorry we never got our independence, might have been a Scottish Honours list produced specially for them, eh?` It was a valiant attempt at humour, given his circumstances.

`Aye, I know what you mean. Heard it was goin` to be called NFO - Numpty of the First Order..! See you in a minute. Fancy a coffee?`

`Aye, thanks, good man.` - the one in front of him was stone cold, after all! Archie realised he was grinning at the Sergeant`s words and wondered if, perhaps, normality might return one day. Maybe.

Ten minutes (and a couple of fresh, steaming and reasonably drinkable coffees) later, Archie was still trawling for information about World War Two bombs and Cam was already organising a couple of uniform cars to go immediately to Erskine and make the area secure. It might turn out to be a complete false alarm but protocol demanded that they treat such matters seriously in case anything did happen. After all, it wasn`t that long since a World War 2 mine had been found just down the Clyde, off Gourock; it had been taken away and detonated, so the threat was still occasionally lurking about. The last thing they wanted was a pile of casualties if it really was a bomb and it went off unexpectedly - a sure fire promotion stopper, that one! Although he had no first-hand experience, Cam did know that armaments from that period were notoriously unstable due to their age and needed to be treated with a bit of respect. The uniforms would move everyone back to a safe distance and cordon the area off until they decided exactly what to do. He pushed the "end" button on his phone and turned to Archie

`Right Boss, I`ve got a couple o` cars on their way now, blues and twos, tae get the area safe. Will we head down?`

`Not just yet, Cam` replied Archie `I`m still waiting for this Major "what`s-his-name" to call me first. Listen, give the site manager a call and tell him to keep this quiet. No press, television, nothing. Last thing we need are reporters or helicopters all over the shop.`

Just as he said this the desk phone phone rang.

`DI Blue`

`Ah, Detective Inspector, it`s Major Donaldson here from the Royal Regiment of Scotland. How can I help you?`

Archie had, for some reason, expected a plummy English accent, a sort of Public School type – he had been brought up watching Dad`s Army, after all! He was pleasantly surprised to hear a polite, yet solid, Scots accent - no trace of privileged education here.

`Major, thanks very much for getting back to me. I`ve just had a report that a possible World War Two bomb has been dug up on the south bank of the Clyde, near Erskine. I haven`t confirmed it yet but we are in the process of securing the area as a precaution and I think we`ll need a bomb team to have a look`

Major Donaldson let out a chuckle.

`Well, well! It`s been a while since we`ve had one of those. I don`t suppose there can be many left now, most of the UXBs were found in London and some of the other cities that suffered extensive bombing during the war, like Liverpool and Coventry. Still, if I`m not mistaken, Erskine is across from Clydebank, is it not?`

`It is` replied Archie. `Of course! There was the Clydebank Blitz.

Is it possible that this is a real bomb, then?`

`Could well be` answered the Major. Archie had hoped that it would turn out to be a false alarm. `the Germans weren`t that accurate and with these enormous blanket raids a good number of bombs fell off target. If this area has lain undisturbed or just lightly farmed, then there is a reasonable possibility that it is a UXB. Anyway, you`re doing the right thing. Keep everyone well back, no going and having a wee look yourself, that`s how accidents happen. I`ll make the call and get an Explosive Ordinance Disposal team over as soon as. Can I have your mobile number and I`ll keep in touch?`

Archie gave the details to the Major and received his in return.

`Might even take a wee trip over myself to break the monotony. Life`s all about form filling these days, and it gets a bit boring tucked away in Edinburgh Castle. It`d be nice to get out in the field with the risk of a large bang to spice things up!`

Archie agreed about the form filling but wasn`t so sure about the large bang part! They said their goodbyes and he turned to Cam.

`Right, my friend, off to Erskine. Oh look, it`s still pissing down. What a surprise!`

Cam was always happy to travel with Archie (although recently such journeys had been a bit strained) and he loved the thrill of being a passenger in the sleek Panamera, which he knew would make short work of the trip to Erskine. He craved a car like this but with a wife and an eighteen month old daughter, it was, at the moment, only a dream! The two, despite their different ranks and backgrounds, were close friends, having joined the force at the same time. They shared a love of science fiction films and, before Cam met his wife, Tracey, they used to spend many an evening getting happily drunk with beer and cheap whisky (a good malt being an un-affordable luxury back then), eating a decent Indian takeaway and wading through the back catalogue of Star Trek, Star Wars, Battlestar Galactica and others of that genre. It happened a lot less often now that Cam was married but they still occasionally talked the "trekkie" talk, sometimes ending a phone call with the famous Vulcan greeting "Live long...and prosper", much to their colleagues amusement!

The car sped down the M8 towards the Erskine Bridge slip road, with the partly concealed blue lights flashing and parting the traffic like Moses parting the waters. They took the turn-off then made their way back along through the sprawling community to the far end of Erskine. Archie wasn`t particularly familiar with the area and was surprised at the amount of new houses, huddled together in their little estates as if trying to shelter from the rain. They were all so similar and so close together it seemed that you could touch the walls of each house if you stood between them (which, in truth, you often could). He could never understand how builders were allowed to over- exploit the plots this way but, as usual, it would all come down to money - the more houses, the more return per acre. If Archie ever had kids he would want them to grow up with a bit of space around them, room to grow and play in the fresh air. If it wasn`t raining, that is...Then it hit him again – he had, in fact, been a father and had just lost his only daughter. He guessed that this would be the way of things from now on, the memory sneaking up on him and dropping on him like a bag of wet cement.

Cam, seemingly unaware of any change in Archie`s demeanour, broke into his dismal reverie `Left here, Boss.`

Archie had been driving through the last complete housing development and he now slowed and turned off the tarmac road on to a rough track that seemed to be surfaced with hardcore and thick grey mud. The car was going to need a serious wash after this! They saw the two uniform cars ahead, blue lights still flashing. A couple of kids on bikes were staring curiously at the gates of the site but the boys in blue were doing a good job at keeping them at bay. He vaguely wondered why on earth they were out on their bikes in this weather, but the flashing blue lights were always an attraction to kids, come rain or shine – he had been no different as a boy. They were probably just looking for a diversion on the way home from school – anything to avoid homework, he supposed. He drove slowly, trying to avoid the filthy puddles, especially as he didn`t know how deep they were, and got to the gate, lifting his warrant card from the binnacle. He showed it to the uniform blocking the gate, trying to open his window as little as possible.

`Afternoon, Sir` the officer said `You fair picked the day for it! The office is off to the left there, just watch your car on the potholes. We`ve got everyone inside and the other boys are heading round the perimeter to keep the curious out. There seems to be a pretty secure fence around the site, though, so I reckon it would be pretty hard to gain access.`

`Good job, constable. I`ll try and arrange a cuppa for you, can`t be a lot of fun out here.` Archie always tried to keep the uniforms on-side, you never knew when you might need a wee favour.

`Cheers, Sir, I`ve been out in worse though!` the cop smiled and waved him through.

Archie manoeuvred the Porsche through the car park, which was beginning to resemble a swamp, and reflected that, perhaps, he should have bought a big four by four instead. At the far end of the yard he could see a couple of cops with a roll of blue and white "Police" tape, cordoning off the area that led out to the building site itself, although there appeared to be no actual building going on as far as he could see.

`Bloody hell, this is going tae be a laugh!` said Cam in a resigned tone – he just knew he was in for a soaking.

Archie parked the car outside the office, next to a black Audi S4 with a personal number plate. They grabbed their jackets from the back seat and got out of the car, trying to pull them on before they got soaked but they were only partly successful and were already uncomfortably damp as they headed towards where the cops were setting up the "do not cross" line. The uniforms turned as they approached.

`Afternoon, Sir. Right carry on this, eh?` said the first. Archie vaguely noticed that the constable looked as if he should still be at school. *Must be getting old...*

`Aye, well, we`ve got tae treat anythin` like this seriously, son.` replied Cam. `So, where is it, this alleged "bomb"?`

`Just over there, Sir, behind the JCB out in the field.`

They gazed across what resembled a World War One battlefield, with trenches, mounds of grey, oozing mud and areas of grass, to where Big Dunk`s JCB stood amidst an area of scrub land, its arm still poised as if in the action of digging.

`Don`t see anything.` commented Archie.

`Big guy who was driving says it`s behind the digger` said the second uniform. `He got well away as soon as he found it. Can`t really see much from here but we reckoned we weren`t going over for a closer look, just in case!`

`No, you`re quite right.` said Archie. `I`ve spoken to the Army and they say to keep everyone well away, even senior ranks. No-one, I repeat no-one is to go anywhere near it until the bomb disposal guys get here.`

`No problem, Sir.` said the first cop.`Any idea when?`

`Nope, I`m waiting to hear from them. Just keep the place secure `til then, guys. We`re away to chat to the driver, see what he has to say.`

They made their way back over to the office block and, by the time they reached it, they were pretty well saturated. They opened the main door and found themselves in a corridor. Hearing voices to the right, they opened the door that said "staffroom" and went in, Archie leading the way.

He could barely stop himself from laughing. As soon as they entered the Portakabin that served as the staffroom he could smell the strong reek of tobacco smoke and the air was noticeably fuggy. He couldn`t quite remember when it became an offence to smoke in a workplace but it was a good few years ago. There were seven men in the room, at least five of whom had a cigarette in their hands but, as Archie and Cam entered, even though they were in plain clothes, to a man the smokers all shoved the hands holding the fags behind their backs, like a bunch of schoolboys caught smoking in the toilet by the headmaster. Out of the corner of his eye he could see that Cam had lowered his head as he, too, was struggling to keep a straight face.

`All right boys, I`m not here to charge you with smoking in the workplace, don`t worry. Seems we might have a bigger problem.`

A short, heavily built man of about fifty, with a head of thick grey hair, walked over and held out his hand.

`Andy Carson, Site manager.`

That explained the Audi in the car park. S400CAR.

`Thanks for coming over so quickly, eh. Listen, mate, we`re on a bit of a tight schedule here and the rain hasn`t helped, so if we could just get this sorted out quick, eh!`

Archie detected the mid Scotland lilt, probably Falkirk area with the added "eh" rising at the end of each sentence. But he

wasn`t this man`s "mate" and their schedule wasn`t his problem. However, he returned the firm handshake.

`Detective Inspector Blue` and, turning his head towards Cam `Detective Sergeant Wilkie` Andy Carson nodded to him. `I`m very sorry sir, but until the Army arrive and confirm one way or another exactly what we have here, no-one will be able to go back on site. Safety is now our prime concern.`

`Detectives?` questioned Carson. `It`s not a crime scene, is it? How come they`ve sent detectives? I mean, you don`t think there`s anything going on here, eh?`

Archie sensed a vague tension in the man`s voice but then it probably did seem a bit strange to find two detectives arriving to deal with a suspected unexploded bomb.

`No, not at all, Mr Carson. We just happened to be the only ones available. There`s a whole lot of events going on in Glasgow today` he paused and glanced out of the window `weather permitting, and a lot of our uniformed officers are helping out.`

`So you just drew the short straw, eh?` Carson said, looking relieved.

`Exactly` said Cam. `Now, could we have a word with the driver who found the...er...bomb?`

`Aye, he`s over in the corner` Carson said `I think he`s in shock. Poor bastard seemed to get a real fright. He`s a good guy, really, but I`ve never seen him so, well, spooked is the way I would put it. Hey, Big Dunk, over here, eh!" he shouted.

They hadn`t been aware of the big man sitting in the corner but as he stood up and made his way over to them, the first thing they noticed was that his whole front seemed to be caked in mud, as if he had fallen. His face was streaked too, where he had obviously made a somewhat unsuccessful attempt to clean himself. He was shaking.

`Have you an office we could use please?` Archie asked Carson.

`Aye, sure thing, just through here.`

They followed him along a short corridor and he opened a door leading into a second Portakabin. The wall was covered with maps, schedules, Health and Safety posters and the desk was a bit cluttered - just like Archie`s. Carson pulled over a few chairs that were sitting against the walls and the three of them sat down.

`I`ll leave you to it, eh` he said. `Could I get youse a coffee?`

`That`d be good` said Archie. `Two please, white, no sugar. And could you possibly arrange one for the officer on duty at the gate please? Poor guy`s soaking out there.` He looked at Big Dunk. `You?`

`Naw, ah`m ok, cheers anyway. Ah`m sloshin` already.`

`Right, a couple of minutes, eh.` said Carson and he left to organise their refreshments. Archie suspected he was probably happy at having something to do but again he got the vague feeling that their presence was unsettling the site manager. Anyway, it was now up to Archie and Cam to determine if the big guy really had dug something up or if his imagination was just working overtime. There was only one way to find out.

`So, Dunk, tell us what happened. And, by the way, like I said to your boss, we`re only here `cos no one else was available, so don`t worry about us being detectives.`

Big Dunk had one of those big, round open faces, a chin covered with stubble, close cropped brown hair and large, round blue eyes that resembled a rabbit`s, caught in car headlights.

Poor bastard`s crapping himself!

Before he spoke further, Archie had him down for an honest enough bloke. Maybe not the brightest but whatever he said was likely to be the truth. Dunk proceeded to tell them what had happened, right up to pulling the "bomb" out of the mud. After that, he had bolted for the office, stumbling in the muddy, uneven ground several times, hence the state of his clothes.

`Okay, fair enough` said Cam `and I can understand it was a bit o` a shock. But, Dunk, you`re still in a hell of a state. Why are you so upset by it all? I mean, you`re awright now, you`re safe in here surely?`

Reluctantly, Dunk recounted the story told to him all those years ago by his then girlfriend`s mother. The two detectives looked at each other as it all poured out.

`So, Dunk` Archie continued when the big man had finally stopped `it`s almost like you`ve been expecting to find something. You`re sure of what you saw. I mean, it couldn`t have been an old drainage pipe, a water tank or something like that? There must have been old farms round about here at one time.`

`No way! It wis kinda silvery like. A drainpipe isn`ae silvery. An` it had sort of fin things on the back. Like a missile. Christ, maybe it`s a missile an` no` a bomb.` He started to shake again.

`Okay Dunk, just calm down. Give us a wee minute, will you` Archie said, standing up and beckoning Cam over to the door. They went outside and he said to the DS

`Cam, you better call an ambulance for this poor bugger, I honestly think he`s in shock. I`ll find out if there`s a wife, family or something and we can give them a call too.`

`Sure thing, Boss` replied Cam, his phone already in his hand.

Archie went back in. `Dunk, do you have a wife or a girlfriend we can call?`

`Oh shit, I`m supposed to be meeting Anna, we`re meant to be going for a curry.` He pulled out his phone, nearly dropping it in the process, but Archie stopped him before he could dial.

`Let me talk to her, Dunk, tell her what`s happened.`

Dunk passed his phone over willingly and Archie spoke to the big man`s partner, telling her that Dunk was going to hospital as he`d had a bit of a shock at work – he was careful not to divulge the details. Anna agreed to meet Dunk at Paisley`s Royal Alexandra Infirmary A & E unit and Archie hung up, handing back the phone. He would get Cam to phone her after Dunk was settled and to caution her about spreading the story. After all, they were still not sure that it was a bomb but the tabloids were always on the look-out for anything out of the ordinary and the public were usually happy enough to receive a few hundred pounds for their information, however inaccurate. And, of course, Dunk and Anna might well feel that it would be compensation for the upset.

`So, Dunk, I`m sorry to have to go over this again but can you tell me one more time what this thing looked like?`

`Well, it was pretty muddy but, from whit Ah could see, it wis about three foot in diameter, kinda silvery, a wee bit shiny like, but no` like it wis chrome or nothin`. But the rain wis makin` it clean. It had whit looked like fins stickin` oot at the top, where it had came oot the mud.`

`Definitely fins? You`re sure?`

`Aye, stickin` oot about a foot or so. Ah could only see two, may have been mair roon` the back. Ah wisn`ae hingin` aboot tae find oot!`

`How much was out of the ground?`

`Ah reckon about four feet or so. Pulled the tractor`s arse right aff the ground so there must be a fair bit still stuck in the mud.`

`Okay Dunk. You`ve been a great help, I really appreciate it. Now, the ambulance will be here soon, they`ll get you up to the Royal Alexandra, and they`ll probably put you on a sedative. Anna will be there so you`ll be fine. Listen mate, I don`t know how I`d react if I dug up a bomb. I`d probably shit my myself! Just one more thing, though. Keep this to yourself until we find out exactly what it is. We don`t want a bunch of sight-seers crawling all over the place, do we?`

Big Dunk smiled, nodding his assent and Archie`s heart went out to him. He was a decent, honest big lump of a guy who had had a nasty shock, especially in light of his fears about the area. Not like the lowlifes he normally had to deal with and it made a pleasant change. That was the trouble with being a detective, you tended, by necessity, to rub shoulders with the less salubrious members of the community. Again his train of thought was stopped short as he remembered the events of the last week and his heart sank. For a while he had lapsed back into being an ordinary cop, getting on with the job in hand and it was a shock to remember that he was potentially a criminal himself. Fortunately his thoughts were soon interrupted as the door opened and Carson appeared with two steaming mugs of coffee, closely followed by Cam, who was putting his phone back in his pocket. Archie reckoned it was probably just cheap instant, but it smelled reasonable and, given the soaking he`d had today, anything hot was welcome.

`Yer man out front`s enjoyin` his too, by the looks of things, eh.` Carson said, putting the mugs on the table.

`Cheers, Mr Carson, I really appreciate that.`

Just as Archie lifted the mug to his lips and took his first mouthful of the welcome, steaming drink, he heard a commotion of some sort coming from the other room. Big Dunk looked up and said

`Oh-oh, trouble`s arrived!`

Archie and Cam put their coffees down, got up and quickly made their way out of the office. The door to the other room was open and, coming out, was yet another big man, easily six foot four, shaven head, a gold earring in one ear. He was dressed all in black, a crisp shirt and well pressed trousers topping a pair of shoes that had been shiny but were now caked in mud. He also sported a big, silver buckled belt, making him resemble an ageing Country and Western singer. Archie put him probably in his mid fifties and felt he looked vaguely familiar, but he couldn`t place him. The guy was shouting as he left the room.

`Ah`m no` fuckin` payin` ye tae hing aboot drinkin` coffee an` smokin` fags. Get yer arses back oot there now or Ah`ll find another bunch o` workers. NOW!`

Archie held his hand up and the loud-mouth stared at him

`Who the fuck are you?`

`Detective Inspector Blue. And your men are not going anywhere. This site is out of bounds to anyone at present, so I suggest you keep your voice down and come through to the office and we`ll fill you in on what`s happening.`

The big man moved a step closer to Archie and leaned menacingly towards him.

`Fuck all`s happenin`, that`s whit!`

Cam stepped in front of his boss.

`I`m going to have to ask you to back off, Sir. Keep your voice down and watch your language`

`Got a problem with my language, sonny?`

Cam looked at this guy. *I could take him. Easy!* - a black belt in Jiu Jitsu came in handy. But he`d try again. He held the big bastard`s gaze for a couple of seconds, glowering up at him from under hooded eyebrows, then lowered his voice to the legendary Wilkie growl.

`I`m not goin` to ask you again, bawbag. Shut the fuck up or you`ll be licking the mud aff my boots.`

For the second time that day, and to his sheer astonishment given his personal circumstances, Archie found himself repressing a smile - in situations such as this Cam was the perfect ally. He waited to see what happened, reckoning it could go either way. Despite the newcomer`s size, he wouldn`t stand a chance against Cam.

Mr Mouth looked like he was going to try and deck the DS but something in the smaller man`s demeanour seemed to make him hesitate until, after a few seconds, he thought better of it - it was a wise move. Instead he took a step back and said

`Aye, right, in here.` He brushed past them in a waft of expensive after-shave tinged with cigar-reek and went in to the office where

Dunk was still sitting. The two detectives followed close behind, Archie resting his hand briefly on Cam`s shoulder and whispering `Nice one, mate!` in his ear. Cam grinned. Archie motioned Dunk to get out and he made off with the relief clearly showing on his face - he obviously wasn`t a fan of this guy! In the distance they could hear the siren of the ambulance and Archie was relieved that the poor sod would soon be out of harm`s way.

`Now, Sir, if you`d just take a seat please.` Archie said.

Cam was still hovering, just in case, glowering at the big man.

`Sorry aboot that.` the man said, lowering his bulk into a chair that looked as if it could barely support him. `But time`s money in this game an we`ve already been held up wi` this pissin` awful weather. Ah`m wantin` this site ready tae pit in founds an` sewers before winter. Oh, by the way` he stood up again and proffered his hand `Eddie McCourt. Managin` Director, HomeFree Builders.`

Archie shook hands reluctantly. There was a vague familiarity about the name as well as the face, but he still couldn`t place it. He certainly didn`t have the honest countenance of Big Dunk, that was for sure.

`So, boys, whit`s the sketch here? Big Dunk`s apparently rabbitin` oan aboot diggin` up a bomb! Pile o` shite, if you ask me. It`ll be some old bit o` scrap or the like.`

`Well sir,` replied Archie, repressing the irritation he was feeling, `Pile of shite or not, we have to take reports like this seriously, just in case. I`m sure you wouldn`t want to be responsible for any casualties or, worse, deaths, now would you?`

`Aye, well, let`s try an` get it a` wrapped up as quickly as possible.`

Archie`s mobile rang - it was Major Donaldson.

`Excuse me a minute, I need to take this.` he said, going out to the hall to take the call.

`Hello Detective Inspector. Callum Donaldson here. How`s things at your end?`

`Hello Major.` replied Archie. `Everything`s secure here, a wee bit of flack from the director of the building company but nothing we can`t handle. Oh, and the site`s almost a washout.`

`Wouldn`t worry too much about that. Have you spoken to the chappie who found the device?`

`Yes and he`s given a fairly good description of what he saw, although I suspect that there`s a fair element of exaggeration.` Archie repeated what Big Dunk had told them and there was a slight pause before the Major replied.

`Hmm. Sounds a bit, erm, unusual, not what I would have expected if he was describing a World War two shell. Usually they`re pretty rusty and dirty after being buried for seventy odd years. Also sounds a bit bigger. Strange.`

`The JCB driver said it looked like a missile` said Archie. `As I said, I did think he was exaggerating a bit - he was pretty shaken by the whole thing.`

`I suppose there is a very slim chance that it was something along the lines of a V1 or a V2, although they came a bit later in the war and generally in the South. Can`t really say though until our boys take a look. Speaking of which, it`ll be tomorrow before we can get anyone up as the team`s based in the North of England. They`ll be coming up by chopper and I assume there`s somewhere on the site where they can land?`

`Should be` replied Archie, `It`s pretty much an undeveloped area at the moment and a good bit away from any houses so there should be a bit of open land. As I said though, it`s pretty wet underfoot . I`ll text you once I`ve found out about a suitable landing area.`

`Right-oh` said the Major. `Can you please ensure that you set up a perimeter well clear of the device, if possible about five hundred metres all round. Absolutely no-one is to go near it, just in case, and that includes any senior officers - they often have a habit of wanting to see for themselves! We`ll talk tomorrow. I`ll call when the chopper leaves. I`ve checked the forecast and its supposed to clear up by tonight. Fingers crossed.`

`Great stuff, Major, many thanks.`

Archie went back in to the office where Cam and McCourt were still silently glowering at each other. He relayed the news and McCourt didn`t seem particularly pleased, but he appeared to have backed down from his earlier stance.

`Best send your men home` said Archie. `No-one`s going back out there until the Army have had a look at the device, if that`s what it is, and I presume your men are off for the weekend anyway. We`ve a perimeter to set up and secure now. Tell me, does the security fence go all the way round the site?`

`Aye, it does, don`t want any of ma plant wanderin` off. Huv you seen the price of a JCB these days?` grunted McCourt. `Anyway, I`ll break the news tae those lazy buggers oot there.` He got up, storming out the office, and they heard him instructing his men to "Fuck off home"

`Nice guy` said Archie. `I`ve the feeling I know him, can`t place him though`

`Eddie McCourt?` said Cam, with a tone of slight surprise. `Big time crook way back. Got eighteen years for murdering wee Puggy Cochrane, his wife an` his teenage daughter. He got oot after fifteen, about four years ago. Good behaviour, apparently! Haven`ae heard a cheep aboot him since but he`s doing okay for himself by the looks o` it. Managing Director, eh?`

`Probably before my time back here` said Archie. "I`d have been in Argyll and Bute about then.`

`Aye, well, he`s changed a fair bit. Used tae have long blonde hair in a ponytail and was dead skinny. Always dressed in white. Now he`s the man in black, covers a multitude o` sins, does that!`

Archie remembered him now. His picture had been plastered all over the front pages during his trial. Back then McCourt had more resembled a rock star, with the white suit and shirt and the dark aviator shades, almost like a Bee Gee who had got away. Now he looked more like Johnny Cash`s older brother!

`Interesting. Think he`s clean?`

`Very much doubt it` replied Cam. `They don`t usually change, do they? But he`s certainly been aff oor radar since he got oot so, if he`s up tae anythin`, he`s keepin` it real quiet.`

`Hm.` Archie paused, thinking. `Listen, remember Stevie Hyslop, the wee runt we pulled in a couple of months ago?`

`Aye, the one with two kilos o` the white stuff in the boot o` his motor. Swore he didn`ae know how it got there.`

`That`s the one. Do you remember the car tyres and his trainers?`

`Aye, they were a` caked in mud. He`d tried tae wipe the trainers but the tyres were still filthy.` The penny dropped. `Mud! Right enough! Plenty o` that here!`

`Worthy of a wee bit of investigation, don`t you think` said Archie. `And I thought the site manager, Carson, was a bit cagey when he discovered we were detectives. Guilty conscience, maybe? Not a cheap car he`s driving either. Anyway, we`ll worry about that another time. Let`s get some more uniforms down and make this place secure for the night. Get me that site plan down off the wall, please, and we`ll see how accessible it all is.`

Half an hour later, they had organised another six uniformed officers to work shifts through the night to make sure the site was safe and secure. All the workmen, including the site manager and McCourt, had left and Archie turned to Cam.

`Right, let`s call it a day. I`m starving – I missed lunch. I hear there`s a good wee Chinese in the shopping centre. Fancy something to eat?`

`Aye, okay Boss, that`d be great. I`ve already phoned Tracey and told her that I won`t be home for tea. Missin` bedtime again, though.` he sighed. Cam`s young daughter, Abigail, was the light of his life. Archie was her godfather.

`Come on then. Oh, before we go, let`s get a soil sample from outside. Forensics will still have the samples from Hyslop`s tyres, it`s worth seeing if it`s a match.`

`Don`t think the sample will be necessary, Boss.` Cam replied.

Archie looked at him quizzically.

`Have you looked at yer shoes...?`

Chapter 11

Saturday morning – the sun was streaming in from behind the curtains in Archie`s bedroom as the alarm on his iPhone sounded, playing 10cc`s "I`m not in love", one of his favourite songs. As he turned it off he realised, to his surprise, that he had slept the whole night through. No waking in a cold sweat, only the vaguest of dreams, no night terrors. He actually felt refreshed for once and it was a welcome change to see that the day was sunny. He sat up and, although the usual thoughts flooded into the vacuum of his newly-wakened brain, he felt he was beginning to gain control over them at last. He also remembered he had been meaning to head down to the Lake District this weekend but that idea was now totally off the cards, despite the dubious advice from his DS! He got off the bed, pulled on his dressing gown and headed downstairs, reflecting on the previous evening. He realised just how much he valued the company of his Detective Sergeant and also just how much the chat had done him good. Of course, he had remained silent on the subject of Kevin King but, following the excellent Chinese meal, the conversation had eventually turned to the topic of Lucinda, as Archie knew it would. He struggled to put his feelings into words – after all, he hadn`t known the girl at all, hadn`t even been aware of her existence until he had been told by Karen Whiteford. But she was his flesh and blood and, naturally, he was grieving. Cam, now with a daughter of his own, had only a vague insight into his friend`s suffering but he listened, for as long as Archie had wanted to talk, until a subtle switching off of the lights in the restaurant had told them it was time to go home.

He breakfasted and showered and was on to his second coffee of the morning when his mobile rang. He looked at the screen and saw it was Major Donaldson.

`Good Morning, Major.`

`Good Morning, Detective Inspector. How are you today? I hope I didn`t wake you up!`

`Not at all` said Archie, `Just having a coffee and waiting to see what develops today. I`m set to go just as soon as you tell me when.

How`s your schedule looking?"

`The disposal team are just about to take off, ETA at Erskine about thirteen hundred hours. How`s the weather looking over your way?`

As was often the case in the West of Scotland after a miserable spell of weather, the sun was splitting the heavens and it was a beautiful Autumn morning.

`Just great, Major. Clear blue skies, gentle breeze, should be a nice enough trip for them.`

He had already texted the Major to advise him that there was plenty of room to land the helicopter in the vicinity, although its presence would be bound to raise a few eyebrows. He was sure the Press wouldn`t be far away from sniffing that something fairly serious was going on but he would just need to cross that bridge when he came to it.

`Good stuff. I`m driving through myself, so I`ll see you on location about one p.m. Look forward to it.`

Archie ended the call and went up to his bedroom to get changed. He knew that, despite the sunny blue skies, the ground would still be sodden so he pulled on a pair of thick hiking socks, followed by his black Craghopper trousers – then he paused, changing his mind - maybe the blue ones would be best... Next he slipped on a pair of Nike trainers, as his hiking boots were still in the car and he could change into them at the site. He had bought a new pair, having carefully disposed of his old ones after the "incident", as his brain now euphemistically referred to it. He sent a text to Cam telling him the arrangements, grabbed his keys and jumped into the Porsche, selecting the "Archie Rock" playlist on his iPhone before starting the car and heading for Erskine. It was time, at last, for some decent music. As he pulled out of the drive, the iconic riff of Deep Purple`s "Smoke on the Water" was pounding out of the speakers and, singing along with the first line, he found himself substituting the location, Montreux, with "We all came down to Erskine..." He wondered if he was, perhaps, on the mend but he was only about a mile down the road when his phone rang. He killed the stereo and answered – it was Gordon Whiteford telling him that Lucinda`s funeral had been arranged for the following Tuesday. They had a brief, stilted conversation in which Archie attempted to apologise for not being in contact and tried to update the doctor as much as he could about their enquiries – the truth being there was little to relate. Gordon Whiteford`s stony silence did nothing to re-assure him and, the call terminated, he proceeded in a silence of his own, weighed down once again by his parallel feelings of guilt and grief.

Feeling only marginally better, he arrived at the site about twelve forty-five and the uniformed cop waved him through into the yard. He noticed that Carson`s black Audi was there already but there were no other cars other than those of the uniformed officers. He pulled the Porsche in next to the Audi, got out and raised the tailgate, sitting on the edge of the luggage space to change into his boots. They were still a bit tight and stiff but they would soon be broken in – anyway, there was no way he could have worn the old ones again... A few minutes later Cam arrived and pulled in beside him.

`Afternoon Boss, bit of a change today!`

Archie tried his best to be cheerful. `Aye, about time though and it`ll still be like a swamp out there. You bring boots?`

`Got ma wellies in the back. Nearly had Tracey`s pink ones by mistake!` replied Cam with a grin.

The two men turned at the sound of a helicopter approaching from further up river - it sounded big, not like one of the smaller ones that the cops used when pursuing stolen cars and escaping villains. As it approached, they could see the army markings on top of the camouflage. It looked a similar type to the ones used by the Coastguard for search and rescue.

`The real deal, then` stated Cam. `I guess we`re about tae find oot if Big Dunk was makin` the whole thing up.`

They watched as it hovered over the site for a few minutes and they could see a soldier leaning out of the open hatch in the side of the fuselage with what looked like a video camera. Archie presumed he was recording images of the site and the "device" (as the Major liked to refer to it). The helicopter circled once more then landed in an adjacent area of grassland that had, as yet, to be cleared. The rotors slowed and, while the pilot stayed inside, three soldiers alighted and walked towards the yard. As Archie and Cam were the only two people in the yard, one of the soldiers approached, grinned and held out his hand.

`Captain Mark Brown, EOD team.`

`Detective Inspector Archie Blue. This is Detective Sergeant Cameron Wilkie`

`Cam, please` said the DS, wincing very slightly at the strength of the Captain`s grip. *Don`t know if I could take this one down. Tough looking bugger!*

`And, Archie, as well, Mark. No need for formalities.`

The captain grinned again. Archie got the impression he was one of those guys who took everything that life could throw at him in his stride and he felt a very slight pang of envy.

`Great. But detectives? Shouldn`t you two be out chasing the bad guys? Is there something I should know?`

Archie smiled. `No, we just happened to be in the wrong place at the wrong time. I`m hoping to hand it back over to the uniform boys by Monday at the latest. Long story

`Okay, fair enough. Probably a nice wee change for you, then! Right, we`ll get started, the boys will unload the stuff and we`ll have a wee look at your contraption!` He winked at Cam, who didn`t seem quite sure how to take the comment! `Any chance you could rustle us up a pot of tea, Cam?`

`Aye, sure thing, I`ll see what I can do.` replied Cam, heading off towards the offices. Archie was amused at his friend`s slight discomfort.

After a cursory look about the area, the soldiers returned to the chopper and unloaded some large, military-style flight cases. Cam brought out a pot of tea, milk and some mugs that he had managed to locate, as well as an unopened packet of biscuits, and they munched and drank as they worked. They erected a small command tent at the end of the yard nearest the device and were unloading the last case when a silver Toyota pick-up pulled into the yard. A dapper man, probably in his late forties and wearing brown combat trousers, a green Army pullover and polished brown brogues got out and walked over. As he neared them, Archie was surprised to hear Captain Brown shout “shun” and the three soldiers stood to attention and saluted. *Of course!* He was a Major and superior in rank to them.

`Stand easy, men` The Major said and went over to the Captain, smiling and holding out his hand

`Good to see you again, Captain`

`You too, Sir. It`s been a while.`

The rest of the introductions were made and the soldiers continued with their tasks. After a short while, Archie and Cam realised that they appeared to be assembling what looked like a small helicopter. The Major explained

`This is the latest thing now, Archie. The drone! They`re frequently used to survey inaccessible areas in buildings that would normally require scaffolding and also for surveillance and photography. We can even use them to fire missiles remotely and, when I say remotely, a guy down South presses the button and the missile fires in some far and distant land. Clever stuff! Of course, we still use the little remote control tractors for de-fusing and recovery but these are great for getting an all round view in situations where you wouldn`t want to send a man in. Only problem is that they`re a bit susceptible to the wind and rain. Should be fine today, though.`

It was just after 2.00p.m. when the soldiers finished unloading and erecting all the equipment. The baby chopper was fully assembled and the Captain picked up the remote control, pressing a few buttons. The engine burst into life and the four rotors started to spin. It lifted a few feet off the ground and hovered there, moving round and tilting to the right and left as the Captain checked all the controls. Archie was amazed to see just how agile it was. He could clearly see the camera fitted to the underside of the machine and the Captain checked that all the various functions were working. The camera transmitted to a computer that was set up in the small command tent, from which a couple of long aerials projected. A small satellite dish had been set up next to the tent and Archie presumed this was to relay images to some distant command centre. This was pretty high tech stuff.

`Right, let`s take a peek at this little beauty.` said the Captain.

He`s loving this, thought Archie as, at the invitation of Major Donaldson he and Cam stepped inside the command tent. The quality of the picture was superb, obviously a really high specification camera was being used. At first it faced straight ahead as the helicopter flew towards its target. Then, as it neared its destination, it panned down towards the ground and they could clearly see the ridges of earth with the muddy puddles in between, followed by the rough scrub land where Dunk had been operating. Some of the trees were already uprooted and lying in piles, presumably to be burnt at a later date, but as the chopper slowed and they saw the JCB come into view they could see that it was surrounded by small trees and bushes, making observation quite challenging. They could see that the door of the digger was still open where Big Dunk had made his hasty exit and the bucket arm remained poised in mid sweep, clearly raised over something in the ground. Captain Brown lowered the chopper to hover as close to the trees as he could risk and zoomed the camera in. There was a faint but audible intake of breath from the small audience. They could see the object through the branches now and it was pretty much as Dunk had described, although maybe not quite as large. It was sitting in the mud at an angle of about thirty degrees to the horizontal and appeared to be only about two feet in diameter, with at least three feet of its length projecting upwards. The tail end did, in fact, have fins, although one appeared to be missing as there were only three. There was quite definitely a hole in the end sticking out of the ground. The soldier at the computer screen spoke

`Okay, it seems likely that, whatever this is, it was self-propelled, I`m fairly certain that`s an exhaust portal for some form of propulsion motor, or rocket, possibly.`

Captain Brown nodded agreement and added `Well, I`m not sure what we`ve got here, gentlemen, but it sure as hell isn`t your ordinary, common or garden World War Two aerial bomb.

Let`s have a closer look.`

He moved the chopper around, trying to obtain a clearer view amongst the branches, then circled the JCB. They gazed in astonishment at the screen as more of the object revealed itself. It looked like pewter, with a slight lustre, but not shiny and there were minimal sign of corrosion. More unusually, there appeared to be no sign of rivets or screws - the casing seemed to be totally smooth.

`This is a right odd bugger, this!` stated Captain Brown.

`Look, there Sir. Is that writing?` said one of the soldiers, pointing to the image on the screen.

The captain hovered the chopper again and zoomed the lens in. There were definitely markings on the side, next to one of the fins.

`Is that Arabic?` asked the other soldier.

`Don`t think so` said Brown. `I served a couple of turns in Afghanistan and Iraq, doesn`t look like anything I saw there.` He peered at the screen. `Might be Chinese?` then he shook his head.

`No, don`t think it`s that either. Haven`t a clue, to be honest. This is new to me. Need to send some images down to Intelligence and try to determine its origin, see what they can make of it. Let`s have another wee look.`

However, the chopper and its camera revealed nothing other than what they had already seen and Captain Brown brought it back, landing it perfectly next to the tent.

`What now, Mark?` asked Archie. This wasn`t gone exactly as he had hoped and the mystery appeared to be deepening.

`Well` said the Captain `I`ll be totally honest. I`ve had a fair bit of experience in this field and I`ve never seen anything quite like this. My concern is...` He paused and glanced at the Major, who was wearing a very serious expression. The Major took up the sentence.

`Your concern is that this object isn`t World War two` he finished. `It certainly doesn`t look that old. Normally these things are shot to bits and unstable as hell but this looks to be in near perfect condition. Then there`s the writing. Don`t know what the hell that is but it certainly isn`t German or English. Or anything else I know of.`

But if it`s no` World War Two` asked Cam, `then what else could it be?`

There was a silence as each man present digested the information and thought about Cam`s question. They were all inwardly asking the same thing and this appeared to be outside any of their collective experiences. It was the Major who broke the silence.

`Well, I suppose if you think about it, we`re pretty close to Faslane. Also, it`s not that long since the US submarine base was in the Holy Loch. Both large nuclear submarine bases with considerable military infrastructure, both located near high density areas of population. Then there was the Naval re-fuelling base at Coulport...Three prime targets, all close together...` His voice tailed off as he frowned at the Captain. `I mean, is there the remotest chance that this thing could date from then?`

Mark Brown hesitated before he spoke, obviously not wanting to commit himself.

`I`m really not sure, Sir. Wouldn`t have thought so but who knows what went on back in the Cold War days. Anyway, I`m going to suit up and go over for a look. Chris, you come with me. We`ll get a cover over the thing, best not to leave it totally exposed to the elements` he looked at Archie knowingly `or the prying eyes of strangers!`

Archie knew exactly what he meant. The presence of an Army helicopter was bound to raise eyebrows and he suspected that, before the day was out, the uniformed officers would probably be fending off enquiries from the media. Also, nowadays the Army weren`t the only people in possession of dinky little helicopters with cameras attached – the price tag of such gadgets had reduced considerably over the last few years. There was also the strong possibility of attempted intrusion by the curious - he remembered the boys on the bikes the previous day and he didn`t like the idea of local kids sneaking in to have a look (as he would probably have done when he was that age!). He would need to try and hand this over to the uniformed branch as soon as possible as it could prove to be a real headache and not something he wished to be involved in, especially on top of the other, more pressing matters that he was currently dealing with. However, he could not deny that he was curious, especially now that the initial reconnaissance had revealed that this was not a straight forward case of an unexploded WW2 bomb.

`Just be careful, Mark.` the Major said. `We really don`t know what you`re dealing with here.`

`Don`t worry Sir, we`ll not get too close. I just want to have a wee look in the places that the chopper can`t access.`

Captain Brown and the soldier called Chris opened one of the flight cases and proceeded to get dressed in an array of body armour, topped with a serious looking helmet. Archie had seen suits like this in films like “Hurt Locker” and knew that, while they could save the wearer`s life, they could still end up missing body parts that he, personally, wouldn`t like to be without. He admired their bravery - it was a job he could never do. They checked each other`s armour and set off across the mud, each carrying a pack of kit.

`There they go.` said the Major, shaking his head. `Don`t know how they can do it, personally. I`ve seen a thing or too, served with Mark in Iraq and Afghanistan. Have you ever seen what a mine or a roadside bomb can do?`

`Not first hand` said Archie.

`Believe me, you don`t want to either. I don`t class myself as a coward but, by Christ, it wouldn`t be me out there.`

`Me neither.` said Archie, watching the two soldiers as they approached the JCB. Cam settled for a simple `holy shit` as they waited to see what happened next.

In fact, very little. The soldiers circled the device, recording images, but they didn`t touch it and, when they appeared satisfied, they erected a small camouflaged tent over it, draping it over the surrounding trees and the raised arm of the JCB, then guying it securely to the ground with long pegs. Eventually they managed to get the locus fully covered, protected from the elements and from any probing aerial surveillance. They squelched through the mud towards the relieved group waiting in the command tent and, once they were back, Archie took out his phone to record a few images of the site for himself, in case any one back at his own headquarters needed confirmation of exactly what was going on!

`Nothing other than what we`ve already seen so we`re no further ahead, really.` said Captain Brown, climbing out of the cumbersome blast suit. `I`ve got a lot of photos so I suggest we wrap things up meantime. I`ll get on to HQ and see what they can come up with. If we need a more specialised team it`s going to be into next week, I`m afraid.`

`Next week?` questioned Cam.

The Major said `I suspect our more specialised men are, em, let`s just say, elsewhere at present?` he looked knowingly at the Captain.

`Exactly` he confirmed, `but I`ll give this priority. Need to keep this area safe though. Absolutely no-one in or out until we`ve cleared it away. Think you might have a problem with that?` he said, looking past them.

They hadn`t heard the big black Range Rover Vogue V6 purr into the car park, but Archie and Cam immediately noted the registration number, E1 MCC. No guessing whose it was. They could hear him haranguing the site manager.

`Aw, no` him again` growled Cam. `I`ll sort it, Boss.`

`Take it easy` he called after his DS as he headed towards the office. To no avail, it seemed. Within a minute Cam had obviously broken the news of the delay to McCourt and the big man was shouting abuse at him, at the soldiers and at anyone in the vicinity. Archie ran across as McCourt made a grave error of judgement and tried to punch the Detective Sergeant. By the time he reached them, the big idiot was face down in the muddy yard with one arm up his back and Cam`s forearm round his throat. One of the uniforms had run over and was already cuffing his free hand. Cam released him into the officer`s tender care. The DS barked

`Book him! Assaultin` a police officer, threatenin` behaviour.` McCourt was shouting `Did ye fuckin` see that. Tried to strangle me. Bastard, I`m havin` you for fuckin` assault!`

`Aye, gaun yersel`, arsehole!` Cam shouted after him before Archie put his hand on his arm and said

`Leave it, Cam. He`s nicked now and out of the way. Let the uniforms sort it out.`

The soldiers were obviously amused at the proceedings and, as the two policemen made their way back over to them the Major said

`The boss, I take it? Seems like a nice sort!`

`Aye, well he`s out the way now for a day at least` Archie replied. `Make our lives a bit easier anyway.`

Captain Brown winked again at Cam.

`Very nicely done, Cam. What discipline?`

`Jiu Jitsu" Cam replied, pleased at the compliment.

"Black belt, I`d guess?`

Cam grinned this time. `Comes in handy with arseholes like him!`

`Oh yes!` smiled the Captain knowingly. Cam was warming to him.

They waited, chatting to the Major, as the soldiers packed away their kit and loaded the flight cases back on to the helicopter. The team returned for the usual round of handshakes then set off back to the chopper, the rotors of which were already starting to turn. It wasn`t long before the big machine took off and Archie felt the usual thrill as it heaved its bulk vertically into the air, tilted slightly nose down, then headed east, back up the river Clyde. Soon peace returned and the Major, too, bade his farewell.

`Archie, I`ll keep on top of this. I don`t want you to have too much grief so I`ll let you know as soon as I hear anything. Let me know if anything else happens at this end. Take care, my man.` He shook hands then returned to his pick-up and set off.

`Well` sighed Archie, `A bit of a shocker, that. What the hell are we dealing with here, Cam? And why did it happen on our watch?`

`Aye, you wonder, don`t you` his DS said. `Seemed pretty

thorough, thae boys. Bloody brave an a`. Odd that there doesn`ae seem to be anything actually happening with it, though. I mean it`s just kinda sitting there, mockin` us` He turned and gave the distant, mysterious object the finger.

`Aye Cam, that`ll really help` laughed Archie.

Cam just grinned and the two set off back to their cars, where they changed out of their muddy gear, chatting easily - a*lmost like old times...*Finally they went their separate ways, Cam to his wife and child, Archie to...well, he wasn`t thinking that far ahead.

The soldiers were, indeed, very thorough. But not thorough enough. On the lower side of the device and, to be fair to them, pretty much obscured by the undergrowth and a liberal smearing of mud, was a small indentation, covered with a thick and somewhat scratched, transparent panel. Very easy to miss. Underneath this covering were four tiny lights, two red, two blue, orientated with the same colours opposed to each other. They had been flashing quickly in a rotating sequence, unseen but not entirely unnoticed since Big Dunk had dug the device up on Friday.

Chapter 12

Commander Urvai 3 Goffella was not a man to whom patience came naturally, although after drifting through far-space for almost eighteen cycles on the ageing craft Zemm, he had learned the hard way that impatience served little purpose. He and his crew had, occasionally, managed to eke out a meagre existence on the few habitable planets that were (relatively) sympathetic to his cause (or, perhaps, just scared of him and his entourage) during their search for the mysterious and elusive weapon, although he had long since come to doubt its actual existence. Legend, old tales – perhaps, but there was little else to give them any hope these days so their search continued. To admit to this, however, would be to admit defeat, so he and his crew continued to search...and to hope!

As he lay awake in his personal cabin, he gazed at the ceiling and wondered, really, what it was all about. He did not have any doubt that his particular faction, tribe, whatever one wished to think of it as, was superior both in physical strength and in intellect. The mighty Atra – hah! Alas, their "might" hadn`t stopped them from being overthrown in the so called "democratic uprising" all those cycles ago, treated now as social pariahs by the weak, liberal planetary governors, thanks to the genetic tagging system that, ironically, his forebears had put in place. Of course, you were free to apply for a decent job, a higher rank in the military perhaps, but at some point you would be told that you were "unsuitable". It was a load of crap really, and he had taken the decision, along with a number of others, that life would be better off-planet rather than suffering the discrimination and humiliation that they faced on Loh. The Atra were an extremely proud people and, even after all this time, there were many of them who firmly believed that their time would come again – especially if they could lay their hands on this elusive weapon.

Of course, it hadn`t been easy, between finding transport and a method of escape (they were forbidden from leaving the planet, destined to remain, unofficially, prisoners on their own world). But they had eventually achieved their objective, leaving what, until then, he had always considered home, filled with some sense of hope and the excitement of a new future in which, just maybe, they would rise to become the superior race once again.

Now, here he was, older, considerably more cynical and no further ahead in his quest. His crew, most of whom had already been friends prior to their escape, were likewise careworn and, over time, their relationships had been challenged - it took a great deal of effort on his part to keep the peace amongst them. They would need to find somewhere to land soon, he realised, otherwise trouble was likely to ensue once more and the last thing he needed was mutiny. Some good old rest and recreation, involving strong drink, good women and maybe even a bit of violence (in which, with a bit of care, they were sure to be victorious) would go a long way towards easing tensions. But it could never change the fact that they were now homeless and, at times it seemed, hopeless. They could not return to Loh – their escape had branded them as criminals and they would be summarily imprisoned should they ever go back, so they were destined to travel space, hoping...

Until his self-imposed exile, he had always believed in the stories of the "great weapon", Samian`s Sphere, some called it. It was to have been the key to finally purifying their planet, ridding it of lesser races (other than those spared to work as servants) and leaving his faction as the sole occupants, their rightful place. He had been told the tale as a child, of how the great weapons master`s creation had been stolen and spirited away by a bunch of cowardly traitors, yet was believed to still exist, although no-one knew where, exactly. But it was all so long ago and, despite their technology and continuing developments in travel within the conduit, the Galaxy was just too incomprehensibly enormous to realistically expect it to just turn up! The last known conduit exit portal used by both the thieves and their pursuers was now known (or thought to be, at least) but, after that, they could have gone anywhere in this particular sector, the one through which the Zemm was now travelling. Urvai was also aware of the existence of sleepers on a number of inhabited planets, quietly and unobtrusively watching for the faintest trace but, as far as he was aware, none of these backward species possessed the technology for trans-space travel so were unlikely to be of much help should the drone be discovered, a possibility that now seemed increasingly unlikely.

He closed his eyes and tried to lose himself in sleep but, like the Sphere, it was elusive, just out of reach. He wished he had a partner, at least it would make the time pass quicker. *Not much chance of that now...*as always, though, the very thought of female company aroused him...

***

He woke suddenly, initially surprised that he had fallen asleep then angry that he had been wakened. The voice that had intruded on his privacy spoke again.

`Commander, can you come to the control area please?`

`This had better be good, Terki, I had just fallen asleep!`

He sat up, scratched his head then stood and climbed into the blue flying suit, whose self-cleaning facility had recently ceased to function. *Need to do something about this, getting a bit odorous....* It always surprised him how exhausting inactivity could be, especially when roused from a fitful slumber and he went to a small cabinet, removed a beaker, filling it from a crystal flask then took a drink of the clear, ice cold liquid, unfortunately now in short supply, that never failed to restore him. *That`s better.* He left his cabin and made his way to the front of the ship, where the main control area was located.

The door to the area slid half open at his approach before grinding to a halt – as usual he had to push it to the side before he walked in. The ship was starting to show signs of neglect, as the on-board computer frequently reminded him, but the crew had little choice but to carry out running repairs as best they could, for there was nowhere to go for a major overhaul. Spare parts were running short too and he didn`t like to think what would happen if there was a major malfunction in one of the primary systems. He glanced at the main forward view screen, which showed the familiar expanse of assorted stars and planets set against the black backdrop of space. There had been a time when it had given him a slight thrill but not now, he had seen too much of it to feel anything. Terki 2 Zeliko, his first officer and oldest friend, was sitting in one of the chairs facing the screen, with communications officer Retso 7 Gergion next to him. Both men were staring intently at one of the smaller communications screens below. Urvai spoke as they looked up.

`Takes me hours to get to sleep and then I get wakened up by a couple of morons. What is so important?`

Terki answered with a grin. He was used to his friend`s abrasive nature.

`Sorry to disturb your sweet dreams, Commander, but take a look at this.` He pointed to the large, three dimensional display in front of them. Theoretically, it should have been spherical but, over the last few months, it had become decidedly elliptical – a faulty field stabiliser, apparently, and just one of the many minor but seemingly un-resolveable technical issues now plaguing the Zemm Nonetheless, Urvai followed the direction of Terki`s finger. He recognised the display as a map of the sector in which they were currently travelling, scanning as they went for any sign of...well, anything, he supposed. The position of their ship was marked with a small blue spot in the centre of the display. At the bottom left hand corner, there was an even smaller pulsating red light. Then it disappeared.

`Well, whatever it was, it appears to have gone` he remarked sarcastically.

`Just wait...look, there it is again.` replied Retso. `And, now it has gone again. Been doing that since we noticed it.`

`So what do you suppose it is?` asked the Commander, his curiosity starting to get the better of him.

`I do not know.` replied the communications officer, `It just suddenly appeared so either it has just come into range or it has just started transmitting. But something is definitely sending some sort of signal.` He turned to a two dimensional virtual screen and touched some of the sensors displayed at the bottom. `There seems to be no content to the message, although that may well be because of the extreme distance. Whatever the source, it appears to be an automatic repetition sequence of some sort. Possibly a location transmitter.`

`So how is the signal getting here if it is that distant?` asked the Commander. This was definitely getting interesting.

`Well, that is the strange thing. The signal appears to be very weak and I would have thought that, by itself, it should not normally travel this far. I suspect that it is being boosted somehow and my guess would be that there are relay beacons somewhere in this sector that are transmitting the signal. They are currently too small to detect. Obviously they are not specifically transmitting to us, though. We just happen to be here.`

`So what you are saying is that someone else has placed relay beacons here. Why would anyone do that unless they suspected there was something to search for? And, more to the point, who?`

`Exactly` said Terki. `Assuming that these are beacons from our planet, which seems likely as any alien beacons would not be coded to relay the signal, then they are here for a reason.`

`Are there any other ships in this sector?` Urvai asked, aware of a prickling at the back of his neck. Other ships could mean trouble if his own craft was discovered.

`I cannot see any` replied Retso `but that does not mean there are none there. Could be hiding, running in secrecy mode. Or could even have landed on a planet that is masking them. And, of course, they could just be too far away for us to detect them. It is a big sector.`

The three men paused for a few moments, silently digesting the information.

`So what now, Commander?` asked Terki.

Urvai 3 Goffella sat down in one of the vacant chairs and stared at the view of space. Was this another futile lead? It wouldn`t be the first time they had headed somewhere, using precious fuel and resources, only to find the remains of an old, decaying wreck on some rock-strewn moon, whose emergency transmitter had suddenly started to work. Little use to the decaying corpses on board, he reflected. And yet, the relay beacons weren`t here by chance. Someone had placed them in this sector, which meant that someone else was searching too...Well, at least it would relieve the monotony.

`May as well have a look. Lay in a course, do not go too fast, it uses too much energy! Keep a close watch for any other vessels, the last thing we need is a fight. Retso, if we get nearer do you think you will get a better idea of what it is?`

`I would think so` replied Retso. `If it is a locator signal we should get a bit more information if we can detect and decode any content. It is just too far away at the moment. That is probably why the display is intermittent. Of, course, there may also be a faulty beacon in the chain. We just can not tell at the moment.`

`Oh well, we will find out in time, I dare say. Good work, I suppose it was worth getting up for after all!`

Terki laughed.

`Did you hear that, Retso, the Commander nearly paid us a compliment. Space must finally be agreeing with him!`

Urvai slapped the back of Terki`s head and smiled as he left the control area. No chance of sleep now, he`d head to the main crew area for something to eat. *Maybe this time...?*

***

And then again, maybe not...

They had been at speed 5 for nearly a day and the red dot on the screen, although closer, was giving nothing away. Urvai was, once again, lying in his bunk staring at the ceiling, wondering if he should abort the journey rather than waste any more time, energy and fuel. But it was something at least, better than fumbling about in the emptiness of space, trying to sleep. And those relay beacons...? He closed his eyes, more in hope than in expectation but he had no sooner done so when Terki`s voice resonated in his private space.

`Commander, I think you will want to see this.`

He was on his feet in an instant, pulling on the blue suit without a thought for its cleanliness. He raced up to the control room and placed his hand on the panel beside the closed door.

Nothing.

`Shit!`

He tried again. The door moved fractionally, then stuck. He shouted

`Terki, I cannot get this door open!`

`Coming.` came the faint reply. Urvai heard Terki banging from the other side and the door moved enough for them to get their hands into the gap. Between them they managed to slide it open just enough for him to enter the control room. It failed to close behind him but he didn`t care anymore. Retso was there, along with another three crew members. He could sense the excitement amongst them.

`What?` he asked.

Retso pointed to the communications screen. `We seem to have come into range to decode the signal. Well, into range of the beacons anyway, the point of origin is still relatively distant.`

`And?`

`Look for yourself ` said Terki, vacating the chair nearest the screen.

Urvai sat down and looked. Such a transmission would normally give information as to what the craft or object was, along with other information on registration and ownership.

`So. It appears to be a drop drone. Interesting. Any clues to what was aboard?`

`No` replied Retso, smiling. `But we know whose drone it was. Look down.`

Khrat moved the information on the screen up to reveal the next portion of the decoded message

Drop Drone 2
Craft Intaria
Loh Gara 4 7
Registered Gara 4 Theasak

He read it again, to make sure. Then a third time. He looked up at Terki and smiled.

`Well, well, well! The filthy traitor, Theasak.` He turned and spat on the floor, as if the very taste of the name offended him.`Finally, something interesting! I wonder what was in his torpedo, my friends. Shall we find out?`

He spoke to the ship, knowing its voice would sound weary.

Just like the rest of us

`Zemm, can we manage maximum speed?`

`It will be an effort, Commander Goffella. The power is low and the integrity of the ship is not all it should be. But we can sustain it for a reasonable amount of time, I suppose.`

`Long enough to reach the location of the transmission?`

There was a pause. The computer was either calculating or thinking.

`If you are prepared to take the risk, Urvai. We will have virtually no power left to return to the portal. But yes, we can reach the destination on full power, if you so desire.`

`Oh yes, I think I so desire. Men?`

They cheered in agreement and held their fists aloft in the forbidden salute of the Atra. No doubt about it.

`Maximum speed. Destination as per source of signal on screen. Let us go and claim it! Whatever it may be!`

Chapter 13

As he drove home from Erskine, Archie realised that not only was he hungry, but also that he had almost no food in his house. A keen cook, he normally always kept a well-stocked larder but recent events had made the task of food shopping, something he usually quite enjoyed, an undesirable chore. He took a detour and headed for the nearest supermarket to stock his shelves and, an hour later, was back en-route with a boot full of food, plus a couple of bottles of decent red wine. He had looked at the whiskies on offer but had refrained from buying any – better to avoid the temptation altogether.

Archie arrived at his home and pulled into the drive. He had always been proud of his cottage on the hillside above Lochwinnoch, the small Renfrewshire village that he considered home. Unassuming yet interesting (a bit like Archie liked to think of himself in his more self-aware and, admittedly, pretentious moments!) it was near enough to civilization for convenience yet far enough away to offer the peace and tranquillity that he desired; and, of course, it had the most spectacular view. Recently, though it had seemed a bit like a prison and a feeling of great sadness descended over him once more as he thought just how quickly his life had changed. He unloaded the shopping and made his way to the front door - once inside, he unpacked his purchases somewhat disinterestedly, leaving out a prime fillet steak and a selection of vegetables.

Can't keep going on like this, Archie, you need to snap out of it. Life goes on. Come on now, where's the bottle opener...

He opened the bottle of Merlot, poured himself a generous glass and took a sip – it tasted excellent and his spirits rose very slightly. He decided that what he needed now was somemusic, something that, although it had slipped out of his life over the last few weeks, seldom failed to cheer him up. One of the reasons that he enjoyed living by himself was the fact he could play whatever he liked, whenever he liked and, given the isolated location of his cottage, at whatever volume he pleased!

Many of his fellow officers considered Archie a bit of a loner. An only child, his parents had died nearly ten years ago, within a month of one another, leaving him quite comfortably well off outside of his Detective Inspector`s salary (hence the Porsche, his one big indulgence in life!) He sometimes wondered if his Dad had died of a broken heart as he had seemed fit and healthy enough until his mother`s sudden death from a heart attack. The devastating sorrow that he had so obviously suffered as a result of the loss of his beloved Lucinda, Archie`s mum, as well as the obvious love they shared for one another was one of the reasons that Archie had been wary of any form of emotional commitment. Of course, his historic earlier relationship with Karen McMillan (as he still thought of her) had probably already established his inherent mistrust of women, as both he and his parents had assumed that the two of them would have ended up happily married. Over the years, he had often wondered how his life would have panned out had she not met Gordon. Maybe if he`d paid her a bit more attention...

No, no point in going there again...

There, there had been a few girlfriends over the years but his was a demanding career with difficult hours and it would need to be an understanding woman who could accept this. Many of his colleagues were divorced or separated, frequently boasting of their "latest partner" and Archie just could not be bothered - for him it had to be for life and he had still to meet anyone who lived up to his expectations, someone he could trust. So, another Saturday night alone with his thoughts – not the most attractive prospect...

Right, time to get the iPhone hooked up and start cooking.

He went through to the hall where he had hung his jacket and reached inside for his phone - it wasn`t there. A further search of the other pockets showed them to be empty too. He tried the pockets in his trousers and his shirt but, again, there was no phone. He felt the sudden pang of panic experienced by anyone who suddenly discovers they have misplaced their mobile and he opened the door and ran back out to the car. He couldn`t find it there either and he returned to the house, picked up the good old-fashioned land-line phone and dialled his mobile number, in case it had fallen down under one of the seats. He went back outside and listened carefully but could hear nothing.

`Shit!` he exclaimed.

Then he remember the incident with McCourt, how he had been

taking a photo of the site with his phone. He thought he had put it in his pocket but he must have dropped it in the rush to assist Cam. He sat down in the car and faced the fact that he would have to drive the half hour back to Erskine to retrieve it.

`Bollocks!`

So much for a relaxing Saturday night. He went back in to the cottage, re-corked the wine and put away the steak before locking the door behind him then pulling the Porsche out of the drive and heading back the way he had come. There was already a faint white skin of frost on the car and, as he knew that the roads were unlikely to have been gritted, he took a bit more care than usual – it was obviously going to be a clear, cold night. He switched on the music system to play some music to ease the journey then realised, of course, that all his playlists played from his phone via bluetooth. *Bugger!* He settled for Radio 2 once again and, as he drove down the narrow back roads he noticed that the fuel light had just come on. *What next!* By now, too, he realised that he really was starving, having eaten virtually nothing since breakfast. His stomach was making very peculiar growling noises!

Forty minutes and a tank full of fuel later, he arrived back at the site gate and he could see the frost glistening on the metallic surfaces of the fence. The marked police car was parked inside the yard and two uniformed officers, witnessing the approach of a vehicle, barred his way, although the Porsche was a bit of a giveaway as to his identity. He opened his window and they approached. The nearest cop bent down to address him.

`Everything all right, Sir?` he asked, his breath steaming in the frosty air.

`Not exactly.` Archie replied with a grimace `Must have dropped my bloody phone earlier, thought I`d better come and get it in case it rains. Although it looks okay at the moment but, hey, its the West of Scotland!` The night sky, though, was crystal clear and a heavy Autumnal frost seemed much more likely than rain.

`Aye, let`s hope it stays off, Sir` the other cop said `A bit nippy out here, mind you.`

`You`ll want this, then?` said Archie, reaching to the passenger seat and lifting over the cardboard tray with two steaming coffees and two Mars bars that he had picked up in the garage - a contingency plan just in case he had needed a spot of bribery! He handed it over to the cop`s eager hands.

`Aw, that`s brilliant Sir, really appreciate it, cheers!`

`No problem, lads. I`m still young enough to remember what it`s like, standing outside on a cold night freezing your bollocks off. Enjoy!`

The second cop opened the gate and Archie drove through. As he gratefully took the hot cup from his mate, he commented

`Aye Gordon, he`s no` a bad sort. Well, for a Detective Inspector anyway...!"

He was right though. Although he might have denied it, Archie was a reasonably popular officer amongst the lower ranks.

He parked at the end of the car park, just next to where the command tent had been set up earlier. Leaving the dipped headlights on, he got out of the car and gazed briefly up at the star filled sky. On cold, clear nights such as this, he always looked up and wondered...then he dropped his gaze back to Earth and walked round to the area where he suspected his phone had fallen. He could just make out the gaunt shape of the abandoned JCB in the distance across the field, but the camouflaged tent covering the mystery object was almost invisible in the dark. He tried to ignore it like the proverbial elephant in the room and proceeded to hunt for the missing iPhone. Fortunately he and Cam had been the last ones away but, prior to that, there had been a bit of activity as the soldiers had stowed away their gear. He wandered about, peering at the drying, caked mud, flattened by many footprints. Then he saw it! Further over than he had expected but at least it was there. He lifted it up and wiped the mud off the screen, hoping that no-one had stood on it. It seemed okay and he flicked the screen, noticing the missed call from his house as well as a missed call from Cam, who was probably just checking up on him. It was a relief to have it back in his possession, though.

After giving it a good wipe to remove the remaining mud he pocketed the phone and was just about to return to the car when he caught a glimpse of something over at the tent covering the device. It was mostly in darkness, his headlight beams illuminating an area to the left of where the JCB sat. He thought he had seen a brief flash of light and his pulse quickened. He stared at the camouflaged shelter for a few moments but nothing seemed amiss. "Just my imagination, running away with me..." he hummed, smiling to himself. *Seeing things now!* He was turning towards the car when he caught another brief flicker of light. This time he definitely wasn`t imagining it. He stopped and stared again and, after a minute, he clearly saw the glimmer of a faint light and, worse, the vaguest shadow of someone moving in the tent. *Holy shit, what the hell`s going on?* He briefly felt like taking the two uniformed cops` coffee back as they had obviously buggered off at some stage, leaving the gate unattended. But the site had a large perimeter and, despite the high fence and occasional patrols round the parts nearer the road, there was a lot of unguarded scrub land that could have afforded entry to anyone really determined to have a look. He glanced over at them and they were happily slurping their beverages. No, he would give them the benefit of the doubt and deal with them later if necessary. *Let`s see what`s going on over here first.*

He set off across the field of mud, which was just starting to freeze over. It was certainly a lot more solid than it had been on Friday but he could still feel the sticky ooze sucking at his feet as he walked. There it was again - there was definitely someone in the tent. Archie reached the back end of the JCB before it came back to him that there was some unexplained and unexploded device lurking on the other side of it. He paused briefly but he needed to remove whoever was there, firstly for their own safety and secondly to give them a right good bollocking and possibly a caution. He approached the tent and lifted the flap.

Detective Inspector Archie Blue was an experienced police officer and there was little that surprised him (or so he believed). Had he been asked, he would probably have said he expected to find

1) Kids up to no good
2) The Press
3) Eddie McCourt (assuming he had got back out of custody that day)

It was none of the above. To his astonishment Archie was faced with a tall female, probably about his own height of six foot one. With his quick, detective`s observation he instantly noted that she was wearing a tightly-fitting grey jumpsuit that resembled some sort of flying overall, and matching grey ankle boots. The material looked thick but quite silky and rippled slightly as she moved, almost rendering her form invisible against the dark background. From what he could make out, she appeared to be quite shapely, but that was of no concern at the moment. However, it was her face that drew his attention. A long, pointed face with high cheekbones. Full red lips with an almost perfect cupid`s bow shape. Her eyes, with an almost, but not quite, oriental upward slant, were the largest and darkest Archie had ever seen - he could make out no pupils and briefly wondered if she was wearing those funny, cosmetic contact lenses. Her hair, which fell down to her collar line and was cut in a slightly unfashionable bob with a heavy fringe, was thick, jet black and shiny, contrasting sharply, as did her lips, with her very pale skin. Fleetingly he wondered if she was in fancy dress of some sort, although Halloween wasn`t for another couple of weeks. She certainly looked decidedly unusual and her dark eyes gazed straight at him with no expression of surprise or alarm, almost as if he wasn`t there. She seemed to be holding a peculiar sort of torch in her right hand, pointing it at the metal casing of the device.

`Just what the hell do you think you`re doing here?` barked Archie, in his best Detective Inspector`s voice.

Nothing.

`Answer me. Who the hell are you and what are you doing here?`

Still nothing. The girl simply stared at him.

`Right. Come with me. Now.`

Archie made towards her and suddenly froze. He couldn`t move a muscle. Somehow he stayed upright but his arms and legs seemed to be locked. He tried to say something but his mouth wouldn`t work either. However, his thoughts were in overdrive.

Oh shit, that`s me stuffed. It must be some sort of chemical weapon and it`s leaking. Her too, she`s finished as well, whoever she is.

However, she didn`t appear to be "finished" at all, as she turned away and continued to move the torch, or whatever it was that she held in her right hand, back and forth across the device. Suddenly, Archie felt the first grip of an unfocussed, yet absolute, panic. He broke out in beads of sweat and had an extreme urge to scream. Still no sound came. The girl, though, seemed totally unaffected and turned away from the bomb to stare straight at him again with her large, dark eyes. Just as quickly as it arrived, the feeling of panic subsided, only to be replaced with...

Archie couldn`t believe it now. He was completely aroused, turned on like he`d never been turned on before.

Aw no....No. No way!

To his absolute astonishment and dismay he felt the first wave of an orgasm approaching but, just in time, it disappeared as quickly as the feeling of panic. God knows what kind of chemical weapon this was - he had heard of some poisons that caused all the body muscles to spasm, inducing the effect he had just felt. However, it would certainly be in demand if it got into the wrong hands. Like McCourt`s, he briefly thought. Then, unexpectedly, a feeling of absolute peace and calm came over him. *It`ll all be fine, no problem.* The girl was still staring at him, expressionless. He saw her mouth move but the sound that came out was totally unintelligible, some odd combination of the Far East, the Middle East and Russia, it seemed to Archie, and he briefly remembered the peculiar engravings on the side of the missile that the soldiers couldn`t identify. But he felt completely chilled and knew that everything would all be okay - if he could have, he would have smiled - he still couldn`t, though. Then the feeling of well-being started to subside as quickly as it had arrived and the girl spoke again. This time he understood the words.

`I am very, very sorry.` she said, her voice soft and deep but with an very odd and unplaceable accent that appeared to carry no emotional inflexion. `I did not mean for that to happen. Are you all right? I did not intend to cause you any distress.`

Archie discovered that his limbs were functioning and he could, once again, speak. He found himself almost shouting at the strange girl.

`We need to get out of here. Right now. I haven`t a clue what that thing is,` he gestured at the object `but it`s doing some pretty damned weird stuff. You and I need to move it. Out, now.` he commanded.

`No!`

`I beg your pardon?` he said, feeling the anger rise. This wasn`t going the way it normally should - a right difficult creature, this! Maybe he should call the uniforms over.

`I said no!`

`You`re coming with me. Move! Now!`

`No. I am not coming with you. I have not completed my investigation.` She turned away from him and continued to move the torch-like instrument over the casing of the bomb.

`Listen lady.` Archie said, drawing himself up to his full height in a vain attempt to tower over her. He put on the most commanding and, hopefully, intimidating voice he could muster and, moving slightly, tried to make eye contact. It usually worked.

`I am a police officer. Detective Inspector. When I say you`re coming with me, then you`re coming with me. Understand?`

She turned back to face him and gazed at him, unflinching.

Then, with an odd (and very slightly menacing) smile, she quickly leaned towards him, bringing her face close to his and causing him to take a step backwards. Imitating his tone almost exactly, she said

`And when I say I am not, then I am not.`

Her eyes seemed to bore into his head for a moment then Archie Blue, the experienced, case-hardened, grief-laden (and possibly murderous) Detective Inspector, did something that, in his entire career, he had never done in a situation such as this... he burst out laughing.

Chapter 14

Archie hadn`t the faintest idea what was so funny but he was almost doubled over with mirth. The whole situation just seemed so absurd, this strange woman, apparently in fancy-dress, totally defying him - that was certainly something he wasn`t used to. And the way she had imitated him had been completely hilarious! The tears were starting to run down his cheeks when, suddenly, the humour evaporated, he stopped laughing and, once again, realised the gravity of their situation.

What the hell is wrong with you – you`re acting like a complete idiot, Archie...

The woman was still staring at him, still wearing the peculiar half-smile. He stared back unsmiling, holding her gaze and trying not to feel embarrassed by his peculiar behaviour.

`Listen to me. Very carefully. I do not have the faintest idea what this thing is,` he cast a nervous glance at the silver object beside them `but it is obviously extremely dangerous, possibly some kind of chemical weapon - I appear to have been hallucinating and I also suffered a temporary paralysis - I can`t believe that you are not feeling similar effects. We need to get out of here for our own safety. Now, come on, move!` Then, as an afterthought, he added `Please!`

`This thing?` she said, looking at the object and snorting derisively. `Dangerous?` To Archie`s dismay she turned and kicked it with her grey booted foot. He cringed involuntarily but nothing happened. `It is not in the least bit dangerous, it is just a big, old torpedo converted to what is called a drop drone. What it may contain is likely to be dangerous but this is quite harmless, I can assure you.`

He stared at her in disbelief

`How the hell do you know what it is, or what`s in it? And how do you explain the effects I experienced? The paralysis, the fear, the...` he didn`t mention the next bit.

She looked straight at him once again. He felt as if she was looking right inside his head and it was freaking him out. But he held her gaze – he had to try and get her away from the device.

`Do you really think the drone caused all that?` she asked.

`Of course. It must have. If not, then what in God`s name did?`

She just stared at him, still wearing the half-smile - it was extremely irritating.

`You?` he asked in disbelief.

She nodded. He shook his head.

`Don`t be bloody ridiculous. No way! You`re saying that you made me feel all those...`

Suddenly, once again he found himself unable to speak. Her black eyes stared at him and he started to feel the vague panic rise in his chest. This time, though, it stopped almost immediately. Archie just stared back, clueless as to what to say or think - this was way outside of his comfort zone. She broke the silence for him.

`Now. First of all, I will leave here, with you if you wish, because my initial task is complete. I am cold and uncomfortable in these damp conditions. Second, I am very hungry. Where can I locate something to eat?`

`What?` Archie, finding his voice again, gasped in astonishment.

`Something to eat, You know, food? Surely you eat? Are you hungry? We could eat together if you like. I feel that there is a lot that I need to explain to you. You appear to be what I would describe as a security operative and I believe that I can trust you with what I have to say. But first, I would like to eat.`

Archie just gazed at her, totally at a loss as to what to do. This odd woman claimed to have controlled his emotions and his body, she was trespassing on a secured (and presumably dangerous) area and now she was asking him to take her for something to eat! He realised that his own stomach was still growling and that he should, by now, have been settled comfortably on his couch, a glass of Merlot in hand and a stomach contentedly full of steak, mushrooms and potatoes. But before he could reply, and as if sensing his hesitation, the woman spoke again

`Please try to trust me. I honestly do not wish to cause you any harm and I am most certainly not your enemy. But, as you have already discovered, you would be unable to coerce me into doing anything against my will. Now, can you please take me to get some food? Or leave me if you wish. I have no preference.`

Archie snapped out of his stupor. At least this would get her (and him, for that matter) away from what he still considered to be an extremely hazardous area. After that, well, he would just have to play it by ear.

`Okay, come with me.`

The strange woman put the torch-like device she had been using into a pocket in her suit that Archie hadn`t noticed at first. Once it was stowed, the pocket seemed to disappear again but he assumed it was a trick of the light. Then she bent down and picked up what appeared to be a pear-shaped board of some sort. It was about eighteen inches long, about a foot wide at the base and about three inches thick. It looked like it was made of a greyish cardboard.

`What exactly is that?` Archie asked.

`It is just a piece of equipment. I will show you later. Do not worry about it.`

He decided to take her advice, his first priority being to get the hell out of there! They exited the tent and walked back across the mud to the yard. The woman walked in front of him and, despite all his confusion and misgivings, he was aware that underneath the grey suit she wore, she appeared to have a great figure. Long legs, shapely...He stopped himself quickly. This was neither the time nor place. But he couldn`t help noticing that, as she moved, the suit blended in to the surroundings, rendering her almost invisible at times. He assumed it was either the darkness or some lingering after-effects of what he had just experienced. They reached his car.

`Is this your vehicle?` she asked, pointing to the Porsche.

Christ, she sounds just like a cop....

`Yes, it is.`

`Interesting. How is it powered?`

An odd question, thought Archie. She must be a petrol-head. Or maybe she was planning on hi-jacking it - at this moment, anything seemed possible! He answered

`A three litre V6 engine. Four hundred and twenty horsepower.` he replied, almost automatically. He knew his car well!

`Horsepower? Really` she exclaimed. `How peculiar. Internal combustion, fossil fuel. And it apparently runs on wheels! Excellent! This will be very interesting.` She opened the back door and placed the pear-shaped board on the floor, but Archie hesitated before getting in to the car.

`And don`t you think those two are going to notice me driving out with a female passenger in the back of my car?` He nodded towards the two uniforms who, fortunately, were facing away from them. `Especially when I came in alone!`

`Oh, do not worry about them.` she said in an off-hand tone. Archie hadn`t noticed that the flying suit had a hood attached, which she now pulled over her head. She climbed in to the car, curled herself up on the back seat and all but disappeared. Archie watched in amazement. *How the hell did she do that?*

`I must be off my bloody head` he mumbled as he got into the car and started the engine. He drove back towards the gate and the two cops stood aside to let him pass. He was convinced they would see the girl lying on the back seat.

`Did you get your phone, Sir?` the first one asked `You were a wee while in their. Thought you`d got lost.`

`Got it eventually, it wasn`t where I expected.` Archie replied nervously –well, it was the truth...kind of! He was expecting them to query his illicit passenger at any moment but they didn`t appear to have noticed her...yet!

`Everything okay, I take it? No-one sneaking about? What about the other patrols?`

`No, all quiet, Sir` the other one replied. `Not a soul, other guys report the same, the whole place is secure. Think the big fence helps. Seems that word hasn`t leaked out yet but I reckon it won`t be long.`

`Probably not.` said Archie. `Anyway, I`m off, `night lads.`

`Goodnight Sir. And thanks again for the coffee, that was just great!`

`No problem` and off he drove. He breathed a huge sigh of relief – he couldn`t believe that they hadn`t noticed the woman curled up on the back seat but, now that they were back on the main road she sat up and pulled down her hood.

`I told you they would not notice me. My suit is has a bio-concealment programme.` she said. `I would like to come in beside you now please. I like to see where I am going.`

A bio-concealment programme. That`s it. She`s totally mental, this one!

Archie checked that there was no-one about. There was a guy in the distance walking his dog and he could see the occasional car at the roundabout ahead, but the road he was on was deserted. He stopped and she swapped from the rear to the front seat.

`Better. Now, where are we going to eat?`

McDonalds. Where else?

`Can you put your seat belt on, please?` Archie asked.

`My what? Oh, the restraint. How does it work? Do you have to do it yourself?`

Archie shook his head, leaned over and pulled the belt across her. As he did so, he caught a very faint, unusual and surprisingly sensual smell as he fastened it in place but the woman seemed entirely unconcerned by his actions or his proximity. He drove off once again but they made no conversation on the road to Linwood, the location of the nearest McDonalds, and Archie was starting to feel decidedly awkward, although relieved to be away from the building site and its mysterious contents. The woman, on the other hand, seemed completely content to sit and look out of the window – she looked totally relaxed. Archie eventually decided to relieve the silence by playing music on his iPhone, shuffling to "Archie Favs 1" - familiar, comforting rock music that should relieve the awkward silence - anyway, Archie couldn`t think of anything to say to her. His passenger appeared to take little notice of the music until one of his all time favourite tracks came on. AC/DC "Night Prowler", one of the sleaziest, sexiest rock songs ever! Archie loved the opening chords then the slow, sensual blues rhythm. She sat forward in her seat.

`What is this?` she shouted over Angus Young`s grinding guitar. It was the first she had spoken on the entire journey.

`AC/DC, Night Prowler.` He turned and looked at her in mild surprise. `Do you like it?`

`Yes. It is amazing. I have never heard anything like it.`

Archie knew that AC/DC weren`t to everyone`s taste and her apparent liking for this particular song seemed strange. The last chord was fading as they approached their destination and he turned the music off, pulling in to McDonalds car park, which was half full with hungry post-cinema customers. He needed to go to the toilet and had decided against the drive-thru, but he didn`t really want to take her in to the restaurant with him as she would definitely look a bit out of place with her unusual looks and attire. This was Linwood, after all. Anything other than a baseball cap, joggy bottoms and Nike trainers looked alien!

`Right. I have to trust you to stay here. Do not leave the car. Do not speak to anyone. I need to, em, pay a visit.`

`You mean you..." she paused and thought for a second `...you need to go for a pee-pee. That is fine.`

`What?` Archie frowned at her as a distant and vague memory of his mother stirred inside him. `A pee-pee? Aye, well, as I said, stay here. Do not leave the car.`

`Would you like to handcuff me to your steering wheel?` she asked. Archie looked for a trace of humour but could detect none - she just stared at him with those dark, unfathomable eyes. He couldn`t think of anything sensible to say so he just shook his head and walked away. As he reached the door of the restaurant he turned to check that she was still there and he briefly wondered if he should, perhaps, have handcuffed her. However, the reality was that he would have been quite glad if she had decided to do a runner!

After visiting the toilet he approached the counter and ordered two Big Macs with large fries and two diet cokes - he resisted the temptation of the Smarties McFlurry, paid for his food and waited for it to be prepared. He kept glancing outside - she was still there. Next thing he heard "Night Prowler" belting out of the stereo – he remembered he had left his phone in the car. A few diners near the window turned and looked to see where the noise was coming from. Archie shook his head again. `Jesus, Archie, what the hell are you doing?` he mumbled to himself, before realising the girl serving him was handing him the bag of food and looking at him in a very peculiar manner. He grabbed it and left as quickly as he could – he felt he had embarrassed himself enough for one night! Armed with the take-away, he walked back over to the car, the music getting louder as he approached. He got in and shouted

`Turn it down, everyone`s staring at us.`

She did as she was asked and Archie passed her the bag containing the food. His mouth was watering - sometimes there was just nothing to beat the meaty burger with its toppings and the bag of hot, skinny, salted fries, dipped in the tangy barbecue sauce. The girl said

`That smells somewhat appetising. What is it?`

`What is it? You`re kidding, you mean you`ve never had a McDonalds before?` She shook her head. `Well, it`s a couple of burgers in a toasted bun, with cheese, salad, tomato, gherkins. Large fries and a Diet Coke. Can`t beat it when you need food quickly.` He started the engine and pulled out of the car park.

`Oh. I see. Where are we going?`

`Just round here.`

Archie liked a bit of privacy when eating and he didn`t usually like to hang around in the McDonalds car park – there was always the possibility of meeting some of his clients! He drove round the corner, parked in the adjacent cinema car park which, by this time, was nearly empty, stopped the engine and took the bag from her. He opened it, handed her the burger and fries, stuck the straw into the drink cup and said

`Right, wire in.`

`Wire in?` she asked, turning to stare at him. She arched an eyebrow slightly.

`Yes, well, I mean eat up while it`s hot!`

She did! They ate in silence, other than the background of some more of Archie`s favourite songs. Free - "All Right Now", David Lee Roth - "Living in Paradise", ELO - "Mr Blue Sky" (the song that had earned him his nickname, Archie Blue Sky, following a whisky-fuelled karaoke performance some years ago) Then the Proclaimers came on, playing "Five Hundred Miles", another song he had been known to massacre at a karaoke session. She turned and stared at him, her burger poised in mid-air.

`They sound like you` she said.

Archie smiled slightly and shook his head. He had been told, occasionally, that he resembled a third Proclaimer but never that he sounded like one – it must be the Scottish accent, he supposed.

When the song finished she said

`I liked that music too. It is very different from what I am used to. And the food...well, I am satisfied now. Thank you.` Archie watched in astonishment as she wiped her hands on the legs of her suit, especially when he noticed the greasy marks vanish almost instantly. `Now, have you finished?`

He was savouring the last few chips and regretting, very slightly, not having bought the McFlurry. Maybe later. He put the empty wrappings back in the bag, threw it in the back seat and wiped his own greasy hands on a napkin.

`Yep, that`s me done. So, a bit of explaining, I think. First off, introductions. I`m Archie Blue, Detective Inspector.`

Having decided that, at the moment, she did not appear intent on causing him any harm, other than costing him a few pounds for the take-away, he held out his hand. She looked at it, looked up at him, then clasped it gently, not in a handshake but as if holding hands. Her hands were cool and smooth, he noticed, if still slightly greasy from the chips.

`Hello Archieblue` she said. `My name is Kharalaya 7 Calfarr. It is nice to make your acquaintance.` She was still holding his hand as she looked straight at him. It was slightly unnerving.

`It`s just Archie.` he said. `Kharalaya Seven Calfarr? That`s a very unusual name. Where does that come from? Do I call you that, or do you shorten it to anything?`

`I will explain the origin of my name in due course. You may call me Khara, it is what my friends call me, Archieblue. and I hope that you will be my friend.`

`Well, we`ll see. And it`s just Archie, Khara.`

`No` she said emphatically `I like Archieblue. It sounds as if it suits you and it is what I will call you. Now` she paused, as if thinking. `Where to start with my explanation?`

`Well, usually the beginning is as good a place as any! And, of course, with the truth. You could tell me where you`re from for starters and what you were doing at Erskine, on a secured site and next to an unexploded bomb. Well, probably...` In reality, he was wondering just what on earth the device was turning out to be.

`Erskine? Ah, yes, where the drone is located. Well, first of all, I am not from here.`

`I gathered that much` said Archie. `So, where are you from?`

`I come from a Galaxy far away`

Archie actually threw back his head and laughed out loud. The old Star Wars line, "Long ago, in a Galaxy far, far away..."

`Aye, right. Like I`m going to fall for that, sweetheart! Come on, where are you from - really?`

She looked straight at him again and still he could hardly discern her pupils - it was most unsettling. She scowled at him, clearly not appreciating his humour, then continued

`I come from a planet called Loh, in a galaxy that your species has not yet discovered. Well, I would assume not, as it is extremely far away and has not been detected on any of your databases. The galaxy is called Pelaria and our people have travelled far and are to be found in many places. We are much like your own species, only considerably more advanced as our galaxy and planetary systems are much older. But although I am a highly experienced far-space pilot and have served on many solitary missions, this is the furthest from my home that I have ever travelled and I can tell you, Archieblue, that, until the drone was discovered, I was becoming quite bored and also somewhat lonely. It is good to talk to another person, albeit from a different species.`

Archie was now at a complete loss and didn`t know how to respond to this. She made the statement in such a matter-of-fact way that it sounded entirely true. Almost. However, in his experience, most prime lunatics (and he had met a few) always looked quite at ease, completely believing in their fantasies. This one was no different.

`Okay, Khara, that`s amazing. Really.` *Humour her, keep her talking.* `Now, I`m obviously a wee bit worried about you, especially as you are so far from your home galaxy...em... Peloria.`

`Pelaria.` she corrected `as I am sure you knew! And you need not worry about me. I am perfectly fine.`

`But how do you know?` He really was making it up as he went along now. `Maybe we should get you checked over to see if you`re coping with conditions on our planet. After all, it must be a bit strange for you here, being so far from home. Probably a different atmosphere too.` He lifted his hand to start the engine. The Royal Alexandra Infirmary was only about ten minutes away, he could get her into casualty, get some uniforms up to deal with the paperwork and get shot of her. He was becoming weary of all this nonsense.

She quickly leaned over and grasped his hand, a bit more firmly this time.

`Archieblue, I sense that you do not believe me. Please do not make me angry by implying that I am lying to you and please do not take me for an idiot. I assure you that I am telling you the truth and if you do not believe me, then take me back to the drone and leave me.

I do not care either way, but please stop wasting my time - that is a commodity that I do not have to spare. You must decide. Now.`

She let go of his hand but, even with her dark, expressionless eyes, he could tell she was glaring at him. Archie was angry now too. This was all the thanks he got for effectively rescuing her, feeding her then having to listen to a load of crap about distant galaxies! He decided, once and for all, to call her bluff, turning in his seat and looking straight at her.

`Fine! So you`re an alien! Great! So, where`s your spaceship?`

She smiled her peculiar half-smile `I thought you would never ask!`

Chapter 15

And so, fifteen minutes later, the highly experienced, slightly cynical and considerably careworn Detective Inspector Archie Blue, of Scotland`s Police Force, found himself driving his cherished black Porsche (currenty reeking of McDonalds take-away) back to Erskine, with a strange and unknown female passenger, who claimed to be an alien, seated beside him. He wondered how he would explain this if it all went wrong and he could imagine his career spiralling away, the odd looks, the comments, "Aye, she told him she was an alien – he believed it, too!" Mind you, in light of other recent events, at the moment this escapade seemed relatively harmless and slightly diversionary. Archie almost felt he was enjoying himself – nothing like a wee journey with a grade "A" lunatic to confirm one`s own sanity. Or so he kept telling himself. But, truthfully, his mind was in turmoil. As an experienced police officer, he was usually a level headed, sensible type of guy who would not put himself in unnecessary danger, yet here he was, heading back towards Erskine, with a total, and seemingly deranged, stranger seated next to him. Worse, he was apparently, going to see her spaceship! *Aye, right...* But, on the other hand, his natural curiosity was getting the better of him and he really wanted to know just how far she would take the delusion and how she was going to demonstrate that she really was the alien that she claimed to be. Once she had failed to do so, of course, he would try his best to get her to the Royal Alexandra Hospital in Paisley, where she would receive the treatment that she obviously needed. But that might not be easy, given her behaviour to date.

This bloody curiosity will be my downfall! You`re a right twat, Archie...

They were listening to more of his songs as they drove, with The Knack currently belting out "My Sharona", when he turned the stereo down and asked

`So, are you going to tell me where, exactly, we are headed?`

`Turn left at the next..., you call it a roundabout.` Khara said.

They had passed through the Red Smiddy roundabout and were

nearly at Erskine. Turning left at the next roundabout, Southholm, would take them towards the sleepy town of Bishopton. Archie indicated and turned left as instructed.

`Turn right here please.` she said.

Certainly seems to know where she`s going...

`This is the road to the dump.` Archie commented, although he was aware that it also led to the Millfield housing estate.

`Indeed. Just follow the road and stop when I say.` she answered. A few moments later they came to the gated turn-in for a narrow overgrown access road, presumably leading to the overhead pylons that ran through the woods. `Right, stop here please.` she commanded.

Archie stopped and switched off the engine. The road was deserted as it was now quite late at night. `So your spaceship`s here?` he said, in a sarcastic tone. *Not long now...*

She turned and glared at him.

`Of course not!` she snapped. `It is in orbit far above your planet. Do you really think I would leave a "spaceship", as you keep referring to it, out in the open? That is quite a stupid thing for an obviously intelligent being to say. No, the transfer shuttle pod is here, in these woods. My craft is elsewhere. Come on.`

`Oh, right, the transfer pod! Of course!` said Archie sarcastically, as he got out of the car. *What next...?*

She climbed easily over a ramshackle fence and headed into the wooded scrub land beside the road.

`And just where are you going now?` asked Archie, a little alarm bell ringing in the back of his mind. It was one thing being in his car, quite another heading into dark woodland with this seemingly deranged stranger.

`In here.` was her reply. `As I said, it is in the woods. I am hardly going to leave it sitting in full view, am I?`

*No, of course you`re not!* `Right, hang on, I`m getting a torch.` he said, opening the boot of the Porsche and lifting a heavy Maglite that would serve as a useful weapon if necessary. He also pocketed a set of handcuffs. *Just in case...*

He followed the girl into the dense wood of willows, silver birches and brambles, the latter tugging repeatedly at his trousers. The ground was wet, soon making his feet, still clad in his trainers, quite damp and uncomfortable and, in the dark, he was also picking up a number of nettle stings on the backs of his hands. He was beginning to feel extremely uneasy and very uncomfortable and he stopped. He felt an overwhelming urge to run back to the safety of his car.

`Hold on. I`m not at all happy about this. Just where are we going?` he asked.

`Oh, I apologise` she replied. `there is a deterrent programme running to keep prying eyes away. Please just try and resist it for a short time. We are nearly there. Come on.` she held out her hand to take his, just like his mother used to do when taking him across the road.

This is bloody ridiculous!

He ignored the hand, swallowed his misgivings and moved on. They came to a small clearing, in the centre of which was a large dead and decaying tree, about five feet in diameter and about eight feet tall. The rain appeared to be dripping from its gnarled branches and it was covered in lichen and fungi. It looked slightly out of place as the surrounding trees were much smaller and it seemed to Archie that the uneasiness he felt was emanating from it, as if it was some evil spirit. He really felt like turning and bolting, not a familiar sensation for him. *Catch a grip, Archie Blue!* The girl stopped and approached the tree.

`Right, here we are.` she said, turning and staring at him. In the glimmer of the torchlight her eyes looked even larger and darker and, for one fleeting moment, he almost believed that she might be an alien.

`It`s a tree. A dead tree.` he stated in a flat tone, clutching the

torch tightly and trying to overcome the almost tangible terror he was now feeling. It seemed to him that they had reached both the limit of her pretence and of his patience and he sensed that conflict, of some sort, was very close. He was now really regretting having come this far and wondered just how she had managed to convince him to bring her here when she should have been safely locked up in the hospital by now.

`Yes, it may look like a tree` she said `but....` she lifted her hand and placed it on the green, slimy bark.

Archie nearly dropped the torch in his astonishment. The tree disappeared, drifting away like mist in the wind. In its place stood a large, dull metal cylinder, rounded at the top. It bore a definite family resemblance to what the woman had called "the drone". On its sides were several protrusions that looked like stubby fins and as Archie played the powerful beam across it he could see that there were some depressions that could have been hatches or access panels of some sort. It appeared to be growing out of the undergrowth but, strangely, the feeling of dread had disappeared completely. She placed her hand on the side of the cylinder and, with a gentle hiss, one of the largest depressions in the surface slid round to reveal the interior.

`Come on Archieblue, inside, if you want to see my "spaceship!," as you seem intent on calling it!`

He took a few steps towards it and stopped, turning and looking straight at her.

`Right, just what`s going on here? What the hell`s this, Khara? Come on, we both know you`re not from space and there is no spaceship. I`m not stupid. Tell me exactly what this is then we`ll go away somewhere and have a nice wee chat about it all. This has gone far enough.`

She glared at him yet again and he took a step back, sensing her rising anger and anticipating that she might actually try to attack him. His grip on the torch tightened but, with no smile playing on her lips this time, she just spoke to him in a tone that reminded Archie of getting a telling-off from a certain Miss Johnstone, his Primary School Headmistress.

`Archieblue, you still do not trust me, do you? I have told you, do not waste my time. Look inside here and tell me what you see.`

Reluctantly, Archie approached the cylinder and poked his head inside, not knowing what to expect. It was lit with a pale green glow and was almost totally smooth, with three small windows just above waist height. Attached to the walls were what looked like two dark grey seats, folded up at present. Nothing else, no mysterious control console, no plasma panels, not a Dalek in sight!

`I don`t see much, to be honest. Just some windows and a couple of seats.`

`No little green men, then?`

Ooh...sarcasm...!

`No. No little green men.` He turned back to face her.

`Now, Archieblue, you have a choice. You can choose to come with me, or you can choose to walk away and you will never see me again. I will not force you to do anything against your will. But if you step in here with me I will open your mind to possibilities you have never imagined. What is your choice?`

Archie had a brief flash of Neo`s choice in the first Matrix film. *Red pill...blue pill...* Yet again, his curiosity got the better of him.

Aw, what the fuck...

With only a slight hesitation, he stepped into the cylinder.

`I believe you have made the right choice` she said, stepping in after him. With a gentle hiss, the door slid shut. `Now, stand with your back to the seat.`

Archie did so and it folded down automatically.

`Now sit please.`

He felt he was being treated like a dog! But he sat down and found that the seat and the wall behind him seemed to mould comfortably to his shape. Khara placed her hand on what looked like the screen of a computer and it lit up with a similar, but brighter, green glow to the lighting. Then she said something completely unintelligible before looking back towards him.

`Safety harness.` she explained and he felt himself suddenly being strapped in by mysterious bands that appeared to come from nowhere. Archie made to pull away. `Do not worry, it is just for your protection. Like the harness in your vehicle that you made me fasten by myself. We are somewhat more advanced, however.`

A disembodied male voice said something equally unintelligible and the girl responded. Archie realised that it sounded similar to the way the girl had spoken to him when he first encountered her in the tent covering the bomb. Some kind of foreign dialect, he supposed.

Christ, am I really starting to believe all this...

`Very well, Archieblue, we will now proceed. The pod will rise quickly and you may feel a bit disorientated but that should pass. Please try not to be sick if you can. We will be at my vessel very soon.` This time she smiled. The green light dimmed then went out altogether, leaving the inside in darkness.

Archie felt the cylinder lift noiselessly off the ground, like an express lift in a tall building. But it didn`t stop, it just kept getting faster. He was used to rapid acceleration with the Porsche but this was mind blowing and although his stomach seemed to be a good bit behind the rest of him, he managed to hold his Big Mac and fries down. *Just as well I never had the McFlurry.....*He looked out of the small window and was amazed to see the lights of Paisley, then the whole Glasgow conurbation, receding at an alarming rate. The world he knew was getting smaller and he gradually became aware of the curvature of the planet before suddenly realising that his view was now the one he had only seen in photos and never dreamt he ever would see first-hand. He was looking down at Planet Earth, in all her glory, suspended in the vast velvety darkness of space. He could easily identify the familiar shapes of the landmasses, Great Britain, The United States, Russia, Europe. The Atlantic Ocean, dark blue where it wasn`t covered by huge banks of white clouds, the Polar Caps white with ice. He could see the sun`s glow around the perimeter of the sphere that he called home and, for the first time, he started to admit to himself the possibility that, just perhaps, this strange girl was what she claimed. He became aware that they were slowing down when he heard the girl speak in the same peculiar manner, answered again by the disembodied male voice. Then she looked at him.

`We are about to dock with what you call my spaceship. It is, in fact, a class 33 far-space reconnaissance craft, one of the latest and best, I am proud to say.`

The disembodied voice spoke again and Archie could see through the window that they had entered somewhere brightly lit, although with that same greenish glow. Then he felt a slight bump and heard some metallic clicks from outside. The door slid open with the same soft hiss, the harnesses retracted on Khara`s unintelligible command and she stood up and held out her hand. His legs felt decidedly unsteady and this time Archie took it willingly as she led him out of the cylinder and onto a brightly lit circular bay. It contained the vessel they had just left along with another exactly the same and a couple of different looking pieces of equipment, the purpose of which he could not readily determine. The walls, which were finished in a matt grey that looked like some kind of plastic material, had what appeared to be several door panels set into them. Below the cylinder there was what looked like a large hatch that, he presumed, led outside, wherever that may be. Khara turned to face him, and, somewhat formally, said

`Welcome, Archieblue, to my ship, Terestal, far-space craft type 33. I am Far-space Security Commander Kharalaya 7 Calfarr. I am pleased that you have decided to trust me and I assure you that your trust will be repaid. You will have many, many questions to ask and I understand that this will be a very confusing time for you. Initial contact with an alien species is often alarming and disorientating but please do not worry, I give you my word that I will not harm you in any way. Please be patient and I will try to explain everything as best I can and in terms that you will understand. But first, can I ask you, do you now believe me?`

Given the events of the last ten minutes or so Archie didn`t really have much choice other than to reply `Yes, Khara, now I believe you, I suppose.` Although he expected to wake up at any minute...

`Good, but do not suppose. Either believe or disbelieve. Now, please come with me.`

Archie followed her through one of the doors which, again, opened silently with just the touch of her hand on a panel beside it. They entered a small compartment about two metres square, with plain walls and a similar door on the other side.

`Safety airlock compartment.` Khara explained, `Just in case!`

He didn`t like to ask in case of what! They passed through the second door, along a short corridor and into a comfortable looking living space with large seats and a soft floor covering that reminded Archie of a meadow - it was green and textured like grass, with what looked like tiny flowers of yellow, blue and white scattered across it. As he walked they seemed to move as if a gentle breeze was playing over them. There were several flat horizontal surfaces but they were bare, as were the grey covered walls. There were areas on the walls that looked like windows but they, too, were totally blank. The air seemed cool and fresh, like the air he breathed when he was hill-walking on a high Lakeland peak, early in Spring. It was all very strange - still, it was a spaceship, after all, although not exactly what he expected!

Too many sci-fi films, I reckon...

Through another door they went and arrived in what Archie assumed to be the bridge, although again there was a shortage of anything resembling controls. There were four serious looking dark grey chairs facing what looked like a large wrap-around window, although it, too, was a dull grey. No view of the stars was visible. *Am I really in space?*

Khara sat in one of the middle two chairs and beckoned Archie to sit in the one next to her. Again, it appeared to mould itself to his shape as he sat in it. She placed her hand on another small panel and spoke the same, peculiar language. Suddenly, a spherical image projected above the area in front of them and Archie could clearly see that it represented Earth and the moon. It was three-dimensional, in full colour and he could just make out tiny satellites in orbit around his planet. She moved her hand and the image size reduced until there was a representation of all the planets in the solar system – it was incredible! Then, on another unintelligible command the dull grey window screen in front of them came alive with the view Archie had expected, one that took his breath away - the stars, Earth far below, it was incredibly beautiful and totally mind-blowing! Several smaller screens appeared from the area below the main screen but their displays were meaningless to him. Khara spoke again and the disembodied voice replied, firstly in the same language and then saying

`Welcome Commander. Communication now in local language. Designated English, local version United Kingdom. I see you have a guest.`

`Yes, this is Archieblue. He is a security operative on local planet designated Earth.` She turned to him `Could you please place your hand palm down on the screen in front of you? You may feel a tingling but there will be no discomfort, I assure you.`

Archie reached out and placed his hand on the screen – the surface seemed almost liquid and his palm sank into it very slightly. It reminded him of the funny kids` slime that he used to buy in joke shops - it felt wet but your hands were always dry after touching it. Then he felt a faint tingling, like a very mild electric shock. He noticed that one of the screens appeared to be showing a schematic of his body, along with an array of meaningless symbols. The computer, or whatever it was, spoke to him.

`Visitor, please state your full name.`

`Archie Donaldson Blue.`

`Welcome Archie Donaldson Blue. How will I address you?`

Khara looked at him and raised an eyebrow. He decided to humour her – after all, he was now her guest. Or prisoner, he wasn`t entirely sure which.

`Em, Archieblue, please.`

`Your designation please?`

Archie looked at Khara for a clue. `Your rank, or position, ` she said.

`Detective Inspector, Scotland`s Police force.`

`Thank you, Archieblue, Detective Inspector. You are now recognised by our system. You may remove your hand.` The tingling stopped and Archie lifted his hand from the panel. Surprisingly, it was bone dry and totally unharmed.

`So, Detective Inspector Archieblue,` Khara asked. `what do you think of the view?`

`It`s absolutely fantastic!` Archie said, realising that his eyes were closing. He was so, so tired. Just a few minutes was all he needed. He felt a coldness creep up his legs. `I never thought I.....`

His eyes rolled upwards and he was out cold. His brain had gone into overload and shut down. Not surprising, really!

Chapter 16

At first he thought he`d been drinking again – he felt as if he was struggling out of the dark, deep pit that seemed to come as part of the hangover these days. He risked opening his eyes slightly, to find a tall, grey-clad stranger standing in front of him, supporting his head with one hand, a concerned look on her long, pale face. He felt absolutely terrible and thought he was going to be sick. *It must be food poisoning*, was his first thought, realising that it wasn`t, in fact, a hangover. *I`m hallucinating,* was his second, as he realised that he was sitting in a seat in some kind of peculiar room, gazing out into what appeared to be the vastness of space. In her other hand the strange woman was holding a small beaker that contained a clear liquid. He had a vague recollection that she had called herself Khara but, other than that, he couldn`t remember who she was or, more importantly, where he was. He certainly couldn`t be in space...could he?

`Drink this, Archieblue. You will feel much better.`

Archie felt too sick and disorientated to argue so he just swallowed the small amount of ice cold liquid that she had given him – it tasted peculiar but very pleasant and refreshing. Immediately, he started to feel an odd sensation and in an instant it was as if he had transported to a day back in his childhood. He was on the west coast of Kintyre, at Westport beach, looking straight out to the horizon of the Atlantic ocean. It was warm and sunny and the sky was a cloudless blue. The clean, fresh waves were breaking in lines of foam on the hot, white sand and he was running into them feeling the cold water on his feet, the smell of salt and ozone in his nostrils, tinged with the fainter smell of seaweed. "The tangle o` the Isles" as his father used to sing. It was the most wonderful feeling. He imagined that the surf was splashing over him, the wind ruffling his hair and his blood pumping through his veins, invigorating him. He looked up at Khara and managed a smile.

`Good, yes?` she laughed. `Better than that strange, brown liquid you gave me earlier, do you not think? With those odd bubbles!`

`What, the Diet Coke? Way better! What happened? Did I pass

out?` Memories of recent events were flooding back but he was struggling to make any sense of them. The woman spoke again, as if sensing his confusion.

`I think you have been given too much information in a very short space of time. This is often the case when a species makes contact with another species for the first time. It is a big shock to your system to realise that you do not inhabit the universe exclusively. But you will be fine, although I was concerned for you. The drink will relieve the symptoms of shock and fatigue for some time, keeping you alert. How do you feel now?`

`Brilliant. I feel, well, I don`t know. Buzzing, I`d say, if you know what I mean..` And he did. He felt like he was ready for anything. *What on earth was in that stuff...?*

`Yes, I think I understand what you mean. I am glad.` she sat back down in her seat. `Now, I think you have maybe been given enough information for the time being, Archieblue. But if you would like I will take you on a quick trip to one of your planets before I take you home. I think you deserve a reward for your trust. And for your discomfort.`

`What? No way! You`ve got to be kidding?` asked Archie, in amazement. He was gazing at the display of the solar system – it just wasn`t possible – or was it...?

`No. I am not "kidding", Archieblue. Not at all. The one that you call Mars is the nearest, I think.` She pointed to a tiny dot in the display.

`There, that is Mars, I believe. And we are here` she continued, pointing to another speck.

`But Mars is about...` Archie tried to recall the vast distances between the planets. `...em, is it not about, what, a hundred and sixty million miles away, or something? It takes years to send an exploration craft there. There`s no way...`

She interrupted, sounding slightly frustrated at his disbelief.

`Archieblue, you are not in an Earth craft. Our technology is considerably further advanced than anything you know of. If you are, indeed, a detective, you should have deduced this – otherwise, I would not be here and neither would you. Now, we will be there, I think, in just over an hour of your time. And, of course, the distance fluctuates dramatically, depending on the relative orbits of the planets.` She spoke to the ship `Terestal, what is the current distance to Planet designated Mars, please?`

A brief pause. `Current estimated distance two hundred and twenty million kilometres.`

`I am sure you can convert that into miles, Archieblue.`

Archie sat in silence, pondering this statement and failing miserably in the calculation. Then he said

`So, the ship must have warp capability, then?`

Khara looked at him with a frown `I beg your pardon? Warp capability?`

`Yes, I mean, it must travel at the speed of light. Oh, sorry, it`s a science-fiction term. From Star Trek. But I guess you don`t know what that is either, do you?` He laughed. *Aye, right, as if she`d seen Star Trek!*

`The answer is "no" to both. I am unfamiliar with Star Trek and no, the ship cannot travel at the speed of light by itself. It can, however, travel exceptionally fast but it is only in the energy field of the trans-space conduit that vessels can exceed light speeds. That is what allows us to travel the enormous distances involved in inter-galactic travel.`

`And what exactly is the trans-space conduit?`

`Well, that is a very difficult question to answer in terms that you would understand. Are you familiar with what you call the "Big Bang Theory?"`

`Yes, of course. The singularity that is believed to have created the Universe.`

She looked at him and raised an eyebrow. `That is very concisely stated, Archieblue. Are you also familiar with...` she paused, as if searching for the correct wording `dark matter and dark energy?`

`Yes, well, kind of. Doesn`t dark matter account for something like eighty percent of the universe?`

`Thereabouts. Well, you will know that the universe is believed to have been formed by an event that released an unimaginable amount of energy, causing it to expand exponentially. Some time ago, our race discovered that, as it did so, multiple channels of energy, what you call dark energy, moving at incredible speeds were formed within areas of dark matter, radiating from the central point where the eventuality occurred. These also appeared to form a kind of loop, so that the energy field is travelling in both directions, the two opposing flows of energy forming an invisible spiral. Eventually we discovered a means of accessing and utilising these energy fields, allowing us to move about the universe at great speeds, although to do so carries a significant risk if not undertaken correctly. Entry and exit from the conduit is via what we call "portals". These are naturally occurring distortions in the surface of the field that contains the dark matter itself - we believe may have been caused by truncation of other branches as the Universe formed. The break in the dark energy field at these points allows us to access the inner core of the energy field. The conduits themselves branch out, forming an immense network throughout space. Dark matter is everywhere and can take us to almost any part of the universe, although there are limits.`

Archie could scarcely believe what he was hearing. `But what`s the purpose of these so-called conduits? I mean, why are they there at all? Is that what`s known as "worm-holes"?`

`No. Worm-holes are a random phenomena, caused by an anomaly in the fabric of space. Although they can, on occasions, be used to travel great distances, they are extremely unstable and unreliable and are seldom used. As to the conduits, we are not entirely sure why they exist. They may carry energy to the outer edges of the universe, which is still expanding. No one has ever travelled that far as, even at the speeds involved, it would just take too long. And, of course, even if you were able to approach the edge of the universe, it is continually accelerating away so, in theory, it is unreachable. Also, no one has ever travelled to the source, the central radiating point. At least, no one has returned from such an attempt. It is still one of the great unsolved mysteries.`

Archie couldn`t think of anything else to ask - even with his extensive knowledge of science-fiction, this was all completely beyond him and his brain was struggling to come to terms with what she had already told him. He was beginning to worry that he might pass out again but, fortunately, Khara interrupted his thoughts.

`So, Archieblue, shall we head off to Mars?`

He sighed and managed a weary smile.

`If you say so. You`re the Commander, after all!`

`Indeed.` She placed her hand on the panel. `Terestal, please set course to orbit nearest planet in local planetary system, designated Mars. Speed eight between planets, slow to speed one within visual range. Harnesses, please.`

Archie sat back in his seat as the harness automatically enclosed him. Already he had an idea what to expect and managed not to flinch.

`Activate acceleration buffers please. Proceed with flight.`

Archie was aware of a faint hum then, with only a slight feeling of being pushed into his seat, the craft shot forward, leaving his own planet far behind him. In a very short space of time they passed what he realised was the moon - he could hardly believe it. Khara noticed him staring at it.

`That is your moon. I have already been there and I will explain my reason later. Maybe I could take you to the surface another time.`

`Aye, maybe` Archie said. At present he was struggling to believe he was heading to Mars. The idea of actually landing somewhere in space was just a bit too much to consider. He sat in an awed silence for a while, overwhelmed by the vastness of the space around him. Khara had altered the display to give a much larger image and he could now determine their position relative to the surrounding space. He shook his head in wonder. She seemed content to remain in silence but, after a while, he decided to make some conversation, despite the awe-inspiring panorama unfolding in front of him.

`So, Khara, your home planet, Loh, you called it, what is it like?`

`Well, where would I start? It is a slightly smaller planet than Earth, with a higher proportion of the surface covered with water. Our population is considerably less too, especially following the long periods of wars that we have experienced but I will not go into the details of that just now, it is quite a tragic tale. Our sun is called Kii, and we have two moons instead of your one. The planet is very beautiful in places and, like Earth, it has many cities where the majority of the population reside. The main difference between our planets is the way they are ruled, or governed, as you might put it.`

`In what way?` Archie asked.

`Well, you have many countries, each with their own ruling or government system. Some good, some bad, from what I have gathered - the ship`s computer has already scanned most of Earth`s databases and I know a great deal about your planet. However, on

Loh, we are a single entity, the reasons for which are historical and quite complicated. The planet is governed as a whole and is not fragmented as Earth is. This has advantagesbut, obviously, disadvantages too and was the primary cause of the wars that I referred to. We are in a time of peace now but there are still factions, albeit quite small, who would wish to regain power. It is a long story and, again, not for telling just now. Geographically, we have some amazing high mountain ranges, in which I love to climb, beautiful lakes and forests and many of the cities are, themselves, quite marvellous. The planet is also home to a number of off-planet species who have integrated into our society most successfully.`

`Really!` exclaimed Archie. `You mean there are other species out there?`

Khara gave him a somewhat disparaging look.

`As I said, you do not inhabit the universe exclusively! Yes, there are numerous other species, although none that we know who have, as yet, mastered the ability to travel as we do. Those who live on Loh have not come to the planet by themselves, they have travelled there with us.`

`Not against their will, I hope?` asked Archie, suddenly conjuring up visions of alien abduction stories.

`Absolutely not!` she exclaimed emphatically. `We certainly do not kidnap alien beings. They have all requested to come to our planet of their own free will.`

Archie couldn`t resist asking `Are there any from Earth?`

`I do not know but it is possible. Our species are very similar and you would find Loh quite habitable, just as I am quite comfortable on Earth.`

`So, how did you come to be here then? I mean, the universe is a pretty huge place. And what, exactly, is the thing stuck in the mud at Erskine?`

`Ah, too many questions that are complicated to answer! Let us just say I happened to be in the vicinity as I..` she paused and thought `I had what you would call "a tip-off!"` She laughed.

More questions kept jumping into his mind. He couldn`t stop himself, it was like having a part in his very own science-fiction film.

`And how come you can you speak English so well?`

`That is quite simple. As I said, the computer has scanned all your databases and transmitted the relevant information to my neural implants. I would be able to speak fluently in any language on your planet if so required.`

`Is the computer in the ship ...well...alive?`

Khara didn`t reply - Terestal spoke for itself.

`Up to a point, Archieblue. I am not "alive" in the sense that you understand it. I am sentient and capable of rapid thought processing. Think of me as an extension of Khara`s mind, what you would possibly call a "backup". Whilst the Commander can obviously function on her own, I cannot function fully without her, although I have a number of automated systems in place for emergency situations. But, as you probably know, even the human brain has massive untapped potential and, as her species is more advanced than your own species, Khara can process considerably more information than you can, even without my assistance. Essentially, I do the hard work and she gets all the fun!`

My God, a computer with a sense of humour!

`There you are, Archieblue, does that answer your question?` Khara asked, smiling at the ship`s reply.

`Yes, but I have to say it`s all pretty incredible. I keep expecting to waken up...!` he paused for a second, then asked `So, back on Loh, are you...em...married, attached...?`

As soon as the words were out he wondered why he had asked. It was none of his business and he felt he had been a bit rude. There was a fractional pause before she answered.

`No, Archieblue, I am not "attached", as you put it. We do not get married in the sense that you do but we try to commit to one another for life so we choose a partner very carefully. Mistakes can be made too easily in such choices.` She paused and sighed. `But such is our way - what about you? Are you married, do you have children, perhaps?`

And there it was again. Even out here, in the vast open space of the Universe, the question that, until recently, would have simply been answered "no". He was suddenly engulfed in a wave of grief which must have shown on his face. She spoke softly

`I am sorry. I did not mean to pry into your personal life. I have upset you.`

`No, it`s okay. Like you say, it`s a long story and not for the telling just now. But, no, I`m not attached and, well...no kids. My parents, who are both gone, had a great marriage and I guess I`m the same as you, I want to make sure that I find the right person and hang on to them for life.`

There was an awkward silence, both of them feeling that, perhaps, they had delved too deep and opened up unseen wounds. Archie stared at the vista of space that was passing him by. Khara spoke softly and, somehow, he felt himself relax and his grief subside.

`Just sit and watch, Archieblue. Like anything in life, there is only ever one "first time". Just enjoy it, there will be other opportunities to talk. For me, it is nice just to have company.`

And that was exactly what he did. Asteroids, stars, tiny comets, distant galaxies, they were all there to be seen. No light pollution, only the faint hum of the vessel, an unfamiliar but, somehow, soothing sound, much gentler than in an airliner. He could not have put into words the feeling he was experiencing but he had never, in his entire life, felt so tiny and insignificant – it was profoundly humbling. After a while he became aware of an approaching sphere and Khara interrupted his reverie.

`There, we are approaching Mars, your so called "red" planet. It is very beautiful, is it not?`

It was! Archie gaped as the planet approached, filling his view with its red mass. It was truly astonishing to see it so close, to see the famous "canals", the mountains, the gaseous clouds. How could he possibly be here in such a short time? The craft slowed and went into orbit, passing round the dark side of the planet. He gazed in awe as the view changed.

`So, Archieblue, how do you like space travel?` she asked, looking straight at him. He held her gaze and replied

`Absolutely fantastic! As they say in Glasgow, "pure dead brilliant!"`

She furrowed her brows at this, then shook her head and laughed. He liked the sound of it, somehow it was unlike any other laughter he was familiar with- he wondered if its infrequency reflected a sincerity that was lacking on earth.

`You are a peculiar species, Archieblue. And you appear to use language that does not immediately appear in your databases!` she said `However, you are quite entertaining! At least, when you are not being extremely irritating.`

Thanks for the compliment...

Once they had completed their orbit of the planet, Khara said

`Now, it is time I took you home, Archieblue. Enough excitement for one night, I think.`

Archie thought it was enough excitement for a lifetime especially as the drink Khara had given him earlier seemed to be wearing off and he was becoming very tired once again. She seemed to be aware of this and said, softly

`I would suggest that you close your eyes and sleep. There is little else of interest between here and Earth.`

Archie didn`t necessarily agree but he was exhausted. The last thing he heard before he drifted into oblivion was Khara speaking to the ship.

`Return to earth, maximum speed please.`

It seemed like he had just shut his eyes when she woke him.

`Archieblue, we are back in orbit around Earth. You need to wake up.`

He rubbed his eyes and gazed out at his home planet. It still looked just as beautiful but he realised that he would never be able to think of it in the same way again, now that he had seen it from above. He could understand how the early astronauts must have felt when they came home, how difficult it must have been to adjust. She seemed to read his thoughts.

`Home, Archieblue. Beautiful, is it not? It gives you a whole new perspective, seeing your planet from space. I can still remember the first time I did so. Now, I will take you back to where your vehicle is parked then I will come back to my ship as I have some tasks to carry out and I also need to rest.`

`Just one thing, if you don`t mind` said Archie, as he stood up. He pulled out his iPhone. `Would you mind if I took a photo?`

`Photo? Ah, yes, an image.` Khara smiled. `Of course. After all, it is not everyday you get to see your planet from above. One word of caution though, be careful to whom you show it, it might not be easy to explain!`

`Fair point! Just for me, then!` He took a couple of pictures of the view on the display screen then switched the camera to reverse and took a sneaky "selfie" of himself with Khara at his side...just in case he needed a reminder...! He put the phone safely back in his pocket as she headed for the door.

Archie followed her back to the shuttle pod and in no time found himself standing in the damp clearing, his feet firmly on his planet once again. Khara led him with ease through the dark woods to where his car was still parked, (in one piece, he was relieved to notice) and, as he got in, she said.

`We have a lot to do tomorrow, Archieblue. I need to give you an explanation about your so-called "bomb", as well as many other things, no doubt! And I need to make plans for its recovery. However, now that I have told you a little about my home planet, I would very much like to see some of your planet, if you would care to show me it. Would you?`

`Of course! I`d be delighted!` Archie heard himself say. Although surprised at her request, he meant it. He suddenly realised that, apart from a brief moment, during the last few hours his troubles and grief had all but vanished and it was only now that they were beginning to seep back in to his brain, along with the cold dampness of the Autumn night. A day out would do him the world of good, especially after a night in space...! As long as he could sleep...

`Excellent! I think that I would like to climb a mountain, if that is possible?

`Seriously? Climb a mountain?`

`Yes, Archieblue. The scans of your planet show it to be mountainous in many places, especially in this area. I feel that I need to take exercise and ease my muscular system as I have been confined to my vessel for some time.`

A mountain! Well, there`s always Ben Lomond...

She continued `I will be back here at eleven on your clock but I will need some more suitable clothes, though, as I cannot go about like this. Could you obtain some for me, please? I will trust your judgement to ensure that I do not look like an alien.`

Archie looked at her and grinned. `Fine, no problem, and I know the perfect mountain, not too far away. As to the clothes, there`s just one thing - I haven`t a clue what size you are. A detective I may be but I`m not that great at guessing ladies` clothes sizes!`

`Indeed. My computer has made the necessary calculations and you will find that the relevant information is all on your communication device, or mobile phone, as you call it.`

Archie pulled out his iPhone and stared at the screen. To his great surprise there was a text message waiting. From Khara.

What...?

Trouser size 14 long
Top size 16
Shoe size 8
Bra size 38DD
Any other relevant garments as required
Eleven on the clock tomorrow.

Khara

There was even an emoticon of what looked suspiciously like an alien! *Bra size? you`ve got to be kidding! And how did she manage to text me?*

`Acceptable?` she said.

`Em, yep, totally...! Okay. I`ll see you at eleven. Here?`

`Yes, Right here.` Then she held out her hand, opening the palm to reveal a small clear sphere, about half an inch in diameter. It looked for all the world like the marbles he had played with as a child.

`What`s that?` he asked.

`It is a small dose of the liquid I gave you when you passed out. I suspect that you will feel unwell tomorrow when you waken up and this will help you.`

`What do I do with it?`

`Put it in your mouth, bite it then swallow it. The outer layer will disappear almost instantly. You will feel much better, I promise you.`

`Is it safe?`

She frowned. `Of course. Do you think I would give you something that would cause you harm?`

`Em, no, sorry...`

`Anyway, you have already had some on board my..spaceship!`

Archie remembered how good he had felt when she gave him the drink on the Terestal. He placed the little sphere in his pocket and simply said `Thanks.` She smiled.

`And Archieblue?`

`Yes?`

`Thank you for trusting me.`

She turned and started to walk away then, as an afterthought, she turned her head over her shoulder

`And thank you for the McDonalds. It was...interesting!`

`Aye, you`re we......`

But she had disappeared back in to the woods.

Chapter 17

Commander Urvai 3 Goffella had long since given up on any semblance of patience. He strode back and forth across the control area, shouting abuse at anyone in his way, kicking out at any piece of equipment that malfunctioned. However Terki, his first officer, reflected that it was good to have his old Commander back! For too long he had appeared to have lost interest, spending most of the time in his personal cabin and leaving the running of the ailing ship to his second in command and the rest of the crew. This was more like old times, when they had first set out from Loh, in search of glory, perhaps, or at least a fresh start. He, personally, had never held out any great hope of finding the sphere. Sure, he had heard all the tales as a child but, just like the threat of abduction by the Queesha, he disregarded them as simply figments of his parents` imagination. But now his old friend Urvai was back in command, as was his rightful place. After all, his great grandfather had been one of the heroes in the now distant revolution, defending what they believed was their birthright of superiority. This was more like it and maybe, after all, the stories of his childhood were not mere fantasy.

`It has been nearly two days!` shouted Urvai. `Are we never going to get there? Maga, can you not make this craft go any faster?`

The ship replied before the engineer could answer.

`Commander, firstly it has only been just over a day and a half, not two. Secondly, the vessel is already at the maximum speed for which it was designed. It is overdue a full maintenance service by twelve cycles. We are already compromising structural integrity by travelling at this speed for such a prolonged time. Please try and be patient.`

Terki cringed. He knew that if any of them had spoken to Urvai in this manner they would have earned a well-aimed punch to the face. Instead, the commander, now red-faced and wearing a slightly mad expression, strode over and kicked the door that was still jammed in a half open position.

`Do not presume to advise me of what this ship is capable of!` he shouted, whilst the crew looked on in surprise as the door suddenly slid shut. Terki hoped it would open again! The ship replied

`I am not advising you, Urvai. I am telling you. After all, I am the ship, just as much as the structure itself. If you have no ship, you have no mission and no means of survival. You would do well to remember that. And I may add that kicking the vessel serves no purpose whatsoever.`

Terki waited for the response but the short, ominous silence was interrupted by Retso shouting

`Commander! I have detected another ship in the vicinity!`

`What?` shouted Urvai and Terki, in unison, turning to the screen. All anger swiftly evaporated.

`Another ship. Next to that planet there. It appears to possess some highly sophisticated screening programme, probably a development since we left...` he stopped just before he said "home" `Since we left Loh. But there is a faint trace, I just managed to catch it. Look, there, see it?`

They did. On the display (which was becoming more elliptical each day) a very faint second red spot pulsated close by the one indicating the drone. Retso enlarged the image of the scan he had recorded and they could just make out the vague outline of some form of craft, unrecognisable to any of them.

`It does not look that big.` said Terki. `Far-space reconnaissance, do you think?`

`More importantly, have they seen us?` muttered Urvai. Given the power they had used on their journey, his vessel would have little in reserve for a battle.

`I do not think so` replied Retso, `I do not think we have been scanned and I am not getting a reading of anyone on board. Not at present anyway. Strange. I think it may be in orbit of that planet. It certainly seems to be within gravitational range.`

`So they may be on the planet. Do you know anything about it - is it inhabited? Can you tell if that is where the drone is located?`

`Hold on, let me see if I can run a planetary scan. We are at the extreme limit for range, though.` Retso touched a few controls on the screen and the Zemm`s sensors managed to carry out a distant scan of the planet, cross referencing it with any known data of the sector held in the on-board memory banks. They waited a few moments, then the ship spoke.

`The planet is inhabited. Species capable of close-proximity near-space travel only. They possess low-grade nuclear capability, standard matter based. This includes weaponry systems with planetary capability only, it would seem. They are no threat. Planet parameters indicate it is capable of sustaining our own species. The drone is, indeed, located on the planet. Records also show that there is, or was, an active sleeper on this planet. They have not been in contact for a considerable time.`

`Really!` exclaimed Urvai. `That is even more intriguing. Do we know who?`

Zemm spoke.

`I will access the database to see if I can find an identity. Although our records are not exactly up-to-date...` the sentence hung in the air – they all knew the reason! `I will display any available information on-screen.`

There was a short, silent, pause, in which Urvai, Retso and Terki looked on expectantly. Maga, the engineer, stood behind them. Then, on one of the small virtual monitors closest to them, the name appeared. They stared in astonished silence. Then Urvai whispered.

`Holy, sacred shit!. I cannot believe it!`

Chapter 18

The alarm on Archie`s iPhone woke him at seven-thirty, supposedly easing him into the day with 10cc`s "I`m not in love.." But, once again, it seemed to be dragging him out of a deep, dark and dreamless pit and he wondered if this was now something he would have to learn to live with. He couldn`t remember getting home, far less going to bed and he realised that, although his jacket and shoes were off, he was still fully dressed and his head was pounding. *What the hell did I have to drink last night?* was his first thought as he sat up. He picked up the phone to turn off the alarm and noticed the message still displayed from the previous evening.

Trouser size 14 long.....

Then it all came back to him and he lay back on the bed, his hands covering his face - it hadn`t been a dream after all. Or had it? Over the previous two weeks he had been waking up to the grim realisation that, firstly, he had become a father and lost a daughter and, secondly, that he might be a killer. Now this...

He sat up again, replaying the previous evening`s events in his mind. He briefly considered contacting someone at the office to ask about psychiatric help but immediately rejected the idea. They would probably lock him away once he started telling them he had been on a trip round Mars and back! But was he really losing his marbles? Or had it happened just the way he remembered?

Marbles!

He suddenly remembered the little vial that the alien woman had given him – or had she? If it was there, at least that might help to confirm his memories. He reached into the pocket of his jacket, which was lying on the floor and, sure enough, he pulled out the little, liquid filled sphere. Dare he take it? He reckoned he couldn`t feel much worse so he popped it in his mouth and, after only a second`s hesitation, bit firmly into it. As before, the liquid seemed chilled and, within seconds, he felt clear-headed and exhilarated.

Wow! That`s some stuff.

He picked up his phone and looked at the screen again, the clothes sizes, the time set for 11.00 (he`d have to get a move on) and

"Khara" – complete with alien symbol! He knew that schizophrenics truly believed in their fantasies - was he turning into one? But, then, if he was questioning his sanity, did that mean he was okay? *Shit!* He got up and headed to the shower, hoping it might wash some sense into his reeling brain. He hadn`t even a clue what time he had gone to bed but it must have been late if he`d been on a trip to the nearest planet at God only knew how many million miles away...or was that kilometres...?

The water certainly left his body refreshed but his mind was still in overdrive as he sat drinking a strong coffee and deciding what to do next. However, before he reached a decision, his mobile rang.

`Archie, it`s Donny, I hear you`ve got yourself a wee bomb...`

Inspector Donny Marsh was the colleague who, by rights, should have been dealing with the so called "bomb" in the first place. He was phoning Archie to let him know he would now be taking over responsibility for the site at Erskine, leaving him off the hook and free to get on his with more "serious" investigations. *Aye, if only he knew the half of it...*

However, given the events of the previous night, he was now not so sure that he wanted to let the matter go, although it would have seemed strange for a Detective Inspector to request control of such a situation - after all, there was nothing to investigate, it was just a matter of keeping the area secure until the bomb squad arrived...wasn`t it...? Archie gave his colleague the run-down on the situation (missing out the previous evening`s events) and told Inspector Marsh to liaise with Cam for any further information that he may require. That seemed to be that, his involvement with the incident was over, although he had asked his colleague to keep him informed – just out of interest, of course!

Following the call and after considerable self-debate, he set off for Braehead Shopping Centre; fortunately, the road was relatively quiet, as otherwise he didn`t know if he would have been able to resist the temptation to switch on his blue lights. That would have been a hard one to explain - `And why were you using your emergency lights, Sir?` `Well, I had to go shopping as I was meeting an alien at eleven o`clock...` `Right, Sir, if you can just blow into this machine...` Anyway, he found himself, at ten-thirty five, standing at the checkout in Next, in Braehead. He was sandwiched between a harassed-looking young woman (accompanied by a howling toddler) and a well-dressed older woman, both of whom were giving him slightly odd looks as he clutched his assortment of t-shirts, jeans, a couple of bras and pairs of knickers (That part had been a bit embarrassing and, after some internal debate, he had decided to go for sensible rather than sexy!) plus a cute little denim jacket. He also carried a bag from Sports Direct with a pair of trainers and a pair of light climbing boots. After all, he was heading to Ben Lomond – wasn`t he? A couple of pairs of warm socks, a rucksack and a lightweight waterproof jacket had completed his purchases in the sports shop.

As he reached the check-out, he noticed a display of trendy, fine leather necklaces, with some coloured beads and trinkets at the bottom. He hesitated, then decided that it would help her look the part; anyway, they were only fifteen pounds...

Back in his Porsche, he headed out of the shopping centre and back on to the M8. "Yours is no disgrace", the classic Yes epic, was playing on the stereo as he gunned the car back down to Erskine and he shook his head - *you are a bloody disgrace!*

Archie made his way back to where he had parked the previous evening but this time the road was fairly busy, with a steady stream of cars taking assorted rubbish to the local dump, as well as traffic coming in and out of the Millfield estate. As he drew close to the fence that he seemed to remember climbing over the previous evening, it felt like it had been in some other parallel lifetime. Now he was back in the normal, West of Scotland world he inhabited, full of ordinary folk going about their ordinary business on a sunny Autumn Sunday. Off to the pub, off to meet friends for lunch, maybe a wee run down the coast. And, guess what, she wasn`t there! Well, of course she wasn`t - what a total moron he was. Feeling the embarrassing, stupid, toe curling feeling reserved for, and so familiar to, those poor souls who have been "stood up", he stopped and prepared to turn the car round and head for home. As he looked over his right shoulder to check the road, the passenger door opened and Khara jumped quickly in.

`Hello Archieblue. You did not expect me to be here, did you? You were about to leave. And I thought you trusted me. You are a particularly annoying being, do you realise that?`

Archie was angry. She might at least have been a bit grateful that he had come back at all, especially as he had rushed to get the required shopping for her. He turned and glowered at her but she just smiled her odd, half smile.

`Oh really, you think so?` he replied sarcastically. `Well, I`m very sorry! But it`s a hell of a lot to take in, all that happened last night. So please forgive me if I suspected, ever so slightly, that you might have just buggered off back to space!`

`There is no need to get angry, Archieblue, I was just stating a fact. I cannot understand why you would say you trusted me then, the next day, decide that you do not. Either you trust me or you do not.`

`It`s not quite as simple as that. It`s not every day you bump into someone who claims to be an alien.`

She raised her voice a notch

`So you are doubting that too now? It is not a claim, it is a fact. You have been in my vessel, seen its capabilities. You are supposed to be the detective - how do you explain that? You need to make up your mind, Archieblue. You are very indecisive. That is most surprising for a security operative.`

`Indecisive! I`m not bloody indecisive!` Archie shouted. `Don`t push me, Khara, or you`ll be walking back to your spaceship. Or whatever.`

`Oh, that reminds me, my transport board, I believe it is still in the rear of your vehicle.`

`Your transport board? What the hell`s that, when it`s at home.`

`It is not at home. It is in your car. Do you not understand me? It is a local transportation device. I will show you later.`

`Oh, for fu...` he happened to glance sideways and caught her smiling,

`Are you winding me up?`

She thought for a moment. `Why, are you clockwork? English appears to be a very odd language!`

He shook his head but couldn`t help smiling, despite himself.

`I am sorry, Archieblue. But you are indecisive. And annoying. But, really, I am sorry – after all, you are here.`

`Okay, fair enough, apology accepted. And, yes, I am here. So, what now?`

Khara suggested that they go back to his house so she could

change into the clothes he had bought. She had quickly rummaged through the bags and seemed to be quite pleased with his choices. He had kept the little necklace separate - he wasn`t sure why, it just seemed a good idea to hold on to it meantime. They headed back to Lochwinnoch, Archie pointing out the various local landmarks as they did so. Khara seemed genuinely interested, asking odd questions that seemed (he thought) to confirm her alien origins. `What`s that, Archieblue?` - it was the railway. He then had to explain what a railway was. `What are those?` - they were cows! She also seemed to really appreciate the countryside that he usually took for granted, and it made him look at the fields, the woods, the lochs, in a totally different light, almost seeing it through the eyes of the stranger that Khara really appeared to be. Soon they were pulling into the drive of Archie`s cottage. The sun had climbed high in the sky and the countryside seemed to be glowing. Khara stood and gazed at the neat,stone built house.

`This is where you stay? Archieblue, it is beautiful, very unlike the houses on Loh. It looks old. Is it old?`

Archie knew the cottage dated from about 1830 and he told her the history. Originally built as a small farm workers` cottage, it had been extended and enlarged over the years, serving as a small dairy at one stage then lying derelict before being converted into a house once again in the 1970`s. He had lived there for about fifteen years and had gradually turned it into what he liked to think of as a quirky, attractive residence, although he would never have confessed to that! They got out of the car and, eagerly clutching her bags, she followed him to the door. Archie unlocked it and he stepped into the hall.

`Come on in, then.` he said and she followed him, looking about her and appearing to take in every detail. She followed him into the lounge, with its real oak floor, a couple of sheepskin rugs and two large, comfy leather couches. A wood-burning stove in a natural stone surround sat snugly in the corner, piles of dry logs on either side. One wall was almost totally glass, with two large sliding doors looking out on to the small garden which borrowed the landscape that rolled down towards Castle Semple loch. To one side of this was a solid oak dining table and four chairs. The outlook was idyllic today, although in winter the wind would come howling across the fields, lashing the windows with rain and sleet. The wood-burner had been a sound investment. As he looked round in the bright sunlight, he realised that the place was in a bit of a mess – he had neglected it somewhat over the last few weeks, although he had every reason. His mind had been very much on other things, after all. Khara didn`t seem to notice, though. She gazed out at the stunning view in silence. Then she turned and said

`My home planet is very beautiful, Archieblue, but this is wonderful, so peaceful. You are very lucky to live here.`

She placed her bags on the oak dining table and looked around the comfortable lounge. Suddenly she burst out laughing, pointing at the little plastic statue of the classic "alien" that Cam had given him as a birthday present a few years back.

`You have a Queesha! Wherever did you get that?` She went over and picked it up and, to Archie`s great surprise, gave it a kiss.

`That`s what we call an, em, Alien.` said Archie, feeling a bit embarrassed as, obviously, it looked nothing like her. Then he remembered she had used an emoticon of similar appearance.`It`s a long story but, back in the sixties, there was a rumour that a spaceship had crashed in America, at a place called Roswell, and that there were aliens on board. I`m not sure where the image came from, but this is what we kind of think an alien looks like.` Then he added `Present company excepted, of course! But how do you know it?`

Khara laughed again, hugging the alien - this was the most emotion he had seen her display in the short time he had known her.

`When we are young, our parents sometimes try to scare us with tales of the Queesha coming to take us away.` She paused and thought. `I suppose it is similar to what you call the "bogey-man", an unseen entity that carries an element of menace. The Queesha looks just like your "alien". How curious.`

`But if you recognise it from your planet, does that mean that they really do exist?`

`I do not know, Archieblue, but it is certainly a surprise to see him here. It is a big co-incidence that two extremely distant planets should possess knowledge of the same peculiar life-form. There are some on Loh who claim that the Queesha were a race who visited us in our past but, of course, there is no evidence to support this. Except, perhaps, until now.` She carefully put the little statue back down, patting his head, then went back over to the table. She pulled the clothes out of the bags and selected a pair of skinny jeans, a red t-shirt (Archie thought the colour would suit her dark hair) and some underwear. `I should change into some of these clothes now.`

`Okay` said Archie, `I`ll show you to the bedroom` he made to leave the lounge but Khara said

`Bedroom? I do not wish to rest, just to change my clothing.`

She placed her finger at the top of the grey jump-suit and slowly ran it down the front. Archie could see the fabric start to separate as if there was some form of hi-tech concealed zip.

`No, it`s just to give you some privacy` said Archie, with some urgency as she moved her finger lower. The material started to gape and she appeared to be naked underneath.

`I do not need privacy, Archieblue. I am proud of my body and do not mind you seeing it. Unless you do not want to see it, if you feel it is unattractive.` she said, with what Archie thought looked suspiciously like a pout.

`No, it`s not that` he said quickly, `it`s just, well, I hardly know you. And...`

It was too late - by now she had unfastened the suit completely and climbed out of it, unashamedly standing stark naked in front of him. She ran her hands up over her curvaceous hips and on to her waist.

`You see, I think my body is perfectly acceptable.` she said, her unfathomable eyes staring straight at Archie as her hands continued upwards over her full, firm breasts. `Now, let me see what I will put on first.`

Archie swallowed nervously as she turned her back to him and he tried not to stare at the most gorgeous backside he had ever seen. In the small of her back was what he took to be a tattoo of some, an unfamiliar pattern that was very brightly coloured – he supposed it had some significance on her planet but there was no way he was going to ask her about it at this point in time! She picked up a pair of white cotton knickers and wriggled into them, then lifted up the matching white bra and looked at it curiously.

`Is this for my breasts?` she asked in a totally matter of fact manner.

`Er...yes` Archie mumbled. He could feel the colour rising in his cheeks. Other things were rising too...

`I see. Now, how does it go on? Oh, I see, like this.` She put it over her shoulders then walked over to him. `Can you help me fasten it, please?` she said, turning her back on him.

Shit!

Archie somehow managed stop his hands shaking for long enough to fasten the clasps, glad that she was facing away from him and wouldn`t see the large bulge that had appeared in the front of his jeans. However, as she half turned and thanked him, she gently patted his crotch, smiled and said `You see, I knew you would like my body. Now, trousers.`

Archie could feel beads of perspiration start to appear on his forehead as she casually walked back over to the table and put on the jeans and the red t-shirt. Then she took out the black and white Nike trainers that Archie had selected, sat in one of the dining chairs and put them on her feet. She looked up at him.

`What do I do with these?` she asked, lifting the laces.

It hadn`t crossed Archie`s mind that she may not know how to tie shoelaces. He went over, knelt down and said

`Here, I`ll help. It`s quite easy, we learn to do this as children.`

He was relieved to have something practical to occupy him and, after double-knotting the laces, he stood up.

`Thank you.` Khara said as she rose off the chair. She put her hands on her hips and asked

`There! How do I look, Archieblue? Will I pass for an Earth-woman, do you think?`

`Absolutely fantastic!` he replied. She did! `You`ll pass! Very human, in fact.`

She then turned and looked in the Sports Direct bag.

`So you are taking me to climb a mountain?` she asked enthusiastically.

`Yes. Well, what we call a Munro. Ben Lomond. It`s just under a kilometre high, not too difficult. It should take us about five hours so we`d better get away soon – don`t want to be coming down in the dark. It`s not too far from here and it`s one of Scotland`s favourite hills - the view should be absolutely brilliant today. I`ve organised a picnic so we can climb up and eat lunch at the summit. We can change into our boots and stuff at Rowardennan..`

He remembered the jewellery. `Oh, I got you this for you as well, just as a wee extra. Thought it would make you more, well, trendy, I suppose. Hope you like it.`

Khara opened the bag and stared at the simple, inexpensive necklace. She lifted it out and gave him a very curious look.

She hesitated very slightly then handed it back to him.

`Don`t you like it?` he asked, slightly annoyed and, well, just a tiny bit hurt, he supposed. Wasn`t it good enough?

`Yes, I do like it, it is lovely. But would you please put it on for me?`

She turned her back to him and lifted her thick, black hair. He placed the necklace round her neck and, with only a slight fumble, he fastened it and she let her hair drop back down. Once again, he caught a vague hint of her exotic, sensual smell before she turned back to face him and glanced down at the little trinket.

`It is very nice, Archieblue, and very special. Thank you. That was most...kind` She fingered the little beads and smiled at him, differently this time, definitely a bit warmer and more sincere. He smiled back, his anger gone, and he wondered just what the hell was going through her alien mind. It was only a wee leather necklace, after all.

Strange.

She picked up the rucksack and opened it then she went in to the pockets of her jumpsuit and took some items out and placed them in the bag. Archie couldn`t make out what they were and a fleeting thought went through his mind, *maybe it`s the keys to her spaceship...*

`Do you want me to put that into the wash?` Archie asked, as she put the grey suit over the back of the chair. There seemed to be very little material in it.

`Wash?` she looked puzzled. `Oh, I understand. No, thank you, it will self-clean.`She touched what looked like a small button on the side of one of the pockets.

`Right, Archieblue, I am ready.`

`Great. Just let me get the picnic and we`ll be on our merry way.`

`Merry? Why is it merry?`

Here we go again...

`Aw, just a figure of speech. Come on!`

***

They drove along contentedly, Archie pointing out the various features that he regularly took for granted. Soon they were on the M8 and taking the slip for the Erskine Bridge, the same turn-off he and Cam had taken only a couple of days previously. It seemed like a lifetime ago and, although he was still struggling to come to terms with the events of the last two days, let alone the last two weeks, he felt lighter of mood than he had done since before...well, before it all kicked off. Once over the bridge, he headed for Glasgow then took the slip road that would take him up through Milngavie, on to Drymen then down to the little hamlet of Rowardennan, on the shores of Loch Lomond.

They arrived in the car park and, as he expected, the beautiful Autumn day had brought out throngs of trippers, although he knew that most of them wouldn`t be climbing the Ben. They changed their footwear, Khara making a valiant but unsuccessful attempt to tie the laces of her climbing boots. Once they had their backpacks on, they set off along the loch and picked up the track that would lead them up the slopes of Ben Lomond. It had been well over a month since Archie had done any serious climbing and he was definitely not as fit as he would have liked. Khara, on the other hand, despite having claimed to have spent some considerable time on her "space flight", seemed to be in peak condition and often had to stop and wait until he caught up. About three quarters of the way up he stopped for a breather and a drink of water.

`You seem to be finding the climb difficult, Archieblue. You told me you were a keen climber. What has happened to you?`

He didn`t rise to the bait – there were some very good reasons why he hadn`t been doing any climbing. He remained silent and gazed at the view. She took off her pack and delved inside. She held her hand out

`Here, this will help.`

It was another small, clear vial, just like the one he had swallowed earlier, its effects having worn off some time ago. He took it and looked at it.

`Is this stuff safe? I mean, I know its incredible and I feel much better after I take it, but what exactly is it? Some kind of stimulant?`

`No` she replied. `In fact, it is only a type of water. It comes from what you would probably call a "sacred" well, in a very remote part of Loh. The water is scarce and only flows when the winter snows melt. It contains some very rare minerals, found only in the rocks where the well is situated. This includes one that gives a sensation of being extremely cold, as the water is when it is drawn. It has extremely effective restorative properties, as you have experienced and it will do you no harm for it is not addictive in itself, However, there are some on my planet who become addicted to the effects it gives and find it hard to function without it. Just as those on your planet who are addicted to drugs cannot survive without them. Ultimately it may kill them, although this water will not do that. I can assure you it is safe.`

At her unintentional mention of drug addicts, Archie felt as if a cloud had passed over the sun. It suddenly came back to him that, on top of everything else, Lucinda`s funeral was on Tuesday. It must have shown on his face.

`Are you all right, Archieblue? Have I said something to upset you? I am very sorry if I have.`

`No, Khara. It`s not you. Just a memory. I`ll tell you sometime. But not just now. Right, let`s swallow this wee beauty.`

He popped the vial in his mouth, bit into it and, within seconds, he was leading the way up the last, steep section that led to the summit.

It was nearly 3.00 p.m. when they reached the top and, to his surprise, there was no-one else there. It was rare to reach the summit of Ben Lomond and be alone as about thirty thousand people a year made the climb, but he was delighted that they had it to themselves for the time being. Khara gazed at the view, apparently mesmerised, down onto the glittering expanse of Loch Lomond and over to the Trossachs in the east. Archie had been right, there wasn`t a cloud in the sky and it was, quite simply, spectacular. They stood in silence for about ten minutes then, at the sound of a party of approaching climbers, they walked over to a secluded spot, took off their packs and sat on the grass.

`Archieblue, on all my travels, this is one of the most beautiful places I have ever seen. You are very lucky to have somewhere like this so close to where you live.`

`I know, it is pretty amazing, isn`t it. And if you look over there, you`ll see that this is just the start. The Highlands of Scotland are that way and there are some much higher hills that Ben Lomond.`

He pointed out the various peaks in the distance, naming them as he did so. Khara seemed amused by the Gaelic names that rolled off his tongue. When he had finished, he unpacked the picnic. He had made a quick trip into Marks and Spencers and had a selection of sandwiches, crisps, freshly squeezed orange juice and a few sweet goodies for afters. They ate in silence, Khara happily wolfing down everything that came her way. When she had finished she lay back on the grass, her hands clasped over her stomach, and a smile of satisfaction on her face.

`That was delicious, Archieblue.`

She gazed up at the sky.

`A picnic...picnic...yes, I think that is a good word – I will remember that. Thank you very much. Did you prepare it yourself?`

`No, I cheated, I`m afraid, and bought it. I love cooking, though, but there wasn`t time today.` He lay on the grass beside her, gazing up at a small white cloud that had appeared. Had he really been way up there the night before? She seemed to read his thoughts.

`You must find it strange now to look up to the sky and know that you have been. I suppose I take it for granted but it changes your perception of things. I hope it has expanded your vision of your planet?`

`Oh yes! Most definitely. Still, you can`t get much better than this, can you?`

`No.` She stayed silent for a few moments, then said `There is something troubling you Archieblue. I can sense it. We are mildly telepathic and, although I cannot read your mind, as you might say, I can tell when you have a concern. Other than me, of course! I have found that, sometimes, it is good to talk of your concerns in somewhere like this. It serves to remind you that your world is still a beautiful place, no matter what. I am happy to listen.`

He remained silent for a few minutes. Then he started. At the beginning.

Fifteen minutes later, and without interruption, he finished his story and lay, still gazing up at the once-again cloudless sky. Khara turned to face him, then touched her right palm to where he supposed her heart was, then placed it over his own heart. As she did so, she said in the strange, alien accent she had used when he first encountered her

`Lehk oawya, Sehk oawya, kheoohe aselto kwi.`

He turned and looked at her, frowning his incomprehension.

`Roughly translated it means "my heart with your heart, sorrow shared." It is an expression of deep sympathy on our planet. I am so sad for you, Archieblue. To gain, then lose a daughter in a day...I cannot imagine it.` She mover her palm down from his heart and grasped his hand tightly. `As to the attack, on my planet we would not consider that matter too seriously, as long as your victim was the person you say he is. Especially not if you believe he was responsible, either personally or indirectly, for the death of the girl, your daughter. Perhaps we are a more violent species, I do not know humans well enough. Our justice can sometimes seem harsh but, well, there are reasons...`

`No, we have our moments, you just need to look at the Middle East, or even closer to home, and see the atrocities that are happening, right now. We`re a pretty rum lot, us humans.`

`Rum?` She frowned as if in thought.`Is that not a drink?`

They both burst out laughing and the sadness and sorrow passed. Archie suddenly realised just how badly he had needed to tell someone what had happened with Kevin King, especially someone such as Khara, who not only was impartial but also would not be put in a compromising position by the knowledge. In fact, there had been no-one else he could possibly have told.

`Thank you for listening. I feel so much better having told you.`

`You see, it was the right time and the right location. I am glad you told me and that it has helped. The sun still shines, the sky is still blue, we have full stomachs, good friends and we are on top of the world! Well, your world, I suppose!`

`I like that!` he chuckled, then sat up `Right we`d better be getting back down before it starts to get dark. We don`t want to be on top of the world at midnight!`

He held out his hand and helped her up then, once their packs were packed with the detritus of their lunch, they slung them on their backs and headed back down the slopes, stopping every now and then to gaze at the glorious panorama as the sun started to go down.

By the time they reached Rowardennan, it was nearly dark and the car park was almost empty. After a quick trip to the toilets, avoiding some rather active bats that seemed to be nesting there, they sat back in the car. Archie turned to Khara

`Hungry?`

`Very, Archieblue, your picnic has worn off!`

`Great. I know just the place. In fact, I booked it this morning.`

***

They headed back the way they had come, this time taking the turn-off for Glasgow rather than the Erskine bridge. As they drove, Khara started to relate to Archie a brief history of her planet, Loh. How, until about one hundred and fifty Earth years ago, it had been ruled by the dictatorship that was the Atra, how the revolution had started and the planet had been plunged into a brutal and almost devastating civil war (to Archie it sounded much worse than either of Earth`s World Wars) and how, eventually, peace had gradually and painfully ensued, with a much depleted stock of population. He could see some parallels to the history of his own planet but it sounded truly horrific. Then she explained more about her mission

`The story of Lumian has almost become a folk tale.` she explained. `It is known that he and his two comrades, Gara, the pilot and Camali, Lumian`s friend, managed to escape the planet and it has long been rumoured that they carried with them some kind of terrible weapon, although the Atra have always denied that such a weapon had been constructed. However, about twenty of your Earth-years ago, some documentation was discovered during construction work, deep in some long-forgotten vault of one of our oldest buildings, that appeared to be some sort of instruction manual. The weapon to which these instructions referred was to be primed with a sample of what you would call the DNA of a specific targeted group, then using some extraordinarily clever programming, created by Samian, who was Lumian`s father and one of the most notorious weapons masters of all time, it transmitted what I would best describe as a kind of radiation pulse wave that caused a genetic disruption, or mutation, if you like, of the chosen group, killing them within a matter of a week or so. In one simple action, with no consequences for themselves and with no possible antidote, the Atra could eliminate a whole genetic group, leaving themselves as the only surviving faction, or Tribe, as you would probably name them. Of course, there is every likelihood that they, themselves, would eventually have descended into their own civil war but they did not consider this eventuality and, fortunately, we will never know. However, the discovery of this information led us to believe that it was this weapon that Lumian and his friends were carrying when they escaped. It is highly likely that the weapon is booby-trapped, as Samian was an extremely clever and sophisticated weapons technician and guarded his work carefully, although the instructions did not refer to this. Fortunately, however, most of the remainder of the instructions appear to be complete and, given our scientific advancements since the weapon was built, it should hopefully be possible to disarm and dismantle it. Then the technology would be destroyed completely, just in case anyone should ever try to re-create it. As you can see, it is of vital importance that the weapon is recovered before it falls into the wrong hands. It could be catastrophic if someone from your planet tried to open it as I could not tell you what would happen and how many people might suffer as a result.`

She paused as if to catch her breath, then continued in a slightly quieter voice.

`Also, despite the peace on Loh, there are still some Atra scattered around who are loyal to the ideals of the original dictatorship. In fact, many of us suspect that there are more than we may like to think, which is somewhat troubling. And just like those in the last revolution, they keep their activities secret. We watch, of course, we infiltrate, but it is very dangerous to do this. Then there are those Atra who have escaped from Loh – we have little or no idea of their whereabouts. Should they find the weapon, and, believe me, they will be looking just as we are, there is no saying what could happen.`

She stopped and stared straight ahead, lost in her thoughts. Archie, too, sat in silence for a few moments after her explanation before speaking.

`That`s pretty heavy stuff, Khara. And I know this probably sounds terrible but, you know, listening to what you say about this weapon, well, maybe there`s an argument for something like that, here, on Earth. You know, there`s a lot of very evil people, races if you like, on our planet. It could be one solution.`

Immediately and unexpectedly she turned and snapped at him.

`Do you think so? "One solution?" Does that not have some shameful significance in your history – was there not a "final solution" once before, in your recent past? Against whom would you use it, Archieblue? Against your perceived enemies? And what if the weapon had landed in their territory? I would be having this same conversation with them, only you would now be the enemy.`

He responded angrily. `Well, I would very much doubt that. You`d be dead by this time - those people don`t negotiate and take you up mountains for a picnic, let me tell you! Beheading, burning people alive! Take your pick!`

`Really! So, what if I had come here say...seventy or eighty years ago. Would you have used the weapon on the same enemy as now, or would it have been a different enemy?`

He didn`t really have an answer for that one - of course it would have been different, but he wasn`t backing down.

`No, well of course it would have been different, I`m just saying maybe it would maybe still have been for the best. It would have saved millions of lives. Are you familiar with our First World War, the thousands lost in a single day on the battlefields, the Somme, Ypres and the like?`

`For the best?` She spat. `You obviously do not have the least idea what is for the best. No matter what, genocide is never "for the best". How can it be? And let us assume that this weapon was retained, would you use it if aliens landed on your planet in the future, either before or after you decided that they were your enemy? Or if you went to war with...say the United States of America. Would that be for the best, do you think? Your perceived enemies change all the time. Who are you to decide who lives and who dies? You sound just like the Atra – that is how they justified the construction of the sphere in the first place! And what gives you the right to assume you are the superior race? According to Earth`s database, that is what the German Nazis believed. You believed that to be wrong, did you not?`

Archie turned and shouted at her – he knew she was right.

`All, right, all right, I get it! Fair enough, you`re right, of course, genocide can never be justified. I`m sorry, it was just a thought and it was wrong. And I`m nothing like your Atra – or the Nazis, for that matter. That was a horrible thing to say!`

There was a tense silence.

`I am sorry too, Archieblue. Like you, I have a temper which, sometimes, I cannot control. It was indeed a horrible thing to say and I do not, for one minute, think you are like the Atra. But this weapon, this sphere, it has become a symbol on our planet of good against evil. Look at us, even here it has caused an argument between us. It has an evil influence, even on our planet where there are some who would readily agree with your views. I have been searching for it for a long, long time and I am weary. I am sorry that I lost my temper with you, but please do not speak lightly about things that you do not, or cannot, understand.` She stretched her arm over towards him and held out her hand. `Friends?`

He responded and clasped hers. `Friends.`

Fucking hell...

`So tell me, after all that,` Archie asked `are you sure that this so called "weapon" is what we`ve found? And, if so, how did you locate it? Space is a pretty big place, after all.`

`Well, Archieblue, we have been searching this sector for some time. We have records that tell us that Lumian was pursued by two Atra fighter craft. We know that they managed to evade one of these but the other followed them and made their last communications transmission from the vicinity of your solar system. Then both craft disappeared, presumed to have crashed somewhere. A few years ago, scanners from another reconnaissance craft detected debris on what you call your moon. Our ship landed and found the remains of two ships, along with the remains of five bodies, Lumian and his friends and the two crew of what was called a Hosil space-fighter, one of the most advanced at that time. The bodies, along with as much wreckage as we could reasonably salvage, were recovered and taken back to Loh, where they were interred with full ceremony. But the weapon was not found and it was presumed that it had been jettisoned prior to the crash. However, no trace of any missile or drone was found on your moon – I have been, before I came to Earth, and I carried out a brief scan of the area just to be sure. We have been searching in this area ever since that first discovery, although it has been almost impossible,` she paused and thought `like you say, it is like looking for a needle in a haypile. When the old torpedo was dug up on your building area, the movement activated a locator transmitter - it was surprising that it still worked after all this time and testament to the high quality of the workmanship; but then, Gara was a master pilot and would have made all the preparations himself. It is likely that he had foreseen the possibility of having to eject the weapon and he would have made sure that it could be re-located at a later date, which was, indeed, fortunate for me. The signal was relayed to a beacon in space that alerted me to its presence and here I am.`

`Yes, here you are indeed!` said Archie, his mind reeling once more with the weight of the information Khara had given him.

`I do realise that this is an enormous amount for you to process, Archieblue` she said, once again as if reading his thoughts. `And I am sorry to burden you with the problems of my planet, especially when you have some serious problems of your own. But I hope you can now see the urgency of my mission. However, there is another problem, which you have probably determined yourself.`

There were many, thought Archie, Which particular one was she referring to?

`For me, the easiest course of action would be simply to remove the drone and leave. But that would leave you with an enormous mystery and might also cause you some problems with an explanation as to where it had gone, as you were supposed to be guarding it. I would, of course, also have to ensure that I was not observed.`

True

`Or I could simply remove the weapon and leave the drone. But, once it was analysed, it would become apparent that it was not from your world, which might be an even bigger problem for you and humanity as a whole. Despite our violent history we are now a responsible race and try, as far as possible, not to cause disruption amongst species who are unaware of other life in the Universe.`

True again

`The final option would be to remove the weapon and destroy the drone. However, that could be extremely dangerous as to destroy it completely would necessitate a very powerful blast and I would not wish to cause any casualties. If the blast were not sufficient, then parts of the drone may not be destroyed, once again raising the problem of analysis of any remaining parts.`

`So what do you propose doing?` asked Archie.

`I do not know at this time which option is best. What do you think, Archieblue?`

By now they were approaching Glasgow`s Merchant City and Archie was cruising round the busy streets looking for a place to park.

`I think we should discuss it over some tapas.`

`Tapas? What is that?`

`Oh, a wee treat. You`ll love it – I hope!`

Chapter 19

Archie was surprised at just how busy Glasgow`s Merchant City area was for a Sunday evening. He figured that the good weather had prompted the populace to eat out after a dose of unaccustomed fresh air and exercise and he was glad that he had taken the precaution of booking Mercado, a Spanish Tapas restaurant sited inside the Candleriggs market. Parking, however, proved to be more of a problem and he ended up quite a distance along Bell Street, just before the railway bridge and in the shadows of some of the large warehouses that remained empty and as yet unconverted. Glasgow could change very rapidly from the trendy, modern Merchant City to what was starting to encroach on the older, and considerably less salubrious, East end, not the best place to leave a car like his, especially as security cameras seemed a bit thin on the ground! However, as they were already a bit late for their reservation, he had little choice. He found a space, slid the car into it and they headed for their dinner, Archie turning and double-checking he had locked the Porsche, just in case...

Soon they were sitting in the bustle of the old Candleriggs, the large indoor former market that was now home to numerous eating places, all with extensive "outdoor" dining areas. Archie loved the tapas in Mercado and ordered a good selection, as well as a bottle of San Miguel (one would be fine...) for himself and a sangria for Khara. She tucked in to the Spanish delicacies with gusto, seeming only to find the calamari rings a bit unpalatable. The conversation now flowed easily, with each telling the other small details of their lives and their home planets - anyone overhearing their discussion of life on a remote planet would have assumed they had imbibed in some mind-altering substances prior to their meal! Archie had also noticed that she was attracting admiring glances from a number of males, especially a bunch of guys celebrating in the nearby O`Neill`s bar. He had first been aware of this on their walk along the banks of Loch Lomond, one particular male observer earning himself a sharp dig in the ribs from his girlfriend. She certainly was a striking looking female, especially now that she was dressed in everyday clothes and was smiling and laughing - he felt a vague and surprising glow of pride that she was with him! Khara, on the other hand, was entirely oblivious to this attention and was happy to concentrate on her dinner and Archie`s company - a very gratifying and ego-boosting sensation! Their meal finished, she swallowed the last of her second glass of sangria, Archie settled the bill and they went for a stroll around the market hall, eventually going outside and walking around the now near-deserted area, window-shopping the few niche shops in the vicinity. It was getting late and the crowd was definitely thinning out. Still, Archie felt he didn`t want the day to end just yet and it was Khara who finally made the suggestion.

`It has been an excellent day, Archieblue, but I am tired and I think we should leave soon. After all, it was quite a vigorous climb that we had today. Also, I still have plans to make. Do not forget why I am here.`

Of course, he had forgotten completely and had been living entirely for the moment for the past few hours. Reluctantly he agreed and they headed back towards where he had parked the car. Once away from Candleriggs the streets were deserted and, despite being a police officer, Archie was always a bit uneasy in this neck of the woods, particularly as it lay in a different, and less familiar, division from his own. As they approached the Porsche he noticed that someone had parked a white Transit van behind his car and he hoped they hadn`t blocked him in. As he passed it and was about to put his hand in his pocket for his keys, he heard a gravelly, nicotine-deepened voice speaking from the shadows of the railway bridge.

`Well, well, well! Look who`s dragged his sorry arse up to Glasgow. Archie fuckin` Blue sky. An` a bint as well. Wee bonus, that, eh Tam?`

`Aye, maybe a wee bit "R an` R" fur the boys, Den!`

Archie looked at the source of this menacing repartee. Two hard looking men, one with an expensive looking hair-cut and wearing a black suit with a collar and tie, the other slightly stockier with cropped hair, dyed almost white, and wearing jeans and a black tee shirt that stretched across the muscles of his broad chest and revealed powerful biceps, heavily adorned with tattoos. The smartly dressed one was Thomas or Tam, McLintock, a reputed but so far unconvicted drug distributor, his more casual associate being the notorious Glasgow gangland thug, Dennis Ralston, or "Dirty Den" as he was known. These men weren`t petty criminals. They were hardened career gangsters reputedly in control of a seemingly untouchable network stretching the length of the UK and reaching into Europe and although Archie was a fit enough individual who could take care of himself, he was decidedly uneasy. This was not a good situation to find himself in and he suspected the Porsche had been clocked by this pair. Somehow it didn`t seem like a co-incidence!

`Back off, Ralston, don`t make trouble for yourself. Always

remember, my gang`s bigger than yours.` he said, in a show of bravado. Assaulting a cop was never a good idea, even for the likes of McLintock and Ralston, as it would inevitable bring a load of trouble for the perpetrator. But as he spoke he became aware of a larger, looming presence emerging from the shadows of the bridge. A heavily accented voice spoke

`So, you`re in a gang too, Blue Sky? And what gang is that?`

Gregor Czarneki. Aka Blok.

`Is that the gang that killed my good friend, Kevin. Left him lying in a car park, bleeding to death, his face such a mess that his poor mother wouldn`t have recognised him? A gang of cowards, who run away. Some gang, huh!` He spat. `No, Blue Sky, I think tonight you will find my gang is bigger than yours. Boys!`

On his command, Archie suddenly felt the coldness of a blade against his throat and realised that there were another two of Blok`s men behind Khara and him. Their wrists were grabbed and secured behind their backs with thick cable ties then one of the anonymous thugs reached into his pocket and pulled out the keys of the Porsche, tossing them over to McLintock. He smiled,

`Nice motor for a cop, Blue Sky. Reckon you`re daein` a wee bit on the side, just like the rest of your filthy mob!`

`Keep your hands off it, McLintock!` growled Archie.

`Aye, like you can fuckin` dae anythin` aboot it, arsehole.` He turned his back and opened the Porsche. `Aye, nice. I`ve already got a buyer lined up. You`ll no` be needin it again.` He laughed as he got in, then he started the engine and roared off.

Ralston opened the back doors of the van and the two thugs manhandled Archie and Khara inside, shoving them roughly on to the bare metal floor then sitting down on a pile of pallets stacked against the bulkhead. Ralston closed the doors, leaving them in darkness, then Archie heard the front doors close, followed by the engine starting. He whispered to Khara

`I`m really sorry, Kh...owww!`

One of his captors had brutally kicked him in the back.

`Shut yer fuckin` mouth, arsehole. Next one`ll be *really* sore.`

They lay in silence, very faintly illuminated in the glow of their captors` mobile phones. Archie was trying in vain to work out the direction they were taking. If he could only get to his phone, maybe he could dial 999 and leave the line open – an unanswered emergency call would soon disclose his number and hopefully alert someone to his plight. But it was in the side pocket of his trousers and his hands were firmly secured behind his back - there was no chance. After what he roughly calculated to be about forty five minutes, the van made a sharp turn and the road surface changed to what felt like a rough track. A few minutes more and the van stopped, the engine died and the back door opened. Archie and Khara were dragged out by the two thugs who had accompanied them, their recent inactivity following the day`s exercise making it hard for them to walk. They stumbled forwards and were pushed roughly down on to their knees. Blok stood facing them, Ralston and McLintock beside him. The other two returned to the van.

`Welcome to hell, Mr Blue Sky filth.` Blok spat again when he finished speaking.

Archie`s eyes darted back and forth as he tried to get an idea of where they were. It seemed to be a deserted farm, with old, crumbling outbuildings and a few rusting vehicles lying abandoned. There was nothing that he recognised and he suspected they were well off the beaten track, somewhere outside Glasgow. There was very little glow in the sky, indicating that there was no town nearby. The only illumination came from the headlights of the van and his Porsche. Blok spoke again.

`Now, I know that you killed my friend Kevin. And, of course, for that you must be punished. What I do not know is just how much you have discovered about my business dealings. But we will find out, we will find out.` He laughed and rubbed his hands together.

`What the fuck are you talking about?` Archie bluffed. `I haven`t seen King for months. We all assumed you`d got rid of him. What the fuck has this to do with me` he nodded towards Khara `or her, for that matter? Let her go. None of this concerns her.`

`Anything that concerns you concerns me.` replied Blok. `The two of you looked pretty close, I thought, in the restaurant. Oh, don`t look so surprised, Blue Sky. My web stretches far and wide!` He stretched his arms wide as if to demonstrate, then continued

`And, of course, often it is the easier way to get to the truth, to hurt someone that you care about. Maybe you could resist my, em...methods yourself but we will see what happens when it is your girlfriend who is screaming like a... you say... stuck pig. I think, Blue Sky, you will be telling me the truth before too long. Then it will be your turn.` He laughed again, the sound guttural and menacing.

`Listen, I don`t know what the fuck you think happened to King, but I haven`t a clue. Like I said, I haven`t seen him around for months. None of us have.`

Blok took a step closer and glared at Archie – he could smell the sour smell of his breath and his sweat, even a few feet away.

`You make the big mistake. You think Blok is a big stupid foreigner. But, no, that is not so. You drive a nice car, Mr Policeman. Very noticeable. Someone saw you pulling out of the secret, little track where you were parked, just before they found poor Kevin in the car park. Even a stupid foreigner could work that one out. I had to bury my poor friend myself. A small farewell, just me and his friends here.` He swept his hand round to include the other four. `No, it was you, Blue Sky, it was you and you will pay.`

Archie had been in a blind panic on the fateful night of his encounter with King. Had there been headlights behind him as he pulled away? Had there been a car driving towards him? A deep memory stirred of headlights in his mirror for a few miles after he had left, catching him up then dropping out of sight at a junction, presumably having turned off the main road. But it was vague – he really couldn`t remember.

During this dialogue McLintock had gone back over to Archie`s car. He returned, carrying their back-packs, which had been on the rear seat of the Porsche. He handed them to Blok.

`So, now, what do we have in here?` He opened Archie`s and

emptied it on the ground – it mostly contained the empty wrappers from their lunch.

`Ha! You seem to have had a picnic together. How romantic.`

As Blok raked through the contents of the backpack, the thugs from the van had returned - one was carrying a holdall which he started to empty in front of them. A hammer and a large, coarse-toothed wood saw came first. Then what Archie recognised with horror to be a nail gun which, presumably for demonstration purposes, the thug fired a couple of times into a handy piece of wood – the nails were about three inches in length. Then he pulled out a gas blowtorch, turned the valve and lit it with his lighter, placing it on the ground. As it hissed, the blue flame danced vividly in the near-darkness. Finally, he pulled out a short bolt-cutter and placed it beside the other tools. Archie could feel his stomach churn and glanced sideways at Khara. She looked completely unconcerned. Blok emptied the scant contents of Khara`s backpack on to the ground. He picked up a silver object that resembled a thick pen and Archie realised he had seen Khara using it when he first met her at the drone.

`What`s this, pretty one?` he asked, holding it towards her. `Some kind of fancy vibrator? Can Blue Sky not get it up, eh?`

His associates laughed at the big man`s joke. For the first time since they had been kidnapped, Khara spoke, her tone completely unemotional.

`Amongst other purposes, it is a neural network enhancer.`

Blok paused, then threw his head back in laughter. `A what, my pretty? Haha, you think you`re smarter than poor old Blok, eh? I know a fancy dildo when I see one. Old Blok has been around, eh? Round the block, you might say! Hahaha!

Again, his associates laughed sycophantically.

`Press the top and you will see.`

`Okay dokey, beautiful. Anything for you. And later, in return, you will do anything for me. Trust me on that.` He pressed the projecting button on the top, obviously expecting it to start vibrating.

Even in the meagre light provided by the vehicles` headlights, Archie could see Blok`s pupils instantly dilate until there was almost no iris remaining visible. His mouth started opening and shutting as if he was gasping for breath, but no sound was coming out and his arms were flapping as if he was trying to swim. The silver object dropped to the ground. Ralston looked on on amazement as the big man fell down, still flapping about and clutching at his throat. He turned and shouted at Khara

`What the f.....` He stopped mid-word and let out a spine-chilling scream, then started beating at his arms and body before he, too, dropped to the ground, where he continued to scream and writhe about as if in agony. McLintock ran over to him then looked over at Khara. As with Blok, Archie saw his pupils dilate alarmingly and he started to swipe at his body, shouting

`Get them aff me, get them aff!`

The two thugs, having finished unpacking the grim contents of their suitcase, stood in astonishment, unable to comprehend what was happening and clueless as to what action to take. They gazed at their associates then turned to Khara. In an instant, one had grabbed the other`s jacket and head butted his fellow thug full in the face. Archie heard the sickening crunch as the victim`s nose disintegrated then the two became locked in a conflict that, on the face of it, would appear to be to the death. The ferocity of their attack on each other was mind-blowing and Archie could see gobs of blood, snot and what looked like teeth scattering in the light of the headlamps. He looked at Khara, who was standing stock still and staring intently at their five former captors, all apparently helpless and completely out of control, in one way or another. She appeared to sense that he was watching her but she didn`t look at him.

`Archieblue, fetch that saw and cut these restraints` she commanded.

Archie didn`t hesitate. He stood up, took a few paces forward then bent down again, managing somehow to lift the lethal looking blade. He took it back over to Khara and, with a struggle, was able to sever the cable-tie holding her wrists. As soon as she was free, she cut his tie, then walked over to where Blok lay, still gasping for breath. Archie wondered if the man was having a heart attack or a seizure of some sort. Before he could stop her, Khara had raised her foot and brought it down with massive force on Blok`s nose, smashing it to a pulp. She raised it again, this time dropping it on his mouth, splitting his lips and dislodging most of his front teeth.

`Khara! Stop! Stop right now! That`s enough!`

Her foot was poised to strike again, but she obeyed and placed it back on the ground, turning to face him.

`And do you think he would have stopped, Archieblue? When they were using the saw, or the hammer, or burning me with that gas torch. No matter how I screamed, no matter how much you pleaded, do you think he would have stopped. Not until I was dead. Then it would have been your turn.`

Before Archie could respond she did a quick pirouette and her foot connected with Blok`s right knee. Even from where he stood he could see the kneecap dislodge. He went across and grabbed her arm. She faced him and he could see hate in her eyes, the first time he had ever seen them register any emotion.

`Enough, now,` he said gently. `We`re safe. Thanks to you.` He bent down and retrieved the little silver gadget.

`Some tool, this.` he commented, handing it back to her, noticing that his hands were shaking badly. She took it and twisted one of several rings round the top. Suddenly, all five captors became completely motionless and silent.

`What have you done, Khara? No, you need to stop!`

`Do not worry, Archieblue, they are now unconscious. They will remain so for some time. I suggest we leave now. But if you were to question them, they will be willing to tell you a great many things of interest, I think.`

`What do you mean?`

`They are, well, softened, terrified, as you have seen. With weaker, non-telepathic species such as yours that will probably last for a few days, although I am not exactly sure. However, for some time they will tell you anything you want to know, for fear of...well, you can guess from what you have observed.`

`And just what have I seen?` Archie was really worried - he had been witness to a side of this alien woman that he didn`t like at all. Violent, seemingly merciless, Had he not been there, he was certain she would have killed Blok. The irony suddenly struck him

And was I any different...

`It is exactly what I said. A neural network enhancer, a development of an old weapon. Using my telepathy, this device senses the victim`s worst fears, nightmares, phobias, whatever you choose to call them. It then makes them believe that these fears are real. I think that the leader, Blok he called himself, is afraid of drowning. The others, well, one was fire, the other insects of some sort, I imagine.`

`And what about the other two?`

`I simply directed them to turn on one another. I made them each believe the other was a potentially fatal threat that had to be removed.`

`And would they have killed? If you hadn`t, well, knocked them out?`

`Undoubtedly, yes.`

`Khara, this is a very dangerous weapon. If this got in the wrong hands...`

`...it would do nothing` she finished his sentence. `It requires my telepathy to operate it. Now, Archieblue, do you wish to

call some of your colleagues to take away this...this...` she struggled to find a word for the human wreckage.

`I suppose. But we need to not be here.`

Together they quickly stuffed their belongings back into the abandoned backpacks and returned to the Porsche, Archie being relieved to find his keys still in the lock. He turned on the engine as he realised that he was shivering, although he wasn`t sure if it was from cold or from shock. Then he put on the Satellite Navigation to find out where he was. The nearest point of reference he could see was Dura Road – the name wasn`t in the least bit familiar. He scrolled the map down and came to the town of Carluke, South Lanarkshire. He scrolled back up. Dura Road appeared to be in North Lanarkshire and served a few, scattered farms. According to the SatNav, he was in the middle of nowhere – the road wasn`t even showing. He started back down the rough track until they came to Dura Road and he looked for a sign. Nothing. He stopped the car and got out, crossing to the verge where the overgrown track left the main road. There was a wooden stump and, in the undergrowth, he found an old, hand-painted sign "North Auchendallie Farm". That would do. He propped the sign against the stump so that it could be seen from the road, then got back in the car and headed for the A71, which would take him to Wishaw and eventually to Glasgow. Once inside the brightly-lit safety of the town, he stopped, lifted his phone and pressed the number for Cam. It was late but who else could he call? Eventually his friend answered, sounding only half awake, which, undoubtedly, he was. His voice was thick with sleep.

`Boss! Whit the hell, dae ye know whit time it is?`

`I`m really sorry, Cam. I need your help. An abandoned farm called North Auchendallie, just a few miles outside Wishaw. Off Dura Road. You got that?`

Silence. Then Cam replied, this time in a whisper

`Boss, whit the fuck`s goin` on? Whit the fuck`r`ye doin` oot there at this time o` night.`

Archie ignored both the outburst and the question.

`Did you get that, Cam? It`s really important.`

`Whit, sorry? Fuck, haud on.`

He was obviously fumbling for something to write on.

`Right, North Auchendallie, Dura Road. That`ll be North Lanarkshire, then. Whit aboot it, though? That`s no` our patch. Boss, are you okay? Are you in trouble?`

`Aye, Cam, I`m okay. Well, I am now, anyway – just! Listen, mate, I really need you to get some officers over pronto and just tell them you had an anonymous tip off. I really have to get away. I`ll explain when I see you. Get there yourself as soon as. Trust me, it`ll be worth it.` *Like I`m going to tell him what really happened...!*

`Whit`ll be worth it? Whit`re ye talking about. This sounds decidedly dodgy Boss. Gonnae gi` me a clue before I haul my sleepy arse over tae the wilds o` Lanarkshire?`

`I`m really sorry, mate, but you`ll just have to take my word for it. Best get a shift on, though. Won`t wait forever!`

`What won`t? Aw, come on Archie!` There was a deep sigh. `Okay, whatever. But you`ve got a fair bit o` explaining to do. Leave it wi` me.`

`Cheers Cam. I really appreciate it. I owe you.`

Aye, you`re right there, mate` Before he hung up Archie could just hear the sound of Abigail howling in the background. Cam would have a spot of trouble of his own now too! He turned to Khara.

`Right, that`s sorted, Cam will deal with it.`

`Cam?` she asked.

`Aye, he`s my detective sergeant. Brilliant guy, great mate. He`ll sort it out.`

Archie took a deep breath and tried in vain to control his shivering. He continued

`Listen, what happened back there, I`m so sorry you got dragged into it. And I take your point about what they would have done but, really, that`s what makes us different from them. Knowing when to stop.` He looked down. `I didn`t. That`s my problem – my temper got the better of me. But I do think you went too far. If I hadn`t been there, would you have stopped?`

`That is hypothetical. If you had not been there, then neither would I. Archieblue, I am instructed not to interfere with local issues, but I have come a long way and I have far too much at stake to be threatened by people such as those. They are evil and they feel that the law does not apply to them, not unlike the Atra that I told you about. People like that must be stopped, most certainly when they pose a threat to my mission. You know that they would have hurt us, probably have killed us, Archieblue, and I could not allow that to happen. You are a brave and honourable man and I know you would have defended me as best you could but, as you see, I am capable of actions that...` she paused and thought `that are beyond your understanding. Now, let us not talk of it anymore. It is finished.`

It wouldn`t be finished though, not for Archie. - not for a long time. He was badly shaken by what had happened, especially following on the heels of his other recent tragedies and he daren`t think of what might have happened, what might be happening now...he knew there would be nightmares. As if sensing this she placed her hand on the side of his face and, instantly, he started to feel better. But he gently lifted it away.

`No, no mind tricks on me, please Khara. I`ve seen enough for one night.`

She smiled and placed her hand back on his cheek.

`That is not a mind trick, Archieblue. Unless the trick is in your own mind because, I promise you, I am only touching you. If that alone makes you feel better, then I am truly glad. Now take me back to your house, please. I need to change out of these clothes, return to my vessel and make some sort of plan for recovery of the drone. We have wasted too much time already.`

They drove back in silence, listening to a Classic Chillout album that Archie had on his iPhone. It was relaxing him only very slightly.

What was helping much more was Khara`s hand stroking the back of his neck. He realised that what she had said was true, it was no trick, just the touch of her hand made him feel better. Forty five minutes later he pulled the Porsche into the drive of his cottage, they got out of the car and finally into the sanctuary of his home. They made it as far as the lounge before her arms were round his neck, pulling his lips against hers and moving her body against his as his hands explored the soft skin of her back underneath her t-shirt.

Chapter 20

The Lauderdale was one of those old fashioned Glasgow drinking houses, a dying breed in the world of fancy night clubs and trendy Gastro pubs. There was a time when it was said that every crossroads in Glasgow had a pub on each corner but these days were long gone and establishments like the Lauderdale were, indeed, a rarity. Many of the clientele, too, seemed to be stuck in a time warp. Men in flat caps ("bunnets", as they were known in Glasgow), women in rollers and head-scarves, the occasional scruffy dog lying beside its master and anxious to continue its walk, all mixed in with a good few younger drinkers, eager to experience a "real" pub before the species became extinct! All that had changed in the last twenty years or so was that, nowadays, the atmosphere was clear and not filled with the blue haze of tobacco smoke that would have been obligatory twenty years ago.

Even on a Saturday it wasn`t a particularly busy pub, but it was welcoming. A cheery nod from the barman, chilled Pilsner glasses in the fridge and, if you were lucky, the possibility of a round of hot, buttered toast about 9.30. A reasonably well stocked gantry, the usual Tennents and Belhaven on tap, toilets that flushed. Everything the habitual drinker could ask for. And Bill McCurdy was certainly a habitual drinker.

He was propping up the end of the bar, already on his third pint of Tennents (extra cold), chasing down a double Grouse. Had he thought about it, he would have realised that, the older he got, the more it took to get him drunk. But he didn`t think about it. He did, however, think about how unfair it still seemed to deny a man the pleasure of a pint and a fag at the same time, instead of shoving him out on the cold pavement to stand like a leper with the other smokers. But, hey, that was progress! He had written a couple of very pointed articles complaining of the infringement of his rights and the editor of the Scottish Sun, the paper he wrote for, had happily published them, being a forty-a-day man himself. To no avail, though, and the legislation went through, condemning him and his fellow smokers to an evening split between the warmth of the pub and the cold of the pavement. Speaking of which...

He downed the remains of the whisky and headed outside, pulling the half empty cigarette packet from his pocket. As he did so, his mobile rang, the classical guitar riff from Tarrega`s "Grand Vals" identifying the ageing Nokia handset. He didn`t give his number out readily so, if someone called him during drinking time, especially on a Saturday, it was usually worth answering. He looked at the screen. "Unknown." Probably a more official source, then. Interesting! He pressed the answer button and held the phone up to his ear.

`McCurdy`

`Hello Bill. Frank Bryce here.`

`Frank. How`s it goin`?`

`Aye, not too bad Bill, not too bad. Listen, there`s a wee something I heard about that you might find interesting...`

Frank Bryce was neither the best nor the worst of cops. Not that he was dishonest or bent, he was just slightly lazy, very disillusioned and now putting in his time until he retired on his sergeant`s pension in a couple of years, at which point he planned to spend his days fishing and drinking beer. He had known Bill McCurdy for a long time, having shared a pint with him on the odd occasions that their paths crossed, and he had been a useful source of information - despite being a functioning alcoholic, he was also a nosy wee bastard who managed to rummage around and dig up all sorts of useful information, which he had occasionally shared with Sergeant Bryce. In return, if Bryce thought he could pass on a story without causing too much harm, he would point McCurdy in the right direction.

`Erskine, you said? Aye, okay, Frank, I`ll mosey on down tomorrow and have a wee look. Could be interesting. Listen, I appreciate the tip.`

`No problem, Bill. No names, no pack drill, though, okay?`

`Aye, you can trust me. Cheers, ma friend.`

McCurdy went back inside and picked up his pint. Might be a wee story right enough. He would head down to Erskine in the morning and see what was what, although he suspected that a later, clandestine trip would reveal more information than standing chatting to a couple of uniformed officers who would tell him sod all. He suddenly remembered he hadn`t had his fag. He returned to the bar and ordered another double Grouse (just to keep him warm, of course!) before heading back to join the other social outcasts.

***

Christine McCurdy opened the bedroom curtains and looked out at a lovely bright Sunday morning. Her garden looked beautiful, still glistening in the morning dew, the leaves turning gold and red in their first flush of Autumn colours. Maybe she`d get a wee hour or two tidying it up this afternoon. She had brought a coffee for her still comatose husband, although she sometimes wondered why she bothered. Coming back in to the bedroom she could smell the whisky fumes and the tobacco reek from his clothes, flung carelessly on the bedroom couch. Still, he had asked her to waken him early (well, 10.30, which was early for him) as he had a "wee message" to go. This meant he was on to something - after nearly thirty years of marriage Chrissy recognised the symptoms. Despite his many faults, she reflected, he was still a decent enough journalist who liked nothing better than to get to grips with a good story although, recently, there hadn`t been too many of these. He had a way with words, too, and she was well aware that, were it not for these skills he would have been out of a job long ago. Still, the mortgage was paid off on their bungalow in the pleasant Paisley suburb of Ralston, she had a nice wee car (Bill hadn`t held a licence for years as a result of repeated convictions for drunk driving) and the kids were doing well - a wee grand-daughter and another baby on the way. Aye, life wasn`t too bad, she thought, opening the window to let some welcome fresh Autumn air into the room.

`Come on, Bill. You asked me to wake you up. Here`s a wee coffee for you.`

Bill McCurdy grunted and rolled over to face his wife. He rubbed his eyes, scratched his grey, stubbly chin and sat up, coughing violently and alarmingly. Chrissy rolled her eyes but said nothing. The chances of persuading Bill to attend his GP to have his health checked were remote at best.

`Oh, aye, so I did. Thanks, Chrissy.` he growled in his deep, phlegm-ridden voice, taking the cup and swallowing a mouthful of the hot, sweet liquid. A four sugar man, was Bill.

`So, what`s got your interest today?` Chrissy asked, sitting on the bed. `It`s not like you to want to get up at this hour on a Sunday.`

`Ach well` he replied, slurping more of the coffee `A wee tip from a pal o` mine. Something happening down near the river. Thought it might be worth a wee look.` He put the empty mug down on the table and got out of bed. `Thank`s Pet, that was just the job.`

Once he was washed and dressed and had eaten a bacon roll, washed down with another coffee, Bill phoned his driver, Shug McHugh. Having no car and no licence had once posed a wee bit of a problem for him but a few years ago he had met Shug in a pub in Paisley. Like many who retire early with no hobbies, interests or family, Shug was bored and lonely and when a few whiskies had loosened his tongue, Bill suggested that he needed someone to drive him about. Shug had jumped at the chance. Any hour, day or night, he was available and, for Bill, he was a Godsend, for not only did it give him unlimited transport but it also meant he could have a drink whenever he liked. It was Shug who drove him up to the Lauderdale, occasionally coming in for a soft drink but never anything stronger. The real irony was, as Bill had once written in a short article, that nowadays it was debatably more economic to employ a driver than it was to own and run a car! Bill knew little else about him although he did sometimes wonder what kind of parents called their son Hugh McHugh - no wonder he preferred Shug!

By midday he was heading towards Erskine in the back of Shug`s Skoda Octavia and soon found himself standing outside the building site, looking at the sign.

"You`ll soon be Home Free...with HomeFree builders. An exclusive development of 2, 3 and 4 bedroom luxury family homes."

Aye, right, wee boxes all crammed together, more like...!

He sauntered over to the two uniformed officers guarding the gate. He could see their car in the yard but there were no other vehicles about. Still, it was a Sunday and, at this early stage in the development, it was unlikely that there would be any overtime on offer. In fact, the site more resembled a ploughed field than a proposed development of "luxury family homes!"

`Afternoon, lads!`

`Good afternoon, Sir. Can I help you?` one of the officers replied.

`Aye, I was just wondering what`s going on here?`

`Going on, Sir?` the officer looked behind him. `Doesn`t appear to by anything going on at all.`

`Very good, very good! So, if there`s `nothing going on at all`

then why are you two here instead of sitting at home tuckin` into the full Scottish, eh?`

The other officer spoke. `I`m afraid that`s our business, Sir. So I would suggest that, as there`s nothing going on, you might want to make your way back to wherever you came from.`

`Ah, well, you see, that`s not what I heard. I heard you`ve found something down here.`

`Found something, Sir?` Bill could sense the very subtle change of tone in the copper`s voice. He`d struck a nerve. `What have you heard that we`ve found?`

`Oh, nothing specific. Maybe a body, something like that.`

Both policeman laughed and they looked at each other.

`You might want to check the sources you listen to, Sir. There`s no body been found here.`

`Well, if it`s not a body, what is it? They don`t send uniformed officers to guard nothing. Come on lads, give me a wee clue, I`ll no` quote you.`

One of the cops winked at his colleague. `Well, I`ve heard that they dug up an old newspaper and, believe it or not, it was telling the truth!`

His colleague laughed out loud. `Aye, that`s it. I heard that too. Or was it the body of an honest reporter maybe?`

`Oh aye, real funny, that.` said Bill, feigning annoyance. He was used to this kind of banter and was far too long in the tooth to let it even begin to bother him. `Och well, I`ll head back then for a nice big fry up and a pot of tea. Shame you can`t join me.`

`That`s fine Sir. You watch how you go, now.`

Definitely something going on here...

Bill headed back to the car where Shug was sitting reading the Sunday Post. During the brief conversation with the policemen he had been surreptitiously eyeing up the surrounding area and he was fairly certain he knew how he could get a closer look. He lit a cigarette and had a few draws before getting back into the Skoda - Shug didn`t like people smoking in his car.

`You free tonight, Shug? About 1 a.m.?`

***

Chrissie was used to Bill going out at odd hours so she she went to bed at eleven and left him watching the television and having a "wee nightcap - just to keep me warm when I go out..." However, on this occasion there was an element of truth in his statement - there was a distinct Autumnal chill in the air. Frank Bryce hadn`t told Bill what had been dug up - possibly he didn`t know himself, but he had indicated a reasonable police presence to keep the area secure and mentioned a rumour that the Army had visited the site on Saturday. Bill hadn`t expected to gain any information from the police during his afternoon visit, but he wanted to get a better look at the area. He knew Erskine reasonably well, as his son and daughter-in-law lived there. Expecting their first baby, too, which would keep Chrissy happy. He knew that, next to the river, there was a large, marshy low lying area called Newshot Isle. A look on Google Maps would show the remains of old barges and a few small ships buried in the silt (including one which, apparently, was the first iron ship used with a diving bell) and the locality had always fascinated Bill. He had also heard that some of these remains possibly dated from World War Two, ships that had caught fire during the bombing raids and were towed across and abandoned in the marshy inlets. The rectangular barges were supposed to have been used as coal tenders or for painting larger ships in the river. He had never really investigated the history fully to corroborate these stories but he had spent a fair bit of time walking about the area looking at the sunken remains, the potential for an interesting wee article hovering at the back of his mind. He knew that if he kept slightly inland from the Isle, he could walk along the low lying area and come up at the rear of the development. He had seen a strong security fence, perhaps a bit unusual for a building site at this stage - maybe the builders had something else to hide! But it meant that the site was unlikely to be guarded by the police in that vicinity and he intended to sneak along, armed with a pair of sturdy wire cutters, and have a wee sniff about undisturbed. In his youth he had been a bit of a hill-walker, before fags and booze took over from fresh air and exercise. But a wee walk along the riverside wouldn`t pose too much of a problem for him, especially if he could get an exclusive story. *Haven`t had one of* *those for a wee while, be nice to go out on a high...*

Shug duly arrived and Bill got into the car, dumping a holdall down on the seat beside him. They greeted each other with a simple "evening" and headed off. Shug never questioned Bill about his activities, he simply charged him by the mile and they chatted about football, politics and anything else that took their fancy. Bill sometimes reflected that Shug probably knew him and his views better than Chrissy did. Soon they arrived in Erskine and Bill instructed him where to drop him off, just near where the road to the various housing estates left Newshot Drive. Once stopped, he changed into a pair of well worn hiking boots and pulled a battered Barbour waxed jacket out of the holdall - thirty quid out of a "vintage" shop just off Great Western Road in Glasgow and plenty of life left in it yet! He buttoned it up and checked the pockets - phone, wire-cutters, small torch, digital camera, fags, lighter, hipflask - *yep, all there.*

`Right, Shug, I shouldn`t be more than two hours, probably less. Just wait here. Any cops come, just drive off and come back about three-thirty. Okay?`

`Aye, no worries, Bill. I`ll be here, you know that.`

For some odd reason, Bill felt a sudden rush of affection for this funny wee man, about whom he knew very little. He reached into the car and patted him on the shoulder, at which Shug looked round, surprised.

`Aye, Shug, I do know that, and I appreciate it. Cheers.`

Bill climbed over the wire fence and scrambled down a grassy bank that dropped about twelve feet to what could best be described as the flood plain, fortunately well below the houses, although there had been a few times when the level had come alarmingly close. Although his son lived in a lovely property, Bill wasn`t entirely sure he would like to live that close to the River Clyde, especially now that it was no longer being dredged. A high, spring tide combined with a couple of weeks of torrential rain and there was no telling just how high the water would rise. Still, tonight the river was well away in the distance, a dark, glistening ribbon reflecting the lights, of Clydebank, on the other side. The recent heavy rain had made the ground quite soft but the going was easy enough. He walked for a bit then paused to have a sip from the hip-flask, just as a wee refreshment, of course. Then he started off again, noticing that, as the main road was curving off to the right, it was getting darker where he was walking. The watery moonlight wasn`t quite enough for him to see the uneven ground clearly so he pulled out the torch to light the way in front. *Don`t want to fall, Bill, not at your age anyway...* The houses were all in darkness but he would have to be careful when he got nearer the site though, as he knew there would still be a police guard. Another twenty minutes and the houses were behind him. He headed slightly inland, avoiding a clump of trees and could see the strong security fence ahead of him. *Here we go.*

Bill pulled the wire-cutters out of his pocket, noticing that he was a bit breathless. Wasn`t the first time either, he had felt this way a few times recently. *Need to cut down the fags a bit.* He pulled at the fence, gauging just how much he would need to cut. He could see the Portakabins in the yard over to the right and he had arrived at just the correct location to ensure that the buildings were between him and the two policemen that he knew would be standing out front. He placed the cutters on the first bit of wire and squeezed. It was tough but he pushed a bit harder and it snapped with a loud "snick" - in the silence it sounded like a gunshot! He waited a minute, prepared to back off into the undergrowth, but nothing happened and he proceeded to cut just enough to allow him to squeeze through.

Once inside, he looked about and could just make out the shape of a JCB sitting far over to the left, amongst some small trees. *Odd place to leave it, maybe its broken down. Or maybe they`ve found something when they`ve been digging. That sounds more like it...*There was a vague shape beside it but he couldn`t make out what it was – he`d find out, though. He decided to head over to the back of the Portakabins first to check what the Police were up to, then he would take a wee wander over to the JCB to see if it held any clues as to what had been dug up - it seemed the obvious place to start. Once safely behind the wall of the building, he sneaked a quick look round the side and was horrified to see one of the uniformed officers heading straight towards him. *Oh shit!*

But the officer climbed up the steps and opened the door; a few moments later, Bill heard running water then the sound of a kettle boiling and he breathed a sigh of relief. This was followed by the flushing of a toilet then the clinking sounds of hot drinks being prepared. Bill briefly considered handing himself in and joining them, as he was frozen, but he resisted the temptation and watched as the cop made his way back to the gate, two mugs in hand and a packet of biscuits dangling below. He took another swig of whisky from the flask and prepared himself for the next part of his mission. *Right Bill McCurdy, let`s get this over with and then home to a warm bed. Maybe Chrissie`ll be up for a wee bit, haven`t had any of that for a while....*

Chapter 21

The four men sat in silence for a few moments, contemplating the discovery they had just made. Terki was the first to speak.

`So what now, Commander? This is, indeed, a surprise, if his identity proves to be as Zemm has told us.`

Urvai didn`t reply immediately. He stared at the floor, still in shock at discovering that the sleeper on this distant, backward planet was none other than Vaki 1 Fensh, direct descendant of revered leader Mossala 4 Fensh, one-time Chief of their tribe, the Atra. He had been summarily executed following what was now known as the "Great Uprising", no trial, nothing, just gunned down on the spot where he was finally captured. His family had been hunted down, most of them eventually being discovered and imprisoned (or executed) but it was widely reported that his wife had escaped with one son, presumed to have left the planet. Since then there had been rumours, apparent sightings, the usual in such cases where a few still dare to hope. But now, it seemed, they had finally tracked at least one descendant down. Possibly...

`Yes, Terki, a surprise indeed, but let us not act too quickly. First of all, we do not know if it really is him or if he is, in fact, still alive. Secondly, he may not even know his true identity himself - after all these cycles his heritage may be unclear to him. Thirdly, many of our race have settled for new lives in remote civilisations - indeed, I would be lying to you if I said it had not crossed my own mind...` he paused for effect `...on more than one occasion. As I am sure it has crossed yours?`

The other three nodded in assent. Theirs was a lonely existence.

`And finally, we are already taking a risk by being here, given that there is another vessel in the vicinity. Imagine if we were to rescue him from his exile, only to be captured or, worse, killed by those on board. We would go down in history as those responsible for finally eliminating the Fensh bloodline! No, we play this game very carefully. Let us see how close we can get, find out if this drone does, indeed, contain the precious Sphere, then make a decision about our sleeper.`

`I agree` said Terki. Urvai continued

`But what a coup it would be if we recovered both Samian`s sphere and Mossala`s descendant. The Atra would, once again, be in the ascendancy. However, I suggest we say nothing to the others. Let us concentrate our efforts on recovering the Sphere, if that is what it is, without additional distraction. Maga, Retso, are you in agreement with this?`

`Absolutely` replied Retso. `Keep it to ourselves meantime.`

`Yes, indeed` added Maga. `I agree too.`

`Good!` said the Commander. `Now, Terki, can you assemble the crew in the main area and we will update them on matters regarding the Sphere.`

`Will do` said the first officer, turning to the console to summon them.

Ten minutes later Urvai sat in the ship`s main living space and regarded the fifteen men who made up the crew of the Zemm. Eighteen cycles in such close proximity had made him painfully familiar with their looks, habits and idiosyncrasies and he could easily detect the subtle change in them all, the registering of hope, no matter how faint, on their faces. None of them was getting any younger, that was for sure, but tonight they all looked as if a few cycles of tension had been lifted from them. They all knew that there had been a discovery of some sort, the ship and crew far too small to keep anything secret for long, and now that they were all assembled they knew that their Commander was going to make some sort of pronouncement. They stared at him expectantly, all except for Terki, Retso and Maga, who already knew what was coming. Then he spoke.

`My friends, my faithful and loyal crew, as you will no doubt be aware, a few days ago we received a transmission from an auto-locator somewhere on a planet in this sector. The signal was weak but it was being transmitted along a series of relay beacons, placed, we believe, by someone from our planet. Initially we did not know what the source of the signal was and, as you all know, there have been disappointments before.`

To a man, the crew nodded in agreement.

`However, as we came closer we were able to decode the signal and we now know that it is being generated by an old drop drone, registered to the traitor, Theasak. And we all know what he had on his vessel.`

He paused to let them digest this information, noting the change in their expressions. He continued

`Now, what we do not know is why this signal has suddenly started transmitting but it seems likely that the drone has been disturbed in some way, either accidentally or deliberately. And we also know that there is another vessel in the area.`

This time there was a collective intake of breath. He really had their attention now.

`So, here is the situation. We have discovered a drone that may, or may not, contain Samian`s sphere but, obviously we do not know for certain. We know that there is another vessel in the vicinity which poses a great risk. Our own ship is ageing and not in the best shape, unfortunately, whereas this other vessel will have the latest technology, including weaponry, I would imagine, and will be in excellent condition. Although it appears to be relatively small, we do not know how many crew it contains. We do not know why it is here but, personally, I do not believe for one minute that it is co-incidence. Then there is the question of the carefully placed relay beacons. It seems that there are some on our planet who have discovered something that we have missed in our long absence. It would appear that, using this relay system, they have managed to locate the drone and are, presumably, intending to recover it, along with its contents. We, however, have the element of surprise as they do not appear to be aware of our presence. Yet! And, of course, we are still a vessel of war. I think it is probable that this other vessel is here for reconnaissance purposes only, although it is likely that it will be armed.`

He paused again to let this sink in. The crew remained silent, waiting for him to continue.

`Now, I am afraid we have a dilemma. As you all know, we have been travelling for some considerable time.` Again the crew nodded in agreement. Like the ship, they were weary. `Our power source is considerably depleted and there has been no opportunity of late, nor is there likely to be any in the near future, to replenish it or, indeed, to service our craft, which is showing considerable signs of strain. We have a difficult choice to make. We can proceed and try to recover the drone, in the hope that its contents prove to be what we are seeking. But this may involve us in a firefight with this other vessel, whose technology will undoubtedly be superior to ours. The end result may be that, if we manage to recover the Sphere, we may not have sufficient power remaining to return to the conduit, far less to Loh.`

`What about this other vessel?` asked one of the crew, Gelnik 7 Gerrikla. `Is there a possibility that either we can commandeer it for our own use or utilise its power source for Zemm?`

Maga answered the question. `As to the energy source, yes, it is highly likely that it is similar enough to ours to be of use. As to the possibility of taking it by force...` he shrugged and looked back at Urvai.

`Well, that is the question. Our scans show that the vessel was, at one point, unoccupied, meaning that the crew are probably on the planet. If this were the case then we would have a chance. But if they were on board, with better sensors, superior weapons and stronger shielding, then, my friends, I cannot predict the outcome.`

The weapons officer, Sulyen 3 Sulat, stood up. For a Lohei, especially of Atra blood, he was short, but broad and muscle-bound, with close-cropped greying hair and a prominent scar across his forehead. His voice, belying his physique, was somewhat high-pitched, although it commanded attention as he spoke.

`Commander Goffella. I have followed you, without question, throughout our entire voyage. Wherever you lead us, I will be there, to the end, and I think I speak for the entire crew. We cannot give up now. Better to die here, fighting for what we believe in than drifting into our dotage, through space, wondering what might have been.`

The rest of the crew stood up and shouted in agreement. There was no doubt now in Urvai`s mind. He smiled and stood up with the rest of them, raising his fist in salute. Then, once they were all seated again, the Commander turned to Maga, his engineer, and asked

`How long until we reach this planet?`

`Best estimate, just under a day at current speed. Assuming the power source holds up. Will we proceed as planned?`

Urvai didn`t speak immediately. Despite the wholehearted support and the enthusiasm of his crew, he knew they were now playing an extremely dangerous game, with so much just within their grasp yet with so little resources left to take advantage of it. Even now, they would struggle to return to the conduit - what purpose would be served by retrieving the sphere, let alone one of the few left alive who could utilise it if they ended up adrift in some remote corner of the galaxy? That was, of course, assuming that Fensh was actually there and wanted to be retrieved in the first place. What exactly was he doing here – was he simply hiding in the safety of this remote corner of space, did he not wish to be discovered at all, or did he, in fact, know that this was where the Sphere had been placed? He wished he had more answers. He replied to the engineer`s question.

`Yes, Maga. We will continue on our present course and speed. Turn off any unnecessary systems to preserve energy, if you haven`t already done so. Reduce climatic control to eighty parts per hundred – our comfort is a small sacrifice to make. Terki, can you check if there is another planet in this system where we may be able to remain concealed? If we can get closer and observe this other vessel, they might actually retrieve the drone for us and save us a bit of power and effort. As I said, we still have the element of surprise which might yet allow us to overcome them and utilise their power source. Let us be optimistic, my friends, I do not believe we are here by chance and fortune may yet favour us. Now return to your duties, or rest if you are able, and we will see what unfolds.`

Chapter 22

Archie woke about 4.00a.m. with moonlight streaming in the bedroom window – he felt completely drained of energy, he was disorientated, his body ached, his head hurt and...He suddenly realised that there was a warm body pressed against his, head resting in the crook of his arm and a hand entwined in the hairs of his chest. Khara, the strange alien woman. Then, as with other recent but considerably less pleasurable memories, it all came flooding back.

He couldn`t say if it had been the relief of their escape, the pent-up frustrations of the last few weeks or just sheer animal lust, but from the moment they had entered his house the physical attraction between them had been overwhelming. They had behaved almost like animals and he was sure there were scratches on his back and legs. His lips felt bruised, his thighs ached, he felt totally drained but he had never had sex like it in his entire life. He moved slightly in an attempt to relieve the pain in his lower back (where he had been kicked by Blok`s henchman) and Khara stirred. The same vague, intoxicating aroma emanated from her, although stronger than before, reminding him of the fresh, mountain air at the top of Ben Lomond mixed with underlying, powerful musky overtones and it was both refreshing and arousing – he briefly wondered if it was some type of perfume or just her own unique body smell. As he stared up at the moonlit ceiling, he felt that his brain was in danger of meltdown yet again, so much had happened in the last twenty four hours. He tried to shut out the pervasive images from the derelict farm but it was impossible - the nail gun, the blowtorch, Blok`s threats...then, to cap it all, he remembered that he had a funeral to attend the next day; his daughter`s. His body tensed and, as if sensing it, Khara spoke in a sleepy voice

`What is troubling you, Archieblue?`

She gently stroked the hairs on his chest.

`Nothing. Everything. I don`t know. I don`t seem to know shit these days. I`m watching my daughter being buried tomorrow, well, cremated, I didn`t even know I had her until a couple of weeks ago. Christ, Khara, we could have been dead by now too! And in a much worse way, believe me. Blok and those animals he associates with are not known for being merciful. They would have taken great pleasure in hurting us, you especially, while I was made to watch. After losing...` his voice tailed off. `After losing Lucinda, I don`t want to...aw shit, never mind, nothing.`

He turned his back on her, lost in his despair and confusion.

She lay silent for a few minutes, then turned and put her arm round him, pulling her soft, warm body against his back.

`Archieblue, you must put last night out of your mind. We are safe. We survived. The threat will be gone, as long as your associates dealt with those...` again she struggled for a word `those vermin. You must not let events that never happened command your feelings.`

`But it`s not just that, Khara,` he mumbled. `Its all the other stuff that`s happened too. Three weeks ago, I was a normal, reasonably happy cop, doing my job, living my life. Aye, sure, sometimes it felt like I was pissing in the wind, well...you know, wasting my time, but I was fine, just getting on. Now, here I am, found and lost a daughter, killed a man, nearly got tortured to death, then, well, now...` he shook his head.

`Now what, Archieblue?`

He turned back to face her. The moonlight seemed to form a halo round her black hair and a shiver ran down his spine as he wondered just what he had got himself in to with this strange, alien woman. He paused before he spoke, then saw her eyebrows raise slightly as if prompting him to continue.

`Okay, cards on the table. Now, I meet you and, hey, guess what, I like you. Yeah, that`s right. You. A fucking alien. From a galaxy far, far away. Here`s me, a poor, defenceless earthling, my life`s a mess and suddenly I fall for some female from another planet. Just great, eh! In to the bargain, I almost get you killed – slowly and painfully. I`m a real fucking catch, me! The sooner you get away from this place, with your precious drone, the better.`

In the glimmer of the moonlight he could see the dark pools that were her eyes as she silently gazed at him. She said, softly

`We have a saying on Loh, roughly translated it means "hold the beam of Kii" our sun. I suppose you would say, hold the brightest moments, or live for the pleasure of the moment. Life passes us quickly, Archieblue, no matter what planet we come from, and we do not know what surprises, good or bad, it may hold. Can you not live for the moment, hold this time, here, now, in your hand and consider it precious and wonderful? Forget last night. It is past. This is where we are now. Who knows what will happen tomorrow? Do not concern yourself. Tonight, you and I are here, together. It may be the last time – do not waste it.`

Archie remained silent but, slowly, her hand strayed downwards, grasping him and, despite himself, he gasped and his body responded.

`Do you remember the first time we met, at the drone, when I was unfamiliar with your species, when I tried to command your feelings?`

`Yeah, at Erskine. I was absolutely petrified at first. Then...` The erotic memory returned. In the moonlight he saw her smile.

Oh...my...God...

***

Archie woke to find that the moonlight had been replaced with beautiful early morning sunlight. He lifted his watch and, to his surprise, discovered that it was just before 8.00 a.m. - given the events of the previous evening and the activities of the night he would have expected to have slept until about midday. Not only that, he felt great. All the pain, the stiffness, the tension, all gone – even the disturbing memories had been subdued. Had she done something else to him, other than...well, he didn`t really care. He felt brand-new. He was also pleasantly surprised to discover that aliens were capable of snoring just as efficiently as humans, as Khara was lying on her back, arms behind her head, mouth wide open, snorting and snuffling like a pig searching for truffles! He gazed at her, thinking she almost looked human, then smiled at his thought. Her black hair was tousled and spread over the pillow, she was still giving off the intoxicating aroma, she was still an alien! He lay on his back, smiled again and shook his head, suddenly realising it seemed a while since he had smiled so much. After a contemplative minute or two he slid out of bed, retrieved his boxers from the floor at the end of the bed and headed downstairs to the kitchen, where a rummage in the freezer uncovered some frozen croissants to go with the scrambled eggs he was preparing. Fortunately he always had a few bottles of fresh orange juice in the fridge and he had just filled the cafetiere with fresh coffee when his land-line phone started to ring. He wondered who was calling him using this method then he remembered that he had switched off his mobile to prevent any unwanted interruptions to the night`s proceedings. He grabbed it quickly before it woke Khara and answered with a quiet `Hello!`

The reply was not at all what he expected. A gruff voice started singing, not particularly tunefully, but he recognised the melody and corrupted lyrics of his favourite ELO song.

`Hey Hey, Archie Blue, we`re so glad to be with you...`

`Cam?`

`Sorry Boss, couldn`t resist it.`

`Everything okay, I take it?`

`Okay? You have got tae be jokin`, man! Oh-fuckin`-kay! Blok, or Mr Gregor Czarneki, as he is now officially known tae us, confessed to just aboot every crime in the last three years. There`s every chance he`ll be headin` back East as it seems he has a record in both Poland and Bulgaria. Child traffickin`, prostitution, drugs, you name it, he`s been involved up tae his fuckin` armpits. Makes oor home grown specimens look like amateurs! Plus we`ve had five raids over the course o` the night. Got aboot a dozen other major suspects in custody, includin` Ralston and McLintock. Oh, and wait `til you hear the icing on the cake...!`

`Go on`

`Edwin Big Mouth McCourt...!`

`You`re joking? You`ve got him as well?`

`No, I am not joking, Boss. Ralston nailed him for a whole raft o` naughty things, seems the two of them go way back, to the days o` Callum Dillon. We`ve got him in custody too but we`ve no` found anything yet. Searched his big, fancy hoose, top to toe, clean as a whistle, he`s obviously a clever bugger! Just a matter of time though, I`m convinced the big bastard is as guilty as sin. Denies it all, of course, but Ralston won`t stop talkin` and there`s no doubt there`s a lot o` people going away for a long, long time. The Procurator Fiscal`s office are creamin` themselves, think they`ll have tae recruit more staff! It is un-be-fuckin`-lievable! The only one missing is Kevin King. Strange, I wis sure he was in big wi` them too, but there`s no sign o` him. Maybe he`d outlived his sell-by date. Who knows wi` that band o` scum.`

Cam paused for a second to catch his breath as Archie`s heart seemed to skip a beat. What if they talked about King`s disappearance too? They obviously knew what had happened, it just needed an inquisitive interrogating officer to ask the right questions and, well...

Fortunately Cam quickly interrupted his thoughts.

`But Boss, seriously, what in God`s name went on last night? Two o` Blok`s men are in high dependency, nearly killed each other, it seems. And Blok`s nose will never be the same, he`s lost most o` his front teeth and he`s got a shattered knee in tae the bargain. And Tam McLintock? Guy cannae speak coherently, keeps flappin` his arms around his heid an` goin` on aboot being bitten, or stung, they`re doin` psychiatric assessment this mornin` and think he`ll probably be sectioned. The guy`s fallen apart. And Ralston`s no` much better either, just won`t stop blabberin` on, but he keeps shiverin` an` the Doc who examined him says he`s showing all the signs o` burn trauma, although there`s no` a mark on him. There wis a gas blowtorch burnin` when we got there, don`t know the significance o` it though, but hopefully we`ll get tae the bottom o` it.`

Archie knew the significance all too well, but he said nothing. Cam paused for breath again, interrupting the near-incessant flow of words.

`An` you know DS Sabrina Wilson, the tall one wi` the straight dark hair? Mind we used to kid on that if you gave her pointy ears she`d look like a Vulcan! Works oot o` the East End?`

`Aye, I know who she is, met her a few times at courses. She`s a good cop.`

`Aye, well, she came in durin` the interview, was one o` the arrestin` officers. Ralston took one look at her and started screamin` blue murder, begging her tae stop. I almost felt sorry for him, he was on his knees, couldn`ae stop shakin`. Just kept sobbing, "stop, stop, please.." I have to say, she wasn`ae much better – should`ve seen her face! Shame really, no` the effect she`d want tae have on blokes, good or bad!`

He actually stopped speaking for a few seconds. Then the inevitable question came.

`So, are you gonnae tell me just whit the fuck this is all aboot, Boss?`

Archie chose his words carefully – he had been prepared for it.

`Cam, I`ve known you a long time. I count you as my closest friend and you know me, you know I`m straight. So I`m asking you to trust me on this one. I absolutely promise you I never laid a finger on any of these guys, although I was there. But I really just can`t tell you what happened. If I could I would. Please, Cam, please don`t push me on this. Just put in your report that they had a massive argument amongst themselves, something like that. They`re not going to tell you anything different, I can pretty much guarantee that.`

Cam was obviously looking for more of an explanation than this but he wasn`t going to let the mystery spoil the moment.

`Aye, well, I suppose that`ll have to do - cannae force you to talk if you don`t want to, eh? Fair enough, Boss. I`ll trust you, thousands wouldn`t! Still, something bloody strange happened, oot there, maybe they got religion or somethin`. I mean, I know they`re the scum o` the earth but, well, fuck me, they`re in some state. It`s kinda scary, you know whit I mean? Anyway, I need to get back and start on the paperwork for this lot, of which there will be a mountain! Comin` in tae help me or are you still plannin` on takin` the day aff?`

`No, sorry Cam, I won`t be in, got things to do, I`m afraid. Anyway, this time was booked off ages ago, by rights I should have been down in the Lakes doing a bit of climbing. And downing a few good ales.`

He suddenly remembered the message from Gordon Whiteford.

`Oh, and by the way, Cam. I forgot to say, it`s the funeral tomorrow. I`ll not be in then either.`

`Aw, shit, Archie. I didn`ae know, Whiteford never said when I phoned him – Christ, I`m really sorry. Whit time is it and where?`

`Listen, mate, you don`t need to come, You`ll be up to your eyeballs in it anyway, last thing you need is a funeral for a wee...` he hesitated `a wee drug addict you never even knew.`

`Archie, I don`t care whit she may have been but she wis your daughter. I`ll be there, no matter whit.`

Archie paused – he could feel a lump rising in his throat

`Fair enough, Cam, and I really appreciate it. It`s at the Woodside Crematorium, Paisley, three p.m. tomorrow. Look, I`ll make my own way and just see you there, I`ll not be much company for anybody. Best I just keep myself to myself.`

`No worries, Boss, I`ll be there.`

`So, anyway, back to the matter in hand. Cam, you need to make this count for you – keep my name out of it, it`s got nothing to do with me. You make sure you get all the credit, there`s a very good chance there`ll be promotion in it, with most of the West of Scotland`s bad boys going down for a long spell!`

`Aye, well, you never know. First stop`ll be Porsche Glasgow to get myself one like yours...!`

`Aye! Quite right!` laughed Archie `You deserve it! But you`d have to sneak it past Tracey! One thing I`ve learned recently though, life`s too bloody short, that`s for sure! Cheers, mate, I really appreciate all you`re doing.`

`Ah, you`re welcome Archie. Have a good day. Take it easy, eh?`

Archie finished preparing the breakfast then took it up to Khara. She was still sleeping and he shook her gently to wake her. Her eyes opened and, for the first time, he was aware of her pupils contracting in the bright morning light. She smiled lazily up at him.

`What is this, Archieblue? Do you eat your food in bed?`

`Well, sometimes, just as a wee treat. Breakfast in bed, we call it.`

`And what if I spill anything?`

`Well, I suppose the bed will get a bit wet and sticky.` he replied.

`That is all right then, as I think the bed is a bit wet and sticky already.` she said, sitting up, taking the tray and tucking in to the scrambled egg and hot buttered croissant. Archie searched her face for a trace of sarcasm but there was none. He briefly thought about asking her if she had done something to his mind that would account for his feeling of well-being, but decided against it. What was it she had said - "Hold the beam of Kii" He decided that it sounded like good advice, climbed in to bed beside her and wolfed down his own breakfast. Apart from anything else, she had given him a decidedly healthy appetite!

***

Breakfast over, Archie had a shave followed by a quick shower. Khara was in the bathroom when the land line phone rang again - he still hadn`t turned on his mobile. Maybe he wouldn`t!

`Boss. Cam here.` his tone was a bit more subdued this time.

`What`s up, Cam?`

Bad news. We`ve got a body. Doon at Erskine.`

Shit!

Chapter 23

Cam related the story. Andy Carson, the site manager, had arrived at the usual time to see if work on the site was able to resume - obviously news of McCourt`s arrest hadn`t yet filtered down as his demise would be likely to put the whole future of the development on hold, unless there were other directors involved in HomeFree who could bale the Company out. It was likely, though, that the finances of any business colleagues would also come under intense scrutiny, given McCourt`s newly alleged criminal dealings. For some undefined reason Carson had, in his own words "gone round the back of the Portakabin for a minute," and had noticed something lying on the ground a short way off. He had gone to investigate and discovered the body of a man, he reckoned to be in his sixties, face down in the mud. Immediately he had called the uniformed cops over and it was now officially a crime scene.

`Any ideas who it is yet?` asked Archie. This development could seriously interfere with his own plans.

`Aye, surprisingly enough we do. D`ye know o` a journalist, works wi` the Sun, called Bill McCurdy? Or used to, I should say...`

`Not personally, but I`ve heard of him. Has he not picked up on a few things over the years? We wondered if he was being tipped off. Wee nuisance of a man?`

`Aye, that`s the one, he`s been roon` the block a few times, a good old-fashioned, hard-drinking hack. Quite well respected in his day, apparently, before the booze got the upper hand. Anyway, we found him a` kitted oot with wire-cutters, camera, torch, hip flask `n` fags! Reckon he wis after a story, maybe someone tipped him aff again aboot the bomb thing. Either that or he just got lucky – well, no` really, I suppose. Anyway, apparently he`d turned up earlier in the day askin` questions, probably giving the location the once-over, planning tae come back later. We found a neat wee hole cut in the security fence doon at the bottom end of the site, so obviously that`s how he got past the guys at the main gate. Seems he walked along the fields doon by the river then cut back up tae the perimeter. Then we found his driver.`

`His driver?`

`Aye. Apparently McCurdy, being a well established alky, had lost his licence a good few years ago and hasn`ae driven since. Had a wee guy called Shug McHugh drive him aboot. We found him sound asleep in his car round Newshot Drive - said McCurdy had asked him to wait for him and he`d be back about three a.m. Seems he never did come back and McHugh fell asleep waiting.`

`Did this McHugh guy know what McCurdy was up to?`

`Says not. Apparently it wasn`ae unusual for McCurdy to go on night trips lookin` for that last big story. The wee guy wis really broken up when we told him McCurdy was dead. We`ve got him in for questioning but I reckon he`s straight as a die. No form, retired butcher, widower wi` no family, nice enough wee man. Just totally devastated. I`ve got a couple of uniforms round at McCurdy`s house as we speak, breakin` the bad news.`

`Never much fun, that` Archie briefly recalled the last, excruciatingly painful time he had broken bad news. He sighed.

`Still, got to be done. So, any ideas what happened?`

`The SOCO`s are there but there`s no injuries, no wounds,

nothin`. Yer pal, the good Doctor Clayton, is on his way and I`ll keep you posted - unless you want tae come along just for fun...?`

Archie remembered the last encounter between Cam and the Pathologist, the banter, the laughs, now it was all just painful memories and the thought of a social evening with Sam Clayton and a bottle of good malt whisky was something he just couldn`t contemplate. The man had carried out the post-mortem on his daughter after all...

Christ, I`ve not even asked what the result was...

`You still there, Boss?`

`Aye, sorry Cam, just thinking. No, I`ll not come down just now, Like I said earlier technically I`m still on leave. You handle it, let me know if anything comes up, yeah?`

`You know, you`re bein` awfy mysterious these days, Boss. You`re usually right in there when a body turns up...aw, shit, I`m sorry, Boss, I didn`t mean...`

Archie interrupted. `Listen, don`t worry, Cam. You can`t go through life treading on eggshells just because of my situation. Anyway, at the moment it doesn`t sound like a murder. Let`s wait and see, eh? If anything changes let me know. You know where I am.`

There was a pause.

`By any chance have you got a woman there wi` you, Boss?`

`Naw, don`t be daft, Cam, just need a wee break, that`s all. It`s been a difficult time.`

`Aye, heard it! You sly dog. You have, I bet you have. Good on you. It`s aboot bloody time! So who is she? Anyone I know? Here, it`s no that pal o` Tracey`s that we introduced you to, whit`s her name...Yvonne? She wis awright, wis she no`?`

Archie smiled wryly – Yvonne was most certainly not his definition of "awright", although he would never have said so to Cam.

`Leave it Cam, no-one here but me. If there was, you`d be the first to know.`

`Aye, okay Boss. Fair enough, none of my business. Can I ask you a wee favour though?`

`What`s that?`

Turn your effin` mobile back on...`

***

Khara came downstairs, wearing one of Archie`s shirts and a pair of pale pink striped briefs, another one of his "Next" purchases.

`Is everything all right?` she asked., seeing the expression on his face. Archie shook his head.

`I don`t really know. Unfortunately, they`ve found a body down at the site in Erskine. Seems its a reporter from a newspaper who was sniffing about looking for a story. Don`t know what happened yet but it does seem to be a wee bit of a co-incidence. But I suppose it could just as easily be be natural causes, the guy was an alcoholic.`

Khara sat down on the couch beside him.

`Archieblue, do you remember I said that there may be members of the Atra who might also be looking for this weapon?`

`Yes.` He paused and considered her comment, then frowned at her.

`You`re surely not suggesting that Bill McCurdy was from your planet too? Naw, he`s just an old newspaper guy looking for a good story.`

`Do not be stupid, Archieblue. I did not mean him. I meant maybe he was...`

`No way!` Archie interjected. `You`re suggesting he was killed by an alien? Christ, I hope not. That`s all we need, as if we didn`t have enough bloody killers of our own.`

That includes me, I suppose...

`Archieblue, do not become so agitated. I am only suggesting it but it is a possibility. Obviously the signal that I responded to could have been picked up by someone else from my planet. I do not believe that there are any other craft in this vicinity but there is another possibility.` She looked concerned.

`And what possibility might that be?`

`Well, there have been instances where the Atra have placed faction members on planets where they believed the weapon may have been concealed, just in case it was ever found.` She thought for a second. `I suppose you would call them "sleepers". They would live as humans in this case, or whatever species in which they were placed, integrating into society, watching, waiting for some sign and then they would contact others of their persuasion if the device was found. It could be some time before the others received the message but they would come, believe me. This weapon is well worth searching for.`

Archie wasn`t liking the sound of this at all.

`So, do you think there is a "sleeper" here?`

`Obviously I cannot say with any certainty, Archieblue. But, if there is, I think we will find out sooner rather than later, now that you have dug up the drone.`

They spent the next half hour or so discussing Khara`s options for the recovery of the weapon. Archie stopped to brew some fresh coffee (which Khara seemed to have developed a liking for) and, when he brought back the two steaming mugs, he said

`Right, I`ve been thinking about how we explain the disappearance of this bomb...well, drone thing! And I`ve had an idea. A bit crazy perhaps, a bit of a long shot maybe, but it`s an idea, at least.`

`Go on Archieblue, an idea would be good.`

`Well, as yet no-one knows what this thing is, that it has come from another planet, galaxy, whatever. Right? With the possible exception of a sleeper, if there is one, but at this stage, they don`t figure in the equation.`

`That is correct.`

`Well, if you took the drone, and whatever it contains, away, obviously some very difficult questions would be asked. But, how about if I were to write an anonymous letter, claiming to be from some crazy student group, maybe Physicists or Astronomers or something, or maybe from anti-nuclear campaigners even. CND was a big thing a while back, pretty active by all accounts.`

She interrupted. `CND?`

`Oh, Campaign for Nuclear Disarmament. They were very much against the possession and use of nuclear weapons. Anyway, I could say that the whole thing was an elaborate hoax, that the drone had been constructed years ago and buried as part of some kind of protest, or something, to make a political point, maybe - I`m just making this up as I go along, remember! Now that it has been discovered and seems to be giving rise to a whole lot of problems, the former students, all grown up to become respectable and responsible adults, of course, have decided to reclaim it and anonymously admit to their guilt. They could say that they never realised how much trouble it would cause, that they were very sorry. They could even suggest making an anonymous donation to some charity or something, as recompense. They would argue that they took it back to prevent anyone getting into trouble on their behalf.`

Khara thought about this.

`But would students in your world do such a thing, do you suppose?`

Archie had seen many odd things that students had got up to over the years. He vaguely recalled a bed going up Ben Lomond once...

`Possibly...probably...who knows? Some of these boffin types have pretty weird ideas, might just be the kind of daft thing a bunch of them would do after a night down the Students` Union, especially if they were anti-nuclear protestors. But, apart from anything else, it would give the Police a "get out of jail free" card.`

`A what?`

`A "get out..." Oh, never mind, it`s part of a silly game we have called Monopoly. Maybe I`ll teach you it sometime! Anyway, it would give the Police an excuse to stop looking and wasting resources on something that turned out to be an elaborate prank. Sure, some cops may end up searching for the perpetrators, but they`re never going to pin it on anyone and the whole thing will just fade quietly away. Assuming, of course, that we don`t have a murder on our hands as well. That could really complicate things.`

They sipped their coffee in silence for a bit, then Khara said

`Your idea does sound rather crazy, Acrhieblue. But sometimes it is the crazy idea that works.`

`Yep, sometimes the silly explanations are the most believable. What was it Sherlock Holmes said? "Once you eliminate the impossible, only the improbable, however unlikely, remains."`

`And who, exactly, is Sherlock Holmes?`

Archie chuckled. `Aye, I forget that there`s a lot you don`t know. He`s a well known fictional Victorian detective. Maybe you`d like the books...anyway, just think about it. None of us wants to believe that it`s an unexploded bomb or, worse, some kind of chemical, biological or even nuclear weapon. No-one would believe it was of alien origin – that`s the impossible bit, of course, as far as everyone else is concerned - and, if anyone suggested it, they would either be classed as nuts or there would be mass panic. A simple, silly prank keeps everyone happy – that`s the improbable bit, isn`t it? Listen, I`m going to type something up, see how it looks on paper. I presume you have a method of getting this thing up to your ship?`

`Of course. You may have noticed some equipment in the docking bay of my ship. There is a cargo shuttle capable of lifting items such as the drone - it is much easier than you may imagine.`

Archie`s phone rang. He had bowed to Cam`s request and switched his mobile back on and, as he lifted the handset he saw that it was the good Dr Clayton. He also noticed the time and was surprised to see how quickly it seemed to be passing. It was well past lunchtime.

`Hello Sam. How`s things?`

`Archie, my boy. Simply grand, simply grand. And you?

Haven`t seen you for a wee whiley, that last sojourn in the seedy Seedhill road I believe`. He guffawed. `We must get together soon and have that wee malt session. I miss your enthusiasm. And your stamina! Anyway. Down to business. Mr McCurdy.`

`Aye, Sam. The body at Erskine.`

`Now, your pet Rottweiler, Cam, told me that you`re not handling the case - some nonsense about being on holiday! That`s why I didn`t phone you about the poor wee lassie in Paisley, by the way, it wasn`t that important, but I filled your good sergeant in, of course.`

Archie winced at the Pathologist`s casual mention of his daughter. Sam continued

`However, in cases such as that of the late Mr McCurdy I know you all too well, my boy, so you`re my first call, just to keep you apprised of the situation! Don`t worry, I`ll get in touch with the good Sergeant in due course. I had nothing on this morning so I had the deceased gent`s body whisked up to my table with almost indecent haste and decided to get on with the post mortem just to pass the time.`

Archie could think of many better ways to pass the time than cutting open a corpse; plus it sounded like the Pathologist wasn`t going to be the bearer of good news.

`Any surprises then?` he asked hesitantly.

`Oh yes. Absolutely!` The doctor paused for effect – Archie had often thought he should have been an actor! But his heart sank. Reluctantly he asked

`And?`

`Well, the biggest surprise was that Mr McCurdy was alive at all. When I cut open his chest cavity and penetrated the lungs, I`m sure a cloud of cigarette smoke wafted across the mortuary. The man was a walking disaster. Advanced cirrhosis, some small malignant-looking tumours on the lungs, probably diabetic, definitely alcoholic. Arteries furred up to buggery. Should have been dead about ten years ago, in my ever so humble opinion! He was only fifty-seven, you know. Looked about seventy!`

`The guy who found him had put him in his sixties, right enough. And cause of death?`

`What gets us all, Archie, what gets us all. He died of heart failure. Brought on by a massive heart attack. Not a hint of injury, nothing. Poor bugger just keeled over in the mud. Best way to go, I reckon. Well, maybe not in the mud...`

Archie breathed a silent sigh of relief.

`Oh well, that lets the boys off the hook, now that we know it`s not a murder. Listen, Sam, I`ll phone Cam and let him know. He`ll be happy about the news. Been an interesting few days, to say the least!`

`Yes, so I believe, First of all you turn up some mysterious bomb, which explains the unfortunate McCurdy`s presence in the first place, I imagine, and now word`s leaking out about a veritable plethora of arrests, seems that half of the West of Scotland`s criminals are in custody. Well done you!`

Archie wondered how he had found out about the bomb. Someone must have opened their mouth – first McCurdy and now Sam. Who else? He decided not to ask the Doctor how he knew.

`Nothing to do with me, Sam. All Cam`s work. I`m hoping there might be a step up the ladder for him after this.`

`Oh, God help us all, Archie, God help us all!` the Doctor guffawed again. Archie couldn`t help grinning.

`Listen Sam, I really appreciate you letting me know the result. We`ll get together soon and sample a few, okay?`

`I`ll hold you to that, Inspector Blue. Oh, there was just one, rather odd, thing. Nothing really, just, you know, odd.`

This post-script was typical of the Pathologist`s style.

`Yes?`

`It was his face. Usually, with a heart attack of this nature you go down like a pack of cards. No time to register anything. But this poor chappie`s face was locked in an expression of absolute terror. As I said, probably meaningless. But it almost looked like he`d been scared to death...`

They said their goodbyes and Archie went back to Khara with a troubled mind. He related the conversation and she looked at him, deep concern in her eyes.

`I do not like the sound of this. As you can probably imagine, it would not be difficult for one of my race to cause such fear that someone with a weak heart would react in this way. This is of great concern, Archieblue. We must act tonight and recover this weapon before anything further transpires. I now fear that someone else is very much aware of the drone`s presence.`

`Is there no way of finding out who it could be. I mean, is there a database or anything that you can access. Pictures? Do you have a list of people who have left your planet?`

`I am afraid that it would not be of any use. The so called sleeper is likely to have been here for many years and integrated into your society. They would have great powers of persuasion, as you may guess. It is also likely that they will hold a position of power. A politician, maybe, military chief, something of that sort. The only thing is that I would probably recognise them as one of my own. But I would have to see them first and that is extremely unlikely.`

`But how would you recognise them?`

`Well, when you first saw me, did you think I looked different in any way?`

`Well, yes, I suppose I did, a bit. But that was partly the way you were dressed. Also, you spoke in your own language.`

`Indeed. And now? Could you honestly say that I look exactly like a human female?`

`That`s hard to answer, Khara. We humans are such a diverse species. But I know what you mean. With all respect, you are a bit...well, different, I suppose.`

`Yes. Of course I am different. It is much more obvious for me, as I recognise things that you do not. How my race look at one another. The way we speak your language. Our eyes. They are much darker than those of your race. Or at least those of you with fair skin. Those with dark skin have very dark eyes, much like ours, but on our planet everyone has skin like mine, very pale. We do not have those curious little spots that you have on your face. No one on my planet has hair your colour.` she reached out and ran her hand through his short, sandy red hair. His freckles had never been referred to as "curious little spots".

`So, if you saw this person who, I suppose, could be male or female, then you would recognise them as your species?`

`It is probable that I would. But they would be likely to be a male, the Atra treat woman as somewhat inferior.`

`Not unknown here, either.` said Archie. `In fact, the police used to be notorious for it.`

They both fell silent, neither unable to think of anything useful to offer. Then Archie spoke.

`How would they know where the drone was though? It could have been anywhere on the planet. If Bill McCurdy did meet this, em...alien, well, this drone thing was only discovered on Friday. How would they know to come here?`

Khara considered this.

`It is possible that they may have managed to make some kind of estimate from the available information. After all, we had an idea that the drone was on your planet and, had the locating signal not activated, then I would have made the calculation once I had arrived. However, the signal guided me here without that being necessary. I think it is probable that the sleeper had been in this country all along. There are many myths and stories surrounding this weapon and the Atra will probably have placed sleepers on any planets mentioned in these tales. Also, it would be easier to rise to prominence in a small, prosperous country such as yours, allowing them opportunities to gather information such as this – if there is a sleeper here, I am certain he will know exactly what we have found and where.`

This was becoming increasingly complicated and Archie was struggling to get his head round it all.

`Okay Khara, I`m not looking for a discussion or an opinion. Just an answer. Do you believe there is a sleeper here?`

`Yes.`

`Do you think he knows about the drone?`

`Yes. Most definitely.`

`Do you think he is responsible, either deliberately or acccidentally, for McCurdy`s, death?`

`Yes.`

`Do you think he will try and retrieve the weapon?`

`Again, most definitely.`

`Then we need to hurry.`

`Yes, indeed!`

Chapter 24

Archie phoned Cam with the news about Bill McCurdy`s cause of death. He omitted the part about the expression on his face. *Best to keep that to myself.* Cam was obviously relieved that it wasn`t a murder he had to investigate, just an unfortunate reporter whose time happened to be up while he was doing a bit of "fishing". However, he tried a bit more fishing of his own about Archie`s domestic situation but he gave nothing away. What could he say? "Right enough, Cam, I`ve met a really hot girl, she`s from another planet." He could just see Cam`s face disintegrating into helpless mirth...

He finished the call and switched on his computer. Having loaded "Word" he started to compose what he hoped would be a believable letter of admission. It was difficult as, when writing any sort of report, he tended to lapse into "police speak", which could be an instant giveaway. Eventually, after a few aborted attempts, he came up with something that he thought should do the job.

To Whom It May Concern

I am writing on behalf of a group of friends, all former students of Physics and Advanced Sciences at a University that I will not specify. I had hoped that I would never have to give the following account but recent events have dictated otherwise.

Some number of years ago, you will recall that there was a climate, especially at academic centres, of Anti-Nuclear feeling, much of it centring on the Faslane Peace Camp. We were part of that movement and, in what can now only be described as a moment of alcohol-driven insanity, we decided to construct a close replica of the particular type of Nuclear Missile held in the UK arsenal at that time. You may well ask why, as I have done over the years. I think we intended to use it as a protest of some sort but it was large, unwieldy and, alas, very authentic looking. There is peculiar writing engraved on the side, a type of `runic` script that one of our learned number came up with. Loosely translated it said, as I recall "Abandon all hope, anyone who uses such weaponry. It will be the demise of our *species." All very pretentious stuff!*

Eventually, after much debate, we decided to dispose of it and, once again after yet another student drinking session (one of many, I regret to say), we decided to bury it in a location where we believed it would not be found until well after our own lifetimes. One of our number knew the area around Erskine and we felt that our "missile" would remain undetected in that location. We intended it to be a "time capsule" and we all placed in it our own selection of memorabilia that we believed reflected the times that we lived in. However, it also contained some highly personal information, as well as our identities that, quite frankly, could now prove to be extremely damaging to some of us.

Of course, back then we could not have foreseen the development of that area and, even now, I would personally question the building of houses in what I believe to be a flood plain. Nonetheless, our "missile" has been discovered and is obviously causing alarm and concern, something we never intended.

By the time you receive this communication, we will have recovered the fake missile. You may well wonder how this was accomplished but I can assure you that there are some prominent, influential and highly intelligent minds at work here so please do not feel too concerned that you failed to prevent its disappearance!

We all very much regret our actions - it was a foolish, student prank that we believed we had "got away with" but I am always surprised at how one`s past can, most unexpectedly, return to give one grief. As I have said, the fake missile is entirely harmless - its contents, on the other hand, are very much not so!

On behalf of the whole group I apologise wholeheartedly for our actions and very much regret the inconvenience that this has undoubtedly caused. I hope you can forgive our actions and put it down simply to the foolishness of youth.

Yours sincerely,

The Ringleader of a band of twelve.

Archie read the letter a couple of times, correcting a few typo errors and changing some of the grammar. He had decided to omit any offer offer of a charitable donation, feeling that it would just complicate matters. Then he pressed “print” to see how it looked on a real page. It looked fine - anyway, it was the best plan he could come up with.

He went into the drawer of his desk and removed fresh, unopened packs of A4 paper and envelopes. He pulled on a set of forensic gloves he had brought with him and, very carefully, removed a few sheets of paper from the centre of the ream, placing them on the printer tray. He then took an envelope from the pack and addressed it to “The senior officer in charge” at Mill Street, Paisley Police HQ. *Best not to quote names, might be a bit suspicious*. He re-printed the letter on the fresh paper and, still wearing the forensic gloves, folded it and placed it in the envelope, then put a first class stamp on it. He put the envelope in a forensic bag and folded it over. Hopefully it could never be traced back to him in the unlikely event that anyone looked more closely into the matter.

He went downstairs with the bag and into the lounge. Khara was sitting on the floor staring at the large plasma screen high definition television. He held the copy out towards her but she ignored him.

`Right, Khara, that`s the letter done, here, have a read and see what you think...Khara, what is it? What`s wrong?`

He knelt behind her and put his hands on her shoulders. She kept gazing at the television and Archie looked to see what was holding her attention.

`That is him.` she said, in a surprisingly matter-of-fact way. `That is the man from my planet.`

No fucking way!

Chapter 25

By now, the apprehension of the majority of Glasgow and the West of Scotland`s top criminals was headline news. Arrests on this scale were unprecedented, especially as they were mostly the result of the confessions of one man, until then relatively unknown by the public – Gregor Czarneki. Archie knew that, once imprisoned (as he surely would be) he would probably spend his entire term in solitary for his own safety but, either inside or out, he was a "dead man walking" - he could never survive this, too many criminal families would hold the grudge until he was eventually "terminated." On the other hand, the Polish and Bulgarian authorities would also have an interest, as it seemed he had managed to escape from both these countries just in time to avoid arrest. He would probably be safer if he were extradited back to Eastern Europe unless, of course, he had antagonised too many criminals there as well! The Scottish news was showing a live press conference at which several of the senior officers of Scotland`s Police Force, including the Chief Constable, were present, all wishing to bask in the reflected glory of the "Purge on Scottish Organised Crime", as they were already referring to it. The Chief Constable, Sir Peter Masson, was addressing the press in his usual matter-of fact way. Archie did not know him personally and had never met him as, prior to the amalgamation of the Scottish Police forces, he had been Chief Constable of somewhere down south, Greater Manchester, he recalled. But he seemed to be well enough respected by officers in general, at least as much as any Chief Constable could reasonably expect to be. He was known to be fair, yet hard on anyone not coming up to the standard he expected from his officers, but one particular characteristic that went in his favour was the absence of the sarcasm or superciliousness so often present with senior officers. He never needlessly reprimanded or humiliated junior officers as many of his predecessors had done and this made him a relatively popular figurehead. There were, of course, the usual detractors, some of them hinting that his sometimes stilted communication skills indicated that he suffered from mild Asperger`s syndrome, but Archie had never yet known a Chief Constable without critics and it was a position he would never aspire to - he was quite content with his own level of Inspector. Archie was also aware that Masson had, in the past, suffered some injury to his left hand that had rendered it partially paralysed, the generally held belief being he had been stabbed in an incident as a junior officer. This also served to help with his popularity amongst the ranks.

But now Archie was gazing at the close-up of his Chief Constable with the benefit of Samsung`s finest high definition 40 inch screen. The cropped, jet black hair, the intense dark, almost black eyes, the pale complexion, the slightly long face, the speech that was correct and yet almost stilted...

`We are, of course, delighted with the actions of our officers and we are entirely confident that these criminals will be brought to the justice that they fully deserve...`

Correct, and yet, almost stilted...

Khara turned to look at him. He could see the anxiety on her face.

`Archieblue, do you know this man?`

`Well, not personally, but I know who he is. Of course I do - he`s Sir Peter Masson, the Chief Constable of Scotland`s Police Force. Technically my overall boss. But I don`t know him personally as I`ve never met him. You`re surely not telling me it`s him?`

`Yes, as you must be able to determine if you look closely. You can see the features, the similarity to me, the colouring. And who would be better placed to find the missing weapon than someone in command of your security, or police, force, with an entire network that would know of such a discovery as yours? Do you know anything about his background?`

`No, but there`s one way to find out quickly.`

`How is that?`

`Google!`

Back at his computer, Archie typed "Sir Peter Masson, MBE", knowing that one of the top five hits would be Wikipedia, probably after the "Scotland`s Police" homepage. Sure enough, there it was and he clicked on the link to the on-line encyclopaedia.

Sir Peter Halliday Masson, MBE
Born - Greenock, Scotland, 20th May 1957
Education – USA, Greenock Academy, Scotland.

Higher Education - Glasgow University
Entered City of Glasgow Police Force 1979

The entry continued and became more interesting. Masson had never married and had no children. An only child, he was, apparently, adopted by an uncle in the USA at the age of five, his parents having been killed in a road traffic accident. His uncle later returned to the town of his birth (where he had been seconded by the computer giant, IBM) and enrolled him in what was considered, at that time, the "best" school, Greenock Academy, an institution that Archie knew as rugby opponents in his own schooldays. Prior to its demolition, it had been used as the location for school-based soap opera "Waterloo Road".The rest was the usual story of a speedy rise through the ranks as, in those days, a university graduate was almost certain to do well if he joined the police. Even in the 1970`s it was still considered a "last-resort" career for the non-academic! Now he was head of Scotland`s Police Force, the pinnacle of an unblemished career. Except, of course, for the fact that he was, apparently, an alien. Archie couldn`t quite believe it and yet the evidence appeared to be staring him straight in the face, in the form of a photo on the Wikipedia website. Again he could see the features that identified his origins as those of the girl seated next to him.

`So what in God`s name do we do now, Khara? This is my Chief Constable, the head of the whole of Scotland`s Police force. I can`t exactly confront this guy and accuse him of being an alien. I suppose, then, he`ll know about us finding the drone and the weapon that you believe it contains?`

`Undoubtedly. And I am also certain that he was there last night and is probably responsible for the death of the unfortunate reporter, although I do not necessarily think that he intended for that to happen. He would not have known that the man was in such an unhealthy state and probably only meant to disable him temporarily, as I did with you. But we must act quickly. My own vessel detected the signal that was transmitted by the drone and, should any other vessels be in this sector of the galaxy, then they will also have received the signal, transmitted by a series of relay beacons that were placed here a considerable time ago. I have not detected any such ship but they may be far away and, after all, I have been away from my own ship for a considerable amount of time and I have not checked any of the scanning systems.` She paused, obviously thinking carefully about what to say next.

`All far-space reconnaissance operatives from Loh are instructed to remain undetected as much as possible and to have minimal effect on other cultures, unless absolutely necessary. Strictly speaking, Archieblue, what happened between you and I should not have happened at all! However, I could not make that guarantee for those still loyal to the Atra. They have a very different outlook from those in my society and have little or no concern for what they consider "inferior" species. They would be likely to land and remove the object with no regard whatsoever for the inhabitants of your planet, either for casualties or for the effect their presence would have. Can you imagine what that could do to your race? I do not think humanity is ready just yet to encounter an alien species, especially in the form of the Atra, do you, Archieblue?`

`No, they`re definitely not. It would cause mass panic, I would think. So, what now? What do we do?`

`Well, I have to return to my ship and prepare the transportation device. But although I can return easily enough without detection, it would be unwise to remove the missile in daylight as I could not carry that out without being noticed. Have you prepared the letter you discussed?`

`Yes, and it`ll just have to do. Honestly, I think it`s fine, but we don`t really have time for anything else now, do we? Right then, do you want me to take you back to your, em, shuttle-thingy now?`

She smiled. `It is just a shuttle, not a shuttle-thingy! But not just yet, Archieblue, I am not quite finished with you yet...`

***

It was just after six p.m. by the time Khara had finished with him - she had obviously decided that, having made "first contact," rightly or wrongly she would explore it to the full...!

However, once their activities were concluded, she dressed in her grey flying suit and boots, leaving the clothes Archie had bought neatly folded on his bed.

As she stood up and they headed for the door, she faced him, her eyes still dark and unfathomable. He could detect no emotion in them as she spoke. - it was as if their recent physical interlude had never happened.

`Archieblue, I can never thank you enough for the help you have given me, nor for the kindness and trust you have shown me. I am afraid that there may be great danger tonight as there is a possibility that your Chief Constable may, again, be present at the site. I do not know if he is aware of my presence here and I think it unlikely, but having now located the weapon he will want to ensure it is kept safe until his associates can come and retrieve it. If that happened, the end result would be catastrophic for my planet and I must do everything I can to ensure that they do not manage to take it back to Loh. I cannot ask you to put yourself in danger for a planet and a race that you do not know. If you can take me back to my shuttle and leave me there, it would be best and safest for you. Your life has not been easy recently - my sympathy is with you, of course, but I feel that I can now only bring more problems and danger for you. I do not wish this so, please, let us say goodbye now.`

Archie held her gaze steadily as he spoke

`Do you honestly think you`re going to get rid of me that easily? After all that`s happened? No way!`

`Please, Archieblue. Do not make this any more difficult.`

`Khara, we are in this together. After all that`s happened over the last few days surely you must realise that? No matter what, my life is never going to be the same. How could it be? Have you any idea how hard it would be to go about my normal routine when I`ve been in space, when I`ve been on a trip round Mars, when I`ve seen all the incredible things you`ve shown me and, most of all, when I can`t tell a single person without risk of being locked away as insane? No, I`m in this, whether you want me or not!` He smiled, in what he hoped was a reassuring manner. Khara shook her head and, as she did so, he noticed that, although she had changed back into her own garment, she was still wearing the leather necklace he had bought her.

`You are a most infuriating and stubborn person. But you are a very brave and loyal friend. Very well, if you insist but, be warned, there may be considerable danger and you must follow my instructions at all times Do you understand?`

Archie nodded.

`Here is what we will do. You can take me back to my shuttle and I will make the preparations to recover the drone. You will also have to ensure that your letter is delivered to explain the disappearance.`

Shit, I`ve missed the last post!

`It would also be useful if you could find out if your Chief Constable has any particular plans for this evening, as that may indicate whether or not we can expect him to be at the site.`

`Okay, I`ll do my best.` although he wasn`t exactly sure how he would find that out. `Then what?`

Khara hesitated, obviously making some calculations. She looked at the clock on the bedside table.

`If you can get me back to my shuttle by seven on your clock, I will travel back to my ship and prepare the lifting shuttle. Then I will return to the site at one on your clock. Exactly. If you could drive there and keep your men occupied, it will take me about...` she paused again, making the calculation `about fifteen minutes to prepare the drone for recovery. I will then lift it and return it to my ship with the shuttle. This would usually be almost silent but, of course, there is a covering over the drone and also there is an excavation machine beside it. As the drone is partially buried, it may make a noise when it becomes free and there is also the possibility of it rotating and hitting the excavator. These are variables that I cannot control. Will you be able to keep your policemen occupied for this time?`

`I`ll do my best.` Archie replied. It was a tall order, somewhat different from handing them a quick coffee and having a brief chat. But he would think of something. He hoped! Khara continued

`Once I have the drone aboard my ship, I will come back on the personnel shuttle and, if you wish, you can come back up to the Terestal and we will attempt to open the drone to ensure the presence of the weapon. That in itself may involve a risk, as I do not really know what I will find. Do you wish me to come back for you, Archieblue?`

`Of course I do! After all this fuss, I want to see what the damn thing looks like!`

`You are, indeed, a very brave man.` She paused, as if choosing her words carefully. `In all my travels I have not encountered anyone quite like you. As I said, stubborn, infuriating, brave, loyal. You are what I think you would call "an enigma," Archieblue.`

`I`ll take that as a compliment, then?`

`Yes, you may. Very well, I will return to the original shuttle site at three on your clock. Exactly. No, wait! I think it would be safe to bring the shuttle here - there are no other houses in the vicinity, it is extremely quiet and I do not think it would be seen. That is what I will do, then. Let us hope the night does not hold too many unpleasant surprises. I think you have had enough of those for the time being.`

`Damn right!`

They set off in the Porsche, heading back towards Erskine. It was quite dark and overcast as the good weather was giving way once again to the the more typical West of Scotland rain clouds. Archie wondered if it would be raining by the time Khara returned with the lifting shuttle, as this might help in distracting the cops on duty. They listened to a few more of his favourite tracks as they drove, a less rock-orientated selection (on his playlists as "Arch Smoochy") that he thought suited their mood. Peter Gabriel "Don`t give up" (seemed appropriate) with Kate Bush`s haunting vocals in the chorus. "Sunshine on Leith", the Proclaimer`s title song from the musical

`I still think they sound like you!` Khara said, straight faced. Archie still couldn`t tell if she was teasing him or simply stating a fact.

The random selection next selected Eva Cassidy singing "Over the rainbow" and he realised that the music was starting to make him feel melancholy as if a chapter of his life was closing – the feeling of despondency, at bay for a couple of days, was creeping up on him once again. Then he remembered he still had a funeral to attend the next day and he experienced a dreadful pang of guilt as he realised that he had not spoken to the Whitefords since the day he had been at their house, other than a brief conversation with Gordon when he had called about Lucinda`s funeral.. He hoped they would understand but, as the investigating officer, he should really have shown them some more professional courtesy. There had been too many unpleasant chapters in his life recently, too many losses and he was starting to really regret his choice of music as they arrived at the road leading in to Millfield. He switched the stereo off as she stopped beside the fence and Khara opened the door, jumping out of the car.

He opened his window and she bent down to speak to him`One on your clock at the site, then three back at your house. Exactly! Good luck, Detective Inspector Archieblue.` She briefly touched his face and she was gone. Once again Archie was astonished at how she seemed to disappear and he remembered it was something to do with the suit. *Must ask her how it works...*

Chapter 26

Archie turned the music on as he drove away but the first song, 10cc`s "I`m not in love" was now definitely played out and prompted him to turn it straight back off. However, after a few minutes he decided on a more upbeat playlist, turning up the volume until it was blaring on the stereo - still it failed to lift his spirits. He wondered if, maybe, this was how his life was going to be from now on, but he seriously hoped not. AC/DC "Highway to Hell" came on and he actually smiled. *That`s where you`re headed, mate...*

On the way from Erskine he had taken a detour along Paisley Road West and posted the letter at the Glasow suburb of Cardonald, as he didn`t want the postmark showing anywhere near his home. He knew it wouldn`t now arrive until the Wednesday, but he hoped that one day wouldn`t make a lot of difference. After checking for any nearby surveillance cameras he carefully popped it straight from the evidence bag into the letterbox, thereby avoiding any physical contact. He jumped back in the car then headed back through Paisley`s one-way system and onto the A737. The rain had started by this time, just a few drops at first but getting heavier as he approached Lochwinnoch. He remembered a saying by one of the village`s long-time residents, concerning the hill, Misty Law, sitting high behind in the nearby Muirshiel Country Park area.

"If you can see Misty Law, then it`s going to rain....

If you can`t see Misty Law, it`s raining already..."

He pulled into the drive of his cottage, got out of the car and opened his front door. It seemed even less welcoming than before and, now, it really was a mess. He couldn`t be bothered tidying anything up though, so he went into the kitchen, put on some coffee, then took out his phone, calling up Cam`s number.

`Hey, Buddy!` Cam said cheerily.

`How`s it going, my friend? Been promoted yet?`

`Goin` just great tae the first and no tae the second! Rushed off ma feet here, still at the office writin` up the reports. Tracey`s goin` spare and I`m worried wee Abigail doesn`ae recognise me! Still, cannae wait tae get the overtime in ma pay packet though, no` long to Christmas! How about you? Still all alone in that wee house of yours, then?`

Archie refused to rise to the bait.

`Still all alone, Cam. I told you, you`d be the first to know. So it`s all panning out okay then?`

`Yeah, fantastic. Mind you, talkin` aboot promotion, I had a visit from "The High Heid-Yin" this afternoon. Can you believe it?`

A little alarm bell rang in the back of Archie`s mind. What was that all about, he wondered.

`What, not the Chief Constable? Peter Masson?`

`The very one, Boss, the good "Sir Peter" himsel`! Hauled his arse all the way up tae the third floor and shook my hand, told me what a great job I`d done and how delighted he was. Said he`d be speaking tae some o` my immediate superiors, apparently they could do wi` a few inspectors of my calibre. Awright, eh? Don`t think the Super looked too chuffed but, hey, maybe he`s feart for his own job! Ah`d have tae try an` speak a bit more posh, though!`

Cam was proud of both his working class roots and accent and Archie had always found it refreshing.

`That`s fantastic, Cam. Only one problem`

`Whit`s that?`

`You`d have stop calling me "Boss"!`

`Aye, right enough, Boss` They both laughed and it felt good. Normal service might just be resumed after all! *Maybe!*

Cam continued in a more sombre tone.

`So, tomorrow. Listen, are you sure you don`t want me tae pick you up. It`s no problem at all, Archie.`

`No, thanks Cam, but I`d really just be better on my own. Listen, by any chance have you spoken to Gordon Whiteford? I forgot all about it, you know, I`ve been so wrapped up in this whole thing myself.`

`Aye, don`t worry, all taken care of. I went over after we`d pulled Czarneki in, told him we had someone being questioned in relation to the murders. Anyway he`ll have read about the goings-on in the papers by now as well. But I`ll call once the funeral`s passed, maybe Wednesday, give them a wee bit of time to recover.`

Archie paused, He dreaded to ask the question but he had to know - he should have asked long before now

`So, do you know what actually happened to her?`

Cam had obviously been expecting it. `Aye, we do. An` it wasn`ae whit you thought.`

`What do you mean?`

`Well, first off, it doesn`ae seem likely that Czarneki was there at all, obviously didn`ae want tae get too close tae the action, although he`s definitely the one behind a` the murders. But Ralston swears she... Lucinda...was, em, deceased when they got there. Dr Clayton pretty much agrees, puts the time o` death aboot twelve hours earlier. So they didn`ae actually have any part in her death, other than with the probable supply of the original hit. Seems she just overdosed, poor wee sowel. I`m so, so sorry, mate. Really. Every time I cuddle wee Abigail I think of you. Shit, I`m getting aw choked up...`

Archie could hear the genuine grief as his friends voice broke and he, too, struggled to speak. He tried to steer the conversation back to where he needed it to be.

`Listen, Cam, just out of interest, did Masson say if there was anything else happening tonight? You know, interviews or anything? I saw him on the telly earlier, basking in your glory!`

Cam had composed himself. He wasn`t used to expressing his emotions in this manner.

`He did, actually, There`s some dinner up in Glasgow, at the Hilton I think it wis. Some association thing he said he wis attendin`, had tae rush off, you know. The usual, can only rub shoulders wi` the minions for so long! Why do you ask?`

`Oh, nothing, as I said, just curious, this`ll do him the world of good, all these arrests on his watch. Probably promote him to the

peerage! By the way, do you know where he stays?`

`I think it`s somewhere oot near Stirling. Whit`s the sudden interest in Masson, Boss?`

`Och, nothing. Just surprised to hear that he was in the office today and it makes you wonder just how the other half live and what they actually do for their money. Some salary he`ll be drawing now, plus a nice pension on the horizon, too.`

`Aye, and no family tae share it wit`either, apparently. I wis gonnae ask him if he wanted tae adopt me, thought better o` it though. I`ll settle for that promotion!`

They laughed again and Archie realised just how much he`d

missed the banter with his Sergeant and best pal. *This is more like it!* Yes, things might just be okay after all.

`You know, he even asked me aboot that stupid bomb. Said he`d heard talk aboot it and asked to be kept informed of any developments. I told him we were off the case now as it wis back with the uniform boys, but he said to keep him posted if I heard anythin`, especially if the Army got in touch.`

`Did he say why?` asked Archie, trying to keep the alarm out of his voice.

`Och, some daft story aboot wantin` tae be there when they finally disposed of it. Said he had an interest, being from Greenock, `cos it was blitzed as well, apparently. I think he wis just pretendin` tae be interested. I mean, whit`s it got tae do with anythin` - he`s got bigger an` better things tae do wi` his time.`

Of course, Archie knew only too well why Masson had an interest.

`Cam, I`m really sorry but I have to ask you another favour. I can`t explain why and I know it`ll sound kinda weird. But, please, don`t pass anything on to him if you can possibly avoid it. I know it`s asking a lot but please trust me on this.`

`You know, Boss - Archie -, you`re asking me tae trust you on a helluva lot o` things these days. And you know I`ll do it for you, but it`d be nice to get a wee explanation of whit`s goin` on. I suppose it won`t do any harm tae keep quiet but I don`t want Masson breathin` doon my neck either if he thinks I`ve kept anythin` from him. Know what I mean? Then, like I said, there`s that promotion...`

`Aye, I know, Cam, but I`d really appreciate it. I`ll explain when I can, honestly, mate! All I can say is it`s really important, I wouldn`t ask you otherwise, okay?`

The sergeant hesitated then, with a heavy sigh, he answered

`Aye, okay then. Seein` it`s you. Listen, d`you fancy comin` over next Saturday for a wee bite. Try and make things up wi` Tracy for keeping me oot late. I`ll get her tae rustle up a lasagne. Hey, you could stay over, we could crack open a few bottles of somethin` decent.`

`You know, that`d be brilliant, Cam. You`re on! And I`ll bring the wine.`

`And, of course, if you want tae bring anyone...!`

Aye, right! "This is Khara, she`s from outer space..."

Archie laughed again, they said their goodbyes and he came off the phone feeling much better, despite his slight concern at Masson`s enquiries about the drone. He poured himself a coffee and went through to the lounge to kill some time until he headed back to Erskine. As a precaution he set the alarm on his phone for eleven thirty...just in case. Wouldn`t do to sleep in...!

It was just as well he did. He was in a deep sleep when, yet again, he heard "I`m not in love" playing beside his ear, the very song that had prompted him to turn off the car stereo earlier. There had been a time when it was one of his favourite songs.

Right, that`s getting binned...

He looked at the time and was relieved to see 11.30p.m. showing, plenty of time to get ready and back up the road. He decided to have a quick shower to waken him up a bit as he suspected it could be a long night – there had been too many of those recently and he hoped that tonight`s events might prove to be a less exciting. Well, in some respects...

After drying himself he donned his usual black Craghoppers, a black t-shirt and a black hoodie - he would get his Berghaus jacket on the way out, as he could hear the rain lashing against the window, a big change from the glorious moonlight of the previous evening. He went downstairs, poured himself a glass of fresh orange juice, put on his new (and now broken-in) hiking boots, grabbed the rain jacket and headed out to the car.

The drive to Erskine wasn`t pleasant. The few glorious days hadn`t been enough to allow the water table to drop and already pools of water were forming on the back roads leading to the A737. However, it would give Archie the perfect opportunity to distract the uniformed cops - they were unlikely to turn down the offer of a coffee and a fifteen minute blether in the Porsche with a senior officer to vouch for them!

He arrived in Erskine about ten to one and waited a short way along the road from the HomeFree site - it wouldn`t do to be too early, just make the distraction a bit longer. He had the perfect reason now, too, as the Chief Constable had expressed an interest in the so-called bomb. He just happened to be passing by and was stopping in for an update that he could pass on to Masson. He had called at the

Erskine filling station on the way and a tray with three steaming cardboard cups of coffee and three doughnuts was sitting on the passenger seat, the aroma permeating through the inside of the car. Just before one o`clock he headed round the corner, down the rough road, the surface of which was almost underwater in the now lashing rain, and arrived at the site bang on time - "exactly" as Khara had put it! Given the foul weather, he wasn`t really surprised that the cops were nowhere to be seen. He pulled up at the gate which, to his slight surprise, was open, and peered through the rain. Then he saw them, sitting in the Police van which appeared to be a bit steamed up. He had a brief thought that perhaps it was a male and female cop on duty and they`d decided to warm up a bit in the vehicle, but he discarded that immediately - it would almost certainly mean instant suspension if they were caught. No, he reckoned they were just having a bit of respite from the torrential rain and who could blame them. He switched his main beam off and pulled up alongside them - if they were already in their van it would make his task considerably easier, as they were facing away from where the drone lay. This was going to be simpler than he thought. He wound down the passenger window so he could talk to them, waiting for them to do likewise. Nothing happened.

That`s odd...

Their window was so steamed up that he couldn`t really see much through it and he wondered if they`d brought a flask, which seemed likely, given the weather conditions. But after a minute, when they still hadn`t responded or acknowledged his presence, he got out of his car and walked round to the police vehicle.

Bet the buggers are sleeping!

He rapped loudly on the window - still no response. He pulled the handle and opened the door. The cop nearest him fell out of the van, the upper half of his torso flopping downwards until his hands were in the mud of the car park. Archie watched in horror then looked inside. The driver was leaning against the opposite window, eyes closed, seemingly unconscious, or so Archie hoped. He lifted the now soaking body of the first cop back into the van and felt his neck for a pulse, relieved to find that there was one. *At least the guy`s alive*. He leaned across to the other cop and, likewise, there was a faint pulse, although both of them seemed as if they were drugged.

He closed the door and stood up, looking around him. There was no-one in sight, the offices were in darkness and it was so wet he couldn`t see as far as the JCB in the field. He had no way of knowing if Khara was there and if she was alone. Then a thought came to him. Unwelcome, unwanted, but it started to grow and spread its wings. Was she in league with Masson? Was she, in fact, the contact that he had made when the "bomb" was disturbed, the Atra member who had come to collect the weapon? All that bullshit about "being in the area." A bit of a coincidence now that he thought about it and Archie didn`t believe in coincidence - well, not much, anyway. They certainly looked similar (granted, she was a lot better looking...) and the way she seemed to be able to control his mind, well...

What a total fucking idiot you are, Archie Blue!

Of course! She`d played him, used him as a cover while she and Masson made their plans. Naturally, he was a good source of information – after all, the Chief Constable was hardly going to get his own boots dirty in a muddy field in Erskine, was he?He wondered if Masson was going to leave with her - how would Scotland`s finest explain that? But they would be away, they wouldn`t care. And him, well, he`d obviously just been a wee bit of fun along the way, collateral damage, wasn`t that what they called it?He was angry now. Never a good thing...

He went back to his car and opened the boot. He couldn`t care less about the inside getting soaked, he was now officially a man on a mission! He knew that, realistically, he would be no match for the two of them, but at the very least he was determined that Khara would know that he had seen through her, that he knew she had played him as a fool (which he undoubtedly was). He opened the little kit bag that went everywhere with him, took out his trusty Maglite torch then pocketed a couple of pairs of handcuffs, *well, you never know...* then he closed the tailgate once again. Pulling his hood up and putting his head down against the driving rain, he walked across the sodden field towards the JCB, still barely discernible in the gloom. As he drew near, he could see its large claw still poised where Big Dunk had left it as he ran back to the offices - it seemed like a lifetime ago now. The tent, however, had been turned on its side and the camouflaged top was facing towards him, leaning on the tracks of the JCB. *Someone here, then, right enough.* Archie kept moving until he was right behind the top of the Army shelter. The noise of the rain meant that no-one was likely to hear him and he paused, summoning all the courage he could to face the two aliens he assumed were on the other side. He lifted the torch high and squelched round the side of the upturned tent.

As expected, there they were, just beside the half-buried drone. Masson had his back to him and seemed to be holding something in his left hand. Archie couldn`t make out exactly what it was but he could see what looked like two small spheres, one above and one below his clenched fist, presumably with some sort of handle joining them. He couldn`t see Masson`s other hand but, by the body language, he assumed that there was something in that as well. He was a big bugger, taller and broader than his photos indicated, and he was heading towards Khara, who was facing him and appeared to be standing still. It was then that Archie noticed her face. It was frozen in absolute terror, her mouth open as if about to scream and, in an instant, he realised that he might have been wrong – maybe she wasn`t in league with Masson after all. At this point in time, the Chief Constable, having obviously used his mind controlling tricks on her, appeared to be intent on causing her harm, just how serious Archie could only guess. Without a further thought he stumbled forward through the mud, Maglite torch still raised, and brought it down full force on his Chief Constable`s head with an almighty crunch. Masson had half turned but he was too late - he went down like a pack of cards, eyes rolling upwards as he flopped heavily in the thick mud. Before he did anything else, Archie whipped out a pair of standard issue, rigid cuffs and locked the unconscious Masson`s hands behind his back, then rolled him over slightly to make sure he didn`t drown. He stood up and went over to Khara, grabbing her by the arms and shaking her, as she still appeared to be absolutely petrified. She stared at him, her eyes as wide as he had ever seen them, then he saw the muscles of her face relax and she started to sob, gasping for breath as she did so. He could feel her arms trembling as she managed to speak.

`Archieblue, I have never been so glad to see anyone in my life. Thank you. I think this man would have killed me.`

She pulled away from him and went over to the prone, rain-soaked figure in the mud. She crouched down and removed the items from his hands, stood up and returned to where Archie was still standing. She held up the object with the two spheres.

`This is what we call an enhancer, or a PTT weapon, the perceived threat transmitter I spoke of last night. It increases our telepathic abilities and allows us to instil fear into the minds of an enemy. It is a weapon that we have used for many years and it has been refined and updated many times. This is an old version, mine is far superior, but I did not imagine that I would be facing this man tonight. I was intent on securing the drone when he appeared and I had no time.`

`This is what you used on Czarneki and his associates?`

`Yes. It is a powerful and fearful weapon, especially in the wrong hands. Fortunately I have some protection in the way of a neural implant, but I think that, although old, this is a highly modified and possibly forbidden version of the weapon that, alas, had a noticeable effect on me. I have not come across this particular version before, but I will be all right now. Thanks to you, Archieblue. I think that now makes us, you would say...even?`

`Yeah, I suppose it does. And what about the other thing?` asked Archie, looking down at Khara`s other hand. She opened her palm and there was a simple dagger, with a lethal-looking blade about four inches long and an elaborately engraved handle that looked as if it might be fashioned from ivory or something similar.

`A very old, but very effective weapon, Archieblue. Probably a family heirloom that he carried about with him. It is likely to have been the cause of many deaths in its history and I would have been the next.` She paused and looked at him. `In two days, I have escaped death twice. I hope I am not faced with it again anytime soon.`

`Aye, let`s hope so.` He stared at her then without any forethought, took her in his arms and held her tightly, as if afraid to lose her. She responded in kind and they stood, rain streaming from them, silently embracing, each lost in the other`s warmth and presence. After a few minutes, she pulled away.

`I must act quickly now, Archieblue. I was positioning the lift shuttle when he appeared and it will still take me some time to remove the drone. What about your policemen that are on guard?`

`They`re out cold. Masson must have got to them first, but they`re alive, at least that`s something. Can I help at all?`

`No. I will be fine, there is little effort involved, just some careful positioning. Are you going to leave this man here?`

`Well, I can`t think of anything else to do with him.` Then he realised that it was his own handcuffs that were locked round Masson`s wrists - when he was eventually found the first thing they would do would be to check them for prints. `Listen, I`ll tidy up here, then are we still on schedule for three o`clock at my house?`

`Yes, three on your clock. Exactly!`

Archie returned to the police car and was relieved to find that the two cops were still out cold. He opened the door carefully, making sure that the unconscious officer didn`t slump to the ground again. He went into the pocket of his jacket and removed a pair of forensic gloves and pulled them on, then he carefully reached to the guy`s equipment belt and removed his cuffs before standing up and closing the door. Realising that his own prints would also be all over the door handle, he pulled up his jacket and used his t-shirt to wipe the handle as best he could. Then, for good measure, he smeared a bit of mud over the whole area.

He made his way back across the sodden ground to find that there was now a gantry-like apparatus astride the device, with a cylinder similar to the personnel shuttle at one end. Khara had her hand on one of the control panels and he could hear the sucking noise as the drone gradually moved out of the sticky, oozing mud. Then, with a dull "clang" it appeared to jump off the ground and attach itself to the cradle held within the gantry, following which a series of fine metallic bands, that looked like braided chain, wound themselves round its body and secured it in place. Again Archie marvelled at the technology but there was no time to ask for an explanation. He looked back down at the sodden form of Masson, fortunately also still out cold. Archie could see the large bump and weal on the side of his head where the torch had struck him and, for a moment he panicked as he thought he may have killed him. He knelt down and felt for a pulse - it was faint, but present. Blood was dribbling out of the wound, being washed away almost immediately by the rain.

Serves you right for attacking my officers – and Khara!

Archie unfastened his own cuffs and put them back in his pocket, replacing them on Masson`s wrists with the ones he had taken from the cop. As he did so, a brief flash of concern came over him.

Poor bugger will probably be in deep shit when they find his cuffs on Masson. Still, can`t be helped.

He stood up and went over to where Khara appeared to be checking the security of the drone. Already the hole it had left was filling with water and soon it would seem that it had never been there at all. Archie knew that the shit would really hit the fan the next day. Two unconscious cops, one of whom`s handcuffs were securing the Chief Constable, also unconscious, at the site of an unidentified, apparently dangerous, device that was now missing. Work that one out...

`I am ready, Archieblue. I will see you at three.`

`I`ll be there!" he called, as he turned back and squelched his way across to the comfort and safety of the Porsche.

Chapter 27

Once he was back inside the car Archie started the engine and turned the heater full on as he could barely see through the condensation that had formed on the windscreen. He was soaked, frozen and covered in mud, and he also now had a feeling of dread, as if he had hammered yet another nail into his own coffin – assaulting his Chief Constable was never a wise course of action! Then his brain deftly used the word “coffin” to remind him he would be attending his daughter`s funeral later that day. He doubted if he had either the physical or the emotional energy left, but he knew he would have to go – it would be the only thing he would ever do for his daughter, after all, but he was dreading having to face Gordon and Karen Whiteford. It was going to be a very difficult day and the night was by no means over yet! He looked at the clock on the dashboard and was surprised to see it was already ten past two. There was still enough time, though, and he waited a few minutes until the screen cleared enough for him to see, then he turned the car round, having a last look into the police van as he passed - there was still no sign of life which, in a way, was a relief, although he hoped the poor guys would be okay - they probably wouldn`t have a clue what had happened to them when they woke up and he just hoped that they didn`t end up in a similar state to the criminals that Khara had disabled. They had deserved it, these cops certainly didn`t!. He drove through the gate and back up the rough road, now resembling a small river, then headed back to the outskirts of Erskine.

He continued through the deserted town and headed back towards the A737 and eventually home. The rain was easing slightly and the roads were deserted, allowing him a clear run, and he pulled in to the drive at quarter to three. He just managed a very quick shower and a change into some clean, dry clothes when he was aware of movement outside. He looked out of his bedroom window and saw the dull glint of the shuttle that would take him to the Terestal. He ran downstairs and outside, pulling the door shut behind him. The door to the cylinder was open but there was no sign of Khara. A vague seed of suspicion rose once again in his mind.

`Where`s Khara?`

The drone spoke, its voice a slightly more metallic version as that of the Terestal.

`She is working on the drone, Archieblue. She sent me to collect you. Time is of the essence, as I am sure she has explained. Please step inside and we will proceed.`

Archie swallowed the niggling doubt that had risen again in his mind and entered the craft, going through the now ever-so-slightly familiar routine of being strapped in. The door closed silently and the craft lifted off immediately.

If Archie`s stomach had felt it was being left behind the first time, this was way worse. He had felt vaguely hungry as he drove home but he was now extremely glad he hadn`t eaten anything for hours, as he had no doubt that any food would have been coming back to greet him! It seemed that it took hardly any time before the shuttle was docking with the Terestal and, once his safety harness was removed, the door opened and he stepped out into the docking bay. Archie gazed around in the bright, greenish light and saw the lifting shuttle, caked in mud, back in what he assumed was its bay. Next to it was the drone, the cause of three days of grief, worry and, he supposed, adventure, with Khara leaning over it, presumably attempting to open it. She turned as he stepped towards her.

`Well, there it is, Archieblue. What I came for. At least, I hope it is, so now I think it is time to try and have a look inside, do you not agree?`

Now that it came to the bit, Archie wasn`t so sure, but he did want to see exactly what the whole fuss was about - after all, it wasn`t everyday he got the chance to see an alien weapon of mass extinction at close quarters!

That damned curiosity again...

He walked up the short ramp from the shuttle and stood beside the drone. It didn`t look as impressive now that it was lying flat and it was certainly smaller than Big Dunk`s original description, but it was still about seven feet long and it did pretty much resemble Archie`s image of a missile, gleaned from numerous action films depicting nuclear threat across the decades! The front end had the ubiquitous cone shaped nose and the rear had three small fins and a slightly blackened orifice that looked like the outlet of a propulsion motor, just as the Army boys had described (Was it really only a couple of days ago?) Despite its trip up through the miserable rain and Earth`s upper atmosphere, suspended underneath the lifting shuttle, it, too, still had traces of good old West of Scotland mud sticking to it, as well as a few bits of grass and leaves. A small piece of Erskine up in space! Khara returned to her work, using various pieces of equipment that were entirely unfamiliar to him. After a few minutes, she put down the tool she was using, sighed, and walked round to stand beside him.

`How do you know where do you start?` He asked.

`That is the problem – I do not know! This is old technology and, at present, I feel a bit like your soldiers must have done when they investigated the missile a few days ago. However, I can only do my best. If you look under there` she pointed below the drone `you will see some flashing lights. These indicate that the location transmitter has been activated and also that the power source is still functioning. It is likely that there will be a control panel of some sort that will allow access to the drone, so I will scan the casing to see if I can locate it. As long as there is power, then the systems should still be operational.`

She picked up what Archie assumed to be a small scanning device, running it over the surface of the drone (every time he saw her use another piece of alien technology he meant to ask her about it, but there always seemed to be some more pressing matter to hand. He`d ask later...) and, as it got near the cone shaped front end, it bleeped slightly and an array of red and blue lights flashed in sequence. She moved it back and forth, zoning in on a particular area until eventually the bleeping became a constant tone and the red and blue lights stayed on. Then she said

`I think I have found the location of the control panel. It will have a protective cover over it to prevent damage as it travels through space. Even when this was dropped on Earth these were already old weapons that had been converted for delivering contraband goods to other planets, so they were built to withstand difficult transit conditions.`

Archie couldn`t help asking `What type of contraband goods?`

Khara gave him a wry smile `Ah, Archieblue, always the detective. But I do not think you would want to know, not just yet!

Your planet has enough contraband of its own without acquiring any of ours!`

`Fair enough. Just can`t help myself sometimes, though. Curiosity killed the cat, after all.`

`What cat?`

`Oh never mind.`

`Well, I am thankful for your curiosity earlier tonight, otherwise I would not be here. But tell me, Archieblue,` she said, putting down the scanner and fixing her gaze on him. `tonight, when you found us at the drone, I perceived that you suspected that your Chief Constable and I were in collusion. Would I be correct in my assumption?`

He knew that there was no point in lying - she probably already knew the answer. `Yes, Khara, it did cross my mind. I`m really sorry, I know should have trusted you.` He looked away, unsure of the expression on her face. He couldn`t decide if it was anger, hurt or a mixture of both. When she spoke, though, there was no mistaking her tone.

`So, despite everything, despite what I have told you and all that has happened, you still do not trust me. Well, if that is the case, you would be as well leaving now and returning to your planet. Leave me to do my job. You are just a distraction and I have no time for distractions.`

Archie snapped. He wouldn`t normally raise his voice, far less swear, at a woman but he`d had enough. He yelled at her

`Aw, just give it a fucking rest, will you, Khara! What the hell was I meant to think? I find two cops out cold then I come across you and Masson looking as if you`re in cahoots! For that matter, how do I even know that you`re the good guy here? Maybe it`s you that`s with this Atra faction. Maybe Masson was trying to stop you getting this...so called lump of scrap that apparently contains...

His tirade was halted by a hard and painful slap on his face, as Khara screamed back at him, an expression of rage on her face.

`Shut up! Shut up! How dare you accuse me?`

He grabbed her wrist as she lifted her hand to strike him again. She glared at him, her fury now highly visible, and he braced himself for some form of mental attack. But she just continued to yell at him.

`What do you know, you stupid, infuriating man? You accuse me of being Atra? I could have killed you at anytime over the last few days. I could have left you to die and saved myself. That is what an Atra woman would have done. Used you, played with you, disposed of you when you became unnecessary. You do not know what they are capable of. They make those vermin we encountered two nights ago look like...like amateurs. The Atra have elevated evil and suffering to an artform. You do not know what happened...`

He felt her arm relax and he released his grip of her wrist. She dropped her gaze and he thought she might be sobbing.

`Khara? What is it?`

She shook her head.

`Christ, I`m sorry, okay? You`re right, what do I know? It`s just so, so bloody confusing, that`s all. Look, don`t get so upset. You`re taking this whole thing very personally. I mean, I understand that you need to retrieve this...thing but you`re so wrapped up in it. Don`t take offence, but how do I really know, even now, that this isn`t all part of an act?`

She looked back up at him and shook her head again. She spoke, quietly

`Because I have no further need for you now. If I ever really did. There is no need for you to be here - I didn`t have to send the shuttle back for you. What help can you be to me now, Archieblue?` She looked back at him. `You are only here now because...`

`Because what?`

She hesitated.

`Because I wanted it. Because it is the first time in a long time since I have trusted anyone and I felt that you deserved to be here, because I thought you trusted me.`

He didn`t know what to say. But he asked

`So what did you mean when you said I didn`t know what happened?`

There was a pause. She leaned heavily on the drone, as if extremely weary.

`The man who dropped this drone, who piloted the craft away from Loh. He was, well, as you would say, my father`s great grandfather.`

She told him the story. Gara, although not Atra-born, had been the finest fighter pilot in generations, being decorated many times for bravery shown during invasion attempts by hostile species (of which there were still a few, she assured him) and also for assistance in suppression of various uprisings against the Atra. He had retired after sixty cycles (just slightly longer than an Earth year, she explained) and had bought himself a ship, the Intaria, a class 7 far-space cruiser (which meant nothing to Archie) kitting it out to an exceptionally high standard to attract wealthy tourists wishing to travel to exotic destinations. Many of these were seeking illicit pleasures, both physical and chemical, many of which were banned on Loh. Hence the use of the so called "drop-drones" to deliver supplies without having to enter the near-space of the various planets on his route. Offering a discreet, safe and comfortable far-space travel service, Gara prospered but, like many at that time, started to develop a loathing of the way the Atra dictatorship was ruling his planet and gradually eliminating all opposition. Like many other ex-military personnel he felt that this was not the society he had fought for and he secretly joined the EC (she explained the tribal meaning, Erti and Cathalla, of the resistance acronym) and ultimately volunteered for the mission to remove the genetic bomb from the planet. By all accounts he was exceptionally brave and a highly skilled pilot, often relying on older technology to outsmart young pilots who relied too heavily, he believed, on the most modern techniques that almost rendered their skills redundant. She was proud to be descended from him and to share his chosen career as a pilot.

She paused.

`Gara, then, was one of the three very brave...revolutionaries, you would call them, who managed to steal the sphere and remove it from the planet, hopefully out of reach of the Atra. Their actions paved the way for the revolution, in which the Atra were finally overthrown. But before that, when his part in the theft was discovered, the Atra decided to make an example of his family – my forebears.`

`I`m so sorry.` Archie said quietly.

`You cannot imagine...` she continued `Those that were caught, they were publicly tortured, for days on end, before being executed. Non-Atra were rounded up and made to watch, as a warning. It is said that it was this show of merciless brutality that finally instigated the revolution so their plan ultimately backfired on them. But the people who commissioned this` she indicated the drone `they killed my family, with the exception of the few who escaped their clutches, otherwise I, of course, would not be here at all. So you think I am taking this matter personally. Maybe now you can see why. That was why I joined the military, why I wanted to be a pilot like my ancestor. I needed...`

`Revenge?` Archie asked

`Yes, I suppose so.` She looked at him. `Maybe you and I are not so different, Archieblue.`

`Maybe not, right enough.` He sighed heavily and shook his head.

She continued, speaking quietly, casting her eyes downwards.

`When I started this mission, I was not alone.`

`Really!` He hadn`t seen any sign of anyone else on board. This was a surprise and, somehow, he felt that it wasn`t going to be a pleasant one.

`Yes. I had a sub-commander with me. Selib 2 Ganno. We were...close...`

`Close? You mean...were you in a relationship?`

`Of a sort, yes. Not very serious, perhaps, but it is a long journey and...well...`

At this revelation Archie felt his stomach lurch. He wasn`t sure he wanted to know but he had to ask.

`And what happened to him?`

Khara gave him an odd look before replying

`Selib was female.`

Archie`s jaw dropped in astonishment.

`You mean...you...`

`What, Archieblue? On Loh, gender is of little significance. If you like someone, if you find them attractive, then you pursue that path. You seem surprised.`

`Well, no, it`s just that...` he didn`t know where to go with this.

`I understand. On Earth you still frown on such a relationship. You are a somewhat un-enlightened species, Archieblue.`

`That`s not fair, Khara. You can`t automatically apply your own principles to our society and call us "un-enlightened" if your behaviour surprises us. Anyway, we`re probably more enlightened than you think these days. It just, well, it wasn`t what I expected, that`s all. It`s fine, really.`

`I do not need your approval. It is neither fine nor otherwise. It just was` she snapped.

Archie could feel his hackles rise but there was no point in starting an argument that he knew he wouldn`t win.

`Okay, I`m sorry. So, what happened to hi...her?`

`When we received the signal from the drone, when it looked as if we may have discovered the Sphere, well...it transpired that her loyalties lay elsewhere.`

`You mean she was one of them, one of the Atra?` said Archie in astonishment. How many more secrets did she have?

`Yes, unfortunately. Although all far-space crew are carefully vetted, somehow she managed to slip through the net. Perhaps because she was female, someone did not check properly. Atra infiltrators have a tendency to be male. It is worrying, though.`

`And?`

`When it became apparent that the signal from the drone may have been of significance, Selib tried to persuade me to change my loyalties. It would seem that she misjudged our relationship and believed that, because of it, I would be happy to support the Atra. As I have explained, that would be entirely abhorrent to me. Unfortunately, I was equally unable to persuade her to change her loyalties. She tried to gain control of the vessel and I had no option but to prevent her. Regrettably, I had to use force to accomplish this and, to my shame, I lost control. I think you can understand.`

Archie understood! Khara`s head was down and he reached towards her, grasping her shoulders.

`I`m so sorry, Khara. With what you`ve told me, what happened to your ancestors, it was obviously just the blind rage, the pent-up hate. You needed to lash out at someone and, well...Selib was the one, I guess. If anyone knows just how easily that can happen, it`s me!`

She looked up at him.

`Yes. Like I said, you and I are not so different.`

She had a point. A very good one.

`So what did you do, how did you dispose of her body? Dump it in space?`

He realised his insensitivity as soon as the words were out.

`No, of course not!` she snapped. `The ship has storage for such eventualities. Her body will be returned to Loh, where I will have some considerable explaining to do when I, too, get back. It will also have to be determined how she managed to be on this mission in the first place, as the outcome could have been very different had she managed to overpower me.`

She paused and sighed.

`So now you know, Archieblue. All my dark secrets. Then you come along, brave, interfering, helpful, distracting. And here we are.`

`Yeah, here we are.` He paused and managed a faint smile as he continued. `Right, Khara, finally, once and for all, I trust you. Absolutely, totally, no more doubts. And, hopefully, no more secrets! I`d trust you with my life. Deal?` He held out his hand.

She hesitated briefly, then took it.

`Deal. Although I am not entirely sure what that means. But I am relieved. You are the most infuriating being I have met.`

`Aye, you said...!

She immediately regained her composure and turned her attention back to the drone. It was as if the entire conversation hadn`t happened and Archie struggled to keep up with her change of mood as she spoke.

`Now, you said you would trust me with your life, well let us hope you do not have to demonstrate that!` she lifted another tool that looked like a small flat plate with an angled handle and placed it against a slight depression on the casing.

`Hopefully this should open the control mechanism for the drone access door.`

She appeared to focus directly on the depression and suddenly it slid back with a slight “click”.

Don`t tell me this thing has some sort of telepathic control?

It revealed what looked like a simple and somewhat Earth-like keypad, covered with undecipherable (to Archie, at any-rate) markings. Khara, however, seemed to know what she was doing and pressed a number of buttons in succession causing two large parts of the casing, about half of its length, to swing upwards and fold back against the lower sides of the body. Archie and Khara stood up and gazed into the interior. Archie spoke first.

`Well, that`s a surprise!`

The drone was empty.

***

Khara stepped forward and gazed in disbelief, bending over and peering inside as if she had missed something - she hadn`t. Archie had never seen her speechless.

`Right!` he said. `There`s got to be an explanation.`

`What explanation can there be, Archieblue? It should be here, and it is not.` She looked close to despair, unsurprising considering the time, effort and emotion she had invested in the mission to date. She knelt down again, grasping the sides of the empty drone. He knelt beside her and put his arm around her shoulder.

`Come on, let`s go through it all, right from the start. On the very first night, when I found you. Did you touch or open the drone?`

She turned and looked at him.

`No, I did not. I was carrying out an initial visual assessment and scan when you discovered me.`

`Okay. Did it seem to you that it had been touched or interfered with in any way, as far as you could tell, other than having been uncovered?`

`No, it seemed to be intact.`

`Before tonight, did you return to the drone at any time?`

`No, I did not.`

`Good. Now, tonight, when you arrived, did the drone appear exactly as it had done on the first night?`

`It was hard to tell in the rain but, yes, it appeared to be the same.`

`Did you arrive at the exact stated time. One a.m.?`

`Yes, exactly as we had planned.`

`Did you arrive before Masson?`

`Yes. I was preparing the lifting drone when he arrived.`

`Do you think he may have had any opportunity to touch or open the drone before you arrived?`

`I do not believe so. As I said, it did not appear to have been touched.`

`When he arrived, what did he say to you, Khara? Can you remember?`

`He said "I see you have arrived before me. I suspected that someone else may come in search of the sphere. With regret, I am afraid I cannot allow you to remove it, assuming that it is, in fact, here. I am sorry." That is a fairly accurate representation, I think. He already had his PTT weapon, the enhancer that I explained about earlier, pointed at me and I had no time to reach for my own. I was helpless, just as you found me.`

`So it sounds as if he believed the sphere to be on the drone too and that he had no opportunity to remove it. Right then. Are you absolutely certain that the weapon would have been in this drone? There is no chance it could have been at the crash site on our moon?`

`No, the previous reconnaissance craft landed and the commander scanned and visually checked the area thoroughly. He found a second drone but it was badly damaged, having split open upon impact. It, too, was empty and there was nothing else there other than the wreckage. Except the remains of the crew, of course.`

`And you`re sure there were only the two drones? There weren`t any others that could have been launched elsewhere?`

`Archieblue, you sound like you are interrogating me! Yes, I am sure. Our records show that the craft contained only two drop-drones. No more.`

`I`m sorry, Khara, I guess I am a bit, just trying to figure out what the hell`s going on. So, it`s not on the moon, it`s not here. Masson hasn`t taken it. You were absolutely certain it was on the ship? What about the pilot, Gara, you called him. Could he have switched the drones, or hidden it somewhere? I know he was your ancestor but it was a long time ago. You`re absolutely sure he could be trusted?`

`Of course he could! Absolutely! His integrity is not in any doubt.` she stated. Archie knew better than to question her statement.

`Right, then, so where the hell is this thing?`

Archie stood up and looked at the drone. The open chamber left about half of the total length of the missile still enclosed. The rear portion, which he assumed housed some sort of propulsion system, accounted for about two-thirds of this but if it was no longer a weapon, what was in the pointed third that was the front end, the bit that looked suspiciously like a warhead. *Just as well Dunk didn`t dig that bit up first...!*

`Khara, what`s in the front end. Just there?` he pointed at the warhead.

`I would imagine that it will be the guidance system. Why?`

`Wouldn`t have thought that, with your technology, it would have needed all that - seems a bit of a waste of space, if you`ll pardon the pun!`

She looked at him and simply raised an eyebrow.

`Sorry, never mind. Right, hold on a sec.`

He got down on his knees again and started feeling around inside the empty storage area, where the bulkhead behind the nose cone was situated. As he pushed, he was sure he could feel a very slight movement, as if the panel wasn`t connected to the main casing. He ran his fingers carefully round a bit more and discovered what felt like a little, simple sliding catch that was holding the panel in place. *Old technology, maybe?* He slid it but the bulkhead still didn`t move.

`What exactly are you doing, Archieblue?` Khara asked, her curiosity now aroused.

`Hold on, let`s see what`s at the bottom.` He moved his hand further round the casing, locating a second sliding catch, and pushed this one away as well. Suddenly, the whole bulkhead slid back, as if on rails, moving easily to the centre of the empty casing. Attached to it was a very secure looking cradle assembly surrounded by a load of complex looking equipment, the purpose of which Archie couldn`t begin to guess at. But there, right in the middle, was a rather beautiful, spherical object, made from a dull metal with a slight lustre. He could see no controls, nothing, it looked like a silver football, although the surface appeared to be covered with a host of undecipherable engravings.

It was the Sphere of Samian.

`There`s your baby!` he said standing up, thoroughly pleased with himself.

For the second time that evening Khara was speechless. But this time she stood up, grabbed Archie and pressed her lips to his in a long, lingering kiss, quite literally taking his breath away.

Chapter 28

Archie was just starting to respond to what he presumed was Khara`s expression of gratitude when they were interrupted by two things. First of all, the drone started to make a very faint, regular clicking sound, much like the noise of a cricket on a hot summer`s day. Then, no sooner had they become aware of this than the ship`s voice said

`Self destruct mechanism activated on drone. Approximately four minutes of local time units until mechanism detonates. Destructive force unknown.`

Khara pulled away from Archie and rushed over to the drone. She looked quickly inside then ran back and grabbed some fresh tools, one of which was an implement which appeared to have two sharp blades, somewhat resembling secateurs. She then returned to the open casing and started to work on the restraints holding the sphere in place. As she sliced through them she said

`Archieblue, you must take the sphere out of this area and keep it safe. It will cause you no harm but do not touch anything at all. Just keep it safe.`

`And just what are you intending to do?` he asked anxiously.

`I have to get rid of the drone. If it explodes the ship will be compromised and we will both die.`

`Can`t you just leave the weapon in it and dump the lot?`

`Archieblue` she replied, sounding exasperated but continuing to work. `I have no idea what this weapon could do to humanity. It will have multiple levels of self-protection, probably some form of highly toxic gas, which would be released into the atmosphere. Although the quantity would be small it could possibly cause harm or even be detected, raising many questions. Also, the weapon may not be destroyed in the blast. I do not know how powerful the self-destruct explosive is but, although it would undoubtedly compromise my ship, it quite possibly would not be enough to penetrate the mechanism of the sphere. Do not be fooled by its light weight - it is constructed of a rare and extremely strong metal that is very difficult to destroy. And, of course, if the sphere landed on Earth, think of the problems that it would cause. Not only that, but remember Masson is still down there. I cannot risk the lives of your people and I cannot risk this falling into the wrong hands. Now will you please shut up and let me extract this fucking thing!`

`What did you just say?`

`You heard! Now will you let me finish, please?`

The ship`s computer spoke again.

`Approximately two minutes to drone self destruct.`

`Acknowledged.`

He didn`t much fancy the “approximately” bit!

Khara finished what she was doing and had obviously managed to free the sphere from the securing harness. She stood up, holding it carefully in both hands and handed it to Archie. It was much lighter than he expected.

`Quickly, into the airlock!` she said, running towards the door they had passed through on his first visit to the ship.

`I`m not going without you!` he replied as he followed her, cradling the sphere in his arms as if it were a baby. `No way!`

`Fine.` she said, sounding even more exasperated, then placing her hand against the panel. The door into the airlock slid open and Archie felt her hand shoving him hard in the back, causing him to lurch across and bang heavily into the closed door on the other side, dropping the sphere on the ground. He turned quickly but the door into the docking bay was closing.

`KHARA`

It was too late - he was a prisoner in the small airlock space. Ignoring the sphere, which was rolling about the floor, he jumped across to the panel and placed his hand on it. The computer spoke

`Welcome, Archieblue. I regret that you do not have clearance to operate entry systems on the Terestal.`

`For God`s sake!` he shouted. `I need to get back out there. Khara`s in trouble. Open the damned door.` He banged on the unyielding door panel.

`There is no need to be aggressive, Archieblue. I cannot allow you access unless authorised by Khara. I am sorry.`

Suddenly Archie heard a loud metallic clang resounding through the airlock and he cringed involuntarily, thinking the drone had exploded. But nothing further happened until, after a few moments, he heard a low rumbling sound which he presumed was the large hatch into the docking bay opening. Another few seconds and he heard the same rumble, presumably the hatch closing again. He was about to place his hand back on the panel when there was an enormous explosion and the whole craft lurched about a foot in the air, throwing him onto the floor. He banged his head on the wall as he went down, knocking himself out cold.

He woke up, his head thumping and the sphere resting against his side. He hadn`t a clue how long he`d been out but he felt absolutely dreadful and he put his hand to where the pain seemed to be focussed, feeling a huge lump above his right temple, on top of the one that was only just receding after his drunken collapse – it seemed like a lifetime ago! He managed to stand up, although his balance wasn`t great, and went back to the panel, placing his hand there once again.

`I am sorry, Archieblue, But I cannot....`

`Will you just open the fucking door!` he shouted. `I don`t give a shit about security protocol. I need out of here. NOW. Apart from anything else, I need a pee.` He didn`t, but somehow he felt it might help his cause – he didn`t imagine the vessel would like him urinating in the airlock! `And I need to find out what the hell happened to Khara. OPEN THE DOOR!` He banged his fist against it but the computer failed to respond.

Archie sat despondently on the floor, the sphere resting gently against his thigh. He could only presume Khara had been killed in the blast and now he was well and truly stuck. What a hell of a way to go, he thought, trapped in the airlock of an alien ship, high above Earth, with only a bloody genetic bomb for company. Holy shit! He considered his options but there didn`t seem to be many. He even took out his iPhone in the vain hope that there might have been reception.

There wasn`t!

He stood up again and went back over to the panel, placing his hand on it. The computer remained ominously silent. He vaguely wondered if it was in the huff!

`Look, I`m sorry, okay? But what can I do here - I can`t get out, no-one knows where I am so if you don`t let me out of here then, basically, I`m going to die, slowly and unpleasantly. What do you suggest?`

`I do not know, Archieblue, but without....`

The door to the bay suddenly slid open and Khara stumbled into the airlock, Archie just managing to catch her before she collapsed on the floor. Her grey flying suit was torn badly at the left shoulder and blood was running down the sleeve. There was also an ominous patch of red at her abdomen – she looked as if she had been seriously hurt and the blood was dripping off the suit and forming a pool on the floor.

`Khara! What the hell happened in there? You`re hurt. What can I do? What`s wrong?`

She mumbled something unintelligible and, at first, Archie thought she was talking in her own language again, Then she spat out a small device from her mouth, gasping "emergency respirator!" Then she continued, her voice faint and shaky.

`I think my arm is broken.` she gasped, obviously in a lot of pain. `And I have other injuries, as yet unspecified.` She looked as if she was going to pass out at any minute.

Archie managed to pull away a bit of the sleeve and have a look before she cried out for him to stop. He thought he glimpsed a fragment of bone sticking out of the broken skin and, by the looks of it, she had lost a fair bit of blood.

`Looks like a compound fracture, I`m afraid. Don`t know about the other stuff, but there`s a fair bit of blood. We`ll need to get you to a hospital and get that seen to.`

Somehow she managed a faint smile. `And what do you think they will make of me, Archieblue? Unrecognisable blood type, peculiar heartbeat, low blood pressure, unusual bone structure! No, I think it best if I stay here.`

`But you`re in a mess, Khara. We need to get you sorted.`

`Do not worry, my ship has a medical bay for just such emergencies. All far-space craft are fully equipped but you will need to help me to get there. Can you help me up please?`

He managed to lift her to a standing position but it was obviously a struggle for her and he could see her cringing with each move. She placed her hand on the door back in to the bay and said

`Archieblue, would you place your hand on the other pad, please?`

Archie left her propped against the wall and placed his hand on the pad on the opposite wall. Khara spoke, trying to keep her voice as steady as possible.

`Authorise Archieblue for security clearance level two. Authorisation protocol Kharalaya seven seven two four nine one.`

The computer responded in what Archie thought was a less than happy tone

`Confirmation, Archieblue cleared for security level two.`

`Now, Archieblue, you can open all doors in the ship. Can you take me back to the living quarters but go to the rear of the ship rather than forward to the control deck? I will direct you as we go.`

He put her good arm round his shoulders and helped her out of the airlock and into the corridor, Khara wincing as he did so. At one stage he thought she had passed out but, somehow, she managed to direct him, in the opposite direction from the lounge area that they had passed through previously. He did consider carrying her but he doubted if he would be able to lift her, although he would have given it a try if he hadn`t felt so unsteady himself.

`Turn right here, please` she gasped, obviously in great pain.

Archie accessed another door and it took them to a rear area of the ship that he hadn`t seen before. There were a couple of doors in the walls of the short corridor they were in and she pointed to one. He placed his hand on the panel and, to his surprise, it slid open. What she called the medical bay didn`t seem to contain much. There was a bed, that seemed to be made of something resembling stainless steel, which was fastened to the floor, beside which stood an extremely complex looking device that appeared to be some kind of mechanical arm. The walls were covered in a very pale blue plastic-like coating and it was lit with the same slightly greenish light as the rest of the ship. On one wall, behind the arm, were what looked like shallow, wide drawers, although there were no handles visible.

`Activate medical support.` she managed to gasp.

As Archie watched the bed, a peculiar, pale blue film started to spread on its surface until it was about six inches thick. It was translucent and resembled a fluid of some description, but there appeared to be nothing containing it.

`Can you help me on to the table?` Khara gasped. `You will need to take off my suit.`

He placed his finger at the top just as she had done in his house and, as he moved his hand, the fastening slid down easily. He pulled off the thin suit which was now soaked with blood. He realised that she still had her boots on and he knelt down to remove them, nearly passing out himself as he did so. As he stood back up, she sat heavily on the table and he lifted her legs, trying to place her centrally, momentarily admiring her lithe body as he did so – the admiration turned to alarm as he noticed the dark, heavy bruising around her abdomen. As she lay down she sank in to the blue covering and it moulded itself to her shape of her body, almost as if embracing her. The blue film deepened until most of her body was enveloped by it. She then placed her hand on yet another pad that was joined to the mechanical arm. In a weak voice she said

`Six five six five two two. Level four. Maximum dose.`

The arm sprang to life as one of the drawers slid open. It stretched over and the "hand" removed a little sphere that resembled the ones that he himself had taken previously, then slid it into a receptacle lower down the assembly. It moved back over and positioned itself against her neck. Archie saw no needle but he could see the clear liquid in the vial disappear. Khara closed her eyes briefly then opened them again, giving a long, weary sigh.

`Painkiller, antibiotic and coagulant. That is somewhat better. Now, Archieblue, I need you to listen very carefully.`

`Okay, Khara, fire away.` He tried to concentrate but he felt his head was about to burst. He was swaying as he stood and he grasped the bed for support. His hand seemed to slip through the strange blue fluid and rested on the harder surface below.

`Archieblue, are you hurt? What happened?`

`It`s okay. I banged my head when the drone exploded. I`ll be fine.` He thought he might have concussion, he was starting to see double.

`No, I do not think you will be fine and I need you to concentrate. Access scan for Archieblue. Compatibility check for six five six five zero nine. Minimum dosage.`

Archie remembered that, on his first visit, he had seen the ship appear to scan his body. *Just what did it learn about me?*

`Compatibility acceptable, minimal risk. Shall I administer dosage?`

`Do not worry, Archieblue, this will make you feel a lot better.

Remember, you trust me now?` She raised an eyebrow, as if in challenge. `Stand close to the bed. Now, proceed with dosage.`

The arm returned to the drawer and removed another sphere that contained noticeably less liquid. The hand removed the empty vial and inserted the full one in its place, then came over to Archie and placed itself against his neck. It felt cold and he was aware of only the slightest sensation of something even colder as the drug was injected into his jugular vein. Within seconds the pain and nausea of his headache melted away - it was incredible!

`Wow! That`s some stuff!`

`Yes, it is an excellent pain reduction compound. Now, are you able to concentrate on what I need to tell you?`

`Yep. I`m good to go, now!`

`As you can see I have received several bad injuries. The damage can be repaired by injecting micro-drones into my body. They will repair the broken bone and the damaged tissue, but it will take several hours at least. I will also receive a transfusion of synthesized blood to make up for what I have lost. I will be scanned to determine what other injuries I have sustained and the relevant course of action will be taken to rectify that, too. For me these procedures are quite routine but they will be carried out under general anaesthetic, otherwise the pain would be intolerable, even with the previously injected compound. Can you tell me what time it is now on your clock please?`

Archie looked at his watch. He felt almost like days had passed since he arrived on the ship but, to his surprise, it was only four-thirty. He suddenly remembered what was happening later that day, but managed to shove it to the back of his mind.

`It`s half past four` he stated.

`Thank you. I will need most of the day to recover and you will need to go back to Earth and rest also, I think. And of course, I remember that you have to attend the...well, you have somewhere that you need to be. Also, I suspect that there will be a lot of explaining to do following last night`s events. You may wish to prepare for that.`

`Aye, you`re right there! What do you think Masson will do, Khara? Will he just disappear, go back to Loh?`

`I think that is very unlikely. As far as I can tell he has no ship here and it will take a while for any of his faction to reach Earth if, indeed, he has managed to contact anyone. Remember, there are many planets where there may be so called sleepers, so it is most unlikely that anyone will be in this area for some time. If there was a ship in this sector I think we would have encountered it by now. No, I think he will continue as he is until someone eventually makes contact with him. Then, who knows?`

`But how did he get here in the first place?`

`That is a very good question and it is the mystery that no-one has yet solved. Atra sympathisers should not be able to leave the planet undetected but, somehow, they do. We do not know how. Obviously he has been here for a long time, as you discovered on your computer. Perhaps his parents escaped with him as a baby. But this is not the time for discussion. I must tell you how to get back to Earth.`

She explained how to use the shuttle, what instructions to give to get him back to his house and how to instruct it to return to the ship, adding

`Remember, the computer is bio-interactive and responds to courtesy. A simple please and thank you is good.`

Archie remembered his recent outburst and felt slightly guilty. He would apologise again, he decided.

`Khara, what happens now? I mean, I know you`ll need to get the sphere back to Loh but are you coming back to Earth when you`re better, before you go?`

`Of course, Archieblue. But, as I said, I will be under anaesthetic for most of the day then I will need to make preparations for my return. The sphere - is it still in the airlock?

`Yes, as far as I know! I couldn`t carry it and help you at the same time!`

`No, of course not. Just leave it where it is and I will retrieve it later. Do not touch it, though. It, too, may have security devices for the unwary.`

Archie had no intention of going near the thing!

`Can I ask what happened in the bay, I mean, with the drone? How did you get hurt? How did you manage to stay aboard - I thought that if you opened a door in space the whole area de-pressurised and you got asphyxiated and sucked out!`

`You are correct, of course, but we have some emergency

plans...`she thought for a moment `as you say “up our sleeves”. The hood on my jacket, if pulled over my head, acts as an emergency helmet and contains the small respirator that was in my mouth. This allows survival for a brief period in such a situation so fortunately I was able to breathe. But when the bay opened I was nearly pulled into space and I collided with one of the railings. That is how I was injured but, fortunately, I was able to hold on with my other arm and my legs until the door closed. I am very lucky to be alive.`

`A bit of a close shave, then!`

`A what?`

`A close... oh never mind. It was a close thing.`

`Indeed. You humans have a most peculiar way of saying things. Why can you not just say what you mean, instead of talking about “shaves” and “cats”. It is most confusing for the translation programme.`

`I`m very sorry!` Even now, lying injured on a surgical table, she was able to needle him. `I guess that`s just one of the things that makes us human.`

`Yes, you are probably right. You are a strange species. Such evil amongst you, but such good too...Anyway, you must go now, Archieblue, I need to be repaired,`

`Huh! And you say we have an odd way of saying things!`

`What do you mean?`

`Never mind! Listen, I hope your “repair” goes well – don`t run off back to space without saying goodbye!`

`I will not.`

`Promise?`

`Yes. I Promise!`

`Pinky promise?`

`What?`

He laughed and turned to leave but she called his name and he stopped, turning round.

`Yeah?`

`Thank you, Archieblue. I really mean it. Thank you. Now go.`

He walked to the door but, just before he left the room he glanced back - the mechanical “surgeon” had already started to dance back and forth, repairing the now unconscious alien.

Chapter 29

`Anything?`

Commander Urvai 3 Goffella barked his question after squeezing through the control room door, which had reverted to its half closed position. Unable to rest, he had returned, as he had been doing for the last three days. Retso, the comms officer, answered. He sounded exhausted.

`There has been some movement between the vessel and the planet below. The last one looked as if it may have been a lifting shuttle of some sort but our sensors were unable to resolve the image. The calibration circuitry is inoperative, I am afraid. There was one life sign on the shuttle but the ship seems to be shielding it now.`

`Why was I not alerted?` he snapped.

`Because` replied Terki, `and with all respect, if there is the possibility of engaging this vessel, I need my Commander to be rested and fully alert. Not half asleep like the rest of us. Had anything more serious transpired I would, of course, have summoned you.`

Urvai glared at him but realised his first officer was probably right. He had slept little since the other vessel had been discovered and he knew that this raised the possibility of misjudgement when quick decisions were required. He made no comment, though.

`Where are we now? I presume this other vessel has not detected us?`

`We are behind the planet`s moon.` Replied Terki. `We have plotted our course to remain hidden by it. Retso deployed three remote scanners in order that we may observe the vessel but it would seem to be completely unaware of our presence.`

`Good. That is something at least. We still have the element of surprise.`

Retso suddenly shouted

`There is something else approaching the vessel. I think it is a shuttle, another life sign aboard.`

They all stared at the two dimensional projected display (the main three dimensional display having finally failed to function a few hours previously) watching the small red dot approach the tiny image of the other vessel. Urvai was aware of drops of perspiration dripping from his forehead - he had further reduced the climatic systems to seventy parts per hundred and they were all feeling the effects - the control room was stinking but he barely noticed. The two images finally merged.

`It has docked` stated Retso. The life sign was no longer displayed.

`What now, Urvai?` asked Terki.

The commander thought for a moment before replying

`We wait. We will see what happens next. Let them do as much work as they can, save our own power. How long will it take to reach weapons range?`

The computer replied `Not long. The moon has little gravity and the other vessel is not far behind it, orbiting the planet.`

`Very well.`

The crew sat in an uncomfortable, stuffy and tense silence. Terki and Retso gazed at their screens, Urvai sat in his chair staring at the image of the moon on the monitor. The failure of the main display had angered him but he knew that the entire Zemm was failing, bit by bit and, despite his dark mood, his eyes would shut every so often before he jerked himself awake. Suddenly they were all aware of a bright flash from the monitors.

`What just happened?` shouted Urvai, out of his chair in an instant.

`Something exploded, just outside the other ship` replied Terki.

`What?`

`I do not know. The ship is still there, although the explosion must have been in very close proximity. However, it appears undamaged.`

Urvai shouted, commanding everyone`s attention.

`Enough of this. We will wait no longer. Terki, take us to weapons range. Zemm, hail the crew.`

There was a noise like a deep foghorn, reverberating through the ship. Urvai spoke again.

`Fellow warriors, we are about to engage this vessel and remove whatever it is they have found. This may well be our moment of glory. Combat alert, everyone, may Kii shine brightly on you today.`

He took his place in the Commander`s chair and, as he briefly scanned the faces of the crew in the control room, he was gratified to see that they each wore a wide grin.

***

Archie had just entered the corridor that would take him back to the shuttle bay when a noise like a smoke detector sounded. The floor of the corridor flashed with green lights, like the emergency lights on the floor of an aircraft. The ship`s voice spoke in a tone of urgency.

`A vessel has arrived in our secure zone. Origin unknown but probably from Loh. They are....`

The voice broke off as there was a loud "thump" and the ship lurched violently to the side, much like it had done when the drone exploded. Archie just managed to keep his balance this time.

`What the hell was that?` he screamed.

`The vessel has fired upon us. A low power weapon, probably intended to warn us. Wait...we are being hailed.`

Silence.

`What`s going on?` Archie demanded. `I thought you said we were being hailed?`

`The Ships` computers communicate directly with one another. This vessel is the Zemm, commanded by Urvai 3 Goffella. They demand our surrender and are preparing to board us.`

`What? You`ve got to be joking? After all this, there`s another ship here? Did you not see that one coming?`

`Of course not! I would surmise it has remained behind your planet`s moon.`

`Oh, that`s just fucking great. So what do we do now?`

`I do not know, Archieblue.`

`You do not know? That`s a fat lot of use.`

There was another thump and the ship lurched again.

`We can`t just sit here letting them shoot us out of the sky. Have you no weapons?`

`Of course we do.`

`Well, for God`s sake use them, why don`t you?`

`I cannot fire without the Commander`s authority.`

`Great! In case you hadn`t noticed, the Commander is lying

unconscious back there with your bloody Meccano doctor poking around inside her.`

`Meccano?`

`Oh Christ, don`t you fucking start!`

`Wait! I am receiving a further communication.`

Silence. Then

`Commander Goffella will count to nine. If we do not surrender he will fire on us and disable the ship. Probably killing yourself and Khara.`

`Nine! Why the fuck nine? Why not ten like other people?`

`Nine is a significant number on our planet. One!`

`Just fire your bloody weapons, will you. Otherwise we`re all fucked. You too, Terestal!`

`I told you, I cannot. Only Khara can give the command. And I will not tolerate any further aggression from you, Archieblue. Two!`

`Aw, shit. Okay, I`m sorry. Right, we need to get her to the bridge.`

He dived back along the corridor and into the room, stopping in his tracks as he saw her. The level of the blue liquid on the table top had dropped a little and Khara lay with most of the skin of her abdomen peeled carefully to one side, held in place by thin metal strips. The machine appeared to be working on her innards, although there seemed to be little movement - he remembered her mention something about microdrones...

`What the hell`s happened to her?` he cried. `I thought she`d just broken her arm.`

`She has some serious internal injuries that must be repaired. Three!`

`You need to patch her up. Now! I`ll get her up somehow.`

`I will activate a battle dressing. It should be sufficient. I will not waken her until she is in the control room.`

The machine immediately stopped its operation and started to spray a milky liquid over her bloody insides, which instantly appeared to dry up. Then her skin was neatly lifted back over the wound and sprayed again, leaving a very pale green membrane covering the whole area. There appeared to be no bleeding and Archie rushed over to the table, lifting her up. She was lighter than he expected and , despite the strange blue liquid that had been covering her, her skin was warm and dry. From a distant memory, he dredged up how to perform a fireman`s lift and, with considerable effort, managed to get her over his shoulder.

`Four!`

Archie somehow struggled along the corridor with the naked alien and managed to get her into her seat.

`How do I wake her?`

`Place her hand on the control panel.`

Archie did so. Suddenly she jolted awake and looked around, obviously dazed and disorientated.

`What is happening, Archieblue. Why are you here. Aaah....` She doubled over and clutched her side.

`Five!`

`Khara, we are under attack. There`s a ship. The Zemm, they`ve already fired on us. We need to fight back. Khara, you need to fire something at them. Khara!` He was losing her. He shook her roughly and she winced. She mumbled

`But the Zemm was lost. Long ago. Archieblue, you are so infuriating. Let me sleep.` Her eyes closed.

`Six!`

The ship spoke. Very loudly, this time!

`Commander, you must authorise weapons use or we will be captured and you will be killed. They will take the sphere. You will fail in your mission. You will have no revenge.`

Her eyes jerked open. She stared at the screen, although there was apparently nothing visible. Archie could see her swaying and he tried desperately to ignore the fact that she was completely naked.

`Now, Commander!`

`Deploy dissector. Weapons authorisation Khara nine one nine one four three.` She was obviously struggling to speak.

Archie looked at the screen. He still couldn`t see a thing.

`Seven!`

`What the hell`s happening? There`s nothing there!`

`You will not see the dissector, Archieblue. It is an extremely slim missile that splits into nine separate devices that can penetrate defensive energy fields. When they approach their target, each one transmits a highly powerful irradiated plasma laser array to all the others Anything in the way is split open into multiple segments.

Observe!`

Archie stared at the screen. Suddenly he was aware of tiny filaments flickering across the previously empty space – he could still see nothing of the Zemm. Then, incredibly, long, straight slivers of bright, intense blue light appeared, forming a glowing network, like a fantastic, complex spider`s web. Briefly, as its defences failed, Archie could see the vague outline of a vessel resembling a long, slim airship, before it was cut lengthwise into a myriad of pieces. Slivers of shiny metal peeled off along with darker structures, illuminated by multiple flashes. Finally, an enormous violet fireball erupted, spewing out a shower of glowing debris - it resembled an atomic explosion, although in every direction. Then, suddenly, the explosion seemed to stand still and in what seemed like a fraction of a second, it reversed until there was absolutely nothing. Although still slightly blinded by the glare of the fireball, Archie thought that he perceived a very slight ripple across the image of the moon, like a pebble dropped in a still pool of water.

`What the hell just happened there?` he gasped, realising he had been holding his breath.

The ship responded.

`Their power source was breached, causing a dark energy explosion. I have deployed a containment device to prevent a dark matter anomaly from drifting in this sector of space.`

`Their power source used dark energy?`

`As does ours. It is a very highly efficient energy source that is in plentiful supply throughout the Universe and replenishment is quite straightforward with the correct equipment. However, it is extremely volatile, especially if the containment fields are ruptured, as you have just witnessed. If left unchecked, there would be the possibility of the creation of what you call a black hole.`

As Archie watched the screen, he saw what looked vaguely like a white-ish jellyfish head rapidly across space to where the Zemm had been. It appeared to spread out then it briefly vanished, re-appearing a few seconds later. Its shape had changed to an elongated sphere and it continued to travel away from the Terestal, diminishing in size then disappearing after a few seconds.

`The energy has been contained. It will now be taken into deep space where it can do no harm.`

`And the crew?`

`Archieblue, there is nothing left of either the Zemm or its crew.`

He sat back in his seat and let out a long sigh. He turned to speak to Khara.

`Khara...KHARA!`

She was lying back in her seat, her mouth open, her eyes staring upwards and with a trickle of blood running down her cheek. The battle dressing had opened and she was bleeding profusely from the gash on her abdomen.

`No, no, no!`

`You must return her to the medical bay, Archieblue. She is very seriously injured.`

With a final, superhuman effort, Archie managed to get Khara back down to the bay and placed her on the table, completely unaware that he was soaked with her blood.

`Is she...?`

`She has stopped breathing. I will attempt resuscitation.`

Various implements appeared from the mechanical arm - they enfolded her, covering her face, covering her chest. He looked on helplessly.

`Is there nothing I can do?` he mumbled.

`No! You must go, Archieblue. I need all my resources to be concentrated on saving the Commander.`

`No. I`m staying!`

He became aware of a terrible pressure on either side of his head. He raised his hands to his temples.

`Do not make me use force. You must go. You have your instructions for return of the shuttle. Go! Now!` The pain increased.

`Okay, okay, I`m going!`

He stumbled out of the room, along the corridor, through the airlock and into the shuttle. Immediately the door closed and he was jettisoned into space - it seemed no time until he was outside his house. As he exited the pod, he turned back towards the door.

`But how will...`

The door slid shut and the shuttle vanished up into the night sky.

Chapter 30

It was more the vibrating of the phone in his trouser pocket than the ringing of his mobile that woke Archie from his now habitual deep, dark sleep. He fumbled to remove it and slid it to answer.

`Boss. You okay?`

`Yeah, Cam` he grunted. `What time`s it?`

`Twenty to two. Ah`m nearly ready tae leave the office an` wondered if you`d maybe changed yer mind an` want me tae come and get you.`

Archie sat up in a panic. If Cam hadn`t called, he`d probably have missed the funeral.

`No, thanks all the same. I`ll just make my own way there and come straight home. I think I`d best just be alone with my thoughts, if you know what I mean. I really appreciate the offer though, Cam.`

`Aye, nae worries, Boss. Are you sure you`re okay though? You sound like shit!`

`Kinda feel that way too. But I`ll be fine. I`ll see you there, yeah?

`Three?`

`Three, yes, at Woodside.`

`Okay, I`ll see you then.` There was a pause.

`Take it you`ve heard about a` the cairry-on at Erskine?`

`No! What carry-on?` Despite still being half-awake, the lie rolled easily off his tongue.

`Aw, just that the bomb, or whatever the fuck it wis, has disappeared. Gone! Vanished, just like that! An` tae top it a`, Masson, oor beloved Chief Constable, was found at the site, lyin in the mud, handcuffed and suffering frae concussion an` amnesia as a result o` being whacked over the head. Oh, and don`t forget the two cops found unconscious in their patrol car, who haven`ae a fucking scooby-doo whit happened. Don`t suppose you know anything...?`

The question hung ominously between them.

`Don`t be ridiculous, Cam. What the hell should I know about it?`

`Well, Boss, that`s kinda whit I`m asking you. You were the one askin` about Masson yesterday, what he was goin` to be doin`, where he lived. Bit of a coincidence, eh? Then that carry on wi` Blok an` his cronies – I mean, whit the fuck were you doing oot in the middle o` nowhere in darkest Lanarkshire? Come on, Archie. D`you think I`m daft?`

Archie hesitated, before deciding to ignore the question altogether.

`Cam, I`m sorry but I need to get ready for the funeral. Look, please just trust me. I`ll explain, I promise. But now just now. Okay?

There was another pause before Cam let out a long sigh.

`Okay, Boss. But you know there`s a limit tae just how much I can cover for you. Listen, if you`re involved in anythin`, well...you know...please don`t drag me in tae it. I`ve got a lot to lose...`

`I won`t Cam. Anyway, I`m not involved in anything, I promise. Listen, I need to go. I`ll see you later.`

`Okay. Ah`ll see you at Woodside.`

He ended the call and sat on the edge of the bed, rubbing the stubble on his chin. He reckoned he would just have time for a quick shave and shower and, trying to put the unsatisfactory conversation with Cam out of his mind, he hauled his weary body off the bed and into the en-suite, turning on the water. Once he had washed and dried himself, he opened his wardrobe, praying that there would be a clean white shirt – fortunately there was! He took out his dark grey suit then rummaged for his black tie and, fifteen minutes later, he thought he looked reasonably presentable, apart from the dark circles under his eyes. He went downstairs and made himself a quick coffee, then set off for Paisley`s Woodside crematorium.

There were a few cars in the car park and, as it was only ten to three, he sat for a few minutes until Cam`s car slid in beside him. He got out and, although the sergeant shook his hand, his grip firm and re-assuring, Archie felt there that their earlier conversation still hung between them, like an invisible curtain. Neither man spoke as they entered the building, where about twenty people were already sitting at the front. Apart from Gordon and Karen Whiteford, he recognised only one, Karen`s younger sister Fiona, although there was a tall young man with short dark hair that he presumed to be the Whiteford`s son – he was the image of Gordon when he had been at school. They sat down quietly a few rows behind but Karen turned and, seeing Archie, managed a faint smile before her eyes filled up and she turned back to face the light oak coffin that sat on the plinth.

The minister entered.

`Dearly beloved...`

Soon it was over. The minister, obviously a family friend, had done a wonderful job, painting a poignant picture of a young life tragically cut short. Alas, Archie knew the cold, hard reality and the words of comfort failed to penetrate his feeling of overwhelming sadness. He was relieved that the family had refrained from producing one of the little order of service booklets that were the fashion these days but, as they stood to leave, Karen came up beside him and handed him an envelope. Cam kept walking, leaving them alone.

`I thought you might like to have these.`

He opened it and looked inside. There were about a dozen photos, the first few he looked at being of a young girl with long sandy hair and freckles, smiling happily at the camera. His head started to spin and he put them back.

`I`ll look later, Karen, if you don`t mind.`

`I understand.` She looked at him, her eyes brimming with tears. `Are you all right, Archie? You look awful.`

`I`ll be fine, Karen, thanks. Just tired. I`ve not been sleeping well.`

`Me neither.`

They walked out in silence, shaking hands with the minister on the way past. He had given Archie the standard bland, pastoral smile and thanked him for coming, but showed no sign of recognition or knowledge of his identity. Presumably he wasn`t actually aware that Archie was the father of the dead girl. Once outside, Karen spoke again.

`Don`t be a stranger now, Archie, you know where we are.`

`Thanks Karen, but I think we both know that`s not going to happen.`

She just shook her head sadly. `So, have you got someone special in your life?`

He paused before answering and she gave him a questioning look. He shook his head.

`No. Just me and the job. As always. You were a hard act to follow, Karen.`

She attempted a small smile. `Its time you found someone,

Archie. You`re a good man. It would be a waste if you slipped through the net.`

`Well, you let me slip, didn`t you,` The words were out before he could stop them.

She shot him a look. `Don`t start, Archie. It wasn`t just me. You could have kept in touch too, you know.`

`Sorry, Karen. I`m just...well, fragile I suppose.`

`I know. I`m sorry, Archie, really sorry. And I should probably have told you about Lucinda years ago but, well, it just didn`t seem right. Not with Gordon...` she bit her lip and stopped.

`No, I suppose not. Anyway, its water under the bridge, now.`

Fortunately Gordon Whiteford came over before the conversation became any more awkward. He extended his hand.

`Archie. Good of you to come. We`re heading back to the house now, just a few friends, the minister, but you`re very welcome to come along.`

`That`s kind, Gordon, but I`ll pass, if you don`t mind. Might be hard to explain.`

`Yes, perhaps you`re right. Well, thanks again for coming,`

`Least I could do, in the circumstances.`

`And you`ve got someone in custody, I believe? Well, more than one, by the sounds of it.`

`Yeah, they`re all pretty much implicated, one way or another.`

`Good, I appreciate that. As long as some clever brief doesn`t get them off.`

`Somehow I doubt it, this time. But I`m afraid you never know.`

`No, indeed. But do your best, Archie. Put them away before... well, before it happens to anyone else. Anyway, we`d better go. Karen?`

She gave Archie a tight hug and he could smell the light scent from her hair. Delicate, enticing, but out of a bottle...

`Goodbye, Archie Blue. And good luck. You take care of yourself now!`

`You too, Kh...Karen. `Bye.`

She climbed in to the Bentley and, with a brief wave, they were gone. Cam, who had been standing discreetly at his car, came over.

`Difficult conversation?`

`No, not too bad. She gave me some photos of Lucinda.`

`That wis nice. At least you`ll have somethin`, Boss.`

`That`s the thing, Cam. I`ve got fuck all!`

***

When he arrived home, Archie decided that the best course of action was to keep himself busy by sorting out his house, which was showing serious signs of neglect. By seven o`clock, though, he had cleaned, tidied and washed and it was starting to look more like a home again. As he toiled, he kept glancing outside, just in case, but there was no shuttle, nothing, just the occasional tractor and a single car heading up the narrow road outside his house. He realised he hadn`t eaten all day and a quick trawl of his freezer produced a frozen lamb tikka, which he shoved in the microwave before opening a bottle of Arran Gold beer – the whisky could wait till later!

His dinner finished, he was sitting on the couch, plucking up the courage to look at the photos Karen had given him. He swallowed the dregs of the second bottle of beer and pulled the precious contents out. They were all colour, good quality prints - Lucinda as a baby, a chubby, cherubic looking infant. As a toddler, playing on a swing - the resemblance to Archie as a child was striking. A school photo, probably late primary, looking slightly more serious. High school...the tears started and soon he was sobbing uncontrollably, the photos clutched tightly in his hand.

He didn`t know how long he had been sitting there when his phone rang. It was Cam.

`Hey, Boss. Just checkin` you`re okay – hopefully that`s the worst over, if you know whit I mean.`

Archie composed himself. Cam was proving to be an even better friend than he had realised. He felt a pang of guilt – his sergeant really deserved an explanation of some sort.

`Yeah, Cam, you`re right, and I`m okay. Just had a curry and a beer, sitting watching the telly.` He was surprised again how easily the lies flowed.

`Good stuff. Listen, Tracey`s askin` for you. I didn`ae say aboot...Lucinda, just said it wis a close friend, but she`s worried about you.` He paused. `So am I, for that matter.`

`That`s kind, Cam. Tell her I`m fine. Honestly.`

`So, are you comin` back tae work any time soon? The Super has been askin` questions, I`ve told him pretty much the same story I told Tracey, but you know whit he`s like. Wantin` value for the taxpayer, etcetera! The usual shite!`

Archie recalled his last conversation with Hamilton and felt a vague and unfamiliar pang of sympathy for the man. He was feeling pretty disillusioned himself, after all!

`Yeah, I`ll be in tomorrow. Business as usual.`

`Great.` He hesitated. `Listen, aboot oor conversation earlier.`

`Yeah?`

`Well...no matter how hard I try, I cannae get my head roond everythin` that`s been happenin`. You and me, Archie, we go back a long way. You know I trust you and I know you`re a good straight cop. But, fuck me, you`re really stretchin` things here! You need to keep me in the picture, Boss.`

`I will, Cam, honestly, I will.`

`When?`

There was a pause.

`Aye, thought so. Listen, Hamilton`s asked me tae head doon tae Erskine first thing tomorrow, see if I can try an` clear up some of this sorry mess. He asked if you`d be...an` I quote, "gracing us with your presence!" Sarcastic bastard! Anyway, how about I meet you there, back o` nine? The place`ll be crawlin` wi` cops but we`ll find a nice wee quiet spot, just you an` me, and we can have a wee chat. No office, no Super, no interruptions.`

`Fair enough. I`ll see you there,Cam.`

`Okay Boss. `Til tomorrow.`

Just what he was going to tell Cam, he didn`t know. He would decide in the morning. What he needed now was an early night.

Chapter 31

The phone alarm sounded at 7.30a.m. - Archie had removed "I`m not in love" and substituted it with one of the generic phone sounds called "uplift", although the ponderous pingle-pongle of the fake piano was anything but! As he slid the control to turn it off he lay back down in the darkness and considered not bothering going in to work – maybe he could justify another day of compassionate leave. Then he abandoned the idea, realising that, sooner or later, his life would have to continue, whatever hurdles he may face. The first, of course, was Cam. No matter how good a friend he was (and he had surpassed any of Archie`s expectations over the last few weeks), he could hardly confess to murder, dealings with an alien and assaulting the Chief Constable. No, he would have to try and concoct something plausible but, once again, entirely untrue. That seemed to be the story of his life at the moment. He headed to the en-suite, his only positive thought being that he had managed another reasonable night`s sleep without resorting to a stiff whisky. He had, however, wakened several times, imagining he had heard movement outside, but a glance out of the window had revealed only the dark, autumn night, faintly illuminated by a quarter moon. As he had lain back in his bed, he wondered if the Terestal was still there, if Khara was still alive. Given recent events in his life, he rather doubted both.

An hour later, shaved, showered and breakfasted, he prepared to set off on the now-familiar journey to Erskine. It was a grey, dry morning, the blustery wind having blown away the rain clouds but, as a precaution, he opened the back door of the Porsche and threw his Berghaus jacket on to the seat. As he did so, he noticed something in the passenger foot-well. Leaning over to pick it up, he realised it was the pear-shaped grey board that Khara had left behind after their first encounter. He lifted it, surprised at how light it was, although he hadn`t a clue what function it performed. However, not wanting to have to fabricate any further stories, he took it in to the house and placed it carefully against the wall of the hall before returning to his car.

He arrived at the building site just after nine to find it crowded with cops and, to his dismay, the army. A helicopter was sitting in the open space behind the offices and he could see Major Donaldson`s pick-up in the car park, the Major himself apparently having a heated discussion with Cam - it was time to intervene. The uniform cops at the gate waved him through then returned to their task of keeping the press and, of course, the television crews at bay. He parked outside the Portakabin and walked over to where the two men were still facing up to each other. As breezily as he could muster, Archie said `Good morning Major` and extended his hand. The soldier turned and, whilst returning the handshake, he didn`t give the slightest impression that he thought the morning "good".

`Archie. This is a bloody disgrace. I thought you and your men were supposed to have this site secure. Now some bugger has removed the device, about which we know absolutely nothing and, to add insult to injury, your sergeant refuses to allow my men to inspect the area. For all any of us know, the ground from which the device was removed could be toxic. You need to use a bit of common sense, man!`

`Major, I completely understand your position. But you must understand ours, too. Our Chief Constable was seriously assaulted here and two of our officers were also left unconscious. First and foremost, we are dealing with a crime scene and we must keep it secure until any possible evidence has been gathered. I accept that there may be some risk but, at the end of the day, the device itself has gone so the risk from that has been removed.`

`But this happened on Monday night, for God`s sake! Your men have had all day yesterday to try and find something. I have a team of specialists here who, quite frankly, have better things to do with their time than stand about waiting for your lot to try and find something.`

Despite his full possession of the actual facts, Archie could feel his hackles rise at the Major`s belligerence. Fortunately, before he could reply, the Major`s phone rang and he turned away, talking quietly into the handset. Archie gestured to Cam and they quickly walked off, heading round the back of the Portakabin and out of sight. The two men leaned on the wall, Cam letting out an exasperated sigh. Then he turned to Archie

`So, Boss. You were goin` to give me an explanation...?`

`Yep, fair enough, and you deserve it. First of all, and you have to believe this, I have done nothing wrong, well, other than morally, perhaps!`

More lies, Archie...

He continued

`Anyway, you were right about a woman.`

Despite the gravity of the situation, Cam grinned.

`You know, I really did have a feelin`. So who is she?`

`Well, that`s the thing, Cam. I can`t tell you. It was nothing serious, it`s over now, but she`s...well...`

`Ah, right, I get you. She`s, em, attached?`

`Aye, you could say. But attached to, well, let`s say someone that we know, someone, perhaps, with a less than savoury reputation, someone you`ve been talking to recently...`

`Aw fuck, Archie, you`ve no` been messin` with one o` that gang`s women! Christ, that`s a death sentence if they find out!

Whose wis she? Ralston`s?`

The penny suddenly dropped.

`Here, wait a minute? Is that whit was goin` on that night, why Blok an` his mob were oot there? Jesus, Archie, yer lucky tae be alive!`

`Aye, I know! And, yes, she was Ralston`s, though she pretty much hated him, poor lassie was petrified of him. And, obviously I kinda knew it was a bad idea, Cam but, you know, fatal attraction and all that crap... Anyway, that night we`d gone for dinner in town, somewhere nice and quiet, where we thought we`d be safe. But someone must have seen us and, when we got back to my car, well, they were waiting and, basically, they kidnapped us. Took us out to that derelict farm.`

He reckoned a bit of truth wouldn`t go amiss. Cam just stared at him, his mouth open in astonishment. Archie continued

`I think they must have suspected her for a while, maybe someone was tailing her and, let`s face it, my car`s a bit of a giveaway. I can tell you, it wasn`t a good situation, in fact it was potentially pretty horrendous. I take it you saw their toys?`

Another morsel of truth...

Cam nodded silently. He knew as well as Archie what these people were capable of. Archie continued

`So, out of the blue, McLintock made some comment about the woman, called her a "fuckin` filth-shaggin` hoor," or something like that. It was strange, but despite what she`d been up to with me, Ralston took serious exception to this and, before we know it, they`re at each other`s throats. We managed to get away, I phoned you and the girl`s done a runner, hopefully to somewhere far, far way.

Oh, you`re a lying bastard, Archie...well maybe the last bit isn`t too far from the truth...

`Seriously? That`s it?`

`Yep. That`s it. Nothing more complicated than wrong place, wrong time and definitely the wrong person! But that`s what happened. At the end of the day, I suppose low-life like that are all out to get each other. Also, I got the feeling that they`d had enough of Blok telling them what to do and it wasn`t long before he became involved and all hell broke loose. As to the other two, I guess they probably just had divided loyalties.`

There was a silence - Archie knew it all sounded pretty feeble but it was the best he could come up with. Then Cam spoke again

`There`s just one more thing, Boss.`

`What`s that, Cam?`

Cam hesitated.

`Well, before I got called away tae deal wi` all this` he gestured over his shoulder `...shite, I was interviewin` Ralston again and I happened tae mention Kevin King. I`d mentioned I wis a wee bit surprised he hadn`ae been there wi` the others. Plus there`s been no sign o` him since.`

`And?` Archie`s pulse had started to race.

`Well, he said a funny thing. Said "Aye, you`ll need to ask yer Boss aboot Kevin."`

Archie tried to look surprised.

`What was that supposed to mean, do you think?`

`That`s whit I`m askin` you, Boss. Thing is, I asked Czarneki as well – he`s still in hospital, by the way, he`s in some state, won`t walk properly again, they reckon. But he kinda said the same thing. Well, he said Kevin had gone and that "Bluesky saw him off." As for McLintock, I`m certain he`s headed for the funny farm, cannae get any sense oot o` him at all.`

`Haven`t a clue, Cam. I don`t know what the hell they`re talking about. I haven`t set eyes on King for months, when we pulled him in to ask about those murders. You interviewed him, said he was a right smug bastard, if I remember right!`

`Aye, I remember well enough, but I wasn`ae there at that farm, or anywhere else for that matter. Listen, Archie, you`ve no` gone an` done anythin`...well, you know what I mean.`

No, Cam. Honestly. I haven`t.`

He felt physically sick.

`And all this carry-on? Masson, the bomb disappearin`. You dinnae know anythin` aboot any o` it?`

`No Cam. Nothing at all. I`ve told you all I know, about Czarneki and his mob, about what happened. That`s the only involvement I`ve had in anything. All the rest, well, its either just pure co-incidence or a bunch of lies. Probably the latter.`

Suddenly he retched and, leaning forward, brought up his breakfast.

`Jesus, Archie, are you okay?`

Archie was bent over with his hands on his knees, gasping for breath.

`Yeah, I`ll be okay, Cam. It`s just been a fucking nightmare, the last two weeks. Ever since...well, you know...`

`Christ, I`m so sorry, Boss. Here`s me givin` you the third degree and you`re still sufferin`. Whit an arsehole!`

Unfortunately, this display of concern wasn`t helping assuage his guilt. Archie stood up, the nausea passing. In an attempt to change the subject, he asked

`What about that big prick, McCourt? Got anything more on him?`

`Naw, we`re gonna have to let him walk. No` a shred, other than whit Ralston said. I`m sure the guy`s guilty as get-oot, but we`ve nothin` solid we can pin on him, it`s his word against Ralston`s. Odd thing though, one of the boys back at the office said that Ralston`s gone all...well, I`m no` really sure. Seems he`s suddenly clammed up, won`t say a word. He`s bangin` on aboot forced confessions, that sort of thing. The other day he wouldn`ae stop talkin` - weird.! Anyway, we`ll keep diggin` on McCourt, though - pity he wasn`ae there that night. I`m just hopin` the whole thing hangs together long enough to get a prosecution. There`s nae chance you could dig up thon woman you were wi`, I suppose.`

Nope! Not a snowball`s chance in hell, I`m afraid.`

At least that much is true...

Archie wondered if there was any connection between Ralston`s change of attitude and Khara`s injuries – had her influence over the gang waned? He answered, trying to sound as natural as he could.

`Aye, that would have been a full house. Except for King. Look, I really don`t like what those bastards are saying. My hunch is they`re trying to implicate me because of, well, my involvement with the woman, I suppose. Even if they hate each other`s guts, its still a matter of honour. Having an affair with a cop is never going to be popular, is it? So my guess is that, somewhere along the line, King overstepped the mark, Czarneki had him killed and now they`re trying to stick it on me.`

`Aye, maybe you`re right. But whit aboot the usual MO? The fingers up the nose? That would have sent a powerful message tae anyone else gettin` oot o` line. King wis quite high up in the food chain.`

`Who knows? Maybe there was another reason, something personal, or even a drunken fight!. Blok`s a rough big bastard, wouldn`t imagine he`d get too sentimental over his associates. Probably we`ll never know.`

As he was talking, fabricating his elaborate alibi, he was gazing down towards the building yard. Somewhere, in amongst the lies, the deceit, the grief, his detective`s mind had jumped into gear again and there was something niggling at him. He couldn`t put his finger on what it was but it was there - deftly, he changed the subject.

`Cam. Remember the morning Carson, the site manager, found the reporter`s body?` he asked.

`Aye, he said he`d gone "round the back" or somethin` like that, didn`t he?`

`Never said what he`d gone for, did he? Look over there. What do you see?`

The two cops looked at the building yard that lay behind the Portakabins, the Army helicopter still sitting idly in the adjacent field. The large enclosure had secure fencing topped with barbed wire, inside which were the other now-redundant JCBs, along with a couple of cement mixers, a few spare crane buckets and about a dozen oil drums, presumably containing fuel for the plant. A stack of concrete blocks stood at the very back. The gate was firmly padlocked.

`Cam, nip round to the office, see if anyone`s there and try and get the keys. If you can, avoid Carson, just in case. And the Major!`

`Will do, Boss.` He trotted round the front and returned in just a few minutes with a bunch of keys.

`Spot o` luck! I met Big Dunk and he just handed them to me. He says it`s pretty likely he`s oot o` a job and obviously doesn`ae feel much loyalty to HomeFree. Cannae say I blame him. Right, which one?`

After a few tries, Cam found the correct key and opened the lock. They pushed the gate open and stepped inside. `They`ve got a secure perimeter fence and then they`ve got this mini fortress for the plant` said Archie. `I know that this stuff can sometimes gets nicked but you`d need a low-loader to get one of these buggers away. It seems to be just a wee bit excessive, don`t you think?`

`Aye, maybe a bit. But it just looks like the normal stuff you`d find on a building site. Doesn`ae seem to be much else here.`

Archie surveyed the area. The ground was wet and covered with the same brown-grey mud that was everywhere, including the tyres of the car that had contained the heroin. What was he missing? All the usual stuff you`d expect to find at this stage, heavy plant, fuel and, in the far corner, the pallets of concrete blocks.

`Cam, do they use concrete block for foundations?`

`No, they usually pipe it in fae those big mixer things, what do they call them, aye, a Jaeger, I think.` He noticed where Archie was looking. `Interestin`. Haven`ae seen any of those in use round the site. Bugger all buildin` going on, if you ask me.`

`Come on, let`s have a look.`

They set off across the yard and, as they got nearer, they could see that a good few of the blocks had been broken up and stacked neatly beside the intact ones. There was a fair amount of fragments spread about the ground.

`That`s a bit of a waste, Cam. Why get them in then break them up? Doesn`t look accidental, does it?`

`Naw, it doesn`ae! Now why would they do that?`

Cam picked one up from the stack on the first pallet and it seemed about the normal weight. He placed it on the ground, sitting it in its edge, then he lifted another and dropped it on to the first, splitting it in two. It seemed to contain the normal mix of aggregate and cement so he lifted another...then another...another...

`Looks like there`s nothin` dodgy here, Boss. Maybe just a load got broken by accident, someone tidied them up` he said, after breaking another six blocks.

`Try some off the other pallet. Maybe further down.`

They carefully lifted blocks off the top couple of layers on the second pallet and took some from the third layer. Cam lifted the first over to his original block and dropped it. Nothing. He went back and selected another, dropping it as before. The two detectives looked down at the sturdy plastic package that had been concealed inside before Archie took a pair of forensic gloves from his pocket and lifted it. Despite the thick wrapping they could both see the white contents it contained.

`Bingo!` Cam grinned.

`Nice one!` said Archie. He realised how good it was to feel normal, to feel that he was on the right side once again. Temporarily, at least. `So, someone, somewhere, makes up blocks with this inside, then once it sets, who would know? Move them anywhere, last place anyone would look for drugs. Brings a whole new meaning to getting "stoned", doesn`t it?" Cam just rolled his eyes. `I wonder if they`re marked. Let`s have a look at the block you just broke.`

They bent down and examined the pieces, comparing them to those of the solid blocks. Then Cam said

`Look Boss, at the end here. Two wee holes, they`re no` on any o` the others.`

Archie looked and saw what Cam was referring to. There were two holes, about two centimetres apart and about a centimetre in diameter, in the middle of one end of the block. He stood up

`Right, see if there`s any more with those holes.`

They went back to the pile and, after a good bit of heavy manual labour, they had found another seven blocks with similar markings. Cam split one open and, sure enough, it contained another tightly wrapped package. Archie said

`Right, I`m gonna call this in, get a bit of back-up. We need to get the drugs guys involved, this looks a pretty big haul to me. There has to be a whole supply chain for this lot and if they can find who makes these blocks, who delivers them and where they`re from, then they should be able to clean up the whole lot. This looks like it`s going to be a right big case, Cam, if we can track it all down. And if we can find out how and where the stuff`s coming in to the country in the first place, well, even better. Did Ralston not say anything about this?`

`Just that McCourt was involved in supply. I don`t think he knew anythin` aboot the actual operation. No wonder he looked clean.`

`I think it`s likely that McCourt`s been Czarneki`s main distributor, maybe indirectly through Ralston – the ones at the top never like to get too close to the sharp end, do they? This is a great cover for them too, no wonder they don`t need to be doing much building, eh? And, given that Czarneki`s from overseas, quite possibly he`s been organising the supply at that end in the first place and using McCourt to store the stuff. You`ll need to see what what else Ralston knows, if he had any idea about this distribution system. Have another go at Czarneki too, see if he`s got anything to say. Christ, no wonder we`ve been struggling to find where all this shit has been coming from. Right, let`s leave these ones intact so they can get the satisfaction of finding some for themselves. Looks like Mr McCourt won`t be going anywhere fast. And I think we should haul Carson in as well. I very much doubt if he`s clean. He seemed a bit edgy when we arrived at first, didn`t he?`

`Aye, right enough. He didn`ae seem too happy that we were detectives. Never gave it much thought at the time.`

`Maybe it was his job to split the blocks open and pass the contents on. I wonder if that`s what he was doing when he found McCurdy?`

`You don`t think he had anythin` tae do wi` McCurdy`s death, do you Boss? You think maybe the poor guy caught Carson in the act, as it were?` asked Cam.

Archie shook his head.

`No, I doubt it. Doc Clayton said it was a massive heart attack and there were no injuries. Anyway, I think it`s pretty certain he was after a story about the bomb, or whatever it was. Nope, I think it was just the poor sod`s time - way to go, really, out on a job rather than dribbling your life away in a nursing home!` Archie was still unsure if it was Masson who had been responsible for the reporter`s death and Sam Clayton`s words still rang in his head "Looked like he`d been scared to death..."

`Yeah, suppose you`re right. Okay, I`ll nick Carson, if he`s there, and pass him over tae one o` the uniforms, get him over tae Paisley to join his pals. You know, Boss, I wonder if this has anythin` to do with Czarneki`s nickname? You know, Blok?`

Archie hadn`t thought of it but it was a possibility.

`Aye, you might be right at that! Why don`t you ask him?`

`Aye, like he`s gonnae admit tae that!` Cam chuckled. Archie continued

`Listen, I`ll wait here and phone Mick Paterson in the drugs team, give him the good news. Once they`re here we`ll head back to the office and make sure McCourt stays securely locked up. There`s enough bloody uniforms here to keep the place secure enough, no-one`s going to sneak in and disappear with anything. It`s bloody freezing out here, see if you can get Big Dunk to rustle us up a coffee, eh? If the poor sod`s still there, that is!`

About ten minutes later, Cam arrived with two mugs of coffee, handing one to Archie. He wasn`t smiling.

`Want the bad news?`

`What`s that?`

`Your friend an` mine, Superintendent Hamilton is here. Wants a word wi` you!`

Chapter 32

Superintendent Alexander Hamilton stepped out of the chauffeur-driven Jaguar and, as he closed the door, he turned and quickly checked his reflection in the window, ensuring that his tie was straight and his hat perfectly positioned on his short, silver hair – he wasn`t taking any chances with all those Press cameras pointing in his general direction. As usual, his well-pressed uniform and immaculate white shirt looked as if they were just out of the cleaners - even his shoes shone almost as if they were patent leather and he frowned at the mud below his feet, as if daring it to adhere to them. He had questioned the wisdom of his uncharacteristic frankness during his last conversation with Detective Inspector Archie Blue but he had hoped that, perhaps, it would serve its purpose and allow him to retire on a high note. But this...well, this situation was going to make him a laughing stock – the man who lost the bomb. No, Superintendent Hamilton was not a happy man. He knew, of course, that this wasn`t directly Archie`s fault but he needed the affair cleared up...fast.

He had sent one of the uniforms ahead to announce his arrival and he reached the front of the Portakabin at the same time as Archie and Cam, who were still clutching their mugs of coffee.

`Ah, Inspector, Sergeant, there you are. I`m relieved to see you back at work, Archie, I believe you`ve had a bereavement. I`m very sorry to hear that but, as you are no doubt aware, things have been going awry in your absence. And I`m glad to see you`ve time to fit in a hot beverage!`

Aye, he`s back to normal – sarcastic as ever!

`Good morning Sir. A bit nippy, just trying to warm up.`

`Yes, well, don`t let the press snatch a photo of you two standing about drinking coffee. We`ve got enough trouble from that direction already– have you seen this?`

He pulled a copy of the Scottish Sun newspaper out of the slim attache case he was carrying and handed it to Archie. Most of the front page was covered with a simple, two-word headline.

"BOMB`S AWAY...!"

Archie was aware of Cam just managing to suppress a snigger, turning it into a cough at the last minute, and he briefly wished that Bill McCurdy had lived to see it. He handed the paper back to Hamilton. The Superintendent glared at the sergeant but didn`t comment. He continued.

`The word "debacle" is being bandied about, Archie and, on this occasion, I believe it to be highly accurate. Quite honestly, this whole matter is an absolute disgrace. Now, I am well aware that you are not personally responsible and, believe you me, you should be relieved. Inspector Marsh is facing a disciplinary enquiry into how he managed to allow all this to happen. I mean, how on earth did Sir Peter himself even manage to gain entry without someone seeing him? The whole thing is, quite frankly, a complete balls-up!`

Archie spoke in an attempt to stem the tirade.

`How is the Chief Constable, Sir? Will he be okay?` He was somewhat curious, after all...

The Super obviously wasn`t too happy at having his flow interrupted but he simply frowned and answered the question.

`Well, of course, that`s another thing. No disrespect, of course, but he is, well, slightly, em...`

Archie knew exactly what he meant and, of course, why!

`Anyway, he absolutely refused to go to hospital, insisted on being taken home. Says he has his own private physician and that he would consult him. Most odd, most odd indeed. However, he has since been in touch and says that he is fine, just suffering from a bad bruise and a bit of concussion. Says, apparently, that he has a great interest in World War Two, wanted a closer look, although God knows why anyone would want a look at a possible bomb that could have gone off at any time. Except, of course, that it now seems it wasn`t a bomb at all.`

Here we go...

From the attache case the Superintendent pulled out a sheet of paper, enclosed in a plastic sleeve, and handed it to Archie.

`Arrived in the post this morning. Glasgow postmark. This is a copy, of course, the original is with forensics looking for prints, etc. Nothing as yet but they`re quite hopeful. Read it.`

Archie, of course, didn`t really need to read it but he made a show anyway. His thoughts were more on just how much care he had taken in handling it in the first place – the least sign of his prints and, well...He still thought it sounded reasonably plausible though and, once finished, he handed it back, but Hamilton held up his hand.

`No, Archie, keep it. I want you to handle this. I want these people found, whoever they are. It seems likely that what they are saying is the truth – I mean, what other explanation do we have? But it would also seem likely that they are responsible for assaulting Sir Peter - and, of course, our two constables in the vehicle. I want you to take personal charge of this, with your Sergeant, of course, and I expect an early result. We`ve already lost enough face here so if we can get some speedy arrests, at least we may regain a little credibility. Mark my words, when you find these people, and note, Archie, that I say "when", then we will be throwing the proverbial book at them!

He beckoned Archie aside, turning his back on Cam`s somewhat hostile stare, and lowered his voice.

`You will recall our conversation, Archie. This is not exactly how I want to conclude my thirty years of unblemished service, with inane headlines proclaiming our ineptitude. I`m counting on you here – don`t let me down.` He turned back towards his car.

`Now, I have a press conference to attend. Keep me posted, Inspector.`

Superintendent Hamilton turned and strode back to the Jaguar, the rear door of which was already being opened by his driver. He slid elegantly in to the back seat, the door was closed and in seconds the car was speeding through the gates and past the throng of reporters. Archie felt like his world was caving in – the lies, the deceptions, they were all coming home to roost. He turned to Cam.

`Let`s get the fuck out of here.`

***

After grabbing a quick bacon roll in the Headquarters canteen, Archie headed up to his office, leaving Cam to question and, hopefully, charge the now heavily implicated McCourt. Even though he had only been absent for a few days, there was a pile of paperwork and correspondence waiting in his "in" tray and he leafed through it disinterestedly, attempting to sort it into piles of ascending priority. His top priority at the moment, however, was the copy of the letter he had written explaining the disappearance of the so-called bomb and, as he sat and stared at it, he started to realise just how idiotic it had been. Of course, he could not have foreseen the incident with the Chief Constable and, had Masson not interfered, the explanation might just have been accepted. But now he was expected to carry out an investigation to find the perpetrators (who existed entirely in his imagination) of an incident that had never actually occurred and the Superintendent had left him in no doubt that he expected a result.

He managed to wade his way through the papers on his desk for another hour or so before deciding to call it a day. As he made a final re-shuffle of the piles, he realised (with some sadness) that he was trying to get away without seeing Cam, whose office would normally have been his last port of call before heading home. He got to the door, only to meet the Sergeant as he prepared to enter.

`Hey, Boss. Buggerin` off early?`

`Yeah, got a few things to sort, then heading home. To be honest, I`m totally knackered. Anyway, I don`t really know where to start with this letter that Hamilton gave me, so I want to sleep on it and come back to it fresh in the morning. I mean, if it`s true, and I`m not saying I really believe it, then these are obviously powerful and clever guys. In fact, it crossed my mind that Masson might even have been one of them. He`s the right age, after all, he went to Glasgow Uni, who knows what he got up to as a student. Just a thought...`

`Aye, well, right enough...` Cam seemed a bit preoccupied. He subtly manoeuvred Archie back into the office and closed the door. He looked straight at him.

`Archie, I`ve known you a long time. You`re a great cop, you`re a great detective. You`re a great mate – Christ, you`re Abigail`s godfather after all, but you are a fuckin` crap liar!`

Archie made to speak but Cam held up his hand.

`No! Don`t say anythin`. Just listen and listen very carefully. I`ve put up wi` "trust me", I`ve put up wi` "I`ll tell you later", I`ve gone along with all your shite explanations, I`ve tried to accept what you`ve told me at face value. But it ends, right here, right now. Any more crap, bullshit or lies and I`m goin` straight to the Super. I`m sorry, Archie, but that`s it. Understand?`

Archie bowed his head and mumbled

`Understand!`

Cam made to leave, then he reached out and gripped his friend`s arm, speaking more softly this time

`For God`s sake, Archie, dinn`ae flush it all away doon the toilet. Whatever the fuck`s goin` on, its no` worth it. You`re on track for promotion, you know that. Chief Inspector Blue – sounds good – and I`d get to call you "Boss" again! Or would you rather be sharin` a cell in some high security unit wi` Czarneki or wan o` his crew?` He paused for effect and shook his head. `No, you know fine well you fuckin` wouldn`ae! You know whit happens tae cops who get locked up an` it`s no` pleasant. Please, mate, get yersel` sorted. You know where I am if you need me. I`m always ready if you need to talk.`

He released his grip, turning and walking out of the room before Archie had a chance to reply.

***

Archie stared at the door, stunned at his friend`s candour. Suddenly he realised he had to get outside, get some fresh air, get away from this place. Grabbing his jacket, he hastily left his office and, avoiding any glances cast his way, he made his way as quickly as he could out of police HQ and into the sanctuary of the Porsche.

He drove home in a daze – in all the time that they had known each other, Cam had never spoken to him in such a forthright and serious manner. The trouble was, his friend was right and he totally deserved every word. Cam obviously knew that what he had been told was a pack of lies and it worried Archie just how much of the truth he actually did know and how much he only suspected. His conscience was troubled, too, as he cared enough to worry about his friend`s involvement by implication. The whole thing was one sick, sorry mess. Problem was, he hadn`t a clue how to fix it.

He made a stop in Lochwinnoch for a fish supper but, by the time he arrived at his house it was lukewarm and he only ate half of it, knowing already that he would suffer from indigestion later. He switched on the television in an attempt to lose himself in the triviality of the programmes but, again, it was in vain so he gave up and headed through to the kitchen to make a coffee – and maybe pour just a small whisky... As he did so, he noticed the odd, pear-shaped board leaning against the wall, just where he had left it. He picked it up, surprised again at its lightness. His curiosity getting the better of him, he placed his palm against it to see if he could activate anything – nothing happened. He placed it on the floor but it remained stubbornly inert. Gingerly he placed his right foot on it and, suddenly, a curved section, about ten inches long shot up from the board and hovered, apparently totally unattached, at waist height. He grasped it in both hands and was amazed at its solidity – it felt like the bar on a child`s scooter. He placed his left foot on the board and immediately it lifted about six inches off the ground, supporting his weight and seemingly compensating for his unsteadiness. Very gently he pushed the bar forwards and the board moved accordingly. He pulled it back and the board reversed. Sideways movements were mimicked and a rotation of the handle rotated the board – he found it quite incredible, the kind of gadget he would have expected in a sci-fi movie and, suddenly, he had the brief thought, "must ask Khara how it works" before realising that he might never ask Khara anything again. He tried to put it out of his mind as he continued to experiment with the board. It responded immediately to any imbalance on his part and he decided to attempt the short journey to the living room – no problem whatsoever! As he became more confident, he dodged easily around the furniture then back and forth between rooms and, as he passed the mirror in his hall, he caught a glimpse of himself and realised he was grinning from ear to ear, like a child on a new bicycle. He hadn`t had so much fun in ages! After about fifteen minutes, he stopped and placed one foot on the ground – the board immediately dropped to the floor. He stepped off and the handle re-joined the main body of the unit and it lay inert once again. He lifted it and propped it back against the wall, wondering, in reality, just what the hell he could do with it. He could keep it, of course, have a bit of fun now and then (until it ran out of charge, or whatever powered it) but what if someone else saw it – how would he explain that? Of course, in reality he couldn`t explain it to anyone, but he couldn`t think of what to do with it. Maybe he could just dump it in a skip, let it get buried somewhere safe...

Wish I could do the same with my probems...

He also realised it wasn`t just the board that had come back to Earth. His troubles were crowding back in again after the brief interlude and, with a deep pang of guilt, he realised that he had been so absorbed in his own desperate situation that he had completely forgotten about Lucinda, the ordeal of her funeral, Karen Whiteford and the pain and grief of the previous two weeks. Not to mention Kevin King...

Maybe I am just a cold, heartless bastard after all.

He went back in to the kitchen, abandoning the thought of coffee in favour of the whisky, when he heard his front door rattle slightly, as if the wind had caught it. He stopped and listened. Nothing - it all seemed calm outside. Then it happened again, a slightly stronger rattle this time, as if someone had bumped against it. He put down the empty glass he had been holding before running to the door and, flinging it open, he was confronted with the dull, silver shuttle pod. He stepped towards it and the door slid open, but inside it was empty, except for one thing. One of the seats was folded down and, on it, was the little leather necklace that he had given Khara.

`Where`s Khara?` he asked. "Is she okay?`

The familiar voice of the Terestal responded.

`No, she is critically injured. She is in an induced, deep coma and the ship is providing life support systems. She must be returned to Loh without delay in order that she may receive the medical attention that she requires. During her brief spell of consciousness, when we discussed the situation, she asked that I return the necklace to you.`

`The necklace?` He had completely forgotten about it.

`But why? It was a gift. Why does she want to give it back?`

`I assume, then, that she did not explain it to you?`

`Explain what?`

`On the planet Loh, when a couple decide to become life partners, similar to marriage on your planet, they exchange necklaces as a token of their commitment. These are somewhat more, well...elaborate than yours, and it is more of a ceremony but, nonetheless, your gift carried a significance of which, presumably, you were unaware.`

Archie frowned. Had he accidentally proposed to her? That certainly hadn`t been his intention.

`But how was I to know that? It was just, well, as I said, a wee gift. I didn`t mean anything by it.`

`Indeed. But Khara was emphatic that I return it to you.`

Archie leaned in to the shuttle and picked up the necklace, pondering on the possible implications of this for a moment. Yet again, his mind was in turmoil but he felt he had to ask

`So, if Khara`s giving me the necklace back, do I take that as a refusal or as an invitation?`

The computer seemed to ponder just as Archie had done.

`Honestly, Archieblue, I do not know. Khara was in considerable pain during our conversation, which was necessarily brief before she was sedated. You must decide for yourself.`

How could he possibly know what she had meant. He stared at the necklace clasped in his hand. What had it cost, about fifteen pounds? Just a cheap trinket, really, and he vaguely wished he had bought something slightly better.

`I need to see her. I need to give this back to her.`

`That is not possible. There is no time and, as I have already told you, she is in a coma. She must be returned to Loh immediately.`

`But I can`t just let her go like this. Not after all that`s happened.`

`You must, Archieblue. I am sorry.`

He felt numb. Her injuries had obviously been much worse than he had realised and he asked the next question reluctantly.

`Do you think she`ll make it?`

`Will she survive? I hope so. I believe that with the correct medical intervention she will recover.`

`If she doesn`t, what happens? I mean, to you, to the ship?`

`If the Commander dies, then all my cognitive power will disappear. The vessel is programmed at a lower level to return to Loh as best it can, but without intuitive guidance, this may not be possible. As you can see, I have a vested interest in Khara surviving.`

The voice paused, then continued

`There is one more thing.`

`What?`

`My inventory shows that a personal transport board is missing. I believe Khara took it with her on her first visit. Is it in your possession?`

The hover-board!

`Yes, it`s in the house.`

`Can you return it, please? I cannot allow any alien technology to remain in your possession. I am sure you understand why.`

`Yeah, sure. Hold on, I`ll get it.`

He went back in to the hall, closing the door slightly. He quickly pulled on his jacket, lifted the board and went back out, pulling the door shut behind him. He dived straight into the shuttle and sat in the vacant seat.

`Please exit immediately, Archieblue. You cannot come to the vessel.`

`No way! Unless Khara has re-programmed you, I think I still have some authority.` Hoping that the computer had less power over him on the shuttle than it had on the ship, he placed his hand on the small control panel. `Shuttle, return to Terestal.`

There was only a slight pause before the door closed and, once again, Archie was strapped in and catapaulted into space. He had only the briefest of moments in which to realise that he had left all the lights on in his house.

It seemed no time at all before he was entering the docking bay, high above his planet. The usual dull clanking noises preceded the opening of the shuttle door and he climbed out and made his way to the airlock door, placing his hand on the panel. The door slid open and, once inside, he repeated the action, exiting the other side. Once back in the main area of the ship, though, he struggled to remember the route to the medical bay. He started in one direction but the ship`s voice spoke

`It is in the other direction. Archieblue.`

He turned too quickly and seemed to lose his balance, almost stumbling on to the floor, but he managed to brace himself on the wall, annoyed at his clumsiness and putting it down to regaining what he now though of as his “space-legs”. He walked down the corridor but, as all the doors were closed, he struggled to remember exactly which room was the medical bay. In the back of his mind was the memory that somewhere on the ship was the body of Khara`s dead crew-mate – he didn`t really want to stumble on that by mistake! Fortunately the computer intervened again, seemingly aware of his confusion.

`This entrance, on your left.`

At his touch the door panel slid open and Archie entered, aware once again of the dull, greenish light that illuminated the room. It was very quiet inside and Khara lay on the table where he had left her, the odd liquid-like surface now enveloping her entire body. Her head was raised, appearing to be resting on something more substantial and he could just make out the curves of her naked body encased in the blue substance – it seemed a lifetime ago since he was exploring those curves...

Don`t go there, Archie...

The mechanical arm stood poised beside her like a sentinel but it was immobile, although the liquid appeared to be connected by thin tubes to the base of the mechanism. He walked over and looked down at her - she looked even paler than he remembered and, somehow, she seemed very fragile and vulnerable. He felt an almost overpowering surge of emotion but was unsure exactly what it was and he dared not try and define it. Instead, he reached into his pocket and removed the little necklace, leaning forward and carefully fastening it round her neck; even in her coma he was very slightly aware of her subtle, sensual smell. She remained completely still and he gently placed his hand on her cheek as he stood back up - she felt cold. He spoke softly

`This belongs to you, Khara. Whatever it means. At least you`ll know I`ve been here. Goodbye.`

`She cannot hear you` said the computer.

`I know.`

He leaned forward again and kissed her cool, white forehead then turned to leave the room. As he reached the door, he stopped and looked back.

`Will you tell her I...`

`Yes? Tell her what?`

He paused. Cam`s succinct choice of words came back to him. "Don`t flush it all down the toilet." That seemed to be all he had done recently, jeopardizing everything - his integrity, his career, his friendships, his whole life, even. *What a total fuck-up!* Now this...no, it was just too big a step, but it was probably the toughest decision he had ever made in his entire life. He lowered his head and shook it sadly.

`Never mind. Just tell her I came. Now will you please just get me home - once and for all.`

`I am afraid that is not possible, Archieblue.`

Archie`s head snapped up.

`What the hell do you mean?`

`Your planet is already many millions of kilometres behind us. You are going to Loh!`

Look out for

Keeper of Souls

The next novel in the
DI Archie Blue series

Coming soon...

#0019 - 040418 - C0 - 210/148/16 - PB - DID2163991